BITTER FRUIT

BITTER FRUIT

Peggy Ann Barnett

CLARA BEAR PUBLISHING

Clara Bear Publishing
Redmond, Washington, USA

Author's website: www.peggyannbarnett.com

Maps and artwork by Peggy Ann Barnett
Author photo © Ronald Barnett 2013
Design by Rudy Ramos

Bitter Fruit
2022 © Peggy Ann Barnett

ISBN: 978-0-9858292-1-6 (trade paper)
ISBN: 978-0-9858292-2-3 (ebook)

Printed in the United States of America

for Emma and Ron forever

TABLE OF CONTENTS

ACKNOWLEDGEMENTS

I have a great number of people to thank for their encouragement and help. First, I want to thank Mary Crane, Kathy Ortiz, Shirlee and Terry Busch, and Regina Bennett, who all read the original manuscript and gave me the strength to keep writing. I especially want to thank my editors Joan Scherman, David Thornbrugh and Eden Graber who all gave so much generous effort to an enormous task. Thank you to T. Clear and Mathieu Talagas for listening to me talk about this project for all these years.

I am grateful to Jennifer McCord for her professional help in publishing this book and to Roberta Trahan for her skills with the final manuscript.

I wish to thank my sister Dr. Erika Michael for always giving me support in my endeavors.

I'm especially grateful to my daughter Emma Barnett for her love and faith in me through the many years of writing this book and for helping me with my website.

I wish to thank the Scottish poet Ian Crockatt for allowing me to use quotes from his translation of Rogenvaldr's original poetry. "Crimsoning the Eagle's Claw: the Viking Poems of Rogenvaldr Kali Kolsson",

And I want to thank my late husband Ronald, who never doubted me for one moment and is still by my side.

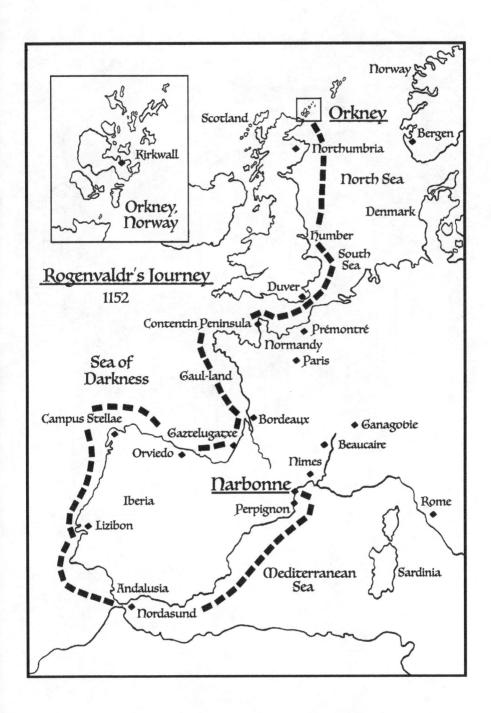

Narbonne 1152

1. Archbishop's Palace
2. Ermengard's Palace
3. St. Just Cathedral
4. Horreum
5. Capitol
6. Royal Gate
7. Caularia
8. Via Domitia
9. Coyran
10. Episcopale Gate
11. Laurac Gate
12. St. Etienne Gate
13. Water Gate
14. Basilique St. Paul-Serge
15. Bourse
16. Raymond-Jean Gate
17. St. Paul Gate
18. St. Marie-Lamourgier Church
19. Lamourgier Gate
20. Beach

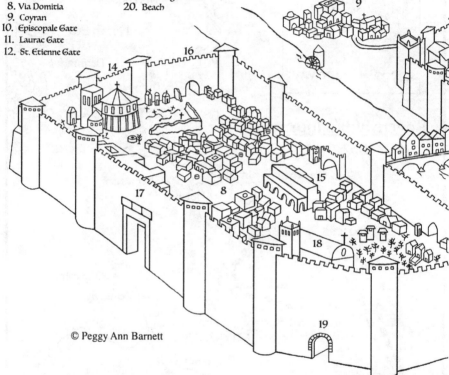

© Peggy Ann Barnett

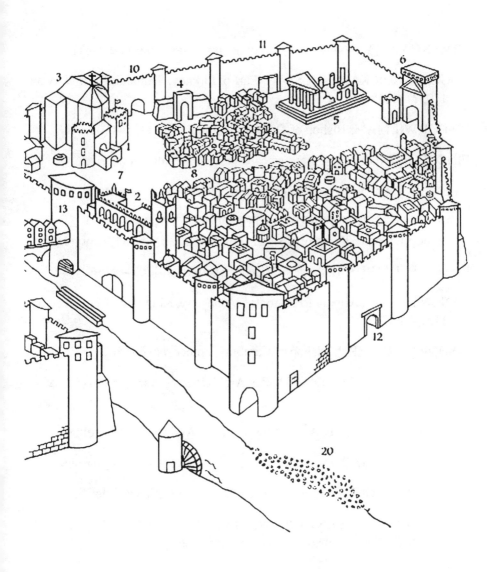

HISTORICAL CHARACTERS

ERMENGARD, Viscountess of Narbonne, born Narbonne 1129?—1196

ROGENVALDR KALI KOLSSON: Earl of Orkney, Scotland, Born Norway, 1103?—1158

BISHOP WILLIAM: Bishop of Orkney, Scotland from 1135–1168

EINDREDI UNGI: Norwegian sea captain, Rogenvaldr's cousin

ASLAK: A young nobleman Rogenvaldr is charged with protecting

SEAMEN IN NORSE FLEET (AS PER ORKNEYINGA SAGA): Magnus, Gudorm, Oddie, Thorbjorn, Swain, Gimkel, Blian, Armod, Thorgeir, etc.

BISHOP PELAGIUS: Bishop of Orviedo, Spain from 1102—1156

CANON HUGON: Abbot of Prémontré Monastery, Kingdom of France, from 1131—1161

BISHOP BURCHARD: Bishop of Cambray, France, envoy of Pope

ARCHBISHOP PIERRE D'ANDUZE: Archbishop of Narbonne from 1150—1156

BERNARD D'ANDUZE: Archbishop Pierre D'Anduze's older brother

ABBOT DON ESTABON: Abbot of Fontfroide, a Cistercian Monastery

HENRY THE MONK: A Bons Hommes Parfait, a heretic preacher

BERNAUTZ DE VENTADORN, JAUFRE RUDEL, RAIMBAUT, D'AURENGA: Troubadours, mid-twelfth century

FICTIONAL CHARACTERS

COUNTESS BEATRITZ DE DENT: Ermengard's dependent, a secret heretic, a Bonne Fille, Cathar, Ermengard's investigator

THIBAULT DE PLAIGNE: Ermengard's liege knight, an older man in love with Beatritz

ALAIS: Countess de Dent's thirteen-year-old daughter

SANCHA ESPAZA: Woman in charge of entertaining Norsemen

BATHSHEBA: A slave, Princess of Begwena, a descendant of Bathsheba

SIGRID ERLANDSDOTTIR: Aslak's kidnapped sister, now named Nila

PETER DE BRUEIL, PETER RAYMOND: Advisors to Ermengard

MAURAND DE TOULOUSE: Part of Ermengard's court, a heretic, a Bons Hommes

BARALA BEN TODROS: Jewish banker in Narbonne

ARNAUD GERARDI: Has stone quarry and two daughters, Ermessend and Gauzia

GUILLIAM MAURS: Templar Knight employed by Archbishop D'Anduze

BROTHER RAMON: A monk whose life is devoted to music

BROTHER GILBERT: A monk whose life is devoted to olives

RAYMOND AND AZALAIS d'OUVELHAN: Parents of Garsend, heretics, Bons Hommes

GARSEND: The heretic Azalais d'Ouvelhan's thirteen-year-old daughter

PONZIA de COMIC: Widowed seamstress to Ermengard, Fabrisse's mother, a heretic

FABRISSE: Ponzia de Comic's thirteen-year-old daughter

GODFREY: Hugon's soldier monk, servant

FROTARD: Jailor in D'Anduze's dungeon

GOMBAL: Jailor in Roman prison

ESCORALDA: Herbalist, keeper of the Mysteries

ABBOT RAMON: Abbot of Ganagobie Abbe

PRELUDE

And I looked, and behold,
a whirlwind came out of the north,
a great cloud,
a fire engulphing itself,
and a brightness was about it,
and out of its midst
as the color of amber, the fire.
                    —*Ezekiel 1:4, King James Bible*

JANUARY 1150, COAST OF THE NORTH SEA, NORWAY

A narwhal died. But the Virgins of the Night, the flames of their luminous green skirts crackling and flickering in the black sky, were too busy dancing above the North Sea to care. Pierced by stars twinkling like diamonds, their glowing, transparent veils streak down to the horizon, then flame upwards with outstretched arms. Red sea foam crashes against icebergs flashing like cracked emeralds floating on a black mirror.

The ice would always thicken as winter turned more frigid, but this year the freeze arrived later than usual, deceiving the pod of twenty-two narwhals feeding in the sea depths. Sharp ice crystals slowly formed under the waves. As the cold water sank, warm water rose, and the thick slush, sensed by each narwhal's long tooth, alerted the pod that it was time—at once—to leave for warmer feeding grounds. The quiet, round black opening in the icy field over them was closing fast, leaving only a ten-foot-wide rivulet leading to the open sea. Whistling and trumpeting high-pitched warnings to each other, mother narwhals surfaced to swim the shrinking passage, frantically attempting to herd their calves to other feeding grounds in the west.

A flash of silver had caught the eye of a hungry young male hunting in the cold darkness below. Diving after it into deeper waters, he slowed his heartbeat and made his excited clicking as silent as possible to avoid alerting his prey. His need for a fat, oily meal made him loose control, and soon he was clicking so fast and loud that the fish always knew where he was, constantly evading him. But eventually his prey tired, at which point he stunned the flapping cod by hitting it on the head with his tooth. Sucking the slippery pleasure into his throat, he devoured the whole fish in one greedy gulp. The narwhal never even heard the frantically calling voices of his pod.

Hearing the loud crack of the passage snapping shut, the narwhal panicked. Heart pounding rapidly he aimed for the surface, though, when he arrived, it was only to thrash frantically under the cold white wall above him. There was no escape. The narwhal's heart, beating slower and slower, gave out as he drowned.

Morning sunlight streamed through the ice to light up his mottled, white underbelly bumping up against its frozen prison. Cold currents gradually pushed his bulk towards land.

The receding tide left him lying on the black stones of a curved beach, a silvery glinting dot at the end of a massive fjord, its snow-speckled mountains reaching out to the sea like a lover's arms.

• • •

Thornson couldn't breathe. His heart was a clenched fist pounding against his ribs. As far as he could see on the high plateau were the corpses of dead reindeer—his reindeer herd. Hanging over rocks, legs sprawled out over the frozen ground, fur singed, the carcasses were already being fought over by wolves, foxes, and a white spirit bear. Bloody pieces of meat hanging from antlers were being snapped at by eagles that screeched down, then swerved upwards to avoid snapping jaws. Heavy, yellow-nosed vultures bent down the lower branches of dark firs, waiting for an opening to join the frenzy.

Last night's terrible lightning storm had stolen his winter food. *There is only hunger in my future,* he thought.

Over and over the giant hammer of the thunder god Dierpmis had crashed down on the mountainsides, sending thunder rolling down into the valley. The Sami had never seen anything like those flashes lighting up the world.

"I fear Dierpmis will slay the sacred reindeer Meandash tonight," Thornson had whispered to his wife as they huddled around the tiny flame flickering in the drafts of their small stone hut, tightly holding their trembling sons. The great, golden-antlered reindeer spirit, with its silver coat, black head, and burning eyes ran all over the mountains to escape the lightning-arrows of Dierpmis' bolt-thrower.

Thornson was worried. *Perhaps Meandash was killed last night. Is that why all my reindeer are dead? I must consult a Noaidi.*

The Noaidi shaman understood, nodding his head. "I will go to speak with your reindeer spirits and ask them." Chanting, beating his drum, the shaman turned himself into a raven and flew away. He returned from the journey with a message for Thornson sent by the animals' spirits.

"It was necessary for us to be sacrificed," he said. "Winter has come early, and many animals are dying from hunger. Sometimes death is the only way to continue the cycle of life. You will be blessed for this sacrifice."

Hunger is a blessing? Thornson hung his head in shame at the selfish thought.

• • •

Pushing aside the layers of sealskin that held in the warmth of his hut, Thornson stepped into the dim dawn of day. The yellow sun was just under the horizon, rays glowing under a pale blue sky. He gazed upwards. The Virgin Dancers were still shimmering lightly, but he could see they were going to sleep. This was good. The paler they were, the less dangerous they were. He didn't want to attract their attention—people had been carried away, or even worse, had their heads sliced off.

"Sussu, I'm going to find amber to trade for food," he said over his shoulder, brushing the powdery snow that tumbled down from the birch branches on the roof from his wiry beard. His sons were still wrapped in deerskins, curled around the fire pit stones with their mother. Eles' thin, bony arm stuck out from the furs. Sussu's eyes were daily growing larger above the cheekbones of her thinning face.

Yes, see how blessed I am, he thought. Sighing, he turned to head toward the beach, where amber often washed up on shore.

Ailo, his black-eyed sturdy ten-year-old, popped out of the hut. "I'm coming with you." Thornson looked at him affectionately. In his brown, furry suit and hood, mittened hands on hips, he looked like a walrus standing on its tail. "No, stay here and help your mother."

"I'm just as hungry as you are. And I want to help feed the family."

Sussu, still wrapped in her reindeer blanket, came out. "Why not take him along? He's got better eyes than you. Go. May the gods bring you luck."

They kept their eyes lowered in the frigid North Sea wind. Salt-encrusted, round black stones crunched beneath their boots as they walked carefully, hoping to spot the orange glint of amber. All around them the frozen day was black, white, gray, and noisy. Screaming black petrels, cormorants, and gulls, wheeling in the air dove hungrily into frothy waves pounding the shore.

An eagle, spotting the tiny red and blue spots of Thornson's and Ailo's hats against the snow-capped peaks, decided they were not edible, and curved away on an air current.

"Remember, Ailo, you must be very respectful of amber. After all, each piece is a tear shed by Beaivi the Sun Goddess, who is overcome with fear every time she travels through the dark ocean at night. Even down in the deep, her tear-rays shine through the waters, and she cries until the time comes when she can rise up into the sky again. Amber is her frozen tears washed up on the shore."

"I found a tear!" Ailo bent down, eagerly snatching up an orange crescent glinting in a crevice between two black rocks. The child examined the triangular piece of amber sitting in the palm of his hand, then held it up to the sky at the bright spot where the sun was shining just below the horizon. "Look—there's an animal in it. So strange. How did it get there?"

Thornson grabbed it from him. A clear black silhouette of a tiny bird was frozen in the golden jewel. Thin wings spread out in flight, stick-like feet with claws curled up against its chest, its narrow little beak, floating in glowing sea of bubbles. Thornson had a sudden sense of panic, as if a god was watching. It was a seiwo-neidoh, a magic bird—a god child!

Snapping his arm back, he quickly threw the glowing stone out into the sea, as far as he could beyond the first line of breakers. "Here, it is returned. You see, we rescued it," he cried. "Don't punish us!"

Firmly grabbing Ailo's shoulder, he turned to walk away. "Never keep amber with an animal in it. Never! Some people who find one sell it for gold. Bad things always happen to them. Remember Gávgu the fisherman? He found a stone with a worm in it and sold it to a trader. The very next day Gávgu's boat was smashed by a grampus whale. Nearly ate him." Amber was valuable, yet it had its dangers.

Walking along, busily kicking rocks, Thornson raised his eyes and couldn't believe what he saw. "There, ahead!" he cried, pointing. "A narwhal!"

The narwhal looked just like the bloated corpse of a drowned sailor. It was lying by the water's edge at the far west end of the fjord. Thornson ran over to claim it: not just for the meat, but for the wealth a long twisted alicorn tooth in perfect condition could bring him when he gave it to the King down south in Trondelog. It easily measured the length of his widespread arms. With calloused hands he examined the brown, twisted tooth carefully, searching for any chips, cracks, or splinters. "It's perfect! Thank you, magic bird. Or is it Máilmi's reward for my reindeer?"

"Hah!" he shouted, laughing as he spun Ailo around and around in the air. "Fetch Eles and the sled!"

The carcass was huge, the size of a bull reindeer's torso. Panting, pushing, and pulling, the heavy weight threatening to break the wooden runners, the three dragged the narwhal home.

Sussu had already started a fire outside the hut. "Put it near the hot stones to thaw. I have to cut the tooth out."

Skilled in these matters, Sussu carefully began to detach the horn from the narwhal's mouth by pulling out the teeth surrounding it. Using a stone flint she cut into the gray flesh all the way up to the skull. Then came the most delicate part of the work. With her fingers and a sharp ivory knife, she snapped off the tooth without damaging its wide base which, Sussu saw with satisfaction, was at least the width of her palm.

She then put the dead narwhal's fresh liver into a clay jar to save for its life-giving oil. The bones would be carved into tools, and the rest of the animal was cut up and buried in a hole in the frozen floor for future meals. A prayer was offered as she burned the remains and scattered the ashes back into the water to appease the narwhal's spirit and thank it for so much wealth.

Then, Sussu melted snow to make warm, fresh water. Chanting, she ritually bathed the horn, cleaning it of blood and sand to purify it. She then wrapped the alicorn horn in the soft, white fur of a spirit bear, and tied the bundle tightly shut with a deer gristle lanyard. Thornson was preparing to set out on the four-day journey south to the King. Sussu heated up some pine resin and wiped the bottom of his pinewood skis with it.

"May the goddess Máilmi keep you safe," she prayed, using a finger to draw a circle with deer butter on his forehead. "It is a cold time to travel. Beware the white spirit."

Pushing on his poles, he set off on the journey to Trondelog. To remain unseen, Thornson dodged between thin, black-branched birch trees, skiing on mountain snow well inland of the coastline. Snow scraped his face as he flew down rocky slopes.

The night was bitterly cold. Afraid of thieves, he didn't make a fire and slept in a pine tree. By morning his legs had turned deadly white and wouldn't move. Pushing himself out of the tree, he fell in a heap. After punching his thighs and hitting his boots against the tree trunk, enough feeling returned to enable him to hobble onto his skis.

Thornson drank some of the stomach-burning fermented fish oil his wife had tucked into a jacket pouch. Gasping and coughing, ignoring his dizziness, he struggled to stay upright and go further south.

Snow packed itself heavily on his shoulders. The next two days sped by in a blur of black trees, white ice, and grey unending rocks. Skimming over the tundra he skirted the edges of fjords to avoid hungry white spirits following his movements. Digging holes in the snow, he slept hidden under its blanket.

Eventually, from the crest of a high ridge, Thornson could see the jagged brown ramparts of Trondelog on the next mountain top. Trudging down into the valley and up the slope ahead, he finally arrived at the gate.

He must have collapsed for he didn't remember being carried in. The warmth of a fire and the smell of hot reindeer stew woke him up. Clutching the white bundle of fur to his chest he ate, fell asleep again, and woke in the morning, still grasping his precious horn. The guard by the door put down his ale and stared at him as he approached.

Thornson demanded, "I must see King Haraldsson. I must see the King. It is my right." After arguing with two other guards, he was grudgingly taken over to the king's meeting hall.

Upon entering, heat from the blazing fire pit hanging from a ceiling beam hit him full in the face. On the walls flickering carved animal spirits bared their blade-sharp teeth alongside double-edged battle axis and brightly painted wooden shields. Wearing cloaks that left one arm bare, sporting heavy gold torques around their necks, warriors lounged beside fur-wrapped women whose jeweled necklaces reflected the flames. When they saw Thornson standing there, everyone stopped talking and stared. A low laugh rippled through the room.

The King of Norway, Sigurd II Haraldsson, stout, strong and obviously annoyed, was restlessly pacing around the room barking at the 'jarls' who served him. Turning his blue-eyed, bushy-haired head to see what everyone was staring at, he found a battered-looking Sami fisherman down on one knee.

"Well?"

"My Lord," Thornson began, then realized he didn't know how to speak to a King. "My, my King."

"Yes, yes," Sigurd II impatiently encouraged him. "Speak!"

"I am Thornson of the Sami people." Not knowing what else to do, he reached out to hand him the long, now filthy, fur bundle.

Sighing, the King handed it to his wife who took a small silver knife out of a pouch on her belt. Standing up, she carefully cut the gristle lanyards and unrolled the bear skin. Smiling, she handed the horn to the King.

Sigurd's eyebrows went up to his forehead. Examining the horn from tip to base, he finally said, "It's perfect.

CHAPTER 1

I brood at her bedside
—I've brought lace, necklaces,
bone combs—who lies, limbs and
lips feverish—wishing
back our glad hours hawking
low-isled water-meadows.
I shape grave words—heart deep,
honed, brief—to imprison grief.

—Rogenvaldr Kali Kolsson, 1103?—1158

JANUARY 1150, ORKNEYJAR

Skálds, those wise bards who knew the ancient stories, were now singing of the old days, when the winters were so cold, and came so soon after summer, that one could almost ski from Iceland to Orkneyjar in Kornskurdarmáudur, Grain Cutting Month. These days, within the memories of living men, the winters had become shorter and warmer, so the sailing days had become longer, often lasting till Gormánudor, Slaughter Month. Sea ice stayed north; ice mountains were smaller. Rivers thawed early, rushing through gorges, creating long, foaming waterfalls in the fjords as far north as Trondelog, Norway.

After Denmark's King Harald Bluetooth was baptized by Poppo the Monk fifty years ago, and declared his people Christian, the Vikings had renamed themselves Norsemen. "We are merchants and traders," they continually had to remind everyone. Heading over the western sea to barter goods in faraway lands, they traveled to distant vine covered islands, around Iberia to the mysterious Persian desert, and up across the Northern Sea to the Land of Rus.

Rogenvaldr Kali Kolsson, the Norwegian Earl of Orkneyjar, was standing on a low hill in Hrossey, the main island of this watery region to the north of Scotland. He spent many days looking north over the sea towards Iceland to watch the Krisuvik volcano spew its dark plume into the smudged sky.

He kept remembering his father, Koli, and the frightening words whispered to him as a child. *Never was rock or stone so hard but that this fire will melt it like wax and then burn it like fat oil. It must surely be from Hell— for it feeds on dead matter, and in Hell all things are dead.* Baptized in his youth, his father had always carried within him a terrifying fear of Hell.

Continual flashes of fire from deep inside the earth lit up the depths of the black, billowing clouds the wind sent south to Orkneyjar. During the day, the sun was a deep orange disc, a dim fire glowing through blue dust. Sunsets took on the imperial purple of a *murex* sea snail; dawns the red of a wild rose. Ash had settled into the winter mud here, turning the ground brownish gray, poisoning wells not carefully covered. Overlapping waves left a necklace of ashes along the shore.

For Rogenvaldr, these were the dark days of his soul. Upset with the painful turns of his life, he felt as if there was a volcano erupting in his chest. After the death of his wife, Vgret Moddansdóttir, while giving birth to twin boys who quickly died, and soon thereafter the fevered death of his youngest daughter Ingirid, he had sworn never to take another wife. God would never again have the ability to so punish him. *I am in dire need of salvation.*

Impatiently, he had waited all that dark, damp spring for Einmánuour, Men's Month, before calling a regionwide Thing in Hrossey. The gathering was set at the time of the Middagsstad Dagmark, or midday daymark, when the sun was at its height for that time of year; a sundial wasn't of much use in these northern climes of long nights and endless days. All the chieftains residing in his large domains were called to gather in the Thingstead, the meeting place centered in the flat field of the Ring of Broadyeur, an ancient circle of forty standing stones. It was to happen at that time of day when the largest stone's diagonal top pointed directly up at the sun's wan disc.

Whenever a Thing was called, all free men and women came from far and wide. It was their parliament and court, an opportunity for conflict resolution, marriage alliances, and honor displays, all played out in a public forum. It was a large crowd of well-dressed Norsemen that spilled out beyond the gaps in the stones towering above them. Draped in cloth covered in intricate patterns, displaying elegant gold torques and broaches that indicated their rank, they appeared, at least on the surface, very different from their ferocious Viking ancestors. Porgnyr the Lawspeaker, who had memorized the Law and served as the Judge, entered and took his place. Excited anticipation filled the air. One never knew what could happen.

Earl Rogenvaldr had inherited the Nordic features of his uncle, Saint Magnus: tall, blue-eyes, broad shoulders; the jagged scars of early battles crossing his back and stomach got him respect. Though in his late forties, he was lean and well-muscled, standing with his back to the sun stone, strong and sure-footed, bare legs set apart. The wind, blowing his orange hair and unbraided beard, gave him a lion's mien. He was a force of nature about to challenge his people.

Looking out on the flat, brown field with its mottled rocks, vast horizon, and pale sky merging with the gray sea, he was reminded how much smaller and different this gathering was from the massively crowded Things in Iceland to which his father had taken him as a child of ten. There, on that sweeping brown plain, its surface laced with steaming rivulets and boiling fumaroles, thousands of bearded, square-jawed chieftains, accompanied by their tall, angular wives, gathered inside the long, straight-sided gash that cut through the inside of the earth. With the black soil wall towering above them, its thick, gnarled roots reaching out into the dense crowd, their muscular bodies, all armed to the teeth with swords, knives, and axes, had swarmed like luminescent beetles. Most had huge carved crosses dangling on their studded leather vests, but some few still wore copper chains strung with gem studded runic symbols.

All those years ago, Rogenvaldr's father had taken him by the shoulder, putting his blue-eyed, crinkled face very close to his own. *Watch, and listen carefully, my son. Memorize the most important chieftains' names. If you always call them by their names, they will be respectful. Yet remember, there are still many un-saved pagans who have come here from the high mountains of Norway, those who follow the old ways of killing, raping, and burning.* A few years later, defending his

Christian faith, Koli had died fighting one of those same Norwegian chieftains that had attended the Thing.

It was different here in Orkneyjar; the light was endless, the soil thin, and one could see forever in each direction. The old site was a dark place for a pagan Thing; this was a bright place for a Christian Thing.

The crowd was waiting for him to speak. Going heavily down on one knee, he announced loudly, in a firm deep voice, "I have called this gathering to declare that I am going to embark on a great pilgrimage to the Holy Land to atone for the many acts of violence perpetrated by myself and the men of my earldom. Though a Christian, I am quick to anger and to kill. It is obvious to me that our blood is still infused with the warrior lust of our Viking ancestors. I confess that the disappearance of my rival to rule Orkneyjar, my cousin Earl Paul Haakonsson, weighs heavily on me."

Rogenvaldr couldn't say it aloud, but he didn't really believe, as Sweyn Asleif claimed, that it was during a battle between Sweyn and Paul that Paul was blinded and maimed. Sweyn then claimed that it was Paul's decision alone to leave the islands forever and live a life of seclusion in a cloister in Scotland. Rogenvaldr actually suspected that Margaret, Paul's sister, wanted Paul's lands and killed him herself. As there was no available proof, he could make no accusations.

"The senseless and drunken killing of the fisherman Arni Spitulegg by my men also pains my conscience. It was careless, and without honor. This callous act is not worthy of a Warrior in Christ. Despair and guilt gnaw at my soul. I fear that the death of all my family is a call from God for true repentance of any violence I have committed, whether in offense or defense.

"Truly, even my own angry nature gives lie to the magnificent cathedral I'm building here in Kirkwall for my holy uncle St. Magnus. I am an unworthy nephew and failed Christian. Over the sea in Iceland, Krisuvik is spewing fire from its depths. God is showing us what Hell is. I see it as sign for me to follow the same path as our holy King Sigurd the Jewryfarer, to take the cross, repent in Jerusalem, and be absolved of my sins by bathing in the cold waters of the River Jordan. Perhaps, God willing, I will also bring a piece of the true cross with me back to Oslo as King Sigurd did!

"If I need to fight, I will fight to save Jerusalem from the Saracens. God willing, I will pray on the Mount of Calvary to ask Jesus for forgiveness." He shouted: "Who will go with me to repent their sins and be reborn?"

Rising to his feet, he turned in a circle, waving his sword in the air.

Many of his friends shouted they would accompany him, for he was a brave man and a good leader. Many were restless and longed for a long sea voyage, and if forgiveness of sin was part of the journey, even better.

"While I am gone, I'm appointing Earl Harald, my kinsman, to govern. I know he is young, and ugly, yet he is wise."

Harald stood on a hillock nearby, his pock-marked face blushing with pride. The clansmen laughed and agreed to let him rule.

Bishop William of Orkneyjar, a serious and educated priest who had clerked in Paris, was loathe to abandon his work in Kirkwall to go on such a dangerous voyage. "I'm much too busy here supervising the construction of the St. Magnus Church. The saint was your uncle. Don't you want it built in your lifetime? And I want to build a palace near it."

Rogenvaldr pushed him. "Come, my friend. I'm just as anxious to build my sainted uncle's church as you are. It's an incredible feeling to watch the stones rise higher to become towers. But it is very costly, and we haven't even begun the interior work. Perhaps we could bring back a splinter from the True Cross, or even, Jesus Be Blessed, the Holy Grail— think of the pilgrims that will flock here! The master mason can work on the church alone for a year, and the plans for your palace aren't even finished. Watching it slowly get built can't compare with seeing where Christ Our Lord was actually born, died and resurrected."

William closed his sad brown eyes and crossed himself. "Christ is everywhere. Paris and Orkneyjar are enough. Besides, I'm too old."

"You're the same age I am! I need you to advise me spiritually. You will thank me later. Besides, how can you die without having prayed at Golgotha where our Lord died?"

Bishop William groaned inwardly as he ran his fingers through his long stringy hair. *That man's impetuousness will land us in trouble sooner, rather than later. I'm afraid to imagine what that trouble will be in a part of the world totally unknown to us.*

• • •

Despite Rogenvaldr's constant complaints, it took far too much time—almost two years—until their departure for the Holy Land.

King Sigurd II Haraldsson had enthusiastically blessed this pilgrimage and promised him a new ship for the voyage. Eindredi Ungi, the Earl's cousin in his father's line, was sent to Norway to bring it back from Bergen to Orkneyjar when it was finished. Rogenvaldr couldn't leave without it, but it was a long, long time coming.

A large forest fire in the western mountains of Norway had burned many oaks, the trees most favored for the hull, so the fulingar, the foreman in charge of building the boat, had to send men much further north to harvest and transport the logs. By law they were to be paid more, and the king began to complain of the extra cost. Rogenvaldr, despite the objections of his bailiff, Stein Haroaldson, had himself sent the extra funds. Then he found out that Eindredi was building his own vessel. Rogenvaldr could only wonder where Eindredi got the money for *that*.

Each dawn, with the ocean endlessly roaring from below as the foam hissed on the waves, Rogenvaldr waited on the rocky strand, standing lost in the sea-haar, the wet heavy blanket of fog covering him in salt, the sideways wind and gales constantly blowing at his coats. Erling Skakki, concerned for his good friend, always stood behind him, alert, counting the waves. Every seafarer knew the ninth wave was the worst and could quickly suck a man into the ocean's depths.

One morning, while Rogenvaldr was standing in the wash, there was a sudden sign from God: an arc blanc. Lit by the sun's rays, its crystals glittering against the murky fog banks, it curved above him, a brilliant shining white rainbow. Under it, a black shadow in the haar slowly turned into the shape of a longboat's prow. Majestically it sailed under the white rainbow towards him.

"It's here!" Rogenvaldr began to shout, running towards it in the surf.

Then a second shadow began to form. Eindredi had indeed arrived. With two great ships. One for Rogenvaldr and one for himself.

Rogenvaldr's longboat was a long and narrow drakkar. The claws of a huge carved and gilded, ferocious blue dragon grabbed the prow, its scaly tail coiling up at the rear of the boat. Under the dragon's flaming, yellow, open mouth were two snarling brandar, the heads of cats with red tongues and green eyes. Under a square wool sail marked with a red sign of the cross, were seventeen double seats for thirty-four rowers. Revolving weathervanes attached to the deck were inlaid with gold and whale bone ivory. The strong scent of pitch testified to its sea worthiness. Rogenvaldr ran his hands along its flexible hull.

"What an insult to the Earl!" Rogenvaldr's men grumbled when they saw Eindredi's ship.

It was even more gilded than Rogenvaldr's, which put the Earl's people in a mind to argue that this insult should not go unpunished. Rogenvaldr knew that Eindredi was really going to Jerusalem because he was a mercenary who wanted to join the Varangian Guard, that elite army that personally guarded the Byzantine emperor. The Emperor's Norsemen unit, taller and fiercer than all his other soldiers, was famous for the savagery of its bloodthirsty warriors who used their double-bladed battle axes to fearsome effect. Eindredi claimed he was descended from his hero Harald Hardrada, who spent ten years fighting for the emperor, and came back so rich he became King of Norway.

As his first penance of pilgrimage, Rogenvaldr decided to put away this business of the second ship—*Forget the ship—Eindredi's still the finest navigator in Norway. And he's still angry I got the Earldom.*

Eindredi had sailed both the North and South Seas and had knowledge of all the whale currents and varder, the important landmarks along the coast of England and Gaul-land where they would have to stop to eat and get supplies. In the last fifty years the Christianized Norse had erected many huge stone crosses on cliffs and beachheads as markers, but Eindredi could find fresh water just by sticking his finger in the sea water and tasting it. And, of course, he had the magical sólasteinn, a sun stone he wore on a gold cord around his neck. Even when the sun was under the horizon, the navigator could look at the sky through the stone and tell you where the sun was, and so which direction was east or west.

No, Rogenvaldr decided. *No argument about the boat from me—I need him.*

That night, the two cousins sat opposite each other on the stone benches that lined the Bu, the Earl's enormous mead hall. The stone building was forty-two paces long, with three-foot-thick walls, and it was always so cold inside that a fire was kept burning, even in summer. Drunken clansmen spent the night exchanging stories of what had happened in the last year. Afterwards, singing in a happy stupor, they embraced each other fondly.

Staring intently over the flames at Rogenvaldr, Eindredi yelled to him loudly over their howling voices. "In addition to the ship, I have a priceless reliquary gift for you from the King. You are to sell it as soon as possible to help pay for the costs of the passage. Meet me in the early morning in St. Nicholas' Church. I want you to gaze upon it for the first time in a holy place."

Eindredi was grinning broadly. Set far apart in a broad swarthy face, his eyes, restless clouds on a gray day, were crinkling with rare good humor toward his cousin. In the firelight, like the crack on a loaf of bread, a new scar from a sword cut ran from his right nostril up past the corner of his eye under the edge of thick, white hair standing out from his head. He loved to describe what happened to make it turn white.

"One night a draugr demon came to claim my soul. It was a terrible battle. I knew I was losing and cried out 'Jesus save me!' and the demon went up in a flash of light! That flash turned my hair pure white. I am blessed with the mark of God."

It's more likely the result of some horrific crime you committed, thought Rogenvaldr. "I'll meet you in the morning."

At dawn Rogenvaldr walked to the treeless mound where St. Nicholas's small, round church stood in isolation.

He knelt to pray at the worn stone altar next to a lonely arched window that allowed in very little light. Large wax candles, flickering gold in the gloom, lit up the apse with its earth-toned painting of a white-robed, stern Christ, his hand raised in either benediction or warning. Next to Christ stood Saint Peter holding an oversized, ornate key to heaven against his blue robes. The holy figures floated above, gazing down in judgment on sinners.

"Jesus, thank you for sending the ship of my salvation." Rogenvaldr prayed.

Hearing footsteps behind him, he rose slowly from his knees and turned. Eindredi was approaching holding a long bundle.

"Here," said Eindredi in a white puff of breath. Looking at Rogenvaldr intensely, he put a waterproof sealskin onto the altar. "Unwrap it carefully."

The king's gift was enclosed in a narrow five-foot-long, highly polished case made of malmfuru fir wood. Opening the two brass latches revealed a lining of precious, deep orange Siberian sable. Nestled in the sable was a long object wrapped in purple silk covered with flowers traced in gold thread. The shimmering fabric protected a long gold reliquary within which lay the brown curved surface of a perfect five-foot-long narwhal horn from the ice-laden waters of the far North Sea. The narwhal's sheath had been carved into a delicate gold lace of tiny, jeweled pilgrims arriving in Jerusalem, kneeling in prayer at the Holy Sepulcher, praying on Mount Cavalry under a crucified Christ, then ascending to the arms of God in heaven. Visible through the tracery one could see the horn's brown twisted surface. Most astonishing of all was a round bloodstone as large as a baby's fist. Set into a gold collar, it was placed under the feet of Christ, where the blood of his fallen tears inside the stone sparkled in the gem's green light.

"A sea-unicorn horn?" Rogenvaldr asked. "Why?"

"The King favors you." Eindredi said, with an edge to his voice. "He orders you to sell this fake as a real unicorn horn to finance your pilgrimage."

Known by the Northlanders as a Sea Unicorn, the narwhal often played in the foam of crashing waves, diving and leaping amongst the icebergs, waving its horn about or fencing with others of its kind. It was rare to find a hard, brown, twisted tooth that ended in such a perfect sharp point.

"The king is not giving me the funds?"

"Only a small sum, and this horn."

I wonder how big a bag of gold coins my cousin pocketed for himself on the journey here. "And to whom does he think I should sell it?"

"You are to sell it to naive and unsuspecting Christians that live in the warm southern lands. The bloodstone alone will work miracles for you." Eindredi grinned.

"I guess I don't have much choice." Annoyed, Rogenvaldr rewrapped the horn, putting it carefully back into the box.

As the Earl left the church, Bishop William, standing just outside the small arched door, grabbed him by the arm.

"I don't approve of selling a fake horn at all. It's the wrong way to begin a pilgrimage. It will bring God's punishment on us."

Rogenvaldr looked at his friend and confessor's earnest face; the brown eyes were troubled, the mouth pursed.

"If the people of the south are so religious that they believe it's real, why not give them some joy? Our Christian king has ordered it to be done. He is a good man who has gone to great trouble to make it into a reliquary. I cannot, and will not, naysay him. Besides, I need the money."

Turning, the Earl handed the fake horn over to his bailiff. "Take this back to my palace." He shook off William's hand to stride away.

"Listen to my warning, Rogenvaldr. Why do you always have to learn the hard way?" Frustrated, he watched the Earl's straight back stomp off.

• • •

William went back into the deserted church and sat on a bench in front of the altar to think. Melting onto an iron floor stand, one tall, lonely candle flickered.

Sometimes being a Bishop is just like being that lonely candle, always trying to shed a small light on the darkness surrounding us before we are snuffed out. Where does our light go when we die?

Blessed St. Magnus, I have witnessed your miracles, keep us safe. When I was blinded, you gave me sight, when I was lost at sea, you gave me land. Yet keeping Earl Rogenvaldr safe will take more miracles than you may wish to perform. You must help me. I beg of you. Be with us as we go on this perilous journey.

St. Magnus was his own special saint. Both born in Shetland, these watery islands were their home. The older man had been kind to the bright, young boy, teaching him how to read and write Latin. His duplicitous murder by Lifolf had shocked everyone, especially when the truth had come out that Magnus, on his knees praying, had not defended himself. Miracles at his gravesite in Birsay followed: Bergfinn's crippled son Halfdán was cured, blind Berfinn Skatisson's vision was restored, Rannveig of Unst was cured of his painful skin boils. Sainthood followed soon after.

William felt the calling to become a priest. As he was a second son, his family was delighted, and sent him off, at the age of twelve, to study in Paris.

Arriving alone in Paris in the year 1115 would have been a trial for a twenty-year-old man, let alone a boy of twelve. Scrambling off the crowded coach, the stench of teeming unwashed people and fecal waste forced the island boy to stand against a stone wall till he caught his breath. Slowly, the heaving of his stomach stopped, and he was able to look around. Endless carts were pushing their way through winding, narrow streets fanning out from the six corners of the square like the spokes of a wheel. A man was hurrying by with a wooden tray stacked with round breads on his head.

Using his best Latin, William asked, "Excuse me, could you tell me how to get to the Cathedral School of Notre Dame?"

The man snarled loudly in French: "Cursed student! Get out of my way."

Down one street he glimpsed the top of a spire sticking out above the two-story buildings. Hugging his seal skin bag tightly to his chest, he headed towards the one place that might help him.

The Cathedral School was immense, with its buildings scattered all around the town center. One side of the square was a brick wall, with a gate through which streamed students in black overskirts. Entering it he found himself in a large stone cloister surrounded by many, many doors, and, it seemed to him, more students than there were people living in all of Orkneyjar and Shetland combined.

At least here his Latin got him in the right direction.

"You are here to enter the clergy. You will be taught a Roman education: the 'trivium' consists of grammar, rhetoric, and dialectic. Once you have mastered this, you will study the quadrivium: arithmetic, geometry, musical theory, and astronomy. You will debate only Holy Scripture in a spirit towards the higher understanding of God."

His new master had sternly warned him: "Beware of philosophical debates based solely on the logic of Aristotle."

But it was just such a debate that he heard from one of the teachers named Pierre Abelard. The master's arguments made William's head spin. Original sin, human reason, baptism, nothing was beyond argument. Abelard firmly believed that by doubting what we know, we come to inquiry, and through inquiry we come to perceive truth.

Then, one day, the master just disappeared. The scandal of his love affair with Bishop Fulbert's daughter, the secret marriage, the love child, the castration—it kept tongues wagging for years.

It was the castration that frightened William the most. *Is this what passion leads one to? Jesus help me to avoid these feelings. It's so difficult to stop these thoughts. These women on the streets with their pink round breasts and hard brown nipples sticking out—stop! Stop seeing them in your thoughts!*

Yet his thirteen-year-old penis wouldn't listen. William's lifelong fight with his body began in Paris and only got worse. Still, he struggled on, and by 1122 he was a clerk working diligently for the school.

Then the master changed William's life again. Abelard decided to be a hermit. He moved to Nogent-Sur-Seine outside of Paris. There, in a flat field of stubble and brackish water, he built himself a reed hut with a simple, stone, oratory nearby in which he could worship in solitude. Solitude was not Abelard's destiny. His brilliance and philosophical logic brought hordes of students to the fields around him. They camped out in tents, built huts, and slept on the rocky ground as they demanded he teach them how to apply logic to church doctrine.

William left his job, packed up a big bag of bread and cheese, moved to Nogent-Sur-Seine and slept on the bare earth.

For weeks he listened to his teacher, then sat under the stars all night puzzling about the meaning of life on earth. About God's plan. About birth and death. The same thought always came, unbidden: *I wonder what it's like to be castrated; to stand there without a penis. Do the others here wonder that too?* He never asked.

One of Abelard's pronouncements stunned William: "A person's intent when he acts, determines the moral value of a person's character."

From these fields William went directly back to Shetland. With enough credentials to be named Bishop of Orkneyjar, he met St. Magnus's nephew, Rogenvaldr Kali Kolsson. With the memory of the Paris Cathedral to inspire him, he persuaded Rogenvaldr to fund a magnificent cathedral to house the relics of Saint Magnus.

And now Rogenvaldr wants me to help him do this. It goes against all my teaching. Selling the horn with the intent of deceiving religious believers is wrong. Still, how can I stop it? Saint Magnus, I beseech you, give me the strength to endure what lies ahead. The candlelight had disappeared. Putting his head down, he prayed in life's shadows.

• • •

From the church a path wound to a cliff overlooking Orjara Bay. Rogenvaldr climbed up to a mound sitting in the sunlight. It was encircled by carefully placed rocks. Walking over to the grave of his wife and sons, he put his hand on the stone cross and looked down. Nearby, down the slope, was a mound of rocks that covered the grave of his daughter.

The memory made him sick. He could still see Vgret screaming in anguish as the two babies were born in a bath of blood. After examining his wife's belly, the náverkkona, the helping woman, began to sing magical galdr songs to "sweep the saddle from the hungry horse". The double birth was going badly, and, fearing the children would not be baptized soon enough, she urged Rogenvaldr to send for a priest. Praying, the priest leaned over the screaming woman. Her strength waning, her voice became soft.

"Rogenvaldr," she whispered through cracked lips. "Put my favorite comb in my grave so I may tend to my hair in heaven." Then she was no longer there.

Gone, he thought.

The first son had been born and baptized, the holy water blending with the blood. The second son's head had emerged, wrinkled, yet alive. The holy water rinsed his face before he died, but the rest of the tiny body had to be pulled out by hand from his dead mother. The older boy, wrapped in his little white blanket, uttered one small gurgling cry before dying. Both children, gone within minutes of birth, taking their mother with them, needing her love in heaven.

I pray you had smooth seas on your journey to God.

As a Christian, he was no longer allowed to burn their bodies. He had to bury them. As an Earl, he could still insist on placing them in a fine boat with the spears, axe, and arrows that were the most valued possessions of a warrior woman.

I will always see you there, lying on your back, holding one child in each arm, all wrapped in a blanket woven of gold, with your red hair spread out on a down pillow like the rays of the sun. As you requested of me, I put your favorite comb on your curls. I know you cared for the babes all the way to God, where angels took them from you. Now, I must leave you, perhaps never to return. I promise to pray for your souls on Golgotha. And, if I die, I will greet you in heaven.

On the way down the mound Rogenvaldr passed stones piled on the grave of his daughter and averted his eyes from the pain.

Gathering his strength, he inhaled deeply and strolled to the reddish cliffs that overlooked the sea. In the early light, yellow tinged and silver, the choppy surf resembled shiny leaping fish. He stood alone on the edge of space, his hair whipped back by the briny wind. The surf pounding at the base of the mossy, red-rocked cliffs outlined the island with a misty haze. Clouds of screeching krykkje darted out of nests in crevices, swooping down, snapping up herrings to feed hatchlings.

Looking to the east he could see square, stone houses set in plains of grain growing right down to the edge of the water. The amount of flat planting land was so much greater here than in Norway; enough for a farmer to feed his family all winter, and still have some left over to ship to Trondelog to sell at a good profit.

The Earl loved his isles. Although he would never admit it, even to himself, the thought of leaving them was frightening to one who had never gone further than Norway.

William's warnings about selling the horn came back, unbidden, interrupting his enjoyment of the landscape with an uncomfortable feeling of annoyance.

I have no choice. The money will pay for my whole trip to Jerusalem and back. The king's gift is devious, yet what a clever way to use southern Christian naivety to my advantage. Besides, think of how happy the one who purchases it will be. Putting it on an altar as a reliquary would bring a fortune in pilgrims' donations to their fortunate church. No, it's a good deed for all!

If, in that church, Christ and St. Peter staring down from heaven truly understood what was happening on their altar below, what would the penance be for the King of Norway and myself?

He forced those thoughts away. There was work to be done.

CHAPTER 2

Joglar, you of a happy spirit,
carry to Narbonne
my endless song
to she who is always
guided by Joy and Youth.

—*Azalais de Porcairagues, c.1150*

July 1152, Narbonne, Occitania

The perspiring right thigh of Vicountess Ermengard of Narbonne stuck to the wooden seat of the chair right through the light silk chemise she wore under her hot, grey outer robe. Carefully, so that Abbot Estaban would not notice, she lifted it up. For five hours they had been negotiating, wrestling, over who owned the earnings of salt, sheep wool, fulled cloth, anchovies, rosemary honey, and tolls on the local roads that passed near both Narbonne and Fontfroide Abbey east of the city. Despite the stone walls and the thick oak forest encircling the church and cells of the twelve monks living here, the heat of the day began to bake the five people sitting motionless in the Abbot's study. It oozed in through the closed wooden shutters and settled on the low, frustrated murmurs of the two combatants. Ermengard wanted to let the light in, perhaps even gain a slight breath of cool air, yet the old Abbot insisted on working by candlelight.

The Abbot stank of anchovies. Flakes of brown fish skin trembled in his wiry, white streaked beard. Together with the odor wafting over from his unwashed nether parts, Ermengard was nauseated.

"We are poor monks trying to live a pious life," Estaban whined through dry, cracked lips. He set them into what he hoped was a sad looking curve.

15

She sighed slowly and quietly. Ever since Count Raymon Berenguer IV had bestowed the land and the abbey on these Cistercians a few years ago, they had been a hypocritical problem. *Poverty indeed! They own thousands of sheep, have power over fifty-six villages, and now have suddenly purchased control over the oak forest where the kermes live.*

This had resulted in a three-way dispute over who owned the tiny kermes insects that fed only on the scrubby oaks in the rough hills here: Fontfroide, Ermengard, or Pierre D'Anduze, the Archbishop of Narbonne. The intense vermilion dye produced from their tiny, crushed wings was priceless. *Just what I needed. Now the Abbot wants his share too. Both oh-so-pious men of the church want the kermes gold—as the Archbishop's avariciousness increases daily along with the costs of his new cathedral.*

Biting her bottom lip, she pushed further. "Abbot Estaban, we are entitled by legal protestativum to the wealth generated by the sale of the dye. We demand one-third of the harvested kermes. If we don't keep up production then customers will turn to the use of less expensive red cinnibar powder, even if our kermes dye is more vibrant. We don't want that money to go to the Spanish mines in Almaden, do we? Narbonne pays the military that guard the city and its surrounding land. We have generously offered, due to its proximity to Narbonne, to protect this abbey and the oaks. Surely Cistercians are not immune to sheep robbers and kermes thieves. You cannot expect twelve monks to guard the oaks when the insects are hatching in October. You are aware their wings must be harvested immediately."

"I'm sure you pay your troops well, Domina," he said dryly. He sat back and stared at Ermengard's face. Orange eyes, the color of thick honey held up to the sun, were glaring fiercely at him. *They look like a raptor's wings. By the balls of Saint Nicholas! What has this world come to that I should have to bargain like a merchant with this insolent young girl. A twenty-three-year-old ruling a kingdom! A holy man such as I forced to negotiate with the cause of all evil in this world. Disgusting.*

Ermengard was wise to his ways. *I know what you're thinking, you old goat. I've been the ruler here for eighteen years and you're not the first abbot I've had to deal with: though you are one of the smelliest.* "Here is my final, very generous, offer: in exchange for one-third of the kermes insect '*in perpetuum*', we will, for five years, charge you no tolls for transporting your wool on the new road I am building to hasten travel between Rousillion and Catalonia."

Her clerk, Peter Raymond, looked up at her, startled at her unusual generosity. He was one of the two clerks scribbling furiously.

If the Abbot knew I could transcribe and read these documents myself, he would burn me at the stake, she thought.

Trying to ignore her full lips, he curtly replied, "We agree."

Good. I'll get you in the end. I'll be making way more money from my soldiers protecting merchants from thieves than from your puny tolls. Ermengard rose from the table and knelt reverently. *Please, dear God, don't let my cheeks be flushed with anger. I can't give him that.* Signaling their departure to the waiting Countess de Dente, she turned to slowly walk out, head held stiff.

"The tail of the serpent," muttered the Abbot to himself, as he stared at the pointed train of her dress undulating across the floor with her footsteps. Slowly it slid over the stone threshold and disappeared.

· · ·

Having escaped the monastery's dark vaults, Ermengard and Beatritz stopped at the old Roman fountain outside. Set into a crumbling wall, whatever god it had once represented was now just a few marble lumps and bumps, yet the basin was full of cold, clear spring water.

Ermengard was annoyed. "Are my cheeks flushed?"

"No, my lady. They're pale." Actually, a red flush ran across the top of her high cheekbones. *I'll not tell her. She'll be in a detestable mood all the way home.*

Drinking with cupped hands, they splashed the refreshing water on their faces. A further short walk down a dusty road led to a blue and gold striped wagon pulled by four dappled horses. The half-dozen military escorts quickly stood to attention.

"Alais! Wake up!" Countess Beatritz called.

A sleepy face surrounded by red curls poked out from behind closed yellow silk curtains. The Countess's twelve -year-old daughter blinked and smiled sweetly.

"Run to the fountain and fill two pitchers with water for the journey home."

"Yes, Mama."

"Alais, are my cheeks flushed?"

"No, my lady." Alais had been well trained by Beatritz.

The coachman helped them up the blue-painted steps into the carriage. Before entering through the curtains they kicked their dusty slippers off onto the ground.

"Countess, help me out of this outer robe before I faint." The gray robe was as voluminous as a Roman toga. Woven of fine wool, it wound around her silk gauzape, a sleeveless gown, to hide the full curves of her body. Also out of sight of the Abbot were two long braids of black hair plaited with gold ribbon and a bejeweled gold affiche medallion that hung over her chest. The sleeves were large and long, almost touching the floor, with the ends knotted at the bottom. A white cotton guimpe covered her throat, then wound about her head to become a large wimple that stuck out on either side with two stiff wings like sails full of wind.

"I feel like a nun in this outfit." Ermengard sighed with pleasure as the weight of the robe and veil dropped off her shoulders. Rubbing her stomach, she smoothed out her turquoise gown and dropped down onto the cushions. Alais slipped in beside her to redo the braids.

"My lady, your hair has gone all curly," she giggled, undoing the gold ribbons that held it together.

"Alais, don't speak to your mistress that way!" her mother snapped at her.

"I don't mind her childishness," said Ermengard. "Here, make use of my comb."

Taking an ivory comb out of the red purse hanging from a green silk girdle on her hips, she handed it to Alais who sighed with envy when she saw the design of pearl rosettes set into gold leaves. Leaning back, Ermengard enjoyed the feeling of young, gentle hands on her hair. She pulled a cord that jingled a leather band of bells to signal the coachman.

The cart's solid wooden wheels slowly pulled out onto the shadowed forest road. *This cool mountain road is the only good part of going to the monastery,* she thought. One could see the little white boles of the irritating kermes insects that textured the rough brown bark of these ancient oaks, many of which had been cut down to feed the insatiable Roman appetite for land to plant wine grapes. The air smelled of old soil and birds' nests.

It was late morning when, after a sharp turn east, the thump of horses' hooves on dirt turned into clopping on cobblestones. The carriage, fringes bouncing and curtains swaying, rocked and stumbled over the worn ruts and dead weeds of the Roman Via Domitia. Still in common use after a thousand years, the road ran from Spain through the center of Colonia Narbo Martius, now known as Narbonne. Then it continued through Occitania as far as the Rhone River, where it turned north into the high mountains above Avignon. *You'd think the Romans still lived here and ran things.*

Ermengard thought excitedly about the new road she was building further inland to bypass this section of the old one. Unfortunately, the constant battles by local counts and Spanish kings for possession of land in Occitania had resulted in defensive castles being built on every hilltop, not roads that connected towns. She wished it was already finished; it would ease this traffic and give her a large income in tolls. Best of all, it would by-pass the center of Narbonne. *This road is always so annoying. It's just too crowded.*

Traffic was moving at the pace of an ox. The road teemed with vendors, farmers, livestock, and thieves; the air smelled of fried pork and grilled octopus as hawkers screamed to sell cheap trinkets and pots; fortune tellers with pointy hats gestured invitations into small tents covered with strange yellow stars and symbols. Lately, it had become increasingly impossible to maneuver a carriage forward. Her soldiers were yelling in frustration at the top of their lungs: "Make way for the Viscountess! Make way!"

Leaning back against the cushions, she vaguely, in transparent images, remembered her father crying when her mother had died birthing her sister Ermessend. Then came the wilting grief after her two brothers had suddenly succumbed to a quick, vicious plague. Viscount Ameryi II's trembling hand had stroked the four-year-old child's head. "You and Ermessend are all I have left now." After that, in 1134, her invincible father was killed in Spain fighting Almoravid Moslems. The five-year-old female child suddenly inherited the whole kingdom of Narbonne, making her one of the wealthiest females in the south. Almost as wealthy as Aelinore of Aquitaine.

More went wrong. At the age of thirteen, after her menses proved her fertile, two forced marriages within two months had left her still a virgin.

First, she was wed to the young Count Alphonse Jordan, who, with the backing of his powerful uncle the Count of Toulouse, had invaded Narbonne in 1142. *I still wonder, maybe I could have learned to love him. Alphonse was reckless, but so handsome.* Unfortunately, right after being given to him by contract, there was no time for noces, the ceremony of carnal consummation that took place after the church wedding. Instead, Alphonse found himself battling for his life.

The Counts of Montpelier and Barcelona were furious with what they considered to be the Count of Toulouse's land grab. Claiming Narbonne for themselves, their armies invaded Narbonne and captured Alphonse. He was given a choice: annul the marriage or die in the dungeons. The union was annulled barely after it had begun. In spite of giving his word, the Count of Montpelier, *dishonor on him for breaking a vow,* had left the young man to die of starvation shackled in the dark.

Ermengard remained a virgin. As soon as she was widowed, nothing was left to chance. The young girl was immediately wed to one of their own faction, Bernard D'Anduze, the brother of Narbonne's Archbishop. Her new husband was an old, bald, widower with grown children, who wanted nothing more to do with marriage, consummation, more children, or Narbonne. On the day of epousailles, claiming he was going on pilgrimage to the Holy Land, he mounted his horse and left the city forever. *Bernard didn't even stay the night. He was probably too old to do anything in the bed chamber and didn't want anyone to find out. Yet not to hear from him for ten years? Never a word for his wife? He's undeniably dead in Acre. He'll never return. I'm a virgin widow again.*

Perhaps I'm just fated to never have a child. One must bow to God's will. I've prayed and prayed. It's getting late and soon I'll be too old. It's so unfair!

The yellow curtain fluttered open to reveal a cracked Roman road marker numbered XXIII. A bitter memory floated to the surface of her mind. The tall stone marked the place where a path went north to a secluded, wildflower filled meadow where a fête had been held three years ago. Once again, she felt her hand resting lightly on the strong, upheld fingers of Sir Justin de Reines as they wandered away from the little blue and red tents with their fluttering flags and curious eyes. Stepping over the threshold of a doorless entry into a circle of broken columns, they found themselves standing on the cracked remains of a once exquisite mosaic floor. Scavenged for its gold tessara, tufts of brown grass were growing in the dirt where fish and mythical nymphs had been scraped up. As they gazed at each other her heart had pounded so hard in her chest that she could barely breathe with the pain. Though his castle was in the north, his black hair, high-cheeked oval face, and almond-shaped eyes bespoke his Spanish lineage through the Count of Barcelona. What beautiful children they would have!

"You can't marry him. You're still married to my brother Bernard," Pierre D'Anduze, Narbonne's Archbishop, had snapped at her.

"He hasn't been here for over seven years. I haven't even seen him since we were wed."

"He's in the Holy Land fighting with other Christians. You should be on your knees praying for him instead of consorting with northern cowards."

"You can't keep telling me what to do! I'm the Viscountess of Narbonne!" Ermengard cried.

Yet he could, and he did. The Archbishop used religion to control her. As long as she was married and alone, he could rule Narbonne beside her. A new husband would take over her domains and disturb the profitable financial order of things.

Always the same answer, she thought sadly. Later, when word came to her of Justin's marriage to a Capetian duchess, she clenched her fists. *I'm going to fight harder next time.* She would ask King Louis to annul her marriage for ratum sed non consummatum. After all, she was still a virgin. *They can all examine me if they want to. Even the king.*

Then they'll all start fighting battles over me again. It never stops. I feel like an animal in a cage.

She watched a buzzing, luminescent blue fly trace circles in the air. *Isn't it pretty how the green wings look against the yellow curtains.* It banged into walls in its frantic efforts to escape. *Just like me.*

The carriage wrenched sideways. It was frustrating. The Via Domitia had not been maintained since the Romans had departed many years ago. *Where are the Romans when you need them?* Still, over time, old military resting stations had evolved into towns with churches and markets; many of her subjects were distant descendants of soldiers who had retired here, who had been paid for their service by a plot of land.

Often, when riding through the scrubby and dry mountain garigue, one came upon a half-buried marble head and shoulders, perhaps an extended arm holding a bunch of grapes. Lichen and moss would have seeped into the white skin, staining it with a motley green and brown leprosy. Or, down in a rocky ravine, missing its statue of a proudly gesturing emperor, was a cracked plinth carved with worn laurel leaves surrounding the words *Pone hic per Caesar.*

Whenever she gazed out the windows of her palace solar, she could see old broken-up pieces of Roman sepulchers haphazardly mortared into the city's ramparts. *Amazing. So many of my people are descendants of marble carvers that Narbonne still does a brisk trade selling marble sarcophagi around the world. Hm-m-m, I must remember to put that tax on any buried marble carvings and statues found.*

The wheels crushed across now dry arroyos that would spring into grassy life when winter rains washed the dust off the old stones. It made her proud to ride slowly alongside the salt marches and seaside lagoons full of waterfowl splashing amongst the sparkling, shrimp-laden tide pools in the estuary of the Aude River. Beyond the tall grasses workers raked dry her white gold, piling the salt into blinding mounds before it was packed into bags and shipped as far north as Paris.

She breathed in the thick, briny air of Narbonne's lagoons, full of merchant's galleys swaying so far sideways that their masts almost tapped against each other. Barges, square-sailed pilot boats, tugboats, and vendors selling food, wine and pleasure, expertly dodged the anchored hulls full of Cordoban leather, Byzantine silk, linen from Alexandria, blond slaves from the icy north, pepper, ginger, saffron, and exotic animals.

Ermengard ruled over a golden land in which all its inhabitants safely participated in the wealth from the harbor trade. Jews and Moslems were permitted their schools. Mozarites, Christians who had gradually migrated up from Moslem-dominated Iberia, and who lived just like Muslims, were tolerated. Persians, Rhadanite Jews, Zoroastrians, those from India and China, all who abided by her laws, were welcome here. Christians wielded power with discretion so as not to disturb the patterns of wealth.

Opposite the Viscountess, sitting on a blue cushion stitched with red stars, was the Countess Beatritz de Dent. An accomplished trobaritz, she played a romantic ballad on her small, gilded psaltery to calm another one of Ermengard's frequently restless moods. The yellow silk curtains, swaying gently in the heat, cast a soft glow on her face. Heavy blond hair bound into a braid was tightly wrapped around Beatritz's head; a strong narrow nose and jaw, and startlingly sky-blue eyes, revealed northern ancestors. Considered exceptionally tall for a woman, Beatritz had a sinewy body that relaxed when she was in voice. Her long- nailed fingers, painted a deep red, plucked vibrating notes as she sang:

> *In an orchard under the hawthorn leaves,*
> *the Lady kept her lover by her side*
> *until the Watchman cried that day had come:*
> *Oh God, Oh God, the dawn—how soon it arrives!*
> *Fair, sweet love, let us play one more game*
> *in this garden where the birds sing*
> *until the shepherd begins to play on his pipe:*
> *Oh God, Oh God, the dawn—how soon it arrives!*

Beatritz was totally devoted to her sovereign; nine years ago Ermengard had saved her life. The Chateau de Dent, so named because of its location high above a pointy ridge that resembled a wolf's teeth, had been her home for the eight years she was married to Arnauld, Viscount of the Plateau of Sault. The blond beauty of this innocent young woman, the daughter of a Provencal minor noble, had instantly captured the desire of the dark-haired, brusque Catalonian. Though he treated his wife with respect, Arnauld was more interested in pulling boulders out of streams to increase mill power, wrapping linen around his pears to make them maggot free, and training the perfect gyrfalcon to sell to the king. Beatritz's favorite time of day was when she sat in the courtyard in the evening light and sang to her two children. In her parents' court she had been trained as a trobaritz, but since her husband was not one to travel and visit other nobles, she became content singing for her children. When her three-year-old son Jean died, Beatritz was inconsolable. She lost herself in deeper lyrics and increased the tragic timbre of her voice. Her daughter, Alais, always sat at her mother's feet.

After six years of isolation in the mountains, the unhappy and vulnerable Beatritz was persuaded into a dangerous heresy.

Her conversion occurred when the chateau was visited by a wandering, self-styled Bishop named Claris de Castres. Accompanying him was the young troubadour, Raimbaut d'Aurenga. Starved for company, Beatritz welcomed them into her home and was delighted that she had such a highly skilled troubadour with whom she could sing.

"Yes, we are indeed Bons Hommes, one of the Good Men," Claris confessed one night to Beatritz and Arnaud, his face bright and open despite the dangers of openly admitting to following a sect deemed heretical by the Catholic Church. "For us, Christ is a spirit and part of God, thus he could never have been crucified." Bons Hommes refused to attend the Catholic Church and take the host; they did not believe in the absolution of sin by confession.

"He's actually a parfait, one of the pure ones," Raimbaut declared. "A spiritual guide, an earthly angel who has guided me to the eternal light of God." It amazed Beatritz when he said that as a Bonne Filles, a woman could also become a parfait and have actual authority to administer rites.

"Your Church mocks God," continued Claris. "It is a den of cupidity and simony with an unending need for wealth and power. We have no need for gold. We never eat meat. We never wear leather."

"They never bathe either," Arnaud snapped to his wife. He had heard of this heretical sect and wanted to send them on their way, but Beatritz had begged him not to do so.

"Please Arnaud, let them stay. I'm a trobaritz and I so long to have another musician to play with."

The next two months were a gentle seduction.

Raimbaut, who actually appeared to her to have a shining light surround him, sang of the beauty of a "good death" that brought you to God's side as a bright star, a fire in the night sky. His songs, full of allegory and pure love, moved Beatritz to the core.

She had lost her only son. Now, on clear nights, she could see him twinkling in the heavens. "Look Alais," she whispered to the three-year-old daughter sitting in her lap, "up there, you can see your brother."

Many nights Beatritz and Raimbaut sang sad ballads together until dawn, crying tears for a greater meaning than this sad, painful life.

"God gave you a beautiful voice," Raimbaut said softly. Her face warm, she looked down in embarrassment. "Come join us Beatritz," he urged. "We can show you how to fly up to God, you will see Jean's face smiling in his star, you will escape these chains for a night."

Beatritz was especially drawn to Sophia, the female aspect of God's wisdom. No one had ever imagined a female part of God; even Mary, the mother of Jesus, was just a holy vessel.

"Ah, but the Hagia Sophia, or Divine Wisdom, has always been female. And who can deny God's wisdom?" Claris was gently unrelenting.

Thus Beatritz was seduced into heresy. She came to believe that darkness ruled the world. Procreation was the work of Satan as it caused humans to be born into misery; she became, to her husband's frustration, newly chaste. She began to look forward to death when would receive the sanctifying consolamentum.

Arnaud was fed up. "I've had enough. Those two have to leave. What if the Church discovers they are living here under our roof? We'll both be burned at the stake while they run off and hide somewhere in their endless caves."

As if the two were warned, they left just in time. A Papal emissary arrived at the Chateau de Dent to find more "Soldiers of God" to fight in his endless crusades. He asked many questions.

"This is your doing, Beatritz. You and your Bons Hommes," said Renaud. "The emissary must have come here because of rumors of heresy. Now I have to declare my faith by fighting in the Holy Land."

In order to protect his wife and daughter from the punishment of fire, Arnaud, angry, but brave, went off to fight in the Crusades.

Beatritz, confused, was left alone with feelings of guilt and betrayal. *What have I done?* she thought. But she could not forget the joy of her time with Claris and Raimbaut.

A few months passed, and word came that Arnaud had been killed in Edessa while fighting a skirmish with the Selkuk Turks.

In nearby Toulouse, Count Raymond IV was pleased. "Arnaud's dead?" This was his opportunity to marry off his youngest son to the widow before the boy's whore disease was obvious to the world and, in addition, gain the Plateau of Sault. He immediately sent a delegation, commanding: "And don't come back without her."

But the Count did not take into consideration the strength of Beatritz's conversion (nor, to be fair, did he have any knowledge of it).

When the delegation faced the widowed Countess, she felt the blood rush to her face. "We are grateful to Raymond, and indeed honored by his noble offer, yet I need time to pray on this matter," she said.

"Ah, yes, of course you must pray. A wedding party will be here in two days to escort you to your new husband."

Fear of living in the Count's worldly hell gave her strength. *This cannot happen! I must foil that old fool's plans.* The same night, avoiding the Count's men guarding the courtyard, Beatritz escaped with her daughter by crawling through the stink and waste of an old midden tunnel on the cliff side of the castle. Speaking softly, so the child would not cry out, she roped Alais onto the saddle of Chanson, her blackest horse. Shaking with fear, she avoided the common paths and set off through the limestone crags of the Corbières, racing towards Narbonne twenty miles away.

Drinking from streams, eating only berries, she forged ahead. There was no moon on the second night. Towards morning, Chanson stumbled in the low mist of a rocky gorge and broke his foreleg.

"Forgive me, Chanson. I must leave you here to die alone," said Beatritz. He looked at her with wet and dark eyes full of pain. "Horses also go to God. I will pray for your soul." His dark form on the rock was breathing softly as, crying quiet tears, she left him lying there alone on the white rocks in the blue dawn.

Bruised from the fall, carrying Alais tied to her back, she started trudging across a calcareous plateau carpeted with prickly garrigue bushes. The scent of crushed lavender, sage, and thyme wafted up into the hot air to mix with the metallic tang of her blood flowing from the dry, razor sharp, grass barbs sticking into the skin of her legs. The frantic barking of dogs forced her to slosh through a freezing stream to put them off the scent of blood. When she saw the stream rushing out of a cave, she hid inside, sleeping on a stone shelf, hugging the shivering and hungry child.

Down, down rolling pebble paths, avoiding workers pruning vines. Lips tight with the force of her determination, Beatritz became numb to pain. On the third day she saw the stone ramparts of Narbonne. Soldiers wearing the Trencavel colors were watching everyone. Braving the road, she saw a peasant driving a cart full of wool. Bribed with a worn coin, he let Beatritz and Alais crawl in and hide until they were through the gate.

Scrambling out inside the town they staggered to the tiny stone chapel built over the birthplace of Saint Sebastien. Sitting exhausted against the altar, she asked the priest to inform Ermengard that she was seeking sanctuary.

• • •

Ermengard despised the Count of Toulouse; she could never forget his earlier invasion of her city. To spite him, she took Beatritz in and sheltered her from his grasping rage.

The two women were of a similar age. Surrounded by a dour court of women whose strict Catholic rules didn't allow for intimacy, Ermengard was immediately drawn to the widow and her child. The Countess, Alais by her side, went to mass every morning, kneeling for hours amidst the jealous and suspicious ladies. Carefully she hid the fact that she was a Bonne Fille; she trained Alais to do the same.

Ermengard soon realized that Beatritz had some very strange attitudes towards life, but ignored them, refusing to let that interfere in their growing friendship. Heresy was never mentioned.

Just once, Ermengard had said to no one in particular: "How can anyone believe in that *Bons Hommes* sect started by that Bulgarian priest Bogomil two-hundred years ago?" Beatritz had looked down at her lap. *My soul will be a bright star shining in the night sky next to Arnaud and our son. I will never be born again.*

It was a long shadow that followed the friendship of the two women, yet it never touched their feet. As an avid patron of the arts, the Viscountess Ermengard was delighted to find that the Countess was an accomplished vocalist with practiced knowledge of the gai sabor, the joyous art of the troubadours. At twilight, with everyone gathered amidst the roof garden's orchids and jasmine blossoms, Beatritz sang a seemingly endless variety of songs and dances, often performing with the jongleurs and other singers who frequently visited Narbonne. Playing the tambourine at her mother's side, Alais came to be loved as a daughter by the childless Ermengard.

Yet, Beatritz remained an active heretic, in contact with many troubadours who were also Bons Hommes. Warnings about searches and persecutions by the Catholic Church was a mission coded into their entertainments; verses held words that gave the time and locations of Bons Hommes secret meetings. Beatritz was an active participant, receiving and passing along these messages, and whenever possible, sneaking out at night to attend meetings. The rest of her time was dedicated to keeping Ermengard content.

• • •

Listening to Beatritz play her psaltery in the carriage, Ermengard relaxed after her annoying altercation with Don Estaban. The royal carriage slowed to a stop as her mounted escorts shouted at someone who was refusing to yield to her right to pass. As blows began to be laid on, the hot and dusty crowd, erupting in anger, tried to defend him:

"By the holy cross, he's just trying to get to market!"

"Next time we'll go to Carcassonne to sell our wares!"

Wrapping a silk shawl around her head, Ermengard pulled back the curtain. "Vidal, what is going on? I want to get home."

The soldier turned around at the sharp tone of her voice. His grisly, round face under a metal helmet appeared at the curtain.

"My apologies, Domina. There's a merchant with a cart full of lemons pulled by an ancient horse who's insisting that he has to get to the market because the heat will cook his fruit. He refuses to yield."

"Fetch me one of his lemons."

"Yes, Domina," the startled Vidal said as he rode away, returning soon, balancing a knobby, yellow lemon in the palm of his old leather glove.

With delicate fingers she picked up the warm, soft fruit. Scratching open the rind with a gaily decorated fingernail, the sharp, acid and sweet scent of citrus sprayed into her nose. Inhaling deeply, she ordered the soldier: "These are exceptionally fine. I will buy the whole cartful of his lemons. Tell him to get out of the way then bring them to the palace kitchen."

The wagon lurched forward again as Ermengard leaned back against the cushions. There was a rushing sound, and the empty sky over the marshes turned into a living tapestry with thousands of honking, rose-colored flamingos rising into the air, their long red legs, bright orange-black tipped wings, and curved rosy beaks moving like colored threads in a loom.

Now what could have caused that? mused Ermengard.

Dozing off to the plonking of music, she didn't wake again until the acrid tang of animal offal baking in the sun informed her that she was crossing the butchers' bridge next to her palace. The fly, smelling blood, went berserk. In its frantic efforts to get out, it knocked itself against the ceiling so hard that it fell into Ermengard's lap, dead on its back.

CHAPTER 3

... skalds can't stint on chanting—
each thrown wave's tune thrumming
through sweet-sheered strakes. Steering
an arc—keel careering
down combers, prow foaming,
spars creaking...
        —Rogenvaldr Kali Kolsson, 1103? —1158

May 1152, Orkneyjar

The wind, heavy with brine and the stench of fish, blew through the morning mist. Finally, after endless delays, the sailing men of Orkneyjar were headed to the docks on the south coast of Hrossey Island where fifteen ships waited in the calm waters of the skalpaflói, the long, flat harbor they called home. Some understood they would never see it again.

Rogenvaldr stood impatiently next to his new ship, running his fingers down the letters on the hull. *Hjálp. A good name for a vessel.* Ornately carved into a wooden scroll, the blue, red, and gold letters reflected the silvery light. *You will carry me to Jerusalem! If we ever get going,* he mused.

"Looks fine, very fine. Well, my lord, are you ready to sail? Eh?" The familiar voice of Magnus Gunnison interrupted his thoughts.

The Earl had picked his men carefully. Months on board a boat watching each other do things they'd rather ignore, eating endless dried halibut and porridge, giving constant attention to changing winds, this needed a reasonably good-natured crew.

"Yes. We're finally ready to leave."

Magnus, the boat's styrimaör, took his seat by the main mast, where, as the navigator, only he was allowed to sit. "Hope you picked a good coxswain. Doesn't matter where I tell you to go if he can't steer the boat."

A grizzled, tough seaman, Magnus was also legally enjoined to make sure that the King's Gulating Seafaring Laws were obeyed. His total power to declare a person lawless, and then throw them off the ship (whether near land or not), was fearsome.

Unfortunately, as good a navigator as he is, he doesn't have a sólasteinn crystal to locate the sun like Eindredi does.

"And who's bringing the rudder?" Magnus asked.

"Brian of Flydruness. Here he comes." Rogenvaldr looked up at the coxswain, who was carrying the ship's enormous rudder on one shoulder. Taller than his Earl by a head, with arms and legs like oak tree trunks, Blian's strength at holding the steering board steady was a legend. Efficiently he set to work attaching it to the starboard side of the ship.

"Good man." Magnus was satisfied with the choice.

Armod the Skald, short and swarthy, staggered up the gangplank carrying a heavy wooden box waterproofed with pitch and seal skin. Strangely, while Armod stumbled when it came to regular speech, he was a masterful singer. He stowed the box by his bench, and, opening it, beckoned the Earl over. Inside was the usual assortment of instruments: lyre, panpipe, deer leg flute, hand bells. Armod took out a large round pouch made of walrus hide that had been boiled in herring oil. With a gleam in his eye he pulled out a magnificent lur, a trumpet made of hammered brass, carved with sacred symbols, and curving around in an arc longer than his arm. When blowing on it, he held it under his armpit, its wide end behind his head: when it sounded, he could feel the vibration in his bones. The ships spoke to each other with these lurs. Their sharp, loud tones could signal danger, stop, reverse, and illness. Its codes were taught to every Norseman in childhood, and it was a valuable man who could blow this horn during a battle or storm.

The crowd gathered on the dock was brusquely pushed aside by John Limp-Leg. "Leave me alone, Blian. I can walk up a gangplank. And row better than any of you. Soon Jesus will cure my leg."

Rogenvaldr's ill-tempered brother-in-law flexed his prodigious arm muscles for the women to admire, then stumped up into the boat, stowing his waterproof sørya, a sheep's wool blanket, under his seat.

Frida, his wife, had stuffed in an extra set of pants and shirt, an animal bone comb, ear cleaner, and tweezers.

The Earl knew John was really going to Jerusalem to be cured of impotence, not his limp. Everyone blamed Frida for their lack of children, but his half-sister had told him the truth. *I wish him well, yet I pray that he will hold his temper.*

Thorbjorn the Swarthy arrived, his round belly the size of the black kettles he was having stowed on board. Over here, you bugger. Bring it over here," he yelled to an overloaded slave who arrived carrying bags of barley, rye flour, fatty slices of dried bread, halibut, and cod. Thorbjorn also insisted on tubs of animal fat; only meat fermented in whey was allowed on the boat.

"You, help get the water barrels on board," he grumbled, "don't just stand around watching. And don't forget the barrels of ale."

Ah, very good. My hairy cook. "Can't wait to eat your porridge day after day for next three months."

"You don't like it, don't eat it. Starve for all I care, my honored Earl. Where's the tinder box?" The cook looked anxiously over the keel.

"Here it is." Walking carefully, carrying a large metal box with a tight lid, came Gimkel of Glettness. During the winter thaw, the earnest young man had spent time on the mainland of Scotland harvesting tree fungus. After slicing it, he baked it in a stone oven until it dried. There was a Viking secret: put it into a vat, ask everyone to pee on it, and boil it for hours until the stinking mixture became a thick and sticky dough. Formed into flat sheets and hung out to dry, it became a smelly, very flammable blanket. Cut up into pieces, it was stored in the tinder box and watched over by Gimkel, who was to sit over it the whole voyage. If lightning struck it, Gimkel would explode in flames.

Aslak came running, breathless and excited, eyes blue and bright, long blond hair coming out of its braid. A soft, pale beard fell from sixteen-year-old cheeks still smooth and scarless. His black leather vest was studded with magic rune staves to protect him from harm. On its back was a bold aegishjalmur, its eight radiant tridents protecting a central point; over his heart was the vegvisir, a compass that would guide Aslak to take the right path in life; on the right side of his chest was Sleipnir, Odin's fearless and brave eight-legged horse that would protect him on his travels.

"Those runes are pagan magic!" declared Magnus. "You can't bring them on this ship!"

"Is there a Law against it?" Aslak challenged the man.

Magnus snarled: "No. But I'm going to make sure there is one in the future if idiots like you bring that kind of un-Christian heresy on board."

Standing alone on a promontory behind the crowd, a broad-shouldered, tall figure, almost hidden amongst the raucous, shrilling, razorbills flapping on the rocks, was Aslak's mother watching him board the ship.

Yesterday, the middle-aged noblewoman, wearing a long, grey cloak, her blond hair neatly tied back, had come to entreat Rogenvaldr.

"Aslak is all I have left. My husband is with God and my daughter Sigrid, his twin sister, has disappeared, probably kidnapped. I don't want him to go, yet he insists, leaving me alone to grind the grain. At sixteen he's a man, but a very young, inexperienced man. I beg you, watch over him. I know he is not your son, but, if she had lived, he would have married your daughter Ingirid. He is impetuous and restless, and, hopefully, this journey will open his eyes to the realities of life's dangers. His grandfather died in King Sigurd's crusade, but Aslak has no knowledge of how far away Jerusalem really is. I think, in his heart, somehow he believes he will find his sister and bring her back to me."

Rogenvaldr was uncomfortable. She was a powerful woman, from a long line of rune readers, and was known to have half of her heart in the Christian world and the other half in the world of old magic. *I can't give him special treatment just because he's her son and so young. And that jacket she made will not help him with the crew.* "God willing, I will return him to you cleansed by the River Jordan."

Her face was stiff. "Please do not fail me. I will sacrifice and pray for the safe return of both of you."

Thorgeir Scotpoll was a bald-headed, fearsome, muscle of a man. A snarl from his angry lips and lizard-like black eyes frightened men into apologies despite having done nothing wrong. His prowess with an axe was legendary; he could split a rock the size of a man with one blow. Yet, in the middle of his wiry black beard, a little orange face peeked out. Green eyes and whiskers above small white paws watched attentively from a snug leather pouch under his vest.

"So who is this little fellow?" Rogenvaldr put out a finger for the cat to sniff. "Will you be our rat catcher on board?"

"This is Freya. I grabbed her from my brother's cat farm a few months ago. Lucky for her, or she'd be a furry hat by now. You'll do good, eh, Freya?" He scratched the little head with a square fingernail. "I've been training her."

The rest of the crew was hurriedly boarding. Nearby, Eindredi's men were pulling in the gangplank. There was one man still missing.

I wonder if the Bishop changed his mind. Oh My Lord God!

A barefoot Bishop William was approaching the docks carrying a huge wooden cross on his back. The square cut vertical piece was taller than his own lanky height and must have been hewn from a huge oak. The crosspiece was at least six feet in length and bolted on with thick iron bolts at least two feet long. William was bent over with its weight. The crowd was falling to its knees in awe as he painfully passed by.

All he's missing is a crown of thorns.

The ship listed to one side as everyone maneuvered to help get the cross on board. Some sailors kissed their hands before and after touching it. William turned to the kneeling crowd and made the sign of the cross. "May Christ bless this pilgrimage and keep it safe."

"Do we really need it?" Rogenvaldr was looking down at the large amount of space the cross was taking up where it was lying in the prow, just where he like to stand near the dragon.

"We will need it."

Sigh. Let's just get out of here before someone brings a church.

Suddenly Magnus stood up and went to kneel on the cross. Hands clasped, the navigator loudly prayed, "Jesus Christ grant us a safe voyage. To this end I have vowed celibacy till we return. Any who wishes to join me will be blessed."

Rogenvaldr rolled his eyes. *That will put them all into an ill temper the whole voyage.*

The clatter of shields being hung on the rails outside the ship stirred the crowd to chant: "Jerusalem! Jerusalem! Jerusalem!," as they threw hats in the air and stomped their feet. Gertrude went to the chapel to pray, as she had sworn to do every day until Aslak returned. And if he didn't return, she would continue to pray; there would be nothing else to do.

Thousands of threatening, screeching boxies dove from the sky to peck at the rowers' heads as they quickly grabbed leather helmets to save their skulls.

"Never mind the boxies! Row me to the front of the fleet before Eindredi challenges my authority. What the—?" annoyed, he nearly fell over the cross as he stepped to stand by the dragon.

Wisely, Eindredi kept his position just behind the Earl.

Echoing their captains' rivalry, the two ships glistened in the sharp waves, competing for the title of most noble vessel. After them came vessels commanded by various clan chieftains such as Erling Skakki, Ungi, Guttorm, and Swein.

A half-mile from shore the út-norör, a brisk north wind picked up. Armond sounded his lur, and the sails were unfurled, setting the large, red pilgrim crosses sewn on them to flap sharply against the rapidly moving clouds. As soon as the fresh, briny taste of the North Sea wet their lips, not one man missed home.

"Look east!" John Limp-Leg cried, pointing at a huge, humped shape in the water moving towards the harbor. "A fish driver whale—a fortunate sign for the beginning of our journey." They all turned to look at the great fish as it generously herded shimmering masses of herring to the shore. "Our people will not starve while we are gone."

Rogenvaldr called out to them: "Let its presence be a warning. As long as we don't fight or shed blood amongst ourselves, the whale will honor its covenant with God and continue to feed our families."

Freya crawled out of Thorgeir's vest and decided it was safe enough to explore. Her orange tail close to the ground, she sniffed at a hairy leg, jumped away when it moved, licked fish oil, nuzzled musty old pants, then disappeared into a dark corner to follow some droppings.

As his slave Oddi set the rhythm by twanging the mouth harp, Armod the Skald began to chant heroic ballads that engaged the oars of the rowers as they pulled against a southern wind off the coast of Scotland. While negotiating the wildly thrown rocks and long sand spits that blocked the mouth of Northumbria's Wear River, the waves began to rise. Armod sang of the journey:

High the crests were of the billows
As we passed the mouth of the Hvera;
Masts were bending, and the low land
Met the waves in long sand reaches;
Blind our eyes were with the salt spray.

When the fleet passed the island of Lindisfarne, a shiver of fear went down every sailor's spine as he tried not to stare at the terrible, burnt ruins of the once thriving monastery. Black, blood-soaked soil was now spotted with bright green moss around its edges. Waves crashed around the cliffs as if still trying to put out the fires. The vista of lonely, empty arches of sacred buildings, brutally ravaged by their Viking ancestors, caused many of them to stop rowing and drop to their knees, praying for forgiveness.

Thank God that we are on our way to Jerusalem and our salvation.

As if to test their resolve, another horrendous reminder of their Viking past appeared ahead, high up on a cliff. Incised into the black surface of the rocky wall was an enormous white carving of an eagle on a man's back. But they all knew it wasn't really an eagle; it was the blood eagle ritual.

Eindredi sounded his lur and headed for the beach below it.

"No, I won't allow it!" Bishop William was livid with anger.

"What can I do?" Rogenvaldr said. "Eindredi is determined to spend the night here. And all the ships are following him."

The beach lay in a curved hollow under the carving. All the longboats anchored themselves in a semi-circle on the strand, their prows trying to avoid pointy rocks sticking out of the choppy waves. The Norsemen stood on the brown sand looking up, as the setting sun shadowed the edges of the carving into sharp relief. It was frightening.

Thorbjorn had dragged his kettle up the beach as he set the Hjálp's men to gather driftwood. Gimkel kindled a fire with tinder stones. Barley, lingonberries, salt, dried shark were set to boiling with fresh water from barrels. Ale was passed around in leather skeins.

After the meal, as night fell, Armod put his harp on his lap. The glow of the dying fire drew a gold line along his beard and lips; his eyes were glass stones. He began to sing the ancient Skaldic song "The Tale of Ragnor's Sons". The further he got into it, the more the now drunken men joined in, encouraging the bloodshed and cruelty, enjoying the victory of Sigurd Snake-in-the Eye, waiting excitedly for King Aella's final punishment: the Blood Eagle Death!

> *I sing of the blood eagle ritual,*
> *the sacrifice of Odin,*
> *the splitting of the knobbed back with an axe,*
> *the white ribs pulled apart to form wings,*
> *the still breathing white lungs.*
> *Make for us the body of the cruelest bird*
> *sacred to the gods.*
> *Throw the burning salt on the mangled flesh.*

"Stop! Enough!" cried Bishop William. "You will bring God's wrath on our voyage for enjoying the old pagan ways. Mark my words, you men will all be punished for singing about those gruesome acts. We are NOT Vikings anymore—we are Christian Norsemen. On your knees— all of you! We will now pray to Jesus for forgiveness and salvation. Especially you, Armod."

"It's just a song," protested Armod.

"It's Satan's power on earth, that's what your evil music is. Now pray!"

Dawn was a gray haze on a flat sea, its surface the oily, silver, sheen of whale skin with no clap of waves breaking, no wind, no birds shrieking. The sailors were afraid to break the silence, gesturing to each other as they left the beach, not looking up at the blood eagle. Sails were useless. They rowed with shallow breaths.

William's prophecy of punishment was fulfilled when, careening down from the north, the huge fist of a thundercloud overtook the fleet. A hammer rolled over them and then they were drowning in a sky-river, a raging flood of water falling from above. Below, the shuddering vessels were caught in the jaws of a sea hungrily eating ships, only to vomit them up again into the watery earthquake of black sea mountains rising forever upwards.

Hailstones rained like arrows into frozen beards, quickly ageing them from brown to frozen silver. Salt spray glued their eyes shut. Frozen burls clung to wooden masts, icy reminders of the trees they had once been. Foam spray on the decks looked like thousands of white fingers chopped off of dead mens' hands.

Aslak, huddled down against the hull, half-buried in seaweed-clotted brine, was clutching his chest in the magical jacket, loudly intoning prayers to the runes.

The gale whipped around their heads: the men grew dizzy as unseen maelstroms spun the ships in vicious circles. In every lightning flash they sought land. Hitting them with the strength of a wrestler's shoulders, brutal gusts punched the ships back and forth between English and Frankish shores.

With desperate relief, piercing through the storm, Rogenvaldr heard Eindredi's lur sounding "Follow me!"

As miserable a man as he is, he's the navigator we need right now.

Magnus had heard the signal and was already telling Brian which way to steer.

Eindredi's *lur* was being blown continuously, and, as Rogenvaldr's ship followed him, Armod blew his own horn to tell ships behind him in what direction to go. On and on the long, high, tones rode the wind, calling them to shore.

Eindredi had surmised correctly that they had been slapped all the way down to the South Sea; tacking sharply, he led them to a deep notch in high, chalky cliffs. Most of the storm was behind them. The exhausted sailors dropped anchor just off some brown sand flats.

Two skiffs had been pulled up on the shore. Rogenvaldr, Bishop William and Eindredi were deciding where to go next. The cross was lying at their feet.

Rogenvaldr's cousin was full of pride at how he had saved the fleet.

William fell to his knees. "Let us pray and give thanks to God for rescuing us."

"No! I rescued us, not God!" Eindredi snapped.

"Three-hundred men watching us from those ships need to understand that you are but God's instrument. Now help me raise up the cross."

Eindredi spit and knelt.

Afterwards, Rogenvaldr rose and brushed off his stiff knees. "We're all exhausted. We can stay here tonight, but we desperately need fresh water and ale."

"This place is Duver," Eindredi said. "The sands here are treacherous. They move overnight if a south wind suddenly blows down the Dour River. Duver is nothing but a bunch of huts built by the Romans to ferry

people across to Calais. Tomorrow we can sail to Normandy. I have
family who settled there."

Soon driftwood was burning, and porridge boiled in kettles.
Rogenvaldr threw some freshly caught fish on the fire, washing it down
with ale. Encircling him, in the darkening light, the fires glowed on the
beach like an amber necklace in the sun. Lying down on the wet sand,
wrapped in fur seal, he gazed up at the storm-cleansed night sky. Inside
the black, endless dome, the stars were bright and sharp, so numerous
they washed across the heavens, pale blue waves on black sand. *I miss
the Virgins of the Night.* A sharp pinch in his chest made his eyes snap
open. *I might never see them again.*

Before dawn porridge was boiling again. Lit by the rising sun, the
white cliffs threw wavering reflections onto the water, lighting up the
faces of the men readying to sail.

Leaving the tide to wash away the ashes, the fleet sailed towards
the sun.

• • •

The Cotentin Peninsula jutted far out into the sea off the coast of
western Normandy. Its foaming surf raged against high craggy cliffs
burning orange against the twilight sky. At long last, tucked into a
corner of the coastline, they found a calm harbor sheltering numerous
impressive fishing boats.

The local fisherman and farmers were the descendants of Rollo, the
first Viking to settle here several hundred years ago. Eindredi sought out
his cousin, "Crooked Neck" Ormosson, who, it appeared, had grown
wealthy and fat whaling in these waters. The two cousins had not seen
each other in many years.

"He looks like a whale himself," Eindredi murmured to Rogenvaldr,
as they sat around a table loaded high with delicacies. "Look at this!"
Eindredi declared. "A meal fit for a king: butter, fowl, chestnuts, rabbit —
a French king that dresses in skirts."

"Ah," Ormosson reminded them, his lips shiny with goose fat, "Yes.
That's what comes of being Norsemen now, respectable traders and
people of this land. You, on the other hand, are still bloody Vikings —
peaceful Christian ones, you claim — but the people you will encounter

won't really believe that yet. It's only been about forty years since we, I mean you, burned Bordeaux, extorted Paris, and killed the Bishop at Campus Stellae in Iberia. One generation of Christianity is not enough time to change people's perceptions of Scandic warriors. We Norsemen living here have worked hard at proving ourselves over the years."

William gave Rogenvaldr a sideways look over the table. He was obviously remembering the events of the Blood Eagle Death.

"The Duke here is a reasonable man who does not tax us overmuch, so we can live in peace. Stay awhile. Perhaps you'll settle. And the winter weather doesn't freeze your balls off either."

"I have two sons, who, being way more men than any of the sodomite argrs around here, have married rich and noble daughters. I'm a grandfather of five!"

"And if the Duke needs us to fight, we go!" boasted one of his well-dressed sons, his brown hair carefully turned under at the bottom on his neck and brow-banks cut straight just above his blue eyes.

"What a soft life—full of demanding women and wine," Eindredi groused later when they were alone.

"Yes, but the wine was really very good," Rogenvaldr replied.

The two were seated by a round window playing hnefatafl on a soapstone table incised with black and red painted squares. Eindredi's hair shone white in the light. His eyes were almost hidden as he squinted at the gaming pieces. A knobby little glass warrior, covered with blue and white swirls, looked too fragile to be held by Eindredi's thick hand. Nimbly, his fingers, with their nails resembling chipped scallop shells, bumped the piece across the board.

Rogenvaldr's fingers, long and strong in his well-muscled hand, the nails clean and carefully shaped, took his piece.

"Ha! This is the only way they fight now. My ass is on a padded chair. Fart on them! Let's get what we need and get out of here."

For once, Rogenvaldr agreed with him. "Fresh water, whale meat, salted herrings, wheat flour, fish oil, your cousins are robbing me naked."

"You're the one who wants wine. Don't look to me for help. It's expensive. It's your pilgrimage, you pay for it."

"Hm-m-m, I wonder how long the cheese they sold me will last."

CHAPTER 4

Oh Priest! Take care!
Or what was said to Christ on the Cross
will be said of you:
He saved others, yet could not save himself!
—Norbert of Xanten, 1080—1134

MAY 1153, PRÉMONTRÉ ABBEY, KINGDOM OF FRANCE

In a desolate valley west of Paris, the frozen mist wrapped its icy talons around the knuckled roots of oak trees surrounding the hidden Abbey of Prémontré. In the mossy graveyard, twelve monks weighed down by brown soggy wool cloaks, their feet freezing in wooden clogs, were gathered on the musty soil heaped around the ragged grave of young brother Gereon. Scrawny as chicken bones, his sixteen-year-old corpse was lowered into the pit, his body rattling when he hit bottom, like dice in a cup. The youth had made a gamble with God: "If I live a penitential life at Prémontré, I will go to heaven." He had not expected to win the wager so soon.

Hugon, Abbot of the Order of Canons of Prémontré, intoned a prayer in a low, accusative voice. Hidden in the shadow of a cowl draped over his long, thin face, his large, heavy-lidded eyes, with no whites showing around the large black pupils, were endless black pits. Flat pouches of gray skin hung under them. Deep straight lines, etched into either side of a large beaked nose, cut his skin down to his chin. It was the face of a vulture, of one who lived on death.

Speaking through thin lips, breath whistling, he warned, "Alas, brothers, this one's faith and body were not strong enough to endure the rigors of our life of penance. Gereon lost the battle, yet he saved his soul; that is the most important thing." *Another disappointment. Another one who didn't live long enough to fully learn the joys of self-mortification.*

41

The monks, in silent agreement, crossed themselves with dripping fingers.

Two barefoot novices in homespun robes, icy water running down their necks from uncovered hair, picked up shovels to fill the grave. A bony cat, just as hungry as they were, crept over to check out the hole. It jumped back when one of the diggers threw a shovel full of soil at it. Undeterred, it snuck back to see over the edge, then jumped in as a small rodent emerged from under a root, snaped it up, and clambered out, streaking away, a black tail hanging from its mouth.

The monks turned to leave, clogs making sucking noises in the mud.

Dripping beech trees, tangled branches forming a tunnel over the narrow path to the Abbey, added to the cold misery. As the monks walked slowly along, heads down, one behind the other, a raptor looking down from his branch mistook them for a plump caterpillar waddling its way down the track.

Norbert of Xanten had founded the Abbey in 1120, and it was home to his Order of Norbertines. Norbert had insisted upon an ascetism so strict that many disciples starved to death, froze to death, or worked themselves to death in a state of religious zeal.

Hugon's measured survival disciplines, including a barefoot four-mile walk every day regardless of the weather, followed by a cup of hot mushroom broth, had increased the number of penitents to two hundred. Still, one had to be tough to stay alive here.

By the time the monks entered the shadowy stone chapel with its heavy round columns to pray for their lost brother it was late morning. Two narrow, shutterless windows high in the damp vault wall feebly insinuated daylight. What illumination they offered fell on the apse, vaguely outlining the spindly wood-carved figure of Christ on the Cross, his painted ochre and black eyes dripping tears of sadness in the gloom. Surrounding Christ were red and blue paintings that told the stories of long-suffering saints, their corroded gold halos tarnished by moisture, their faces cracked by white lead paint curling off the walls.

The faint smell of incense was now overwhelmed by the rancid stink of the sheep fat used to waterproof the cloaks. Then a sharp smell of old urine wafted upwards when the monks lifted their habits to kneel and pray. Bare knees knocked against the sharp cold of unpolished flagstones. Twenty-four hours of starving prayer was their gift to Gereon. Every few hours there was a low thump as one of them fell over into an exhausted lump.

The Abbey's religious routine, devoid of Mother Mary's compassion, and driven by the absolute belief in the salvation of mankind through the deprivation of human comfort, was basically unaffected by the youth's death.

• • •

Hugon, seated at a table in his study, was responding to a request to become a resident of the Abbey.

"Unfortunately," he wrote, "we are unable to accept your submission for penitence. Being extremely selective of the type of person allowed to find salvation here, we are not convinced of your passion, and truth be told, that happens so rarely. Another monastery may be a better fit for you."

And let them accept your pittance of funds offered, he thought wryly.

The weather had finally turned dry, yet the trees shadowing the algae-smeared roof tiles kept the eaves drip-drip-dripping onto the stones below. *That dripping is my penitence*, he thought. The translucent light of an arched window covered with linen soaked in tallow stroked the side of his bald, bony head, which sat on a neck so long that a bend in it forced his chin forward. A round lump the size of an egg protruded from under the jaw. It poked unattractively through his wispy brown beard.

His eyes kept glancing at an unfolded letter with a broken red seal. It was from his family. Normally he didn't really care what they wrote. It was an attitude they were totally aware of, yet, nonetheless they felt it their duty to inform him of births, deaths, and marriages.

> *...sad to inform you that your Uncle Armande has*
> *gone to be with our Holy Saviour Christ our Lord...*

Quite unexpectedly, the words touched a place buried deep in his heart (though there were many who doubted he even had one anymore). Armande had been his Aunt Martha's brother. Saintly Aunt Martha, named after the patron saint of women in the home, had taken in the sickly babe Hugon when her sister died birthing him.

"Every boy is worth saving," she said gently, lifting him into her arms.

For years, time after time, when the family thought the thin, morose Hugon dead, Martha had put him, wrapped in a sacred linen used by Saint Genevieve to dry her hands, directly onto the altar in her little chapel. He could remember lying on the marble top staring up at the small round apse with its large painting of Christ, white eyes and black pupils staring down on him, one hand raised in a blessing. Perhaps it was the warmth of the candles, the stillness of the incense-laden air, or Christ's love, but he had miraculously survived each crisis.

One day, just after Advent, he began to run a high fever. Martha had as usual wrapped him in Saint Genevieve's linen and personally carried the underweight eight-year-old boy to the altar. Carefully she laid him down on it. Kneeling on the stone floor she began to pray. Deep in the night the fever got worse as his face flushed redder and redder.

Martha, who was on her knees fervently praying, cried out loudly:

"Jesus, my saviour unto death, if thou desirest a soul take mine and spare the child. I give my life to you."

Horrified, her maid watched Martha fall over dead.

That same evening, his fever miraculously disappeared. The family, blaming him for her death, decided to send the child away to a monastery. Before leaving he ran to the chapel and snatched up Saint Genevieve's linen and stuffed it under the old tunic they gave him for the journey.

"You should be grateful you have shoes," his uncle snarled, with all of the cousins standing tight-lipped and angry.

The next dawn they shoved him, all alone, out of a side door into the mist covered courtyard. There he was grabbed by a hooded monk in a damp cloak who lifted him up onto the seat of an old cart. For two days, sleeping upright, he watched the horse's bony rump in a sullen silence never once interrupted by the faceless monk. Morning and evening he was handed a piece of brown bread and water. The mist turned to freezing fog as they neared Prémontré Abbey. Soon the cart rolled through a thick wooden door in a high stone wall.

The little postulant spoke to no one for a whole year; he found the ascetic routine and the stringent rules a comfort. The constant cold invigorated him. Eventually, Abbot Norbert called the child into his study. Upon finding out that Hugon could read and write, he was given letters to copy. The intense child was diligent; growing older he never wavered from the proper path to salvation. When he was fifteen, he discovered the pleasures of self-flagellation.

Only once was there a problem. When he was eighteen, Norbert decided to send him to the Vatican for six months.

"I don't want to go."

"Are you disobeying me?"

The young man bowed his head in shame.

"You will give the Pope this book we have copied for him. I want you to see what corruption exists in the church today. Satan has entered the sacred precincts."

Hugon had returned disgusted by the luxurious apartments, gold plates overflowing with rich food, and all the sinful women. The Pope's men were glad to see the back of him, for his endless tirades against lust and wealth were annoying them no end. He had learned his lesson well. Now he truly recognized Prémontré as the sacred path that protected him from Satan, which led to eternal grace by the side of God.

After many cloistered years of unquestioning obedience, the position of Abbot was willed to Hugon by the dying Norbert.

"Be vigilant, my son. Do not allow Satan in the gate. It is our pathetic human lust for procreation that stirs the basest emotions. Just one monk's desire for bodily comfort can destroy all I have built. Here, accept this cross—it will always bring you comfort when you pray to it. It will be your one possession."

He gave Hugon a wooden cross about four hands long. Attached to it with iron nails was an emaciated, ivory saviour with sticks for arms and legs, looking for all the world like a mantis religiosa, a praying mantis.

It was actually his second possession, for Saint Genevieve's sacred linen was his first.

• • •

His musings were interrupted by Anselm, knocking on his door.

"My Abbot, Bishop Burchard of Cambray has suddenly arrived."

Without warning? Oh, no. His visit is worse suffering than my hair shirt. "Tell Anselm to bring him to me."

Hugon hated these visits by churchmen who lived like pigs in luxury; he was always determined to make them feel as uncomfortable as possible.

He waited with his elbows on the table, resting his chin on his hands after hastily stacking the papers on the window ledge, the letter on top. Behind him hung a roughly woven wool curtain that covered the entrance to his living quarters. Anselm arrived with Bishop Burchard, politely offering him a hard, wooden chair opposite the Abbot.

Burchard lowered his bulk and tried to make himself comfortable. He could feel his fatty backside bulging into the air on either side of the seat.

Anselm poured some wine from a clay pitcher into two quartz goblets, bowed, and disappeared.

They had not seen each other in the many years since Hugon had left the Vatican.

Hugon felt grossly offended by the huge stomach and ornate red robes that spread out from under the Bishop's fur-lined cloak. *He's bigger than ever.* Eight bright, jewel-studded gold rings pinched the fat on his fingers, of which the nails were oval and buffed to a shine. Nauseated by the thought, he knew that novice nuns pared the fingernails and toenails of Bishops with tiny knives, then smoothed their edges with white pumice stones. Burchard's triple chin hung from ear to ear like a nun's wimple. Beneath the wide-brimmed red hat, small brown eyes, long trained to hide his thoughts, exuded warmth and cordiality.

We really are in separate worlds, Hugon mused haughtily, with difficulty suppressing the sin of pride. Speaking in his soft, whistling tone, he greeted the Bishop. "Welcome, your holiness. I hope your journey here was uneventful?"

"Yes, thank you," Burchard answered a bit too quickly. *And I can't wait to get out of this godforsaken place and return to Cambray. Christ on the Cross! This man frightens me more than ever. He would condemn me to Satan for eating and drinking. That bony face! Those eyes are two openings to Hell. And that yellowish vulture's nose*—he caught himself and spoke more slowly, modulating his tone to one of utter politeness and respect.

"I have been sent to you by Bernard of Clairvaux himself." With dismay he watched his words form a cloud of mist. The fireplace was a small pile of ashes. A vague lingering scent of excrement in the air emanated from the Abbot. "He has a special holy task for a Canon of known depth and discretion. You are that man."

Lowering his head, Hugon murmured humbly, "I am at the service of my church and Christ." *Lord, what do these servants of Mammon want with me?*

By the balls of Saint Peter, his breath could make Hell smell sweet. Burchard subtly moved his backside from side to side. "It's about heresy," he said bluntly.

Hugon was now interested. He sat up straighter. "Heresy. Yes, it is ever increasing. To which heresy are you referring?"

"No doubt you have heard of the Bons Hommes down south in Occitania?"

"Of course, The hermits of Étienne de Muret. The ones near Toulouse. They are exemplary Holy Men. Pious, austere, and as severe, if not more so, in their deprivations than we are here. What could possibly be the problem?"

Burchard snapped, "Would that those were the Bons Hommes that concern us. No, now there is another group that called themselves by that name: the Cathars, 'the pure ones'. This is bad, very bad. These heretics hide in the mountains surrounding Carcassonne and Montpelier and have converted many there. Narbonne is the next vulnerable target. Fortunately, the Viscountess Ermengard is a true Catholic and totally loyal to the King.

"These 'pure ones' are followers of that son of Satan, Bogomil the Bulgarian. He's preaching the vile heresy that Christ was not born on this earth as the Son of God, and that confession and absolution are useless. His followers include female priests! Women who wander the land seducing good Christians with promises of salvation. Our church has lost control of them. And they're migrating north. They must be stopped!"

"Ah, but Satan is always sending his agents to try us. What do you want of me?"

"Bernard has just returned from a vain attempt to stamp out the scourge. Even after he burned heretics at the stake in Minerve, he was still chased out of churches and reviled in Albi. Narbonne is vulnerable because of the weak Archbishop there. D'Anduze is incompetent. All he wants to do is build a big cathedral. His parishioners are out of control.

These heretics are multiplying. You will go to Narbonne and spy for us. As you are a Canon Regular, no one will question your presence; it is part of a Canon's job to wander and preach."

Hugon shuddered. "At my age? I'm in my fourth decade. I can't get on a donkey and ride around from village to village." *And I certainly won't leave here and have someone else rule my monks!*

"One must break the egg that hatches new heretics!" bellowed Burchard, banging the table with his fist.

Hugon flinched. "I can't go."

"You can go, and you *will* go. The Pope demands it." Burchard fumbled a pouch out of his robe. "Here is some gold. I promise it won't burn the skin fingers off your fingers. And, by the saints, get a new robe. Yours is so filthy it sticks to your bones, and I can see the vermin crawling around your hair shirt. Make sure you're back by Advent."

Irritated, Burchard scraped his chair loudly as he heaved himself to his feet.

"Will you stay the night? Hugon rose as he held his arm out with an inviting gesture. *I dare you to stay.*

"Forgive me. I must return immediately. I am hosting some priests from Canterbury." *I wouldn't suffer the night here—Matins on my knees on a stone floor? Never.*

They bowed slightly to each other, and the Bishop turned to leave as fast as his dignity and bulk would allow. Egon, his servant monk, was waiting for him at the gate.

"Here, take this," Burchard threw his cloak at him. "Have it cleaned of lice and whatever else is crawling in it. Give me the other one. Are the stones hot?"

"I started a fire and kept them warm. They are on the floor of the coach."

"Well put some on the seat too. We will stop overnight at Vauclair Abbey. They have heated chambers, and, if I remember correctly, they'll have roast lamb for a Bishop."

Ah, that feels better. Burchard, his bulk settled under the soft heated warmth of a white wool blanket embroidered with a gold cross, ordered the coachman to depart. With a heaving lurch, the carriage rolled off, its huge wooden wheels leaving deep furrows in the damp earth.

• • •

At first Hugon was furious at the thought of wandering around the untamed south on an arduous mission spying for that overfed pig. The nobles down there were constantly warring with each other, especially the Count of Barcelona who felt he owned the whole of Occitania. It was social chaos ruled by an age-old rule of law they called paratge, which, to him, seemed to be the constant swearing of loyalty to one ruler and then breaking that oath when another ruler made a better offer.

Unnerved by his desire to disobey, being still a servant of the Pope, Hugon went to pray at the Norbert crucifix hanging in his bed chamber. As he knelt down, he could immediately feel the suffering it exuded.

"Anselm, fetch Brother Godfrey."

Godfrey was a master of scourging. With his weathered leather lashes he knew exactly how to deeply crisscross a bared back with knife-like precision. The pain would increase and plateau with such exquisite beauty that his body would eventually shudder from within.

Afterwards, Hugon remained on his knees, oblivious to the passage of time. When the cold shadows of night smothered the day, Christ on his Cross became a shining light. Hugon, feeling the heat of his Saviour's passion, saw the hands and feet begin to bleed. He saw a wave of hot, dark blood moving across the floor towards him, its warm stickiness wrapping itself around his aching knees. He saw broken eggs, their yellow, running yolks floating in Christ's blood! He saw the ragged, white edges of cracked eggshells surrounding him!

At that moment, a ray from the rising sun scratched its way through a gap in the shutters to land on his face, showering him with its radiance. In a miraculous flash of clarity, the true meaning of the mission revealed itself.

Heretical eggs must be broken before they hatch more heresy!

A fiery, blinding flame of passion flared up before his eyes. "Thank you, Jesus," he gasped, as tears of joy streamed down his sallow cheeks.

One week later, Canon Hugon, wearing a relatively clean brown habit, a newly woven goat's hair shirt firmly tied around his chest, and a glass vial of Saint Paul of Tarsus's blood bumping against his ribs, sat sideways on a donkey heading south. Norbert's cross, wrapped in Saint Genevieve's linen towel, was packed in a leather bag behind him. They would protect him from marauders and any wandering illness Satan would throw at him. Godfrey, his devoted ex-soldier monk, walked ahead, leading his own donkey with a rope.

Toulouse, Carcassonne, Beziers, Narbonne. . . repeating the names to himself, Hugon stoked the hot flame in his head, its holy light showing him the way to truly serve God.

CHAPTER 5

Ride the spray-maned sail-horse!
Sea-ploughs don't grub field-gorse!
Bows plough the blue wave's course
to Byzantium! Norse-
men, claim that caliph's gold!
Cut through steel-storms, be bold!
Feed wolve's red grins! Withhold
wit while kings' tales are told!
   —Rogenvaldr Kali Kolsson, 1103?—1158

JUNE 1152, THE SEA OF DARKNESS

Dawn illuminated the pink cliffs that rippled along the edges of Gaul-land. The weather had turned a bit milder as the fleet wound its way further south. Just offshore, made inaccessible by the pounding surf, monasteries perched perilously on top of pointy rocks. Varders, stone crosses left by previous Viking sailors, were becoming less frequent.

The keels slapped against choppy waves the mottled color of shark skin. There was no land to be seen in the west. No more markers guided them.

"We are entering the Sea of Darkness," Eindredi announced one night. "We must cling to the Eastern shore."

The sailors crossed themselves.

In order to avoid panic whenever there was wild weather, Bishop William ordered the crew to hold up his huge cross so the other boats could see its comforting shape. It wobbled and tipped, yet they managed to hold it upright.

Progress was slow. This was partly because, three times a day, Magnus the styrimaör, ordered the fleet to halt and eat on shore. It

51

was the Gulating Law, and they knew it was the only way to survive a long voyage.

A week later they came upon a small estuary.

"This must be the Gironde," said Eindredi. He was holding up a dirty, old linen map that he had purchased in Trondelog from an aged navigator whose father had been a map reader in the Norwegian crusade to Jerusalem fifty years earlier. "Upstream is Bordeaux — a rich city."

"Our ancestors already destroyed it forty years ago. Forget those thoughts — we're going to Jerusalem to fight for Christ," said Bishop William.

• • •

"We're entering the waters north of the Iberian coastline." Rogenvaldr looked up from Eindredi's map. They had gone ashore for water. "For now we keep heading south. Eventually we turn west along the coast of Gallizaland and arrive at Orviedo."

William, sitting on a rock next to him, had the distinct feeling he didn't want to hear what Rogenvaldr was about to say.

"Christ's blood!" Rogenvaldr exclaimed. "Orviedo is the beginning of the way to Campus Stellae, the Field of Stars. I want to make a barefoot pilgrimage to pray at the tomb of Saint James. I must do penance for the acts of our pagan ancestors forty years ago, attacking and ransacking the town, then killing Bishop Sisenand II. We were pagan animals. I must find absolution."

William threw up his hands. "God in heaven, Rogenvaldr. I just hope the people of Campus Stellae are holy enough to forgive you and not cut off your bare feet. Let's just get supplies in Orviedo. Hopefully, it will be a large enough port."

When Eindredi heard what Rogenvaldr wanted to do, he rolled his eyes. "Are you crazed? Me go barefoot to Campus Stellae? I want to get to Jerusalem." His white hair shook with disbelief.

Rogenvaldr snapped, "Have you forgotten that Saint James is the protector of Christian soldiers? I want to go to Campus Stellae. Now, how do I get there?"

No one knew the answer to that question. And if they did, no one said anything. They all just wanted to get to Jerusalem in one piece.

Navigating south in the Sea of Darkness required vigilance; fast changing currents threatened to bang the ships into high cliffs along the rocky coastline. A stony lace of tunnels, arches, and caves cast shadows on curved, white beaches. At night, the men anchored offshore, rowing back and forth to sleep on land. Often, they set up camp in a hundred-foot-high crack in the endless stone curtain, a falling white ribbon of fresh water pooling below.

Pinpoints of light reflected in Rogenvaldr's eyes. "The stars are almost as bright as those of Orkneyjar," mused the tired Earl as he feel asleep.

One murky night, a thick blanket of fog lay over the water. Towards morning, as it slowly began to lift, the night watch began shouting.

"Look, over there—spirits on the water. Jesus protect us, wake up, wake up!"

Indeed, a tall golden light with a halo was flickering in the distance above the black waters.

"Holy Mother of God! It's the spirit of Saint Magnus guiding us." Magnus Gunnison fell to his knees, crossing himself over and over. The men began murmuring prayers of protection.

Rogenvaldr felt as if spiders were running up and down his back. His uncle Saint Magnus—the one he was building the church for in Kirkness! *What could he be here to tell me? He knelt in prayer watching the frightening vision.*

Then, as the revealing light of dawn drew a line on the horizon, it outlined a small church high upon the crest of a rocky island offshore. Candlelight glowed in a narrow, round-topped window. A priestly shadow passed by. Morning revealed a long, winding stone walkway from the shore to the church.

Rogenvaldr felt calmed. "I'm going there to ask for directions to Orviedo," he said. "William, come with me. I'll probably need you to get a monk to speak to us."

The crossway was the width of a man, with boulders cut to fit the contours of the cove. Strong wind gusts forced them to crouch down behind the stone walls and pushed them through the rectangular wooden door. The church was made of red bricks, with a grey tile roof thickly covered in the droppings from thousands of birds screeching above, fighting for food. Inside it was dark, and relatively quiet.

The three monks were not pleased to see the travelers. When they saw William's robe, one of them agreed to speak only to him.

"We are sixteen Benedictine hermits living here in the hermitage of San Juan on this island named Gaztelugatxe," the monk explained in heavily accented Latin. "Orviedo is the capital of the Kingdom of Asturias. To get there, follow the coast west to the port of Avilés, perhaps two days with a good wind. Ask to speak to Bishop Pelagius. Now, please leave. I will light a candle for your pilgrimage. But only if you go. Otherwise I will curse you."

Walking back down the gusty causeway, Rogenvaldr teased the Bishop. "Well, William. Here's your next home."

"The way I feel about this trip, I'm tempted to stay."

The ship sailed west. Rogenvaldr sat down on the cross and composed a nasty song about the rude monks. Grabbing a harp, he sang:

> I've seen them kirk over,
> apple-cheeked Eves, weave their
> girl-gaggles. Girls, sixteen,
> I'll swear it—isle-spinsters
> with hair hacked in circles,
> half-baled heads. We skaldsmen
> goad them west—Shaven! Blessed!

The sailors guffawed, making mincing gestures as they grabbed their crotches. Bishop William, sat on the cross with his back to Rogenvaldr.

• • •

Avilés, on the coast of Asturia, was a busy port. Reflecting into quiet waters, its stone walls and towers surrounded busy streets lined with warehouses and money exchanges. The salt trade had always been a good source of income, but for the last thirty years there was more money to be made from toll-paying pilgrims on their way to Orviedo, all anxious to walk the King's new Camino Way to the Campus Stellae.

"I've sworn to go there barefoot," announced Rogenvaldr. "You must come with me."

Eindredi was adamant. "I won't go. King Sigurd the Jewryfarer sacked it forty years ago. I'm tired of being cursed by angry cities."

Rogenvaldr couldn't understand. "Sigurd was on pilgrimage—why did he kill Bishop Sisenand and burn such a holy place? There must have been other, more Christian, options."

"Well, maybe it was before Vikings lost their balls and became Norsemen."

William and Rogenvaldr went to find Bishop Pelagius. He lived in Orviedo, a two-day walk on a heavily tolled road protected by knights in castle fortresses large enough to shelter, feed and overcharge hundreds of pilgrims on a daily basis. The paved road cut through fields of apple trees as far as the eye could see. Occasionally the ripe scent of boiling apple cider filled the air.

Pelagius was a tall, energetic, round-bellied whirlwind. Bouncing on the balls of his feet, he was bursting with anticipation at entertaining noble pilgrims. Surrounded by an enormous mane of strait brown hair, his alert black eyes were set close together above a long snout. He had the look and build of a hungry bear.

"Yes, yes, welcome, welcome! You're in the right place. The only way to Campus Stellae goes through Orviedo," he enthusiastically answered Rogenvaldr's question. "And it takes about two months to complete."

"Two months?" William glanced quickly at the Earl, who chose to ignore him.

"Your ship may remain anchored in the port of Avilés as you make your way across the mountains. It won't cost you too much. Bishop William, didn't we meet in Paris some years ago? Yes, yes! Wonderful to see you again."

"My honored colleague, I didn't know you were here." *And a greater rascal there never lived. I wonder if he's still up to his old tricks; forever borrowing money, never paying it back, stealing other students work, forging completion certificates—I wouldn't trust him with anything.*

"So much to do here—and my scriptorium is my life. You must come and see it. And the reliquaries here are truly as holy as you will find anywhere. Yes, yes! You must see them."

"While we're seeing your magnificent city, perhaps my men could buy supplies for the fleet?" asked Rogenvaldr.

Yes, yes! Anything you need. Just tell them to ask the port master. Be careful, he drives a hard bargain."

And count everything twice before it goes on board, thought William.

Breakfast at the Monastery de San Vicento was surprisingly delicious: fried fish, sausage, cabbage cooked in apples all washed down with a strong fermented cider.

Pelagius met them at the Church of Santa María de Naranco, once a Roman Temple. Unlike the ruins of Roman temples in England, it was in perfect condition. It was like going back in time. Pelagius led them up the outside stairs to the main floor of the rectangular basilica. Carved gilded stars were strewn across the high vaulted ceiling. Long, tall windows threw light and shadows on colorful wall paintings depicting Christ's life. It was very simple and felt very sacred.

Pelagius began to talk again. Once he began, he never seemed to stop for breath.

"Let me tell you the story of the Campus Stellae. Two-hundred years ago, King Alphonse II, "The Chaste", began to build this city. At the same time, Bishop Theodemir of Iria was preaching west of here on a wide grassy plain surrounded by rocky shores. That's the Campus Stellae, where the stars shine so brightly one can almost reach up and pick them, like jasmine flowers on a tree!

"One star, brighter than the rest, led Theodemir to find the bones of Saint James hidden in a crypt. A miracle!" He crossed himself three times. "Many miraculous cures happened at the shrine he built. Our King decided to build a road so pilgrims could worship there. Of course, that project was interrupted by you Vikings attacking the shrine. That wasn't so long ago."

Rogenvaldr was uncomfortable with that history. "Can we go now to see the relics in the Cámera Sancta?"

"Yes, yes."

The road winding down to the modest, barrel-shaped church was paved with black Roman stones.

Pelagius had told the truth. The relics were indeed marvelous.

Against the back wall of the small chamber was the Arca Santa, a heavily carved cedar chest covered with gold candle holders. On the wall above it stood a gilded, life-sized marble sculpture of Christ shining in the light. Attending Christ were the Apostles holding candles, their pink, brown and black faces flickering, their eyes staring.

Pelagius turned quiet and serious. Gesturing them to kneel, moving aside the candles, he prayed before opening the lid. Looking inside the Norsemen gasped. They had never seen such sacred objects.

"We have here the Cross of Angels, the Victory Cross, a gold Agate box used by Saint Ursula, and, most sacred of all, the Sudarium of Orvieda, the cloth used to clean and cover the face of Jesus after the crucifixion."

William was moved to tears. "How did the cloth arrive here?

"It states clearly in the bible that 'Simon Peter, following him, also came up, went into the tomb, saw the linen cloth lying on the ground, and also the cloth that had been over his head; this was not with the linen cloth but rolled up in a place by itself.' It was originally brought to Iberia from Jerusalem through Carthage and carried to safety here to Orviedo during the Moslem invasion four-hundred years ago. You must understand, we were never invaded here. The mountains protect us."

Rogenvaldr, overwhelmed at the spirit of holiness emanating from these objects, silently prayed. *I've never felt so close to Christ... will it be this way in Jerusalem? And, God help me, on the Holy Mount?*

After they had been shown the toenail of Mary Magdalene, a sliver of St. Peter's cross, and a vial of Saint Simon's blood, the three were guided down a busy street to visit the scriptorium. They had no choice in the matter.

Bouncing along beside them Pelagius continued his monologue. "Yes, yes. Recording the history of the Christian world is a long-time project of mine. I mean to preserve and copy documents from Scandia all the way to Syria. I have many thousands of pieces already in our library."

And I wonder how many are forged and how many are history re-written for the church, mused William.

Awnings above craftsmen's workshops offered a welcome shady path. The smell of heavily spiced lamb and horsemeat in a densely flavorful smoke floated out of open doors. Rogenvaldr had to eat, so they stopped for a few moments at an outside grill. Gnawing at a tender chunk of meat, he had a thought.

Looking seriously at Pelagius he asked, "would you like to buy a genuine unicorn horn?"

William nearly groaned out loud. Pelagius put down his cider and peered at Rogenvaldr, putting his snout-like nose very close. His hair was standing out around his head. With a particularly serious expression, which looked as if it would, without difficulty, turn into a laugh, he replied.

"Thank you, no. I believe we have enough Godly power here to protect us. Still, I appreciate the offer."

Later that night, at the monastery, William was stomping around in a fury. "How could you have been so disrespectful? Did you really think that a scholar like Pelagius would be taken in by your thievery? In the morning I'm going back to the ship."

"And what about my pilgrimage to Saint James?"

"Go by yourself. And if they hang you, so be it."

Reluctant to go on a two-month walk by himself, Rogenvaldr dragged his feet back to Avéira in a foul mood.

The high tones of the lur called the Norsemen out of the brothels and taverns back to their ships.

The sails snapped as they caught the wind.

William sat silently on his cross, leaning back on his arms.

Rogenvaldr hunched on the foredeck rail, hanging on the dragon, stared at the blue-black waters. He had not spoken to William in three days. *I can't believe he refused to go with me. How dare he treat me that way!* His fury grew worse when the vessel began to navigate south. Slowly, the ship sailed along the curved coast of Ibiza. The green fields of the Campus Stellae, surf pounding on its rocky edges, disappeared behind him in a wet haze.

• • •

Eindredi, studying the faded lines on his map, could identify most of the Iberian cities that marked the way south. "When we were in Normandy, a wool merchant from Toulouse told me to avoid Lizibon. King Alphonse is in a continual war with his cousin Alphonse VII. He'll try to buy our men to fight for him."

"We're short on food, we have to stop there. I'll just be vigilant," answered Rogenvaldr.

Fortunately Lizibon was not a problem. Terrified by the last Viking boats that had attacked his city, the King gave the fleet all the food it needed at no cost. *Feeding them is easier than fighting them.*

"Please, just go," Alphonse, the king of Lizibon requested politely, yet firmly.

As the weeks went by, the heat grew steadily worse.

Rogenvaldr's face was red and his eyes were aching from the bright sun reflected off the water. "Our blood isn't used to this heat. It's too thick."

"My leather pants are too hot. This heat is boiling my balls," groused Thorbjorn the Swarthy. "Yesterday, I took off my boots and burned my feet on the sand."

"Hah!" smirked Eindredi. "It's going to take a week for your feet to get back in your boots."

"What in the Devil's name are you all complaining about? You sound like a bunch of women!" Gudorm snarled.

The cool winds followed them ashore each night.

One morning as the bickering about the heat began again, Aslak followed a trickle of fresh water running across the beach and found a crevice in the cliffs with a cool waterfall that fell into an overflowing pool. Three hundred Norsemen stripped off their clothes. After scrubbing themselves, adroitly removing ear wax with long ivory scoops, and combing the knots out of their hair and beards, they washed their clothes and spread them on some flat rocks to dry. Grunting like pink walruses on a strand, they all went to sleep in whatever shade they could find. Laughing voices from above the cliff woke them. A gaggle of curious women looked down at them, pointing and giggling.

"Hey, come down!" Blian yelled. In a burst of inspiration he held up a coin.

Soon, several dozen naked women came running down the beach, clambering over the rocks.

Negotiating a peaceful voyage around Iberia was not really too difficult for what appeared to be a small army of Vikings. Occasionally, merchants timidly approached them from a small harbor on the coast. In addition to fresh fruit and wine, the men bought medicinal salves to put on their sunburnt skin. Rogenvaldr bought a pair of woven linen pants and tunic with a wide brimmed hat; even a black sooty cream to put under his eyes to cut down the glare.

"I wouldn't be caught dead in those pants," snickered Eindredi.

Gradually, discarded leather boots were piling up in the center of the ship, their black mouths exhaling foul air.

The setting sun was a burning red ball. Eindredi sat himself down heavily on a rock next to Rogenvaldr. His white hair looked like it was on fire. "The lines on this map are getting vague. I can't figure it out. Maybe you can."

He tossed the floppy linen to Rogenvaldr, who turned it around a few times before he could understand the crude lines that were Iberia.

"We follow the coast south until we arrive at what the map calls the Nortasund, two rocky islands that are the gateway to the Mediterranean Sea, at the far eastern end of which lies Jerusalem. It shows their ancient name of The Pillars of Hercules."

Doggedly, the fleet sailed south. It took another two weeks to round the curve of Algarve and pass Andalusia. Ahead of them the shoreline unrolled like a dry parchment scroll, whose scrubby trees, islets, and rocks told an ancient tale scratched in clay. During days when the sultry air barely moved the sails, they slept in the shadows of trees in a cove and rowed at night under the lantern of a bright moon and the sharp candle flames of stars.

The fleet turned east, and a sharp wind turned the waves choppy. Without warning, one hazy dawn, the pilgrims found themselves looking up at the two triangular rocks of the Nortasund floating on the water in a mist. Necks craned, their fifteen insignificant longboats bobbing on the gray water, the mariners stared up at lichen-streaked vertical walls rising to sharp peaks that cut the silver sky into jagged fragments. Flying crazily in circles around the island mountains, thousands of screeching petrels, cormorants, gannets, kites, and gulls screamed with ear-splitting shrills.

"It's like two Nordkapps of Norway side by side," breathed Magnus.

The crew laughed to cover their fear. Standing under the taut red cross with his drum, Armod enthusiastically improvised a song praising the bravery of the Earl in contrast to a churl who's afraid and stays home for the week:

> *The fire-gold giver's comrade*
> *given himself seven*

daylong-contented days
carousing in the house.
Rogenvaldr vigorously
gallops the spray-veined stallion;
bright-painted, shields blinking,
we breach Nortasund strait.

Ahead of them, the barely glimpsed opening between the giant rocks portended a frightening gateway to a very different world. Without warning, the Poniente, a strong Western wind, moist and hot, began to push them through the gap.

Persistently it filled their sails, funneling the ships from the foamy waters of the Sea of Darkness into the brilliant sun and turquoise waters of the Mediterranean Sea.

The dry air suddenly smelled of lavender and sage. Rogenvaldr breathed it in deeply, squinting at the bright blue sky, trying to take in this new world.

CHAPTER 6

Treacherous Rome! Your avarice is clear!
You shear and steal all the wool
down to their flesh
from the sheep that are your flock.
May the Holy Spirit made flesh
hear my prayers
and break your beaks, O Rome!
              —*Guilhem de Figuera, troubadour, 12th cent.*

The thunder of crashing masonry lifted the Archbishop's bed up into the air. Pierre D'Anduze, jarred awake, was startled into fear. Screaming curses were emanating from the back of his palace where the workmen were repairing the old church.

Groaning, he rolled out of bed. *Lord Jesus, help me! I pray it's not the apse!* The chamber was still dark, as his monk servant had not yet raised the curtains and brought his morning sweet wine, milk bread, and cheese. Still clad in his long, linen shift he shuffled down the long connecting corridor to the Cathedral of Saints Justus and Pasteur, tripping over his loose leather sandals.

The thick-walled old church was wedged between his palace and the city ramparts behind it. Bright, dusty rays of sunshine were shining through several jagged, new crevices in a section of collapsed apse. The sharp light outlined red bricks and curved stone blocks now scattered across the dust-covered floor.

It's unbelievable. Massive stone walls, yet they fall apart whenever you try to fix them.

Squinting at a pile of rumble next to the old altar, he noticed, with annoyance, that the workmen had not protected the brightly painted wooden image of the Twelve Apostles attached to the front of it. Ancient, dry, mortar powder swirled up to the ceiling through the scaffolding. Using his sleeve, he wiped red dust out of his thinning hair and square face, his slit of a mouth grim under the narrow nose. With angry brown eyes blinking rapidly in irritation, and his rectangular body rigid with anger, he sought out the masons responsible for this mess; they had all disappeared.

Collapse was an unending problem: insect-eaten wooden beams, loose clay infill, and long-buried walls of ancient basilicas under the present foundation destabilized the floor and the crypt ceiling. Fire-stained marble columns, which appeared to be stable, fell sideways and cracked.

The original ninth-century church that he was trying to rebuild contained six small, dingy, round chapels. The flickering lights of votive candles were barely able to brighten up the dark interiors of the old apses with their centuries old, faded, wooden statues of the Virgin Mary and obscure saints. Building a new wall to connect around them was a logistical nightmare.

Not helping the problem, a group of black-veiled old women, ignoring the fact that at any moment a masonry block could fall on their heads, insisted on praying in those old chapels. As a matter of fact, three were there right now, kneeling silently in front of some ancient wooden statue of a Madonna with peeling paint and foreign eyes.

"Go somewhere else to pray. Go to St. Paul-Serge, or St. Marie!" he yelled at them. They didn't care; she was their Madonna. Not even an Archbishop could move them elsewhere.

He kicked at a spotted cat that jumped into the rubble. Every time a corner cracked, vermin ran out from the walls. A scruffy tortoise shell cat was slinking over a fallen column to pounce.

When crypts full of bones collapsed, the workmen, struck with terror, would run away screaming from the "souls of the devil and dead spirits flying out of there". D'Anduze had lost count of the number of times he had re-consecrated the site to get them to back to work—but only after every last bone had been removed and put into old marble ossuaries to be re-buried in the necropolis on the other side of town.

Emperor Constantine had built the first basilica here in 313. Destroyed by fire in 441, it was rebuilt by Bishop Reticus in 445.

Later, it was dedicated to Saints Justus and Pastor, two martyred Spanish children, aged six and nine, who were flogged and beheaded by Roman soldiers because they refused to give up their Christian faith.

For hundreds of years it was used but neglected. It was D'Anduze's fervent dream and ambition to construct a cathedral in the soaring style of the northern Frankish Kingdom, just like the one Abbot Suger had built at Saint Denis. After all, Abbot Suger had declared that "the dull mind rises to truth through that which is material."

The master mason who was working on the installation of the new portal to the old Madeleine Chapel showed up. He was a huge man, a hammer of a man, towering over the Archbishop.

D'Anduze, bracing himself, snapped, "Can you explain what happened here?" He hated looking up at people, but he often did.

"It obvious. Theodemir used shoddy materials. My men could have been killed. Should have lasted a lot longer than two hundred and fifty years. Not our fault. Or yours. I need more money to pay my men to work in such hazardous conditions. Also, there's a problem fitting the new door into the old crumbling walls—too much loose rubble from the original choir that was there."

The mason's voice had a low, grumbling tone that reminded D'Anduze of a rocky landslide. The glint of greed was in his sharp eyes; he knew he had an obsessed client in his net. What the master mason had intuited was true; this cathedral was the indeed the Archbishop's obsession.

• • •

As a young child Pierre loved to stand watching the construction of the Cathedral of Rouen, happily breathing in the mortar dust, sometimes carrying water to the laborers.

"Please, why can't you take me on as an apprentice?" the eight-year-old begged, as the master mason took a large block away from the child.

The master had laughed. "Because you're small for your age—look at the size of these other boys even younger than you. Besides, you're noble, your family would never allow it. They'd hang me if anything happened to you. But first they'd chop my hands and feet off."

His mother, in constant fear for her stubborn son's life, was always sending servants to seek him out and bring him home before a rope broke and a stone fell on him.

Pierre was small, yet he was smart. When his parents offered, the church was eager to take him in. As soon as he arrived at the monastery, he started working on the buildings. Whenever he had the time, in-between the trivium and quadrivium, daily prayers and chapter meetings, he was re-paving walkways, mortaring failing walls, and re-hanging doors to shut properly.

Over time, his persistence paid off. Eventually people clamored for his help. "Where's Pierre? The scriptorium roof is leaking! Where's Pierre? The steps are loose in the wine cellar!"

By the time Pierre was eighteen the church was sending him to various cathedral construction sites to inspect the work being done; and woe betide the mason who tried to cut corners.

When the Bishopric of Narbonne was offered to the D'Anduze family by the powerful Archbishop Guifred, they grabbed it for their son despite the high cost.

Narbonne's new Archbishop Pierre D'Anduze was by now familiar with all of the new building techniques being used in the Kingdom of France. He decided that Narbonne was the perfect place to construct a magnificent cathedral. As soon as he moved into his palace, he began to draw up plans for rebuilding the old church behind it.

D'Anduze envisioned flying buttresses supporting the highest apse ever built, pointed spires soaring over Narbonne, and walls pierced with brilliantly colored, tall leaded glass windows that made the interior glow with the light of God.

But building it would be expensive. Very expensive.

His family, busy enlarging their sheep estates and buying up water mills, did not see any need to indulge his building fancies with more funds from the family coffers.

"We bought the Bishopric for you, that's the end of our largesse," they announced. "If you need money, we advise you to tax your flock. Lots of taxes."

There was never enough money. Even the considerable income the Templars collected for him from his farming and sheep domains wasn't enough. Often the thought occurred to him: *I wonder how much those Soldiers of God are stealing from me*.

Cathedrals were being built all over the land. The masonry guilds, short of men, were charging more and more exorbitant fees for their work. He had never expected such difficulty finding good craftsman. It was frustrating to be forced to hire Spanish sculptors to cut new faces of saints for the tops of old support columns. D'Anduze was jealous of Abbot Suger, who, using the King's money, had all the great French artists working for him.

Even the local sculptor Gilabertus of Toulouse, so arrogant that he actually signed his work 'Gilabertus, Who is not a Stranger, Carved Me', had refused to come the short distance to work in Narbonne. After D'Anduze had seen the figure Gilabertus carved of the 'Death of Saint John the Baptist' in a new Toulouse cloister, he went to entreat the master.

"Please," he had begged. "For the love of Christ's glory, just carve one capital for one column. You carved a head of Saint Peter for the Abbot of La Grasse. Why not for me?"

Gilabertus would not be persuaded. "I'm way too busy to come myself. I'll send one of my apprentices. He's very skilled." The apprentice was also very expensive.

Just how in Christ's blood did the Abbot of La Grasse pay for Gilabertus? And now the Italian painters need more gold leaf for halos shining in the new wall paintings. One artist had actually had the nerve to admonish him, "Holy figures have to be properly clothed in lapis blue, sienna red, and saffron yellow robes. And, of course, all the saints' robes need gold trim."

Doors required brass hinges, the floor needed special marble tiles to make a labyrinth, and the carpenters working on the roof demanded long beams of the finest oak from forests up north.

Salt, wool, lead, silver and gold-bearing mines, wheat and fulling mills, oven taxes—all went into the bottomless pit of construction to keep watering his vision.

D'Anduze knew that even the faithful were whispering behind his back, "don't go to mass at Saint Just, for the Archbishop will stand behind you and take your cloak to sell to the pelhier, the rag buyer, for his construction debts!"

The most aggravating fight was with the town council. D'Anduze had applied for permission to enlarge the size of the west transept that butted up against the town ramparts. It was a logical request—the narrow streets were bursting with merchants, convents, markets, and taverns. There was no place to expand into the town.

"You want to breach our protective walls? The ones that protect us from Moslem invasions?" the council had asked, terrified.

"But there are no more Moslem armies approaching us anymore!" he had argued. "The Spanish have pushed them back to Carthage— they'll never come back!"

"And if the enemy comes from the East? Why do you think we have a militia on those ramparts you want to tear down?"

The Archbishop's frustrations went back as far as the visit, seven years ago in 1145, when Bernard, the Abbot of Clairvaux, had journeyed south to Narbonne as part of an urgent crusade to squash heresy. It was an ill-advised time to request construction money from the church.

Bernard had fumed, "I'm here to return those Bons Hommes heretics to our church, not to hand out funds to an incompetent Archbishop who can't squash heresy in his own city."

The Abbot had preached in every church for miles around. He ranted and raved with great passion, denouncing heretics, and burning Bons Hommes in town squares. The people, whether heretics or not, were so frightened of his powers to denounce a person in the morning, and have them burning in the flames that afternoon, that they hid in their homes. In the meantime, the sect's leaders disappeared into gorges and caves in the mountains and waited for him to leave.

D'Anduze didn't give up. "A magnificent new church will lure the heretics away from the Bons Hommes. People need to see other images than grinning skulls and long-tailed devils. High, colored glass windows would tell the stories of the Bible with light and ecstasy. A soaring vault will lift them up to heaven. Please, I need your support."

"Do you think you're the only one who wants more glass and higher towers?" snapped Bernard.

Brusquely, he chastised the Archbishop. "By Christ's holy cross stamp out heresy here! Instead you spend your time building a church. Unbelievable. The Song of Songs warns us, 'the vineyards of the Lord are destroyed by little foxes'. Exterminate the vermin in your vineyard. That wandering Cathar, Henry the Monk, is still spewing his vomit everywhere! He's a ravening wolf in the guise of a sheep. The sacraments are not sacred, the baptism is denied—it's shocking that he could have such a large following. Find him! Torture him! Burn him! I tell you, you're trapped in an obsessive passion of the soul that allows evil to spread. Pray for Christ's light before it is too late!"

In his heart D'Anduze knew the Abbot was right. Heretics were like rats in every corner: gardeners, bakers, rich women, whores, and especially those troubadours spreading sin all over Occitania. *Especially Ermengard's trobaritz,* he thought. *She's an abomination unto God. I know she's one of them. I can smell her burning flesh already. Satan owns those vegetable eating Manicheans. Still, if Bernard of Clairvaux can't get rid of them, what can I do? I'll build a church—that's what I'll do! But if I don't build it before I die, it will never be built.*

The thought of failure was a constant threat bonging around and around in his head like a church bell. *I'll mint more coins to hire more masons, and argue with Ermengard about the salt revenues. She can't take all the money for her cursed road. Talk about obsession! And that bread oven on my side of the river—it belongs to the church, not her. I'll increase the water tax on the Jews' cloth fulling mills. And the carnalages tax— those wealthy butchers slaughtering all those beasts can afford it . . .*

Crestfallen, D'Anduze stood in the rubble. The fallen nave would have to be re-built and replastered before installing the new window frames. Set deep into the thick walls, bird droppings had, for hundreds of years, eaten away the mortar.

Am I the only one here who knows what it means to build a new church?

CHAPTER 7

Greetings Narbonne!
With your beautiful countryside,
your walled city and fortifications,
your healthy citizens, your markets,
your gates, forum and capitols,
your fountains, lagoons, river and bridge,
your grand sea...your vineyards,
pastures, olive trees...
— *Sidonius Appolinaris, 465 CE*

JULY 1152, NARBONNE, OCCITANIA

The turquoise Mediterranean Sea mirrored the burning sun overhead, glaring painfully into blue Scandic eyes. Norway seemed so dark green, icy cold, mountainous — and comfortable. The northern sun was a yellow luminescence, not this white-hot metal fired in God's forge. The men grudgingly put on straw hats and smeared black soot around eyes that felt like dry fish-scales whenever they blinked. Red arms and necks were greasy with useless oil that was supposed to stop skin from blistering.

"We're being roasted like capons," grumbled Magnus.

The fleet was sailing northeast up the southern coast of Iberia. In the far distance, sharp peaks formed a ridge down to the sea. The blue, hazy light turned the white, lightly snow-capped slopes into delicate veils draped gracefully over gray rocks.

"Those must be the Pyrenees!" William exclaimed. "I never thought I'd see them in my lifetime."

"Aren't you satisfied you came along now?" said Rogenvaldr. Distractedly he observed a ship approaching them.

"Hail!" The captain of a Norwegian karve was sailing his shallow merchant ship towards them.

"Hail! Come drink with us," called the Earl, eager for some information about where they were going. Other ships were fearful of approaching the fleet unless they had something to sell them.

Captain Skarde Cleft-Chin turned out to be an old trader operating out of Bergen. Sitting himself on the cross (after taking a good look at it), he took a horn from his belt so Rogenvaldr could fill it. Smiling, his wind-lined face with a beard that showed the world a wondrously cleft chin, he toasted the crew's health several times before settling down to talk.

"I recognized your boats, so I want to warn you of what's coming. There's a rain-filled, southerly wind they call the Ostro. When it begins, put to shore as fast as you can," he warned. "You won't be able to see your hand in front of your face. I'm trying to outrun it, but my cargo is very heavy."

"I noticed your ship is low in the water. What are you carrying?"

"Sarcophagi. The city of Narbonne, a day east of here, is famous for the quality of its carved marble sarcophagus. It has quarries and carvers second to none. My ship is specially built so I can tie large pieces of marble to the bottom of the keel with heavy ropes. This gives me outside ballast. Makes for smoother sailing in choppy weather. I'm sailing up the Seine to the Franks in Paris. I get good money for a sarcophagus from Narbonne."

"Narbonne. Tell me about Narbonne."

"It's an old, rich city," the captain explained. "Very old. Goes back to the Romans. There's a bustling port—you can buy and sell anything in its markets and auction house. Goods come from Egypt, Persia, even India. The city is one of the friendliest you'll find: Jews, Moslems, Catholics, Zoroastrians, all in one pot."

"Is the king friendly to visitors?"

Skarde threw back his head and laughed, showing brown stumps of teeth. "There's no king. It's ruled by a queen!"

"By herself?" Rogenvaldr had heard of strong Norse women ruling a clan without a man, but it was rare.

"Yes. And she's only twenty-three. Viscountess Ermengard rules with an iron hand. The city is so prosperous they all love her. And, as she's unmarried, no one except her closest advisors get near her.

"Why isn't she married? Women want to marry and produce heirs. That's what they're for."

"The story is that she was married once for a short time before he died in a battle. Then she wed again, and he disappeared, or died, again. Twice married, maybe twice widowed? Who knows. People don't speak of it. Everyone wants the political situation to remain unchanged. Nobody wants some incompetent idiot to marry her, take over, and ruin everything."

"Hm-m-m," Rogenvaldr said. "Is she a devout Christian?"

"Now I can't speak for her personally, but it's said that the city has a powerful Archbishop who makes sure she doesn't fall off the straight and narrow path. There's supposed to be quite a power struggle between them. Well, I've got to be on my way—don't want to be caught in the storm. Watch out for the sandbars when you get to the lagoons—they move around like eels."

When the downpour began later that afternoon, they were forced to drop anchor in the busy fishing port of Perpignan. The harbor's beach was a sandy crescent, which, even in the rain, was a lush setting of palm trees and dunes. Behind the town was a green, bush covered plain that rose up into craggy, erratic peaks covered in fallen rocks, with torrents of water that flowed from engorged streams to carve rivulets in the sand on the way to the sea.

Warm rain was streaming down the yellow stucco walls of the modest dockside tavern as Rogenvaldr and Eindredi arrived. Under a wooden shelter out front, two wrinkled fisherwomen were mending nets. Their hands never stopped moving as they looked the two muscular men over. Water-soaked red bougainvillea drooped in clay pots on either side of the arched doorway. The owner came to the door to greet them. A full-figured woman, with dark hair and large black eyes, she wore a colorful flowered dress bound tight around her body and a white head scarf starched into the shape of a sail. Bowing respectfully, she sat them at one of four clean tables. The others were empty.

"Do the gentlemen wish ale or wine?" She spoke modestly, in a low voice, her eyes down, avoiding Eindredi's stare.

"Ale. Cold if possible."

The ale, served in large blue ceramic cups, was very chilled. A white oval plate of salted oil-cured anchovies was served with warm crusty bread, olives, and green onion stalks. They quickly finished off duck eggs pickled in sweet herbs and vinegar.

"Delicious!" Eindredi was wiping the oil off his frizzy beard with the rough cloth she provided. Contemplating her breasts, he wiped the sweat from his forehead.

"Thank you. I'm honored you find the food to your taste. Our town's specialty is preserving anchovies, She pointed to some large ceramic pots against the wall, filled with layers of salted fish covered in a green tinted oil. "We do it the way the Romans taught us to do it."

"Well, as Norsemen I must say we appreciate this Roman way of curing the fish. The flesh and bones are very moist. We'll have to buy some barrels for the fleet. And maybe have some sent home."

It was hot and humid in the tavern. Occasionally, through open blue shutters, the wind blew a wet spray onto their table. After three more cups of ale, they got down to talking about the sale of the 'unicorn horn'.

"Narbonne sounds perfect," said Eindredi. "A young, rich, unmarried queen?"

"I'll have to make her trust me," Rogenvaldr said.

"You? Thor's balls! Every woman you meet falls at your feet. Why should she be any different? Just don't let her buy it outright. Make it a gift, obligate her into giving you a monetary gift in return. Get its value in gold coin. No ruler wants to appear less generous than another. And don't let her forget you're the Earl of Orkneyjar."

Rogenvaldr stood to leave. Eindredi crossed his arms and, leaning back, stretched out his legs. The tavern owner, eyes still lowered, was filing another cup of ale for him.

• • •

Dawn was clear and comfortably cool. Well supplied with anchovies, fresh water, ale, and a crusty brown bread, the fleet eagerly sailed east towards Narbonne.

Old Skarde was right. These sandbars are treacherous. Could suck a man right under. I've never seen such vast lagoons. Rogenvaldr stayed alert as he watched the shoreline appear and disappear in and out of tall, endless reeds waving in the sharp wind. Occasionally he cried out, "Sandbar ahead!"

At one point, startled by the big ships, there was a rushing sound, and the empty sky over the marshes was filled with thousands of honking birds, their rose-colored bellies bumping in the air. Amazed, everyone watched until the birds, still screaming in annoyed alarm, gathered themselves together again, finally settling in a quiet spot further away.

Fishermen in brightly colored flat-bottomed boats floated in and out of green curtains growing in the shallows, throwing their large nets over flat marshes. Vying for the catch of shrimp, fish, and crabs, squawking yellow and red birds greedily swooped right into the nets to scoop up a meal. It was a continual fight with the birds, as the men yelled and swatted them ineffectively with palm fronds. Herons skidded across the water to grab the bigger fish.

Vineyards, sheep, wheat, olive trees—this is a land of plenty. Rogenvaldr wasn't the only one thinking this; in all the ships the men were standing at the rails staring at how much green land there was here to cultivate. And it was all being put to use. Compared to their narrow strips of rocky farmland winding around the edges of fjords, this was the Garden of Eden.

All this played out against a sweep of the deepest blue sky the men from the north had ever seen, with azure water as clear as the finest glass from Egypt.

• • •

Ahead of them, rising above the lagoons, a shimmering dream in the heat, was a golden city. Purple shadows dappled the orange stones of Narbonne's towers and crenelated ramparts. The music of many church bells was like overlapping waves crashing through the air.

This where I sell the horn. Excitement jumped in the pit of Rogenvaldr's stomach.

The fifteen longboats slowly sailed forward to find an inlet. Locating it was not hard; it was dense with ships. Smaller coastal cargo boats, their sails full, were scurrying to depart as quickly as possible, following the faster galleys that had begun to row as soon as Viking ships were sighted. Larger merchant vessels, heavily weighted down with corked clay amphorae of wine, oils, or anchovies, stayed put, resigned to their fate, hoping to sell their way out of trouble. Flat-bottomed barges hauling timber bobbed on the water, not moving, fearful of being noticed by one of the warrior ships.

A path silently opened for them as they arrogantly sailed through into an enormous lagoon. Rogenvaldr waited as a low galley with a man in a blue tunic and turban standing in the prow, rowed hurriedly towards him. When he arrived within calling distance, the man bowed.

"I am Frezols," he said with an air of authority. "The navigator for the harbor. Please identify yourself and state your purpose here."

"I am Rogenvaldr Kali Kolsson, Earl of all Orkneyjar, and I will navigate up the river to Narbonne."

"But who, what is. . .?" Suddenly understanding, Frezols stopped speaking. Glancing fearfully at the visitors, he turned to the crew and quietly commanded that they guide the newcomers to the mouth of the Aude River.

The escort led the fleet north through the curves of the Etange de Gruissan, the lagoon's flat surface reflecting sky, clouds, and streaking birds. In the distance the shallow water erupted into humps of brown sand surrounded by green algae. The route avoided small islands of gray boulders resembling hump-backed whales journeying through windblown brown weeds towards the sea. Fiery sunlight on wind rippled wavelets, reflected on their faces, blinding them.

The mouth of the Aude River was wide and shallow. The current was lazy and heavy, and the longboats easily rowed up to Narbonne.

Along the banks were numerous wharves, landing stairs, and warehouses. At one point, to their right, were white, undulating fields of salt. Workers in flat, wide brimmed hats, their feet bound up with cloth to protect them from the corrosive mush, were using rakes and paddles to air dry the crystals.

"Now *that* is a lot of white gold!" remarked William, squinting at the sparkling crystals.

Near the river was the ruin of an ancient amphitheater. It appeared to be a small city of its own having taverns and shops, with mostly scurrilous sailors milling about by the look of it.

Narbonne appeared to be two cities connected by a bridge. Neither appeared to be very well fortified. The heavy walls, curved outward at the bottom, were only about the height of ten men. Granular mortar interlocked older, yellowed larger stones at the bottom. Smaller, whiter stones at the top were covered with carvings.

Old Roman buildings were taken apart to build those walls. This is a weakness. Rogenvaldr checked his thoughts. *We are not here to conquer. We are on pilgrimage. We are here to make some money, and leave.*

"We're close enough. Stop the fleet," he commanded, holding up his hand. "I want to look." Far to the west he could see the snow-capped Pyrenees bumping down to the sea. *Iberia is now behind me. I'm half the way to Jerusalem.*

Small villages, their red-roofed houses painted in bright colors, dotted the flat plains around the city. A mess of ramshackle wooden huts on a narrow path were nestled against the fortifications. The river foamed heavily as it encountered the triangular stone pillars holding up seven arches of an old Roman bridge lined with buildings. Past the bridge were numerous water mills.

William came up beside him. "Those large towers are called Mauresques. The Moslem Caliphate built them when they ruled here. It was quite a popular style in Paris for a while."

William had a bad habit of flaunting his Paris education. "You'll notice," he continued, "the same porous mountains we saw in Perpignan are north of here. Hah! Actually, everything is north of here. And look at that wonderful, dense forest beyond the plains. Looks to be oak. Old oak. That's *just* what I need for the roof of Saint Magnus's cathedral. I wonder if I can order some from here to send to Orkneyjar."

Messenger doves, dotted black shadows silhouetted against white-washed walls, flew in and out of tiny, square, columbarium windows, as hands reached up to the sky to catch them. Flowers were draped on every empty wall, hanging bushes of cascading pinks, reds, and yellows, climbing plants with enormous purple blooms the size of platters, sharp-edged fronds of palm trees rippled above the walls of hidden courtyards.

On flat rooftop gardens, women wrapped in gaudy dresses and white hats to protect them from the sun, watered ferns waving in the wind.

Entranced, they were oblivious to the church bells which were sounding frantic warnings of a possible attack. There was frantic activity as every man grabbed a crossbow or pike. On top of the walls, soldiers hid behind crenellations, their arrows pointed at the invaders.

Frozen in fear, the people of Narbonne watched the fifteen longboats begin to move slowly forward in a stately procession until they were floating quietly in the still water below the walls of the entrance to the harbor.

Watching them carefully was Viscountess Ermengard of Narbonne. Despite the loud objections of her bodyguards, she had raced to the ramparts. Archbishop D'Anduze, panting with fear, arrived to stand beside her.

In the lead, glittering in the sun, was a blue and gold ship. It carried a full white sail that had a large, red cross sewn onto it. The blue dragon, with its angry, staring eyes, red tongue and jaws belching yellow flames, was truly frightening. From the city rose the murmuring sound of everyone praying to Jesus. The gates to the city were quickly bolted.

Ermengard, her hands clutching the rough stones, turned to her liege knight Sir Thibault De Plaigne. "How many men are there?"

De Plaigne squinted. "Fifteen ships, at least thirty men in each, must be near five-hundred. It's the size of a small, dangerous, Viking army."

Damn my fifty-year-old eyes. I hate squinting. Trying to hide his anxiety, he turned his tall, rigid body away from her. From habit, he put his left hand on his sword, nervously tapping the tip of a large, knuckled finger on the hilt.

A small blue skiff was being lowered to the water from the dragon boat. In its prow stood a tall monk holding up a huge wooden cross with both arms. He was floating towards the pebbly beach at the foot of the Mauresque tower. The water was completely calm, yet he moved without a sail.

It's like a scene from the Bible, thought D'Anduze.

Ermengard could clearly see it was a Man of God crossing the harbor towards them. Turning D'Anduze, she respectfully entreated: "Please, your Holiness, go down to the shore and greet him."

"Why me? I'm no warrior."

"But you are a warrior of the church. It is our only hope for a peaceful engagement."

"Jesu preserve me!" the white-faced D'Anduze mumbled. Hands trembling, he grabbed an old gold cross that a monk had brought up to the ramparts for protection in order to use it for his own salvation down on the beach.

Stumbling in his long white skirts, a gold-striped miter on his head, fingers tightly gripping the jewel-encrusted cross in front of his chest, he cautiously made his way down the winding stairs of the tower to emerge on the strand. Looking up, he could see everyone's faces above him staring down. Fearfully he stepped forward.

The hull of the boat scraped on pebbles near the shore. The monk lifted the heavy cross and gently put it into the water. Then, gathering his brown sackcloth robe around him he stepped out, wading barefoot over the wet stones. Carrying the cross on his back, he went to meet the churchman waiting for him. Soon they were face to face, the dark cross looming above them.

Dark brown eyes, sad and honest, gazed at him through long and tangled black hair covering high cheekbones. William had shaved his beard from the front of his chin, but left his jaws and cheeks unshaven, and there his hair hung down in two scraggly points. His robe, tied around the waist with a hemp cord, was dank and filthy. A pungent smell, like old mushrooms, surrounded him.

Obviously, he believes bathing is an offense unto God, thought D'Anduze.

Then the monk spoke in Latin, gently, but loudly, so that his voice carried up to the ramparts and the people listening: "We are not Vikings. We are not here to pillage and burn. We are Norsemen from the lands of Orkneyjar. I am Bishop William, and I accompany our Lord Earl Rogenvaldr Kali Kolsson on his sacred crusade to Jerusalem to atone for past sins. We wish nothing more than some shelter and the opportunity to buy supplies for our ships."

"As a pilgrim you are welcome here, my child. I am Archbishop Pierre D'Anduze," he replied in Latin.

Steadying his burden, Bishop William knelt, giving obeisance to an obviously pompous Archbishop. *Here we go. Now the farce begins,* William thought. *A dangerous game.*

Dazed, D'Anduze looked down on the lice crawling around the monk's bald spot. *I hope that cross doesn't fall on me.*

Ermengard understood Latin but spoke in Occitanian to De Plaigne. "We have to keep them calm. See to it that nine of their nobles plus their Earl are housed and given what they need. Put them outside the city walls in Coyran. If any other sailing men want to leave the boat, they are confined to the old amphitheater near the salt flats. They are used to that low type there. Don't let the nobles into the city without an escort.

Watch them every minute. Send a message to the Count of Carcassonne immediately to warn him. Oh, and make sure you house them near a bathhouse."

Rogenvaldr paced the ship's deck, watching the little convocation on the strand.

Eindredi was watching Ermengard give orders. "Seems the Viscountess really *is* the absolute ruler here." His large knuckles turned his silver walrus horn round and round. Sitting on the edge of the rail, he tipped the horn back and drained the last of the wine. "This wine from Perpignan isn't bad. A little sweet, but very rich."

Throwing away the dregs, he hitched it onto his belt. "So what are your plans, Rogenvaldr?"

The Earl stood still, put his hands on his hips and looked down. *The heat rising from the deck is unbelievable. Will it get worse? Can it?* "I want to see her as soon as possible. We're already deep into summer. I'm sending William to negotiate the exchange of gifts. If that's Narbonne's Archbishop out there on the beach, William has to convince him more than anyone else that the horn's real. Let's see how naïve they all really are."

If King Sigurd II thought it was that easy, why didn't he sell it himself? Suddenly, a wary feeling grew in Rogenvaldr's stomach.

Eindredi, as always, was practical. "Somehow, I kind of think that it would be to the church's definite advantage to have a real unicorn horn here. Think of all the paying pilgrims. Just make sure you can see and count the gold when you get it. They're southern folk—I don't trust them."

When a messenger came from Ermengard to tell them about the housing arrangements, a long argument ensued over who was to go ashore and live in town.

Eindredi wouldn't leave his crew.

"I told you. I don't trust them. I'm going to stay on my ship."

In the end, Rogenvaldr, along with nine of his own men, disembarked from their longboat at a wharf below the walls. He ordered the rest of his crew to moor the ship at the dock in case he had to leave quickly.

A tall, elderly man covered in chainmail was waiting for them.

"Sir Thibault De Plaigne, at your service. I am your guide to Narbonne. I will escort you to your living quarters in Coyran."

"Earl Rogenvaldr Kali Kolsson. Please lead the way." *How can he wear that metal outfit in this heat?*

As soon as Rogenvaldr left, Eindredi took the fourteen remaining vessels back through the lagoon and anchored in the Mediterranean. All the men were ordered to remain on board, but after a lot of angry grumbling he allowed them to go in pairs to the amphitheater taverns and whorehouses once a week.

Only God knows if we'll be out of here in a week, he thought.

CHAPTER 8

Who'll challenge my nine skills?
I'm champion at chess,
canny recalling runes,
well-read, a red-hot smith—
some say I shoot and ski
and scull skillfully too.
Best of all, I've mastered
harp-play and poetry.
              —*Rogenvaldr Kali Kolsson, 1103?-1158*

De Plaigne was in no mood to play host to ten over-muscled Norsemen. *Nobles! Pilgrims! Hah! They're just devious Vikings hiding their balls.* Impatiently he gestured for them to follow him.

Filthy from living on a ship for months, the sailors trudged behind him along a river path beneath the ramparts. On the wharves, jute bags stacked high, some lying tumbled on the ground, released a heavy mélange of cinnamon, saffron, pepper, and turmeric into the warm, damp air. Suspicious, defensive glances measured their every step. The pounding of water rushing through the arched bridge piers, combined with the churning wooden wheels of the many fulling mills, made a thunderous racket. Wagons loaded with piles of dark, foul-smelling cloth from the mills were being hauled by four iron-collared oxen.

The path was murky and slippery with squashed manure, human and beast, thrown from a bridge packed with merchant's houses, their red-tiled roofs leaning on top of each other. Nimbly, they ducked from side to side, avoiding the discarded sheep offal and pig parts that butchers above them were tossing into the river. Screaming children dove into the water to grab dinner.

"These flies are the size of herrings!" groused Thorgeir, attacking them with his hands, "and just as hungry."

Rogenvaldr had purposely chosen him to accompany the group. His impressive size would act as a deterrent to any impulsive attack. Unless the whole town got up in arms, which could always happen.

At the east end of the bridge stood a pointy topped tower in which a circular staircase led up to a Water Gate.

"This is one of ten guarded gates." De Plaigne emphasized the word *guarded*. "Five lead into Narbonne and five into what we call The Bourg which is across the river."

Soldiers of the militia, their crossbows cocked and ready, were staring down at them from above. The Norsemen had to climb the stairs into Narbonne one man at a time. One of the soldiers decided to challenge Rogenvaldr's right to carry arms in the city. All the tall Viking had to do was put his right hand slowly across his chest firmly on the hilt of his broadsword and stand there, staring down at him. The soldier took a quick step back.

Once through the gate, the Norsemen found themselves in a crowded market square lined with stone buildings. On their left, the unbuilt top of a church tower loomed above a yellow stucco wall with an elaborate entry door.

That must be where William is living with the Archbishop, Rogenvaldr thought. When William had been invited to stay with D'Anduze in his palace, Rogenvaldr ordered him to get the Archbishop to accept the purchase of the unicorn horn. As one churchman to another, William would be able to persuade him of its worth to the church.

William had been indignant. "I resent your equating me with this puffed-up church bird. And you know my feelings about selling a fake horn."

"Well, our King has given us little choice. We've got to get to Jerusalem one way or another," Rogenvaldr had said. "You might as well help."

De Plaigne was trying to get his attention. "This is the caularia, the vegetable market." The knight really didn't know what else to say. *I'm not a guide,* he grumbled to himself

The vegetable market was a jumble of merchants' carts selling spices, dark roots, and rough green vegetables mounded next to red and yellow fruits. Beyond it, carts of fish, strange talismans, and brightly colored weavings clogged the narrow main street as far as the eye could see.

Dust flew in erratic circles through the hot air under fluttering yellow sheets overhead. Hung up with hooks and poles to shade the street, they gave scant relief from the harsh noon sun. Heat cooked the horse manure left underfoot on black stones, its odor mixing with the smell of grilling horsemeat. The scent of warm jasmine honey floated under the sharp, raw smell of garlic and salty sheep's cheese.

When the ten Norsemen strolled into the market, all motion stopped. Men held bags of grain above their heads, women grasped soft fruit too tightly, fish slipped back into baskets.

The man in the lead was obviously a nobleman. Tall, orange-haired, dressed in a heavily patterned overtunic, he wore a thick sword longer than a man's arm, its scabbard studded with square jewels set in gold. His companions wore sleeveless leather vests that showed off tattooed arms, huge-muscled due to months of rowing. Their leather pants sat tight and shiny on buttocks and balls. Their shanks were tree trunks.

De Plaigne urged them on. "Your residence is in Coyran. We must go straight ahead. This way."

Rogenvaldr faced him, thinking—*he looks like a bunch of metal pots stacked one on top of the other.*

The market began to smell musty as the odor of human desire permeated the air. It emanated from armpits, was exhaled on hot breath, and rose up from under the folds of sweating groins. The Norsemen smiled broadly as they explored the stalls owned by women, munched on the free offerings of sweetmeats and olives, gazed intently at the curves of breasts and hips, watched brightly patterned skirts swing over rotund asses. Thorgeir's height and obvious bulge made women ache. Several crowed around him, gazing boldly up at him.

The women here are definitely a threat to Magnus's vow of celibacy, thought Rogenvaldr. He watched the navigator lean on the edge of a dark-haired woman's cart, smiling and fingering her fruit suggestively as her man stood nearby scowling and ready to kill him. Magnus couldn't have cared less about the man; one quick blow and he would be cut in half. The Earl was trying to gauge any threats. *The men here seem small and what? Effeminate?* He examined De Plaigne again—*maybe that's why they cover themselves in metal to fight. To save their skins.*

"But we're Norsemen, not Vikings. Have no fear," he heard Magnus say in the French of Normandy. Looking at him sideways the woman coyly dropped an apple, then kicked it under the wagon toward Magnus's feet. He squatted to pick it up and got a pleasing vision of her thigh. Rising, he saw the Earl watching him, and flushed.

Suddenly the air began to vibrate as the city's church bells rang for sext prayers. The clanging reverberated against the ramparts and bounced back and forth down the alleys. A deafening cacophony to men that had been at sea for months.

Jesus help me, my head feels like it's being hit by a hammer. Rogenvaldr put his hands over his ears and looked up, turning in circles. His head was still buzzing after they stopped.

De Plaigne saw his chance. "Let's go. It's time to go to your residence." *Absolutely degrading. Nobles, shopping in a market. Christ help me, I'd like to throttle everyone one of them.*

"Calm yourself, De Plaigne. Where do these streets lead?" Rogenvaldr pointed south.

A wall of stucco storefronts lined a barely passable lane crowded with tables and wagons piled high with dry goods. Dark-haired men wearing yellow hats with knobs on top, busily carried rolled-up cloth in and out of deeply set doors, their ornate iron bars open for business.

"That's the Jewish quarter. They sell the finest fabrics in the world here. Fit for a king. At kings' prices, too," he answered grumpily, then spit over his left shoulder.

"I've never seen so many Jews in one place."

"Well, don't be wandering around there at night. Especially stay away from the Jews' Gate in the wall. They're the only ones allowed to use it, and sometimes their devil religion makes them close it at strange times. We watch it carefully on their holy days—one never knows what they're up to. I have no idea why the Viscountess Ermengard permits them to live here."

But Rogenvaldr wasn't listening. A crowd of merchants trying to peddle their wares had closed in around him. He was getting very uncomfortable. A swarthy man in a linen robe, having pushed through, was trying to sell him some intricately carved hide belts. *These are so thin they'd never carry a sword. What are they for?* "Are these for women?"

"No, my lord. These are suitable for the finest nobleman."

"Well, not this one. Leave me." When the man persisted, Rogenvaldr pushed him away so hard he fell. *These people can't take no for an answer.* The crowd picked the man up, discarded him, then pushed in again.

"Quiet! I said leave me!" Everyone backed away in silence, afraid of his temper.

Ermengard's palace was built right on the river next to the Water Gate. The solarium had windows overlooking the caularia, and when she sat at her worktable the familiar calls and cries of trading were always in the air. Sunlight drifted in, filtered by green silk curtains draped across arched windows, its dappled reflections rippling lightly in the warm breeze coming off the river. White tiles with brightly painted flowers and birds covered the floor, matching the occasional swallow or lark that flew in, winging its way across the room. Pink flamingo feather fans hung from the ceiling with thin gold ropes that reached the floor. Four barefoot little boys, wearing little gold Byzantine tunics and floppy Phrygian caps, lazily pulled the ropes to work the fans. One trembling fan was still as the child had fallen asleep. Set against lime-colored walls, purple orchids grew in luminescent Egyptian vases. Red flowers floated in a large brass water basin. A thin clinking sound came from transparent blue curtains weighted down with gold coins.

Just outside the tiled, arched doorway to the room, was a corridor leading to a tiled staircase up to a large roof terrace used at dawn and dusk when the air was cooler.

But at this time of day the sun was high and hot. Ermengard had ordered her clerk, Peter Raymond, to go home for his mid-day meal, and sent her ladies away to take their afternoon naps. Only Valencia, her old Catalan nurse remained, dozing on floor pillows against the wall. Draped across her thighs, also asleep, was a white, long- haired cat.

I've just got to get a more comfortable table. Really too many things to do, and I'm tired of working all the time. Scrolls and parchments were piled on the table in tumbling stacks. Grumbling to herself, Ermengard wiped black stains of hawthorn bark ink from her fingers. *Oh! Mother Mary! Now there are spots on my sleeve too.* Dabbing at the yellow silk only made it worse. She had deliberately ignored Valencia's advice to put on a writing jacket.

Maybe I should just stop working and read. Ermengard looked with longing across the room at her favorite book lying face down on the floor by her reading couch: a delicately illustrated volume of Li Romans d'Alixandre, the exciting, romantic adventures of the handsome Greek hero, Alexander the Great. Many a sultry afternoon had been spent enjoying the conquests of the bold, blond chevalier as he journeyed from Macedon to Armenia, from Persia to mysterious India. Circumstances having left her a love-starved young woman, she imagined situations in which they would meet, and Alexander would instantly fall passionately in love with her, kneeling at her feet, vowing chivalrous love forever. Ermengard's longing made her thoughts morose. *Still, whatever God wills, I must bear it in silence. But I think it's now time for me to stop working. That's strange. The street is so quiet. What could have happened?*

The cries from the market were usually loud and raucous. In the silence a lark in a golden filigreed cage on her desk began to sing.

"Troubadour, my little friend, did the quiet wake you up?" Ermengard tapped lightly on the cage with her quill.

The continued absence of noise persuaded her to put down the quill and go to a window overlooking the market to find out what was going on. To her surprise the Norsemen were in Narbonne exploring! Leaning on the stone sill, she found herself laughing. She actually enjoyed the antics of the foreigners as they ignored De Plaigne's annoyed requests to move on. She watched him give up and sullenly lean back on a stone wall, stroking the pomaded, white-streaked bush on his chin.

Poor Thibault De Plaigne, he's just rattling along in his armor. These blond Norsemen are like a herd of my wild Commarge horses, she thought. Living freely in the open marshes, bounding along the flat grasslands, very few horsemen could tame those white steeds, let alone ride them. Muscular legs rippling, they galloped through the sea foam, glistening droplets flying off silver manes. Ermengard rode one herself. It had taken two years of intense training with an ungelded foal named Orion, who now saw himself as her protector, kicking and biting as well as a destrier when he thought her threatened.

A deep voice with a heavy Spanish accent abruptly snapped. "Get off me, Luna!" Green eyes, the color of sea foam, opened wide as Valencia dumped the cat off her thighs. Her ebony walking stick clacked on the floor as she shuffled up to look out the window. Her tiny bones were held together by skin that looked as wrinkled as a deflated pig's bladder. Obsessively terrified of falling, she grabbed Ermengard's shoulder with a surprisingly tight grip.

"Ah, what healthy looking bulls! And that one with the sword must be their leader. He's the handsomest bull—look at his haunches!" She laughed deep in her throat. Memories of past bulls were not forgotten. "Alexander the Great has arrived in Narbonne!"

"Though not for me."

"Sadly, as things are, this is true." Valencia's gnarled hand rubbed Ermengard's shoulder. "Yet, you must decide, babies or power. You see how Aelinore had her marriage to Louis annulled to get the Aquitaine back along with her freedom. A very strong, determined woman. And a woman who's been on crusade! Who knows if she will ever marry again. If she's smart, she won't."

"Is that their Earl just below us?" She watched him with curiosity.

Sensing he was being observed, Rogenvaldr looked up—straight into honey-colored eyes shaped like larks' wings. Enveloped by an undulating green silk curtain was an oval face surrounded by black curly hair.

Perhaps a servant girl? Rogenvaldr smiled and bowed lightly. Her eyes widened as her hand went over her mouth.

Ermengard sprang back from the window so quickly that she nearly knocked Valencia over.

The afternoon heat was increasing. Soon the Norsemen decided it was time to follow their guide. Munching grilled octopus, and pastries stuffed with honey and pistachios, they wandered along the Via Domitia, the ancient way paved by wide, glossy-black Roman stones. It still ran through the center of the city a thousand years after Caesar's armies had departed, but it was now known as Straight Street.

"You're stuck inside these ramparts—how do you keep the streets so clean?" asked the Earl.

The knight liked the question. "One of the few Roman constructs kept up through all the years of Goth, Visigoth, Muslim, and finally Spanish rule, are the old water sluices and drains located at intersections where the crossing stones keep feet dry during winter rain floods. Even the cisterns under the city's wells are still fed by underground aqueducts that bring fresh water from the mountains north of here. Townspeople are fined if they throw garbage out the windows. It must be collected. Ermengard has taken the instruction of a Persian physician who is an expert in diseases very seriously, and she is very adamant that these rules be followed. The sluices are cleared each dawn with river water carried in carts by the town water cleaners, a hereditary profession. The water cleaners claim they're direct descendants of Domitian's Legions, and considering the body size, they very likely are. Marrying into their families is a very expensive proposition, unless beauty is the coin."

After the Archbishop's palace, the men turned left to find a large cathedral under construction. Walking single file, they warily avoided rope-covered scaffolds and winches carrying up carved stones. Sweating, shirtless men jumped from beam to beam, their metal chisels and hammers clanging on broad leather belts. Always eager to learn more about stone building techniques, Rogenvaldr wanted to watch. The marble and mortar dust was choking everyone.

This time it was his men who got him away. "You can always go back. We're choking on dust, we're hot and tired," said Magnus, "and still hungry."

Ahead, set deeply into the ramparts, were the towers of the Episcopal Gate. A huge marble frog, its throat bursting with air, was carved into the top of the arch. Thick wooden gates were open to allow pushcarts to leave the market.

• • •

Outside the walls they entered a quiet, sunny, green landscape watered by countless small culverts layered between white-stone terraced walls. Leading gently down to a bend in the Aude River, the land was edged with plots of small holdings still yielding peas, legumes, and stalks of black rice waving lightly in sparkling wet shallows. The sound of humming bees filled the air. Hands on foreheads, the Norsemen shaded their eyes while gazing open-mouthed at thousands of hives filling the horizon in neat rows. The fuzzy insects swarmed busily from lilac bushes to lavender to oregano.

Beekeepers, veiled in white gauze hanging from round straw hats, stood amongst the little wooden boxes cleaning their interiors of mildew and cobwebs. Some were smearing a brown mixture onto the outside of the hive.

"This is astounding!" said Rogenvaldr. "I've never seen so many hives in one field. Who owns them?"

"They belong to Ermengard. Honey is a very important ingredient in our cuisine. And of course there is the finest candle wax." De Plaigne spoke seriously.

"What are they putting on the wood?"

"A thick mixture of dung and wood ash. The heat here can be intense. When it hardens it's like a clay shell which keeps the interior cool, so the bees have a place to shelter from the noon sun. If they can't forage, we leave out bowls of mush made of raisins, barley and wine. Don't you do the same?"

"Our summers are short," responded Rogenvaldr. "For us honey is in short supply most of the year. We make it into mead to drink on special occasions, but only the wealthy nobility can afford it. We don't often eat it in our food. Mostly we drink ale. This is great wealth."

"Yes, Ermengard has great wealth. May we continue to your residence?"

Above them, the flapping wings of pelicans, throats full of harvested fish, mingled with the raucous laughter of gulls streaking down to the sea to claim their share of the bounty. A knot of hawks, hungry for a rabbit dinner, floated in circles on warm air currents.

Again some of the men wondered, *have we landed in the Garden of Paradise?*

In a field just north of Narbonne, an intimate cluster of stone houses formed a small town.

De Plaigne stopped walking. "The Viscountess Ermengard welcomes you to Coyran. It is a town she owns, and its people have been ordered to extend a gracious welcome to you."

He waited as an angular man in a tan cotton robe and a broad-bosomed woman wrapped in a brightly flowered dress walked down the road towards them. The man wore a wide-brimmed straw hat over a tight-fitting cap tied under his chin. The woman was wearing a wide headpiece made of stiff white linen folded into wings that stuck out on either side of her head. Her firmly folded hands sat on her stomach.

"Raolf lo Campanes, please bow to Lord Rogenvaldr of Orkneyjar," De Plaigne commanded.

Raolf went down on one knee.

"Please see to the safety of the Earl and his men while they are in Coyran."

De Plaigne then addressed the woman. "Sancha Espanza, please look after the needs of these visitors."

She curtsied deeply.

A stoutly built, handsome woman in her early fifties, Sancha clearly had no compunctions about dealing with these men from Scandia. With dark lines of kohl ringing sharp black eyes set in a round face, and a generous mouth rouged in red, she brusquely nodded in the direction of town.

"Let's go. Follow me," she said in a strange accent, yet at least she spoke Norman French. Sancha picked up her skirts and set about the walk into town, her rump shaking the flowers of her dress like an oversized bouquet.

"Stay." De Plaigne held Raolf back with one hand, waiting a minute before speaking. "Tell Sancha to make sure they eat, drink, and whore heavily enough to keep them from putting their noses in where they don't belong. Hopefully, they'll be gone in a week."

Leading her gaggle of geese, Sancha walked them to the cobbled main street of stores, taverns, and open-fronted workshops. Narrowly winding in a curve through the town center, the road sloped downhill to the river where one could hear the splashing of waterwheels pushing grain stones and smell wet cloth being washed in fulling mills.

Merchants watched them warily from the doorways of two-storied stone buildings whose outer walls leaned on each other, each holding the other up.

No wooden buildings, no empty spaces, just gray stones against stones. I feel like I'm in prison, thought Rogenvaldr, as they wound around corners. *Our homes aren't built like this. We have room to breathe in Orkneyjar, to see land and the sea.*

Tortoise-colored cats lingered on rocky walls. Toms stalked howling females, who escaped from their leaping rapists by running into the shadows of crooked alleys. The stink of cat-piss wafted out of a darkness that sunlight never reached to dry up the dank corners.

Dark female eyes peeked curiously through curlicued window latices. Standing in an arched doorway surrounded by red blooms, a woman lifted her skirt provocatively while making kissing noises. They bumped into each other looking.

In the town square stood an open, wooden-roofed market. It was deserted, except for hungry cats tearing up discarded bits of meat dropped by an old man bent over a charcoal grill. Horsemeat smoke filled the air, and the men began to salivate.

Rogenvaldr looked at Sancha, cocking his head at the meat. His stomach hurt.

"Oh you can eat it. Ifan is always here after the market closes. I love his marinade."

Ifan was not prepared for ten over-sized Norsemen encircling him. At first, the man, stringy-haired with watery eyes cringed, yet when his customers turned out to be voracious meat eaters, he couldn't cook fast enough.

Chomping away on fresh meat that they hadn't had in a month put them all in a good mood. "We'll come back tomorrow!" Gimbel cried, clapping Ifan on the back so hard that he nearly collapsed.

At the end of one street, standing apart, was a larger, white-domed building covered in blue and red tiles cleverly laid out in a wave pattern. White clouds rose from behind it.

"What's that place?" asked Rogenvaldr.

"A bath house," Sancha said, looking him up and down. She sniffed. He got the point.

Eventually, at the end of a short lane, they stopped to look up at a high stone wall. Rogenvaldr groaned inwardly. *This is going to be an impossible prison for us. I've got to sell that horn and get out of here.*

Ducking through the low door they emerged, astonished, into a large courtyard garden open to the blue sky, awash in colors they had never even imagined existed in nature.

Norway was a gray, misty dream of the past.

• • •

Watching Norsemen walking through Narbonne was such an exciting event that no one, not even the militia nervously patrolling the ramparts, took notice of the dusty travelers on two worn donkeys entering the city through the Royal Gate from Beziers.

One donkey carried a tall, scrawny monk in a brown cassock under a black cloak. A deep cowl hid the face of a man with the hungry, heavily lidded eyes of a vulture. Bony hands held a cross. The second donkey, carrying a leather saddle bag and filthy rolled-up blankets, was led on foot by a burly man who had the easy walk of an ex-soldier. A bowl of grey hair topped a round head whose dark slate eyes seemed to look everywhere at once. Empty jowls hung below lips that did not enjoy smiling. A scruffy beard hid an old noose scar. Yet it was a forgettable face.

The burly man asked the gatekeeper, "Where's the Archbishop's palace?"

"Are you blind?" Annoyed by the man's northern French, he responded in Occitan. "It's the biggest building in the city. Just go towards it."

When he saw the monk's cross, he knelt and crossed himself. The monk looked at him like he was a beetle on ox dung and moved forward.

Entranced, Archbishop D'Anduze was in his church examining a newly painted image of a winged, white-robed Christ separating the saved from the damned at the Last Judgement. The saved souls, depicted as a herd of sheep, were to his right. The damned were goats being herded away by a blue, dragon-tailed Satan. Under the feet of goats ready for the roasting, were yellow flames outlined in red.

He jumped when a stranger appeared unexpectedly beside him. With him came a strange miasma in the air.

"This is all vanity," the man sneered. "It will not last."

"And you are?"

"I am Canon Hugon, Abbot of Prémontré Abbey, the chosen heir of Norbert of Xanten."

Oh my Lord, who needs this extremist Norbertine here? Flagellation, starvation, constant prayer the only paths to salvation? He looked him over. *Nothing but a skeleton held together by sinew.* D'Anduze shivered. *Those staring eyes make even me feel condemned to eternal damnation. And that huge beak. I swear, I think I'm going to have a vulture for a houseguest. And that huge lump in his throat—ugh! What's that stink?*

To his relief the Canon refused the offer of comfortable sleeping quarters upstairs. Instead, Hugon found an unused, ground floor guard's chamber with rough stone walls and no window. It was conveniently located near a small door with access to a narrow alley leading to the market square. The Canon was quite pleased to find out that just across the square was Ermengard's palace.

"I need a wooden bed with a straw mattress, one wool blanket, a bucket for my soils, and hot broth with dark bread sent to my room twice a day after matins and vespers. My servant will sleep on the floor by my door."

Afterwards, D'Anduze saw the Canon wandering through the unfinished cathedral, gliding like a dark phantom of doom. Catching up with Hugon at the altar, he asked, "Why are you here?"

"You will never live to see it completed. You do realize that don't you?"

D'Anduze felt cold fingers walking on his spine. "Who sent you here?"

"The Pope! Heresy! I have been to Toulouse, then Carcassonne, and now am come to Narbonne. Bernard said the whole region is crawling with heretics. And he is right. How did this happen here? Are you so busy rebuilding Sodom and Gomorrah that you didn't notice?"

"This cathedral is for the glory of God, as is Saint Denis, in case you didn't know," the Archbishop responded testily. "Yes, they are here — and in growing numbers. I *am* very concerned. Even the nobility, especially the women, are sheltering the Bons Hommes. And what are you planning to do about the heretics?"

"I will wander, as a Canon does. I will visit churches and preach. I must talk to the people, find out their secrets. Bernard wants reports of what I find, and who is suspected of heresy."

He narrowed his eyes and inspected D'Anduze. *It might even be you.* "We must stamp it out!" His voice rose, becoming fiery. "We must break the egg that hatches heresy!"

Break the eggs that hatch heresy? Whatever is he going on about? Peculiar man. D'Anduze turned to leave. "You must forgive me, I must go. I have a pressing meeting with Bishop William."

"And who is this, Bishop William?"

"The confessor of a Norseman just arrived with a flotilla of ex-Vikings."

"How intriguing. I would be pleased to attend and meet him. Thank you for inviting me."

"Well, come along then," the irritated Archbishop said.

• • •

Bishop William was examining D'Anduze's study. It was pleasantly cool despite the day's heat, with a stone-vaulted ceiling, large arched windows to let in the north light, and wooden cubicles to hold thick books, tagged old scrolls, and unused parchment. Amidst some ivory carvings he found an exquisite container with a round lid. He was closely examining it when D'Anduze arrived accompanied by an emaciated monk.

What does he think he's doing wandering around my study? D'Anduze thought. But politely he said, "That's a pyxis. It's carved from a single piece of ivory and was made for an Arab king. I keep the host in it." Turning to his uninvited guest, he made the necessary introductions. "Bishop William, this is Canon Hugon of Prémontré Abbey."

"Yes, I know of it." *A place of extremist flagellators starving themselves to death.* "God be with you." William decided to be very careful of what he said.

"And may God be with you, my son." *Well, at least you don't appear to be a complete glutton.*

After they were seated and offered wine and dried fruit, which Hugon gruffly refused, D'Anduze looked at Bishop William.

"Why did you wish this urgent meeting?"

"I am here about the great holy item Earl Rogenvaldr has brought with him as a gift to be exchanged with the Viscountess Ermengard."

"What holy item?"

"A unicorn horn."

"A WHAT?" the other two exclaimed in unison.

CHAPTER 9

Any person who reproaches me
for loving you, is a fool,
as it is so pleasurable for me.
They do not understand me—
they do not see you with my eyes.
                    —*Castelosa de Auvergne, 12th century*

Rogenvaldr and his men stood and stared at the profusion of flowers growing in the courtyard of their house in Coyran. Blood red pomegranate blooms dripped from trees in blue ceramic pots, intense pink and yellow bougainvillea climbed up white painted walls to intertwine with clusters of purple irises. Lavender bushes exploded out of corners where the wall met blue and orange floor tiles. White, trumpet-shaped flowers emanated a heavy, sweet aroma. Confined to the inside of the courtyard, the smell was overwhelming. Some of the men began to sneeze. Others just closed their eyes for a few moments to adjust to the brightness of the sun reflecting off the tiles.

Slightly dazed, each man was led to his own room. Windows opened onto interior tiled hallways where balconies dripped flowery waterfalls all the way down to the courtyard.

Rogenvaldr was shown to a large corner chamber with a view of distant grain fields. On a nearby green mound was a small church with scattered sheds and an enclosed cemetery. Shimmering in a blue haze, rock mountains shaped like iron anvils cut through the land, their points splitting gnarly forests in half. The Aude River, water mills lining each bank, curved eastwards in a wide loop. Just below the window, pruned orange trees provided shade in a small walled garden furnished with marble benches, tables, and a fountain with a statue of a naked nymph bending forward to pour water into a basin.

His room was large and airy. On the floor, under a window divided into arches by a flower carved column, was a heavily stuffed mattress covered with brightly colored woven cotton blankets and pillows. Against the yellow wall stood a white marble table shaped like a church font. A damp, clay water-filled pitcher stood nearby on a wooden chest. Next to a silver cup, a pile of neatly folded cotton towels were placed with a wedge of green olive soap.

Looking for a bucket to relieve himself, he opened a narrow wooden door to find a brightly tiled room overlooking the garden in which there was a tiled bench with a privy hole underneath. Another clay water pitcher was next to a basket piled full of green leaves and moss. On the wall hung a bucket with a handle and chain that he could pull to tip water onto his sweaty body. There was even a channel and drain for the used water. *By the saints, this is so different from the gardhús in Norway. And by the Saints, I stink.*

Hot and tired, hair sticky from endless salt washings, ears itchy, and his toenails killing him in his boots, he stomped down to the courtyard.

"Sancha, where are you? Take us to that bath house!" He yelled loud enough for everyone to hear him. "*All* of you," he barked, "get your filthy skins down here. Now!"

Amidst cranky groans and grumblings, the men dragged themselves out of their rooms to take a bath.

"What, we're washing indoors?" Armod asked. "What's wrong with the river?"

William came over to talk to Rogenvaldr. There was a definite look of relief on his face at being back with his companions. "This strange Abbot Hugon arrived at the palace from the north. With him distracting the Archbishop, I decided to move out and live here. Hugon asked too many questions about the unicorn horn. I think he knows I'm lying, but he isn't saying anything. He just makes a wheezing laugh whenever he sees me. I surmise he thinks the Archbishop is a heretic lover."

"Never mind him. Did you and the Archbishop come to an agreement for the sale of the horn?"

"Yes. He understands the financial benefits to the church. Now, I just want to relax in some hot water."

Sancha had cleared the bath house of locals and made sure there were enough masseurs. Rogenvaldr ordered the men to leave their clothes and short swords by the door. Magnus, naked and disgruntled, was elected to guard the big pile of filthy linen, iron, and leather.

The huge bath house dome had a small round window open to the sky. The men jumped into tiled, hot baths heated by wood fires under the floor. The pools reminded the Norsemen of the steaming springs and outdoor geysers of the north, but the lack of frigid outdoor air made it hard for them to breathe. And the cold baths available, while refreshing, did not seem very cold. These were men used to northern extremes.

Ah, I really do miss the Deilartunguhver, thought William. He leaned back, remembering the hot rocks on his back, the sulfurous smell of steam, and the green ferns against the dark, damp soil around its edges.

Sancha arrived with clean outfits suitable for the heat, and ten women.

"I'll take these vermin-infested leather clothes and have them cleaned. They will be returned to you." She gave the girls a knowing look, saying in Occitan, "You clean the men."

Upon seeing the well-muscled Norsemen, the women quickly stripped off their dresses and jumped into the pools. Hair and beards were trimmed, washed and re-braided, backs got scrubbed, sexual needs were met, and Rogenvaldr got his toenails cut. The men's' tattoos led to all sorts of raucous comments.

Magnus was sitting on his bench with his need on display. William felt sorry for him, so he went over and got dressed. "You said you wanted to be celibate on pilgrimage."

"I didn't think it would take so long to get to Jerusalem."

"I'll watch the weapons. Go ahead and get cleaned up, if nothing else."

Magnus raced to the water.

• • •

William, tired of ruminating about things he could do nothing about, decided to go sit on the steps outside and get some fresh air. The tiles stairs were warm in the bright sun. He leaned back against the wall inhaling the smell of jasmine and mint, trying to calm himself. Next to him, leaning on a red clay flowerpot, was a ragged black tomcat.

Gray streaked fur stood out like feathers around his neck. One bitten ear twitched when William sat down. Then the tomcat opened up round, milk-white eyes. William put out one hand to stroke him, but then remembered that his mother had always told him to never pet a blind cat. Carefully he pulled his hand back.

A tall, slim woman, walking down the street in long strides, was heading towards the bath house. Deliberately she stopped in front of the steps. Looking down at him she asked, "Are you the Norseman priest?"

"Yes, I'm Bishop William. And you are?"

Her back was very straight, her arms bare under a silk veil, her shoulders and neck smooth and lustrous. An oval head, with black braids falling down her back, framed the most beautiful face he had ever seen. Her eyes, too large for that delicate face, had unblinking black irises that captured his and would not let go. Looking at her eyes made him feel slightly dizzy.

"I am Princess Bathsheba of Begwana, once the Kingdom of Aksum. My mother was a descendant of Makeda, the great Queen of Sheba, and King Solomon, ancestor of Jesus through the line of King David."

William was shocked. "And you are here? How did that happen?"

"Pirates. My ship was attacked near Rhodes. I was foolish to be there. The coast is full of hidden caves and has always been a place of lawless thieves. Even Gaius Julius Caesar tried unsuccessfully to get rid of them."

She shrugged her shoulders smoothly. "I was a virgin priestess dedicated to serving the church that guards the ancient Hebrew Ark of the Covenant in Lalibela. I was sold to a slave trader who sold me to a brothel here in Narbonne. Now I am given to many men, yet I am forbidden to take my own life. I ask you, as a priest from far away, how I can continue to live?"

Throughout this narrative, William had been watching the curve of her breasts, the line of her long legs, and wondering what she looked like under the veils. He shook himself, *what's the matter with me?* He was also dumbstruck. *How could such a holy woman have come to this? And how do I know she is telling the truth? Women are clever, and scheming.*

"I know you are thinking: how do I know she is telling the truth? I will prove myself to you."

Folding her long legs beneath her she knelt to the ground, touching the stones with her forehead and palms. After a minute she straightened up, her eyes closed. When she opened them, they were as unseeing as the cat dozing next to him. Turned totally inwards, she tilted her head back and began to chant in a strange language. It was obviously a Christian prayer, but it took some time before he recognized it as an ancient language he had once heard in Paris. A priest from Aksum had arrived to meet with the King.

The next morning, at mass, dressed in white robes, the priest had chanted prayers in an old language he claimed was spoken by King Solomon. The ancient, haunting words had had a mystical effect on his mind then, just as her words did now. The priest and this woman had a similar aquiline nose and pointed chin.

She had stopped chanting and was looking at him intensely.

"You believe me now. I can see that."

"Yes, I do."

"What is my fate to be?" she asked.

"We must accept God's plan," William said quietly.

"Yet there are times when we must try to find God's other way for ourselves."

How true. I wish I had insisted on going that other way before we started out and arrived here in this place.

"I beg of you, in God's holy name, help me to go home." Her voice had a mystical quality; she gazed deeply into his eyes.

William's soul felt invaded, as if someone was taking over. Without volition he was about to give in to an urge that he should ignore.

"Yes, I will help you. I will buy you and set you free. You must go home."

"You will be forever blessed. I will wait for word from you. Sancha knows where I am enslaved."

"You must wait until I have the money."

In one sensuous movement, she rose and strode away, head held high, her body swaying like tall, green grass.

William watched her walk away, an intense look on his face. He rubbed his eyes with his palms. Bathsheba had stirred up long gone feelings in him. Or he had thought they were long gone.

Not that fight again, he moaned to himself.

• • •

With swords strapped over dark blue cotton trousers, linen tunics, and despite the heat and their newly polished old boots, the men arrived back at the house. A plentiful mid-day meal was waiting for them under the palm trees in the courtyard. Having eaten nothing but some barley porridge for their dagverther before leaving the ship that morning, their stomachs were rumbling like hungry dogs.

Confused by the food, they had no idea what to eat. There were cracked-open pomegranates, their seeds bleeding red juice stacked up in bright blue ceramic bowls, cut lemons piled up in baskets, pungent green sauces in yellow saucers, heaped purple grapes, dates, almonds and raisins mixed into orange rice, and ceramic pots full of stews that scented the air with cinnamon, cloves, mint, and pepper. Orkneyjar was far away, drab, tan, a different world; there, food was for the teeth and stomach, plain and hearty, meat and porridge. It was not a feast for the eyes.

These fearless warriors were afraid of foreign food.

Thorgeir, standing at full height, said it plainly. "Where's the codfish, reindeer meat, salmon, and sour lingonberries? I can't eat this. I'll starve to death. This is woman's food."

A smiling servant quickly brought him a plate of lamb stew. She fed him a piece with her fingers.

"It's strange, but at least it's meat." He sucked the sauce off her fingers and ate some more.

"And this is?" asked Rogenvaldr, picking up a platter and sniffing at it.

Sancha explained, "That's Raymonia. Boiled chicken chopped into pieces and fried in walnut oil served in a reduced sauce of sour pomegranate juice, ginger, saffron, ground blanched almonds and honey."

His cheeks puckered at the sweet-sour explosion in his mouth. The tart pomegranate reminded him of the lingonberries back home. He looked around for butter, boiled mutton, pork fat, cottage cheese, and some crusty dark bread, and couldn't find any. Picking up another plate, he held it to his nose. "And this?"

"Salsa de Cerpol, a wild thyme sauce made with pepper and verjuice served on fattened goose that's been roasted for half a day in a clay trapa buried in hot ashes."

"And what's verjuice?"

"A fermented juice pressed from unripe green grapes."

"Can I get the goose without the sauce?"

"Tomorrow. How about the matafeam? It's lamb stew with salt, pepper, ginger, and cinnamon. You eat it with a flat, white bread made with the finest flour."

Rogenvaldr took the lamb, bread, some salted anchovies and sat down on a stone bench. The anchovies were excellent—large and fatty. He was crunching on the bones when a young girl, her eyes outlined in black, her golden skin decorated with red dots and swirls, knelt before him with a silver tray. She poured a cup of dark red wine and handed it to him. It had a cloying, musty taste. She offered him a plate of dried spices smelling of cinnamon and ginger and gestured to him to put the spices into the wine.

"No," he said, gesturing with his hand. The drink was already too sweet. He felt a headache coming on from all the tartness, bright light, and sugar. *Drinking sweet mead at a special occasion is one thing, but why do these people have to put honey and sweet wine into everything?*

Now that they had figured out the food wasn't poison, his men were eating everything without any thought, just hunger. The ale was pale, and deceptively strong, and their thirst, increased by the fishy sauces, made them drink heavily. The afternoon temperature was rising. The exhausted, clean Norsemen collapsed to sleep in the cool corners of their rooms.

In his own chamber, Rogenvaldr threw himself onto the pillows under the open windows. Outside was a cloudless sky and he fell asleep listening to twittering birds and the scent of lavender.

At twilight, the deafening croak of frogs woke him—thousands of them, all making gurgling-throated mating calls in the darkening rushes by the river. Reflecting into wet shallows, the setting sun was a furnace of pink and orange flame, followed by a transparent blue evening with a crescent moon wearing a star for an earring. Shadowed on the horizon, thin black palm trees bent in the breeze, shaking their fronds against each other. Leaning on the windowsill, he watched, enchanted.

"Rogenvaldr, get down here."

Shaking himself from the spell, he got dressed.

CHAPTER 10

Coined 'wine-oak' for woman;
wooed, all autumn taught her
hawk's tricks, Norse-talk's pleasures.
'Tell me, Mademoiselle
—wine bruised lipped who born of
bed boasts such pedigree?'
Lime cracks, stone falls; crimsoned
hawks claim flesh, mon amour.
                    —*Rogenvaldr Kali Kolsson, 1103?-1158*

Down in the courtyard his men were gathered around the ever-present Sancha.

"Where's the best whorehouse?" they all asked at the same time.

Eager to please, and following orders, she led them through a cool evening breeze towards Narbonne. Turning east along a winding path under the battlements, they stepped around low terraces and well-tended vegetable plots reeking of human waste.

Aslak trotted behind, totally excited, looking forward to his first such adventure. He had combed his straight blond hair till it shone and put on an embroidered hat purchased in the market earlier that day.

Rogenvaldr was curious about Sancha. Guiding her by the elbow around a mound of horse manure, he questioned her. "You can speak northern French yet I can't place your accent. Where are you from?"

"I'm originally from a city named Wurtzburg in Eastern Franconia. I was a seamstress in my husband's tailor shop. We had three children. Five winters ago my family was killed in riots by peasants who thought we were Jews hiding food.

A sharp pang of sadness caused her to stop walking. She fingered a large lapis blue cross hanging on her bosom.

"The house was burned down with my family locked inside. I was outside the city delivering garments to a noblewoman when the riots started, and I couldn't return until they were over. I was despondent, inconsolable. I sold what was left in the ashes, some burnt silver, a few books that strangely enough survived, and persuaded a peddler with a wagon full of cures and cooking pots to take me with him.

A short laugh puffed out of her.

"God plays many tricks. My savior, Benjamin, turned out to be a Rhadanite Jew. We made do with each other. I encouraged the women to trust him so that they would purchase more. We wandered together through many towns. When we got here, I was too tired to wander any more. I stayed and Benjamin left to go on—and probably visit his wife in Barcelona, though we rarely spoke of his family. Occasionally he comes through and stays with me for a short while."

Raising her hands, she clapped them on her thighs.

"And I am here still. Let's go into the city now. Here is the gate."

Torches around the thick wooden doors of Narbonne's north-eastern Porte-Laurac revealed an arch dotted with fractured Roman marble sculpture, faces and legs flickering in the light. A brisk wind, swirling around corners, swept the smell of frying fish, garlic, spiced wine, and burnt honey into the air. Enormous wagons, their six oxen standing sullenly in piles of old and fresh manure, were lined up along the road outside. Merchants were busily loading their wares into the smaller carts allowed in the narrow streets.

"They never stop buying and selling here, do they?" Rogenvaldr said.

"No, never. It's the only way to survive," Sancha answered. "But our people are not hungry."

Leaning over the crenellations, tense soldiers watched them enter the city. Just inside, covered by shadows, a tavern was leaning up against the city walls. Outlined by the flames of oil-filled clay pots, drivers swarmed over rickety tables arguing endlessly about money. A candle flickering in a window revealed a hand fondling a bare breast. Torches were glowing through a round stone arch up ahead.

"Keep moving, please. We must go through there," Sancha said, pointing.

The ancient Roman basilica, looming above them in the middle of a large square, was a sudden surprise. Known by the locals as La Capitole, it stood in an open forum once used by the Romans for public gatherings. On a cracked concrete platform, a dozen thick, fluted, marble columns were topped with heavily leaf-carved capitals. The triangular pediment above the doors had cracked ages ago when the wooden roof fell in; flecks of tarnished gold paint could still be seen in the letters MINERVA carved into the cornice. Over the centuries the crumbling temple had retained its original dignity. The Norsemen had never seen a nearly complete Roman building. The ones in Britain were mostly ruins. Its presence awed them. Glimpsing this temple, already standing here at the time of Christ, the pilgrims had their first inkling of what lay ahead in Jerusalem. Necks craning, oblivious to the crowded taverns and jugglers somersaulting on its crumbling stairs, the men circled the building.

It was obvious that the Narbonnaise were not in such awe of La Capitole. Leaning against the columns, lounging on the steps wantonly displaying their bodies, whores called to them, quickly arriving in a wave of perfumed lust hanging in the air.

Aslak, the wind blowing flaxen strands around his sixteen-year-old face, was flattered by two women running their fingers through his hair.

"Oh, aren't we young and beautiful," murmured the younger one in his ear.

"Not too young for me," snapped the older one, pushing the first out of the way.

"No!" loudly snapped Sancha. "Get out of here!"

She shouted at the women, who answered her with curses and raised fists. Shoving Aslak away, she aimed them all towards a narrow street off the square.

"In there." Rogenvaldr jerked his head at the still lingering Aslak, who jumped to follow him. As they walked, he kept remembering Orkneyjar. *I'll never get used to these cracked facades and narrow streets—just spread my arms and I can touch the walls on both sides.*

The black sky was a narrow, jagged gash above him. *I can't even see the stars.* A spacious longhouse built of wood and thatch, with its large friendly rooms, high ceilings, and outdoor pools, was a luxury that he had never really appreciated enough.

And the fresh air of the longboats! The oppressive stench of urine, spices, and sweat was a constant reminder of how many people were crowded inside these stone houses.

Soon, a guard opened a wooden door that led into a brightly torch-lit courtyard. Lounging around on colorful couches were women beautiful enough to have stepped out of an exotic dream. Kohl-rimmed eyes examined their customers up and down with curiosity. Some moved sinuously over on their couch to make room, as others went upstairs with a man they fancied. One of them approached William.

"Shall we?" she asked, pulling open the rope around his waist. After all, he wasn't the first monk she had taken.

"No thank you. I have a mission I must take care of." William took her hand off his crotch and headed for the door so quickly that he tripped on a small rug. Gathering his cassock and his dignity he went out to laughter.

Thorbjorn happily dropped his bulk beside a tiny young woman.

"Hey, don't suffocate her!" Swain yelled across the room.

Rogenvaldr was looking at the food set out on tables. Again, there were pitchers of verjuice. Platters were heaped with fish grilled in a sweet pomegranate marinade next to thick crusted pies filled with minced meat and raisins. Venison wrapped in bacon, fried in olive oil and ginger, sat in a vinegary green sauce thickened with breadcrumbs. Thankfully for Rogenvaldr, who was still hungry, there was a plain lamb stew with onion greens. Baskets were heaped with flat breads, small rye loaves, and ground almond patties.

Again all this sweetness, thought a displeased Rogenvaldr. *Instead of plain red wine, which they have so much of, here's this hydromel drink again. Can't they even keep honey out of the water?* He was about to grab some bread and lamb stew, when he heard a girl scream.

Aslak had been swaggering around the courtyard, thumbs in his belt, acting exactly like a nervous sixteen-year-old in his first whorehouse. Several women had attempted to approach the blond, slender young man, but he had turned his back on them. It was hard to tell whether it was from fear or indifference to their looks. As he walked past some pillows on the floor he suddenly stopped, staring down. Bending over, he grabbed a young girl by the forearm and dragged her away from Armod.

"Hey, get your own girl," complained Armod.

"No!" she screamed. As she struggled to free herself, a table full of clay pitchers and platters of food crashed to the floor-tiles, shattering into sharp, sauce-covered shards.

"No! No!" the girl was still screaming. "Let me go! I don't know you and I won't go with you!"

She was pale-haired and tall, with Nordic features. Lomanha, the brothel's owner, ran over to find out the cause of the commotion. Nila was one of her most expensive women, and no man was going to abuse her unless he paid extremely well. And a beautiful one like her, who never got pregnant, was worth her weight in gold.

Lomanha and Rogenvaldr arrived at the same time.

"What's going on?" Rogenvaldr tried to get Aslak to let go of the fighting and kicking girl.

"She's my sister!" Aslak was protecting himself without letting go.

"I don't know him!" Nila cried hysterically.

"I just want to talk to her!"

"Can you do it calmly and quietly?" asked Rogenvaldr.

"I don't want to talk to him! I don't know him!" She was frantically clawing at his fingers on her arm.

"Look at her—she's Sigrid Erlandsdóttir—my twin sister," Aslak said quietly, now serious. "She was abducted from our fields in Norway three years ago."

Everyone stood there, open-mouthed, looking from one twin to the other, for it was obviously the truth. The same pale oval face with a small mouth, silvery straight hair, and blond lashes that outlined startlingly blue eyes. Disconcertingly, each had two prominent, very white, front teeth under a triangular nose. Snarling at each other with their upper lips curled in, they gave the appearance of two angry rabbits fighting.

Rogenvaldr conjured a memory of two children hiding behind their mother's skirts.

Nila collapsed down to the pillows as Aslak gently let go of her arm. She sat there staring at the floor, rubbing the bruise he had left.

"Just let me talk to her," begged Aslak of the madam.

"You want to talk, talk, however you will pay to do this. Nila, go to your chamber with him. And stop crying, it makes your eyes red."

"I'm coming with the two of you," Rogenvaldr said.

Lomanha looked at him, ready to protest.

"I'm their Earl, it's my right."

"Then you will pay too," she said agreeably.

• • •

Resignedly shrugging her broad shoulders, Nila led them upstairs to her room. Red weavings decorated plastered yellow walls above a low bed standing on sturdy wooden legs. In the corner was a small bathing pool lined with colorful mosaic tiles. Two square windows high in the wall were draped with blue curtains. A carved closet in the corner had veils and skirts hanging on its open door.

Tucking her long legs under her, she curled up on the bed cushions to tell them the painful story. Oil lamps on the floor and a small table outlined her face with a wavering glow.

The Earl stood leaning against the wall, one foot bracing himself. Sitting on the floor made him aware of his aging knees.

She looked at the Earl. *I must make that arrogant man understand that he has to leave and take my ignorant brother with him.*

"Yes," she began, "I am Sigrid Erlandsdóttir. Three years ago, I was gathering lingonberries in the field near our farmhouse in Tromso. I had only some goats for company because the men had gone pillaging in the longboats and mother was at a birthing. Some horsemen from the western lands over the high mountains came riding by and saw me. I ran as fast as I could, but they were on horses. It was useless."

Aslak tried to sit down next to her. "No," she said, pushing his chest to get him to move away. *Go away! I don't want you near me,* she thought.

Aslak settled on the floor close to her knees, looking at her intently. *What's the matter with her? I'm just trying to rescue her.*

"The men were brutes from Rus. They took me with them on their way south. They avoided larger villages, pillaging small farms, viciously killing anyone who fought them, raping any woman in their way. I was bound up at night so I could never escape. It was no use screaming—who would hear me? Who would even care? Each man used me according to his will, day or night, it didn't matter."

Her hands rubbed her thighs, still feeling the weight of the men. She glanced quickly at Aslak.

"I was fed just enough to survive. Sometimes I ate shrubs and berries next to the road, even grass, like a cow. For fun, the men poured water down my throat as they violated me, almost drowning me, watching me gag as they laughed. And now I can't drink water. Wine or ale, but never water. After a while I performed any horrible act they wanted of me. I became an animal. Their horses and dogs were treated better than me. My cloths turned to filthy rags, my body stank, and I became infested with vermin."

I think I'm going to be sick, thought Aslak, hugging his knees tighter to his stomach.

Sigrid wrapped her arms around her body and shivered. Her fingers were like crab claws digging into her skin. "Sometimes they let a stranger pay to whip me and have sex. Getting to her knees on the bed, she turned her back to them. Opening her blue and yellow flowered dress, she let it drop open enough for the wrinkled red scars crisscrossing the bones of her back and shoulder blades to show.

Oh, Sigrid! How do I persuade you to come home with me—back to mother, back to the farm.

Closing her dress, she turned around to face them, slowly tying the red sash.

"They needed money and were tired of me, so I was sold to a slave trader who took pity on me. He turned out to be Benjamin of Tudela, a Rhadanite Jew, a merchant who wandered from the western ocean to far eastern lands.

Where have I heard that name before? Rogenvaldr tried to remember. *It was just recently.* He was not shocked by Sigrid's story, just saddened.

"Benjamin traveled back and forth, far from his wife and children in Spain. He would stop in a town and, in some way, always manage to send money to them. He was a decent man, yet still a merchant. Everything he did for me was to ensure a profit and, frankly, I was past caring. I was bathed, massaged with oils to make my scars less swollen, fed well, and given a clean linen kirtle.

Small, short sobs burst out of her. *Oh Mother Mary, forgive me for what I have done! How can I tell these two men from the old country? But I have to—it's the only way to get rid of them. Aslak must hear this!*

"But that is nothing compared to what I did. Jesus forgive me! I didn't want to kill the child inside me, but the thought of the evil that spawned it was too much to bear."

Aslak turned away, hands over his face, eyes tightly closed. *She will go to hell for this!*

Sigrid looked at the ceiling. "I screamed and screamed until the blood came. So much black blood. I nearly bled to death. The curing woman stopped it with herbs and made me drink willow bark and the juice from a flower that stopped the pain. I slept for three days."

Sigrid pointed to a pitcher of wine on the table. Rogenvaldr gave her a cupful and she took a long drink, turning the cup around and around. Sighing, she quieted her sobs.

"When I awoke, they told me I was too damaged, that I would never have another child. I'm sorry, it was the only way. I knew then that I could never go home again. I never wanted to see my family, for what am I but a damaged woman whom no man would want to marry. Benjamin understood that. He brought me to Narbonne, and sold me to Lomanha, who paid him well for a young blonde woman from Scandia who would not ever conceive."

She leaned over to her brother and gently took his fingers off his face. The twins looked at eachother, their tear-filled, red-rimmed eyes mirroring each other's grief. The girl spoke quietly, but firmly.

"Better to be here than a whore in Norway."

"We would help you—mother will find someone—"

"You idiot, what would I do there? Sit in a cold, dark hut all day by a fire reading runes? Go away—and never mention Sigrid Erlandsdóttir again. Tell mother she is dead, gone. Only Nila remains, the corpse of Sigrid."

Turning away, she threw herself down on the bed. "For the love of Christ, leave!"

She's right. Let her stay here. Barely able to breathe, Rogenvaldr could practically feel Sigrid's mother's runic spells hovering over him. Putting several gold coins on the table, he said, "This is for you. I will pay the madam separately." He turned to Aslak, "We're leaving. Let's go."

"No! we have to take her with us!" He tried to grab his sister.

She quickly backed away on the bed and kicked at him. *Will he never leave?*

Rogenvaldr grabbed the stunned young man by the arm and dragged him out of the room. Lomanha was waiting at the bottom of the stairs.

"Madam, Nila is yours. Thank you for the time with her." A gold coin satisfied her, and bought her silence, for no doubt she had been listening at the door.

Once in the street, Rogenvaldr pushed Aslak up against the stones of the rampart walls. "Never, ever, repeat what you know again. Do you understand? You *never* found Sigrid. Never. If this story were to get to your mother, it would kill her."

Finally, they're gone. Nila rose to slam the door shut. Closing her eyes, she leaned back hard on it, until the door latch pressing into her spine felt as if it would crack the bones. Rousing herself, she ran over to the table, expertly sliding her hand to gather the coins. The gold would be her secret. She hid it in a compartment in a wooden leg of the bed. There was a hidden pouch behind the bed that she knew Lomanha regularly checked and stole from. *Let her.*

Sitting down on a low straw stool at her make-up table, she puffed out her cheeks and blew out a breath. *He was always an idiot. And mother was no fun. Besides, who wants to get pregnant anyway? Certainly not me.*

Picking up a black paint stick she began to paint her eyes, smiling sensuously at her reflection in the copper mirror. *My hair is a mess. Leon is coming later. He always pays extra to lick my scars.*

CHAPTER 11

Lady fair! Thy form surpasses
all the loveliness of Maidens,
though arrayed in costly garments,
and adorned with precious jewels:
silken curls in radiant splendor
fall upon the beauteous shoulders
of the goddess of the gold-rings.
　　　　—The Orneyinga Saga, Anon., 13th century

JULY 1115

Brother Ramon, the caput scholae of the choir, was leading a circle of monks chanting a hymn he had composed for Saint Martha on her Feast Day.

Holy Saint Martha—
daughter of Bethany,
send us your Dragon
to fight against Sin

Ramon's strong tenor voice flowed up, then rippled down a musical river, each holy word a melismatic note streaming in fluid prayer, such that the golden lilies carved into the ceiling waved in the wind. A lingering echo shivered as his pure tones vibrated like overlapping waves on a stone shore.

Viscountess Ermengard, absolute ruler of Narbonne, let the music settle in her bones and calm her. She sat, proud, rigid, and hot on her gilded throne under the apse of the old basilica attached to her palace. Having gone to enormous expense to renovate the chapel, she loved showing it off. Above the apse, Spanish masons had built a dome with an ocular window through which a light beam fell through dust motes onto the altar. Around the dome, windows illuminated the glittering chips of a mosaic set by Byzantine artists from Ravenna. The Virgin Mary, swathed in a blue gown, sat with the Christ child on her lap looking down protectively from a heavenly gold sky. Winged angels playing harps and trumpets floated in a circle around her.

On the wall above her, shining in a mosaic oval, was a magnificent 'Christ Pantocrator' seated in majesty on the arc of heaven, the earth beneath his feet. His ivory face, with its wavy brown hair and curly beard, was surrounded by a wide gold halo. All-seeing round, white eyes outlined in black, bore witness to the Light that Shines in the Dark. One hand was raised in a blessing, the other held a book on which was written: "I am the light of the world." The Greek letters Alpha and Omega floated on either side of him in a gold heaven.

In front of her stood an ancient altar decorated with a painting of Saint Peter and the Apostles, all walking stiffly in their purple Roman togas on a red background. A fine linen cloth, gleaming in the bluish-white light of the oculus, was draped over its surface.

Surrounding the standing worshippers, on walls framed by solid arched columns, life-sized mosaic figures of saints walked towards Christ in a procession. Draped bodies moved in a luminescence of rainbow hued precious stones. Halos, edged in red, floated behind faces all turned toward salvation. The saints' chests appeared to breathe in the flickering light of a hundred candles.

All the arches were covered in mosaics; Byzantine artists were trained to dazzle the eye. Iridescent blue peacocks, Ermengard's favorite bird, flew in corners over red, trumpet shaped flowers whose lush leaves grew down marble columns. Blue sea-waves rolled along the ceiling. Interlaced geometric patterns wound their way around a white marble floor covered with blue stars.

Ermengard wanted her jeweled chapel to overwhelm the soul, to give awe and joy to all who came to worship. She had succeeded.

Everyone there was in a state of anxious anticipation.

When it was announced that the Norseman Earl Rogenvaldr Kali Kolsson of Orkneyjar was presenting the Viscountess with a magnificent holy gift on the Feast Day of Saint Martha, the whole court erupted in a frenzy to obtain an invitation.

On both sides, down the length of the hall, Ermengard's court intimates were lined up shoulder to shoulder, outlined in the stripes of light and dark shadows thrown by windows set high in the walls. Emotions were running high. There had been significant arguments relating to the protocols of who could stand where.

The Countess Beatritz de Dente stood to the left of Ermengard with Alais, her daughter's face covered by a thin white veil. *I really have to be strong and steel myself to endure this charade of magical thinking.* "Alais, keep your eyes down."

Archbishop Pierre D'Anduze, arrayed in gold-trimmed red vestments, was standing to the right. The richness of this small chapel was a source of constant envy for him. He knew the cost of every tiny mosaic tile set into the walls. *The amount of gold tessera here alone could pay for three stained glass windows in my church.* The thought irritated him.

His round eyes staring, trembling in his black robe, the rotund sacristan of Saint Paul-Serge stood beside the Archbishop. *God in heaven, save us from whatever unholy event might happen. I don't trust these Vikings. How do we know they didn't get us here together to slaughter us all at once?*

Directly behind them was Canon Hugon. He had unexpectedly appeared at the palace early that morning to accost Ermengard about the choice of Saint Martha's Feast Day. Despite the heat he wore a wool cassock and hooded cape with his face hidden deep inside. He was incensed that Ermengard was degrading the memory of his Aunt Martha.

"Why have you chosen the feast day of the modest, virtuous, and holy Saint Martha to perform this lascivious ceremony? Have you no shame?"

"Martha welcomed Christ to her home, just as I am welcoming the Earl to mine. I have prayed to her every day from matins to terce. I will do as I please."

Hugon was repulsed by the brilliance of the chapel. *Here, indeed, lives Satan. He has seduced this woman into the seven deadly sins: she lives in an earthly world of vainglory, envy, covetousness, and gluttony with, no doubt, lust, royal anger, and sloth.* His eyes wandered around the chapel, alighting on various prosperous looking families. *I wonder how many of them are secret Bons Hommes—I can smell the heresy right through the incense!*

Bishop William held close to the wall in the shadows behind Hugon, watching him intently. *I feel it in my belly. This monk is not to be trusted. There is an evil fire burning in him, a madness. And I must be mad to have allowed this to be happening. I should have thrown the cursed horn overboard during a storm.* He sighed.

Ermengard's advisor, Peter Raymond, standing with his arms firmly crossed, had tried to talk his wife Frida out of coming, but she would have none of it. "I want to see the gift."

"I'm telling you Frida, I don't trust this Norwegian Earl. There's a duplicitous reason he has picked Narbonne, of all cities, for a sudden visit. His peaceful words are a cover for some scheme we have yet to find out about. I want to protect Ermengard from him, but how?"

Sir Thibault De Plaigne, being a knight protector of the Viscountess, was permitted to wear a sword. Of course, this also meant that he had to wear his armor, so the sweat was running down his armpits and crotch. *All this fuss for that arrogant bastard. I know who and what he is that misery of a Viking.*

Near to Beatritz de Dente, stood Raymond d'Ouvelhan, his wife Azalais, and their daughter Garsend, three heretics locked in mutual belief. Garsend, zealous in her fervor, lived only to become a parfait. Her mother had to restrain the thirteen-year-old from giving Ermengard open glances of disgust at this outrageous display of wealth. Azalais, offspring of an interlude of Ermengard's father with her mother, was locked in a familial relationship with the Viscountess. Raised at court, she suspected that Ermengard knew of her beliefs, but as the subject was never raised, they were able to live their lives in a companionable silence.

A wary expression on his tired, gray face, Raymond I Trencavel, Count of Albi, Beziers, and Carcassonne, stood with his wife Saure and their youngest son Roger II Trencavel. *I promised her father—it's my duty to protect Ermengard with my life. They call themselves Norsemen, yet they are still nothing but Vikings hiding behind Christ's skirts. Kill my grandparents in Bordeaux not fifty years ago, yet you want me to believe you've changed? Pah! You're pillagers, not pilgrims.*

Raymond was another heretic hiding in a Catholic court. Covering up the family secret was a dangerous game. If found out they would all burn, and Ermengard could do nothing to protect them. The thought of his wife and son screaming in the flames exhausted him, made him sick. The glitter of the court was an earthly tie he wanted to sever, but his oath to Aymery II bound him to this life.

Ponzia de Coumic did not have the time to venture out often. All she could think about now was all the stitching yet to be done. Ermengard, enamored of her skill with a needle, had ordered another three of those pointed collars. The problem with her eyes was frightening. *If only I had to hold the work closer it would be fine, but the further away it must be for clarity, the harder it is.* A widow permitted to live at court, how was she to hide the problem? Every morning she dragged her daughter Fabrisse to mass. The child had no patience for her mother's endless piety. But piety, and being on your knees in church, was the only way to keep the Inquisitor away. Fabrisse was too scattered a girl to be told the truth, she chattered away all day. She would betray Ponzia with her childishness. Ermengard's invitation to this ceremony could not be ignored. *What gift? Another piece of gold to tie one down to this life?*

Abbot Esteban couldn't resist coming to see what was going on. Fontfroide, as a Cistercian Abbey, was always eager to help Ermengard manage the religious affairs of Narbonne, especially if it involved steering her away from the notorious excesses of Archbishop D'Anduze and his endless cathedral construction. The Abbot and the Archbishop threw hostile glances at each other.

Today had been in Ermengard's thoughts all week, invading her prayers to Saint Martha. Clenching her fists, she tried to calm her stomach by praying *Our Father who art in heaven, Our Father who...*

She was blinded by the sun when the arched doors at the far end of the hall were flung open. In the white light stood the Norseman. Loose waves of shining orange hair framed a strong-boned, mature face. Deeply set, his lapis-blue eyes sat above a high-ridged nose; his angular chin sported a braided beard. A broad chest filled out a tight-fitting, red linen tunic that fell to his knees. It was very elegant, with inset sleeves covered in geometric patterns and gold knots. The left side was tucked into a broad black leather belt held together with the wings of a gold, ruby-eyed eagle. The carefully draped tunic revealed, not inconspicuously, his heavily muscled thighs which filled out blue leggings tucked into knee-high leather boots. Despite the fact that he was entering a church, a large, jewel-hilted sword was prominently visible on his left hip.

In his outstretched arms he held a long wooden box. Taking several steps forward he paused in mid-stride to stare at Ermengard of Narbonne. Seated at the far end of the chapel bathed in a sunbeam, she was a glowing rainbow. *By all the saints! It's her—the woman in the window at the market.*

In his most dignified manner, Rogenvaldr stepped towards her. From above, the sun's rays bounced off the shining face of Christ who stared at him, accusing him with eyes of fire, *as if he knows what's going on.*

Ermengard sat motionless, an ethereal flower on a gold throne that radiated jewel-studded peacock feathers behind her head. Gold-flecked eyes, shaped like lark's wings, sat over high oval cheekbones, as her long straight nose descended from a white forehead to end above full lips. A dark, curly hairline was visible under a crimson silk veil. A gold diadem, spiked high with rays of the sun, was covered all around with precious jewels set into flowers.

Under the veil, a white wimple was wrapped tightly around her firm oval chin. A circular, blue glass eye, set into an old Roman gold fibula, held together the top of a sheer, waist length purple cape. Edged with a broad crimson wave pattern, the cape fell over a square gold breastplate heavy with jewels nestled into a rounded bosom. Around her, falling in soft, long folds was an extraordinary green silk dress, the green of a "parrot bird" the Earl had once seen. Red sleeves, woven with sheer gold stripes, touched the floor with a small knot. Slit on both sides to expose a blue chemise, the skirt was carefully draped in waves around pointy red shoes tied tightly around the ankle with gold ribbons.

Sit still! She told herself. *But I don't know how to handle this. What do I say? What is he going to do? This is unbearable. My stomach hurts and sitting in this heat is misery. He is like Alexander the Great in the poems I read! Mary, mother of God, help me get through today.*

Similar thoughts were flying through Rogenvaldr's mind, too. *I don't know if I can do this. All this gold shining into my eyes blinding me, mosaics everywhere, candles, people dressed like peacocks, so much incense—Saint Magnus, help me! No, I can't ask you, you'd be really enraged at what I'm about to do. Jerusalem—think of Jerusalem and step forward. She's just so young to be ruler of this place. And she's so rich. Yes, Jerusalem!*

He walked slowly forward holding the box in front of him. Upon reaching the luminescent circle of the altar, he carefully put the box down in the light. Stepping back, he lowered himself to one knee.

"Viscountess Ermengard, here is my gift to you. A Unicorn Horn."

There was a collective intake of breath. Everyone stared at the box. Murmurs rose and raced around the chapel. Brother Ramon stopped singing.

Oh, no, thought Beatritz. *Another false idol.*

Archbishop D'Anduze moved forward and found himself standing next to Bishop William. Unacknowledged conspirators, for the blink of an eye, their eyes met, then quickly looked away.

Ermengard rose and walked straight-backed to the altar.

She's shorter than I expected, Rogenvaldr mused.

She held out both hands to him and he put his forehead to the back of them. *My God, his forehead is sweating so much.*

Her hands are trembling… and hot. Jerusalem! Jerusalem!

"We accept your holy gift with due reverence and gratitude." *His hands are calloused. I wish he would get up. What's he thinking about for so long.* "Please, you may open the box so all should see this miraculous horn."

Rogenvaldr slowly got up. *Jesus, this kneeling is getting harder and harder on my knee bones.* When he opened the box, there lay the purple swathed horn on its orange fur bed. The air got warmer as the heavily breathing courtiers saw the glint of gold and pressed closer. He took the horn out and laid it on the altar in front of her.

Ermengard stared. It was five feet long! *So how do I unwrap this without dropping the whole thing?* It was heavy and wobbled in the air when she picked it up. He steadied her hands and helped her hold it. With a rustle of fabric, her long fingers unwound the covering.

Revealed was a long gold sheath that covered the unicorn horn from end to end. Its finely crafted lacework showed a jeweled procession of miniature pilgrims walking, riding donkeys, and sailing towards the walls of a tiny Jerusalem. At the end of their journey, on the tip of the horn, was an ivory Christ crucified on Calvary. Beneath his finely carved cross was an enormous bloodstone catching the blood rubies dripping from his feet. Caught by the green stone, the red drops glowed, emitting waves of sadness into the air.

Ermengard felt like crying. *Just looking at this bloodstone makes me want to weep for the pain Christ endured. It's the largest I have ever seen. The stone alone would be an enormous gift.* Through little openings she could see the swirls of a light brown unicorn horn coming to a perfect point just under Christ. *The horn has a strange glow in the light from above. Is God watching?*

Archbishop D'Anduze signaled to Ramon to start chanting again, then he knelt and began to pray.

I don't like this. But Bishop William had no choice. He knelt, but his prayer was for absolution. *Forgive me, Oh Lord, forgive us all our sins.*

Annoyed, Rogenvaldr also went down. *Cursed knees.*

• • •

The public presentation of the unicorn horn was to be in the Cathedral of Saint Sergius-Paulis that coming Sunday. Rogenvaldr and William were obligated to participate in the long religious procession.

William was in a terrible mood. "This deception is dragging out in time. It's getting more and more dangerous."

"Calm down. After it's over we'll get the money and leave."

"Don't tell me to calm down," William snapped.

"The King told me to sell it, so I'm going to sell it. Be quiet or you can go back to the boat."

Surrounded by chanting and weeping worshippers, they plodded over the Roman bridge. It had taken two days to scrub it clean of its bloody offal. Now it wafted the perfume of soft rose petals being crushed underfoot.

Without warning, a hot mistral wind began to blow. The rose petals flew into the air, soft fingers swirling around their heads.

Then, traveling on the wind, came sand from the African deserts.

Ermengard, barefoot, felt the grains rolling on the stones beneath her toes. She tried to protect her eyes by holding up the silk sleeve of her ivory dress, but the wind whipped around it. The ruby brooch fastening her sky-blue cloak together at the throat broke open, so the cloak flew away, billowing over the ramparts, flapping in the sky like a lost heron. *Why is this happening? There was no sign on the horizon at dawn. The hand of God is here.* She shivered, then gripped her jeweled cross tighter to her chest.

Behind her in the procession, for all to gaze upon, was the unicorn horn. It lay on a purple cushion under a gilded, roofed bier carried by twelve Templar Knights. Ignoring the wind and sand, red crosses snapping on white tunics, they marched on, Soldiers of Christ who had been to the deserts of the Holy Land and back.

The wind whipped up the smoke of large, swinging, acorn-shaped incense burners filled with hot coals and frankincense carried by four burly monks. The smoke made Archbishop D'Anduze squint as he held on to his gold miter. Half-blinded, he stumbled towards the church. *Is this a warning from God?*

Sand blew into the mouths of chanting Cistercian monks from Fontfroide Abbey.

Sand blew into the bleeding wounds of penitents scourging themselves, their whips happily grinding in more pain.

Sand blew off the hoods of monks dragging large wooden crosses across the cobblestones. Kissing the crosses as they passed before them, sobbing worshippers hobbled forward on their knees, falling on their faces, stepped over by those coming behind them.

Sand blew the apart the tattered rags of lepers, revealing their pus-laden sores—abandoned souls forbidden to be inside the city walls, hiding under wagons and in wooden casks, desperately praying to be cured as the holy aura passed near them.

Just outside the church, dozens and dozens of buckets were being filled with the piss and soils of the crowd. Hired urchins stood in a brigade that emptied them into the river as fast as humanly possible.

Abbot Hugon, avoiding the smelly throngs, crept through windy side streets to get into the church through the sacristy. *Hah! God's wrath will punish them all. Fornicators, sinners, every one of them.* Totally ignored, he squeezed himself into a dark corner reserved for the monks to watch this spectacle of Mammon.

The church was old and thick-walled, with a large round apse that was located on an ancient Christian necropolis over the tomb of St. Sergius, a Christianized Roman Proconsul sent here by Pope Fabian to be Narbonne's Archbishop in the third century. Penitents surged into the wide aisles: those who wanted to be cured of illness, the old seeking salvation, and the rich seeking absolution from the sins of greed and gluttony. Around columns of horizontal pink and gold stone stripes, wide enough for ten men to put their arms around, some miracle-seekers had sat for three days, eating and sleeping on the stone floor.

In high, candle blackened corners, the carved faces of prophets and skulls looked down with their usual disapproval. Narrow plinths stood empty; their statues of the Virgin and saints had been removed and hidden in the crypt, where, unseen, lepers had crawled in and hidden.

Eventually, those who had earlier prostrated themselves on the stone floor became a living carpet; some had the life crushed out of them by those who walked on their backs. Yet no one cared. If one died in front of the sacred unicorn horn, one would surely go to heaven. When the gold reliquary was placed onto the altar with an enormous lit candle, a collective moaning began. The temperature in the church, usually cool in summer, became sweltering. The smell of unwashed and sick bodies was overwhelming. The sacristan ordered more incense. The air was choking everyone.

Everyone in the church was expected to spend the day and night in prayer, including them. Archbishop D'Anduze was intoning Mass. Forty Knights Templar covered in chainmail stood in the round apse. Armed with swords and spears, they had been sent to guard the horn day and night.

Ermengard and Rogenvaldr were on a bench beside William facing an ancient altar painted with a red wooden panel telling the story of the Archangel Michael; how he protected Christians in battle, how he overcame the terrifying, tail thrashing demon, Satan, by piercing his heart with a spear. Beneath the battle, the yellow flames of hell scorched the devil's cloved hooves. Painted above in the apse God was blessing the world, and beside him, Saint Paul, held the sacred book and sword.

After Mass, Ermengard cried out "Saint Paul, protect me!" then threw herself face-down on the floor in front of the altar to pray through the night.

William, also going face-down in front of the altar, whispered to Rogenvaldr, "Lie down!"

"Absolutely not!" he mouthed back and settled to his knees. *This is bad enough. Maybe I can get a cushion?* He had to settle for a bunched-up wool cape.

It was an agonizing night punctuated by the smell of the dead and groans of the dying.

The hot mistral wind stopped blowing sometime during the night. At sunrise, a ray of the sun pierced through the open doors of the east wall and came to rest on the unicorn horn in its splendid gold reliquary. It shimmered and glowed. The bloodstone appeared to drip red drops on the altar cloth. Looking up at the sacred light, the worshippers cried with joy.

Abruptly, a black cloud covered the sun as a cold wind rushed through the church and extinguished the altar candle. The horn became dark.

Afraid of this portent, people rushed to leave, pushing and shoving each other out of the way.

Later that day, one of the old women, who had seen many bad omens, whispered ominously to her friends. "First the mistral, that I understand. But from whence came that cold, ill wind?"

CHAPTER 12

One day it happened as the Earl sat at the feast
that the Queen came into the hall
and many women with her.
She was dressed in the best clothes,
had her hair loose as maiden were wont to have,
and had put a gold band round her brow.
She poured the wine into the Earl's cup,
as her maidens danced before them.
The Earl took her hand and the beaker too
and set her on his knee,
and they talked much that day.
         —The Orkneyinga Saga, Anonymous, 13th cent.

AUGUST 1152

Waiting in her shuttered parlor for Barala Ben Todros to arrive, Ermengard became lost in thoughts of Rogenvaldr. *His hand is moving from my waist to cup my breast. I turn up my face and feel his warm breath. His hard chest.... he clears his throat... he clears his throat?*

"Ahem." Ben Todros, a short, older man wearing a dark blue tunic and the prescribed yellow hat for Jews, cleared his throat again as he stood waiting in the door frame for permission to enter the room.

How long has he been standing there? I can't sit here and have him watching me.

Annoyed, she said, "You may enter. Sit. We must attend to business."

After the presentation of the horn had come the Feast of the Assumption of the Virgin. Entreating, she had prayed, "Mary, Mother of God, please make him love me."

121

Today she had decided to take real action. *If I can win the battle of Tortosa, I can win this man's heart.* "Enough prayer. Send me Ben Todros."

Her be-ringed fingers tapped impatiently on the inlaid ivory pattern of the eight-sided table. Bought from Egypt by her father, it was one of her most valued possessions. It gave her a feeling of power to sit at the same table at which he had negotiated with kings. "Now, tell me the financial state of my mines."

Ben Todros was in charge of her metals, selling the gold and silver extracted from mines owned by Ermengard in nearby Villemagrie. "Production is going well," he said carefully. He always spoke carefully to her. *I have a definite feeling where this is going.*

"I need one-thousand Almoravid moribatani gold coins."

Oh-oh, thought the worried Ben Todros. "In order to purchase that many refined gold coins from Moslem Al-Andalus you will have to mortgage one year's production from your mines."

"Double the number of slaves digging it out. That way I will mortgage only half of a year."

"Doubling the workers won't necessarily double the output." When he saw the sharp glance she gave him, he changed course. *Big mouth. You should know better by now.* "Yes, of course, we will manage it as you suggest. You are always wise in your judgement. May I inquire the purpose of this vast sum?"

"No, you may not." *My gift to Rogenvaldr in exchange for the horn is none of your concern.* "Just have the coins ready at the Gold Exchange for me. How long will this take?"

"Three weeks, Domina."

"Make it two weeks. You may leave."

Feigning disinterest, he bowed his way out of the room. *Of course, this is all about that fake unicorn horn. She's giving him a reciprocal gift, yet she's really buying it. Foolish woman—that Norseman is a thief if I ever smelled one.*

"Send in Pedro and Faydida," Ermengard called to a servant just outside the door. She drummed her fingers on the table again until the head cook and palace châtalaine came running in.

"I wish to have a magnificent banquet to honor Earl Rogenvaldr."

The palace slaves jumped to work cleaning up sticky spider webs, throwing out dried-up old bunches of thyme and lavender hanging from rafters, re-washing soiled tablecloths to pure whiteness, and removing every splinter and seed dropped by dirty rushes. Hundreds of clay chamber pots were washed with ashes and put into tile-lined pissoir rooms and into corners.

Young boys went out to climb trees to collect bird eggs and fresh chestnuts. And always, escaping their yard and getting underfoot, were the naked, annoying geese. Freshly plucked for new pillows, they wandered around honking at the top of their lungs until roasting silenced them.

The festivities were to be held in the palace's inner courtyard, a bright open space with tall, narrow, marble columns that supported graceful pink and red brick arches. At the age of five, when her father died, Ermengard had inherited a dark, heavily walled fortress with tiny arrow slits instead of windows. It had always frightened her, so she decided to hire an Andalusian architect to rebuild it; it was now an airy, light filled palace.

To shade guests from the sun, large white sheets were tied horizontally to iron hooks embedded into the walls. The old floor mosaic of African animals, once enjoyed by a wealthy Roman, was scrubbed and waxed. Benches and tables had been set up organized in the northern tradition, with chairs for nobles seated at a high table covered with white linen. Standing on it were Ermengard's precious gold goblets inset with red cinnabar crystal flowers, an inheritance from the long-dead mother she had never known. Blue tubs of red roses and white orchids lined the walls.

Laughing, Ermengard had said, "We will not use pillows and carpets to have our banquet on the floor. These Norsemen just don't know how to eat on them. They sit with legs sticking out like cranes as food constantly falls into their laps."

• • •

During Ermengard's week of prayer, Rogenvaldr and his men wandered freely around Narbonne, eating tasty snacks and mounting any willing woman, neither of which were lacking. Quite comfortable with the situation, they clearly didn't care about the animosity of husbands and fathers. They were looking forward to the banquet. It was sure to be an opportunity to seduce higher quality noblewomen.

William kept himself separate, hiding the secret meetings with Bathsheba in the Bourg's olive groves. He kept telling himself his attraction to her was of the spirit and that he only wished to save her. *How can I get the money from Rogenvaldr to buy her? He must be getting a vast sum for the horn. I must ask. Yet how? And when? I can't leave here until I know she is free and on her way back to Ethiopia.*

Bathsheba was strict with herself. *I'm still a priestess, whatever happens to me. I must hold myself aloof from him; it is the only way to gain my freedom. I can never lie with him. And yet now I must prepare to lie with many strange men at the banquet. They will touch my body, but not my holy being. I will prepare my mind by fasting and chanting.*

"Mother Mary, please shut her up!" The other whores were sick of hearing her strange prayers and chants.

• • •

"No, leave my hair loose and weave gold threads in it." The hairdresser was pinning it up.

"But you are a married woman." València mistakenly said.

Ermengard rounded on her, explosively yelling, "I've been widowed twice and abandoned. As far as I'm concerned, Bernard is dead. And I'm still a virgin, so I'll wear my hair like a virgin."

Her thick black curls had been massaged with the clearest olive oil, brushed and brushed again, then combed until their blue highlights glistened in the sunlight. On the point of the gold diadem encircling her forehead was a jeweled dove putting its beak into an owl's forehead, a gift from a love smitten Grecian prince. Upon placing it on her head he had whispered, "This crown will give you the wisdom of Athena's owl through the path of your third eye."

The crown held in place a white veil that floated down her back. Moving in circles, she watched the lapis blue folds of her silk dress and long sleeves swirl around. A low, square neckline tightly held her breasts as high as possible. Gold-threaded veils pinned on her shoulders were attached to jeweled bracelets on her wrists.

Downstairs in the courtyard, servants in blue caftans were ready to serve verjuice and red hippocras wine chilled in bowls of ice just delivered from the ice caves of the La Grasse Abbey.

A mild, damp wind, redolent of brine, blew in from the lagoons. The sharp aroma of spices frying in oil wafted out of stone kitchens standing in a walled-in field overlooking the river. Pits full of glowing coals were roasting lambs, pigs, and a large boar, all dripping fat that sizzled and smoked. Long skewers held strings of plump, stuffed birds, their skin turning crisp and black with herbs. Hot rye, chestnut, and milk bread was pulled out of man-sized clay ovens. Unwanted scraps were thrown over the wall to crippled beggars.

Many guests were already seated when, after the heat of the day had lessened, Rogenvaldr arrived with his nine hungry men dressed in colorful thigh-hugging tights.

Sancha had taken them to the Jewish quarter for a rush order of proper, banquet-worthy outfits. Nobody could tell their rank, and the Norsemen were very casual, sitting wherever they damned well pleased. Usually they sat down next to a woman—who all moved over to let the men squeeze in. The townsmen were tired of these well-muscled warriors strutting around, they wanted them gone. Yet which one had the courage to confront them? Most resigned themselves to raising little bastard Vikings next springtime.

Rogenvaldr found his seat at the high table next to William. *And where is Ermengard? By the balls of Saint Peter, I'm hungry. I smell meat—there better be meat. And that strange music—like bees buzzing around my head and snakes in my ears! Those little drums, and that jingling metal... Finally, here she comes.*

Everyone rose as ten ladies gracefully formed an aisle for the Viscountess to enter the courtyard. The blood rushed to Rogenvaldr's head: Ermengard was a shimmering mirage in the diffuse sunlight glowing through the gold silk veils wrapped around her luscious curves. A gold diadem sat on black hair tumbling over bare shoulders. She halted to be adored. Everyone bowed. Rogenvaldr rushed over to escort her to her seat. Placing her hand lightly on his, she stared straight ahead as he boldly looked at her.

Arriving at the high table, they did not sit, but stood in place, waiting for something. Rogenvaldr leaned over to whisper to William, "What's going on?"

"Just wait, remember what I told you about the customs here," William replied.

Before the banquet William tried to teach Rogenvaldr some of the Parisian rules of dining. "Once you have touched a morsel of food, don't put it back on the plate. Don't touch your ears or nose with your bare hands. Finish chewing what's in your mouth before drinking. Never, ever, put a dish to your mouth...."

Despite Williams efforts the Earl had thrown his hands in the air, irritated with it all.

Impatiently, Rogenvaldr stood there as a servant put a large bowl in front of each of them. Another came with a brass lavabo, a pot that had two spouts so he could easily pour hot water sideways into two bowls. The scent of lavender rose up as he was handed a thin slice of soap and a white towel. *I have to wash my hands right now?* The room remained standing. Ermengard was finishing up. Everyone was watching him. William kicked him under the table. *This smell of this cursed water makes me want to sneeze.* Self-consciously Rogenvaldr washed with the little piece of soap and dried his fingers. When the servants removed the bowls, Ermengard finally sat down. Benches were pulled closer to the tables in anticipation of the feast.

Ermengard could barely breathe from the scent of muscles and manhood emanating from his body. *Oh Mary, I hope he can't see my stomach shivering. Quick, pick up a wine goblet.* She turned to Rogenvaldr and made herself look directly at him. "To your health," she murmured. To herself she commanded, *Stop flushing!*

"I say skaal to a most beautiful and royal Queen," he replied in his most elegant and seductive way, touching her goblet with his. *My God, those oils and perfumes—I'll bet her skin is really hot.* The jewels on the cup felt rough under his fingers as he brought it to his lips. *Agh! So heavy and sweet! Who can drink this wine? Again—there's more honey than wine in it. It's even sweeter than mead.*

Rogenvaldr signaled to a servant, "Get me some unsweetened wine, or ale. I can't swallow this." He then turned to William, but the Bishop just sat in his chair, a brooding look on his face. *What's bothering him?*

He had to lean back as, in a rush of activity, the first dishes were set out on the table. Oranges, their zesty skins cut in the shape of water lilies, arrived floating in bowls of Persian rosewater. Fresh picked, furry borage leaves, dotted with their blue starflowers, swam in walnut oil and salt. A puree of mint-flavored fava beans was encircled with little circles of soft milk bread.

Where's the real food? I'm a Norseman. I don't eat green leaves, oranges, and white sauce.

Obviously, a few of his companions felt the same way. "Bring us meat!" It was a friendly request with an undertone of ravenous hunger.

Wooden slabs loaded with steaming juicy cuts of roasted meat, topped with a squinty-eyed boar's head, were placed in the middle of tables. The men fell on it, tearing it apart with their hands, licking the fat off their fingers. *By all the Saints, Sancha must have told them to stop the sauces on the meat. I must thank her.* Taking a thin silver knife from off his belt, he speared a large slice. It smelled of roasted fat, thyme, oregano, and olive oil. Ermengard was sharing the same gold tailloir with him, for no noble lady was thought clever enough to manage her own meat. Using the knife to cut it up, he fed her some tiny pieces, then watched intently as she sucked it up greedily between pursed lips. Her tongue went in a circle around the outside of her mouth, leaving a sheen of grease.

A gelatinous looking pig arrived. The slices were covered in a sweet glaze and studded with garlic and parsley. *They certainly ruined the pig. How did they manage that?*

"And what sauce is that on the pig?" he asked as politely as he could through puckered cheeks.

"Oh, it's verjuice," she answered smiling, delighted to have something to talk about. "It's very good for the body's humours. Together with the garlic it restores the balance of melancholy and anger." She looked across him at William, who just sat there. "Perhaps you should offer some to your Bishop, he looks a bit melancholy for such a merry evening. Here, have some pepper," Ermengard proceeded to put on enough pepper appropriate for a Viking.

A trumpet heralded the arrival of a stuffed, roasted swan, its neck upright and its smooth, white feathers re-attached as it sat on a mound of chestnuts, almonds, minced clams, oysters and shrimp. This was followed by an enormous baked peacock, its skin crackling, its green and blue luminescent tailfeathers fanned out behind it. On either side of its stiff head, beady black eyes looked angrily at Rogenvaldr, apparently blaming him for this indignity. Another dish arrived. *Oh, no! More birds?*

Ermengard's eyes opened wide with excitement as the huge platter of fragrant, tiny hortolan was placed before them. Plucked, then roasted whole, the little birds sat in a puddle of hot olive oil, piled up on their backs, their claws and wings sticking out rigidly, like the twigs they had been sitting on before being trapped in nets.

Impatient, she served herself. Picking a bird up by its feet, using the tablecloth to keep the juices off her dress, she opened wide, delicately popping the whole creature into her mouth, head, feet and all. Rogenvaldr could hear the bones crunching as he watched a dribble of greasy bird juice run from the edge of her lips down her chin. The juice smelled of burnt bird fat and sweet wine. Between each bird she cleaned her fingers, wiped the grease off with the tablecloth, and ignored the bowl of scented water with white almond flowers next to her elbow.

"Don't you want one?" She offered him a bird by its head.

"No. Thank you." He couldn't help staring. *What is the use of eating fried bird bones and feathers?*

She looked him over. *Well, I guess Norsemen eat mostly meat. But it sure seems boring. Still, they sure have a lot of meat on their own bones.*

He noticed her look, but was interrupted by the fresh grilled oysters, lamprey eels, sardines, and anchovies, silver skins crackling with dried thyme, mint, sweet basil and rosemary. To an eruption of applause, huge black pearls of salted fish roe from Ruthenia were served with spoons carved out of oyster shells. The guests ate the roe as if famished, washing it down with more thick wine.

Will the food ever stop? Goose livers, baked in a clay pot in a trapa oven with crushed arugula seeds, came floating in a woody vinegar sauce flavored with sorrel, cloves, and pomegranate juice. Then came a tureen of boiled mutton in a fragrant gramase soup of almonds and olive oil flavored with watercress, all surrounded by soft milk bread baked of the finest white flower, perfect for sopping up the meaty sauce.

Rogenvaldr kept passing the spice plate back to wherever it came from. He was starting to feel a familiar pain in his gut. *These southerners have the stomach of a goat.*

Carefully eating only roast boar and bread, he was in the middle of asking for more ale, when he was startled half out of his seat as Eindredi came up behind him. Pushing him down by the shoulders, his breath stinking of garlic and blood, he growled into his Earl's ear: "So where's the money from the horn, eh? We know you sold it. Send it to the boat or we'll come and get it. All of us. And that won't be nice, though it might be fun."

Rogenvaldr looked up into his cousin's face. Eindredi's gray eyes were six inches away from his own, the red scar looking like a lightning bolt. "I'll have it ready in a week. I'll send half of it to you."

"Hmmm, I have fourteen boats—you, you've got one. I'll be generous. You can keep one fifth, I'll take four-fifths. Don't forget, the rest of us have been sitting in hot anchored boats for several weeks while you and your noble friends have been enjoying the delights of Narbonne. Maybe it's time for the rest of us to enjoy the delights of Jerusalem."

This is the wrong place for an argument. "You can't leave without me. I'm the Earl of this crusade. I'm trusting you."

"Oh, you can trust me—though not forever. The question is, can I trust you?"

"A week is not forever. I'll give you your money," said Rogenvaldr. "But we go to Jerusalem together—is that understood? In the meantime, eat and enjoy the women here."

Eindredi cocked his head at Ermengard with a questioning look.

Shrugging off his cousin's hand, Rogenvaldr turned back to Ermengard as Eindredi sauntered away to sit down beside a delighted woman.

The noise was getting louder. Acrobats twisted and tumbled as joglars sang ribald songs. William just sat and watched, elbows holding up his chin. Twilight was turning the air blue. Servants circled the courtyard with long wooden poles lifting the white awnings off their hooks, allowing the evening breeze to blow away the sharp smells of food and sweat. The evening star was revealed, shining alone in a lavender sky. Ravens circled down, lusting for leftovers, avoiding starlings impatiently swooping down for crumbs.

Now drinking from the same goblet, Ermengard and Rogenvaldr fed each other candied ginger with their fingers. Flushed with wine, Ermengard allowed him to slide her onto his lap. At first, she leaned away, but he saw her chest heaving and pulled her towards himself.

Without warning, a fire-roasted lamb with its head split down the center was placed in front of them. Distracted, Ermengard picked up a thin wooden pick, delicately speared the left eye, and offered it to him.

Oh, no, he thought. *You're supposed to be a Viking! Just eat it!* He chewed slowly on the slimy sphere as he watched her eat the right one. *I'm really getting tired of eating staring eyeballs.* But he wiped the sauce off her lips with his fingertip and put it in his mouth to clean it.

William looked down the table to catch Beatritz's eye. She was sitting beside Ermengard, watching.

This is not going to end well, thought William.

This is not going to end well, thought Beatritz.

Her senses heightened by hot spices and wine, the musty smell of Rogenvaldr's skin made her draw closer to him. His hands were rising to her breasts, caressing her ribs. A platter of roasted boar ribs landed in front of them. Distracted again, her white fingers covered in sparkling gems, she reached for a rib that dripped fat onto the table. Ermengard offered it to him and they ate it together, mouth to mouth, cleaning it off to the bone. The skin was so crisp and salty, she heard it crackle when he bit into it with his strong, white teeth. Rogenvaldr wasn't even tasting the food; the way she was feeding him was driving him to distraction.

Sitting on his lap, she was aware of her effect on him. *Hmmm, I think he likes me. . . I think I'll let his hands keep going.* "Oh," she suddenly cried, her eyes lighting up. "By all the Saints! It's Jaufré Rudel!"

The troubadour, just arrived form Queen Aelinore's court in Poitiers, had appeared in front of their table and was kneeling to Ermengard.

"My dear honored lady, I am here to entertain you and make you jolly."

Ermengard laughed and slid off of Rogenvaldr's lap. Standing up, she leaned over the table with both hands, her greasy breasts heaving. "God be with you, Jaufré. How delighted I am to see you. Yes, yes, please sing for us!"

Rogenvaldr rolled his eyes. *Every time I think I'm getting somewhere with her she gets distracted by something else. If it's not a pork loin, it's a troubadour!*

Jaufré was tall and fluid. The straight black hair pulled back into a knot on his neck framed a fine-featured face with a noble, straight nose. He blinked his heavy-lidded black eyes, fringed by impossibly long lashes, seductively at Ermengard. Silvery tights, topped with a short red jerkin, left nothing to a woman's imagination. There were continual rumors about him and Ermengard. Either the two were very discreet, or as was the truth of it, the rumors had no merit. Still, many could not believe that she spent hours in his company just to hear him sing.

Pacing slowly, fingering the mellow strings of his lute, Jaufré began to chant a planh in his throaty tenor's voice. His sad ballad of unrequited love was deepened by a musician blowing a cornmeuse pipe. Its mournful, whining tones slithered around the singer's words like a slippery snake. Women sighed, using the points of their sleeves to wipe away tears.

> *It is no surprise that I love an unseen lady.*
> *That we may never meet is a joy to me,*
> *for I can always hold her in my dreams.*
> *Nothing would give me greater pleasure*
> *than to know we will unite in the house of death,*
> *as the golden lion sleeps quietly in his bed.*

The chirping of birds filled the silence. Putting his instrument down he nodded to Beatritz, who always had her psaltery to hand. Nodding respectfully back to him, the trobaritz came forward and sat down on a low wooden stool. She had to let him know she had understood his message—that she would be at the secret meeting of the Bons Hommes tonight. Strumming lightly, she sang a reply in a high, intense voice full of passion, expressing infinite sadness at the trials of love, and hopefully giving Ermengard a warning.

> *A lady who devotes herself to chivalry*
> *should indeed set her sights on a pure knight.*
> *Only once she knows his worth*
> *should she dare to love him openly.*
> *Yet how open can her heart be permitted to be?*
> *Someone must console her when life ends*
> *in the house of death.*

Jaufré was about to resume singing, when, startled, he bowed to give way to Rogenvaldr, thinking, *And who is this man? Why do all noblemen think they can sing?*

I've mastered poetry. I've won poetry jousts. Let me show them how it's done. Rogenvaldr placed himself front and center, then began to improvise a verse in a deep voice that carried across the courtyard:

> *Who else hoards such yellow*
> *hair, bright lady—fair as*
> *your milk-mild shoulders,*
> *where milled barely-gold falls?*
> *Chuck the cowled hawk, harry*
> *him with sweets. Crimsoner*
> *of eagles' claws, I covet*
> *cool downpours of silk; yours.*

Ermengard was confused. *Why all the blonde hair? I don't have blonde hair. Eagles? Hawks?*

Beatritz didn't understand all the strange, hidden meanings in his Northern French words either, yet she knew enough to answer him with a warning verse:

> *Clean hands bespeak a clean heart,*
> *though are your hands washed in truth or lies?*
> *Gifts from a great man often melt the heart*
> *and a wise sparrow will receive them with care*
> *when she is tempted to fly with the hawk.*

Rogenvaldr challenged the trobaritz in a seductive voice that enraptured a number of the women, including Ermengard.

> *Ah fate, I fear you tear*
> *my heart from Ermengard's.*
> *That rare man's matched with hers*
> *must live a slave to love.*
> *Where is beauty's lair? There*
> *in her brow. To bed her,*
> *just once—oh for the chance—*
> *I crave French hivehoney.*

Beatritz cautioned both of them more bluntly. By now, every woman in the court knew what was going on.

> *Beware Caesar!*
> *Eastern marching legions*
> *should leave no tracks in the sand.*
> *The red-clawed hawk seeks*
> *to love the sparrow,*
> *but beware the branch that breaks*
> *the body and the heart.*
> *Fire can melt ice, yet*
> *melted ice can put out fire.*
>
> *Beware fair lady!*
> *It is nature for a hawk to fly and hunt.*
> *In the garden of love*
> *an arrow pierces the bitter fruit*
> *that hangs too long on the branch.*

Every woman in the court held their breath. Ermengard stared at both of them. Rogenvaldr and Beatritz looked at each other in silence. The Earl threw back his head and began to laugh, his open mouth showing his strong white teeth. Beatritz, relieved, politely smiled.

Regaining his seat at the table, Rogenvaldr grabbed Ermengard and pulled her to him. Chin down, she stared at him out of the corner of her eyes, watching his eyes roam her shoulders and breasts. His nose was sniffing at the scent of lavender and jasmine emanating from the sweaty sheen on her cleavage.

Armòd the Skald had been listening to the troubadours and poets and was disgusted with their limp music. *Their music has no balls. Nor do the men here. I'll show them how it's done.* Throwing someone's wife off his lap he rose from the table. Elbowing his way to the musicians in the corner, he grabbed for the largest flat drum.

"You call this a drum, you turd?"

Blanching, the musician handed it over. The Skald strode to the center of the room, grabbed a stool, and placed the drum vertically on his lap.

Carefully patting down his beard to keep it out of the way, he made a huge fist and began to bang the drum hard and loud, in a slow, ancient Viking rhythm. Howling and grunting, he chanted hungry bear growls and whale mating songs, called to life the Virgins of a Night Sky left so far behind, perhaps never to be seen again. He hissed orange mountains of fire and pillars of steam, walked over black beaches and white snow, and sat at the home's hearth. His song flew above sparkling icebergs lit by the midnight sun and over huge creatures swimming in the deep, cold waves of an ocean far, far north. Tears ran down his flushed, drunken cheeks. All the Norsemen in the room cried with him, their beards wet. When his wailing stopped, it was as if all the animals of the north had died in a freezing wind.

The silence in the courtyard was total. The birds had flitted away in fear; the dogs were cowering under the tables.

Slowly the room returned to life. The dogs began to gnaw their bones, but the birds were gone.

As the sky turned from lavender to dark blue, God lit the stars and dessert arrived: pears, dates, cinnamon and honey-flavored figs poached in rose water, sugared baked walnuts, sheep's milk thickened with ground almonds poured over sweet rolls laced with clove and saffron, tiny honey-coated flakey pastries garnished with dried raisins, all washed down with sweet honey mead in tiny cups. Jaufré sang to an appreciative group of ladies who threw their jewels to thank him. In a dark corner musicians played softly on lutes and tenor flutes.

Drunk Norsemen slowly began to pull women away from the tables. They stumbled their way into cushioned corners in dark hallways and into chambers lit by oil lamps and candles. Murmurs of desire were followed by slaps and grunts of conquest echoing under the arches.

William, trying to ignore Rogenvaldr and Ermengard exploring each other's mouth and neck, sat staring down at an empty plate. At the sound of cheering he looked up and was immediately thrown into a panic. A group of well-dressed whores was being shown to some drunken Norsemen. The townsmen had ordered them in to get them off their wives.

Among them was Bathsheba, who had been grabbed by Eindredi. "No!" William shouted.

Everyone ignored him. His chair fell backwards as he jumped up from the table. "No!" he shouted again. Running over, William grabbed her by the arm, trying to pull her away. Eindredi was already groping her under her dress.

Eindredi look up surprised, and then laughed. "You too, William? Well who would have thought! Let's share her—you can even go first."

He held on tight to her as she bent over in pain and shame, her eyes glistening with fear.

"Let go of her. As your Bishop, I command you to let her go."

"As your Bishop you command what?" Eindredi began to laugh so hard that tears began to roll from his eyes. His white hair shook around his head as his hand let go of Bathsheba. William pulled her away and ran for the door. Other Norsemen tried to clap him on the back as he left.

"About time, Bishop!"

• • •

Outside the palace it was dark and quiet. Bathsheba turned away in shame. William put his hands on her shoulders, and she let herself burrow her face under his chin.

During secret meetings, walking outside the walls, telling intimate details about their past lives, they had become very close, but never intimate. Now, not saying a word, he took her hand and walked to the Villa Limon, where he guided her to his room.

Hopefully I can trust him, she thought. *But I will do what is necessary to return home.*

After sliding his hands down her arms, he led her to the floor cushions where, exhausted, she threw herself down. Watching her fall asleep, he became more and furious with himself at the arousal he felt. *Why do my loins ache? I got rid these desires years ago. Why now? What is this place doing to my mind? St. Magnus, dear teacher, guide me to walk the holy path. She trusts me, I cannot betray her.*

• • •

Rogenvaldr didn't notice what William was up to. Ermengard, who had been sitting on his lap and allowing all sorts of intimacies, put her hand on his thigh and got up to leave. Rising in confusion, he watched her speak briefly to Beatritz, who looked downcast, yet nodded in obedience.

Floating across the courtyard with a little wobble, Ermengarde departed through a small arched door behind some columns. Like a small flock of little chirping birds, her handmaidens followed after. He stared after them. *Well, that was rather insulting. Am I left to pleasure myself?*

Beatritz, her eyes half-closed to hide her dismay, with her mouth set into a straight line, came over to speak to him. Quickly she left a message in his ear, then followed her mistress through the door. He could hear a bolt snap into place.

Well, well. It seems that I shall also have to leave. Now how, by all the Saints, do I find this Roman pool?

CHAPTER 13

Chaste Ermingard hastens
to serve—the snow curve of
her broidered brow silver—
poured-wine beauty shining.
So swung swords gleamedtempered
in fire's sheath, warm-flame wreathed—
when war hardened heroes
assaulted that castle.
                    —Rogenvaldr Kali Kolsson, 1103?-1158

B elow the palace, down a crumbling, curved staircase, Ermengard relaxed on the tiled shelf of an ancient Roman bath fed by a cool spring for a thousand years. Niches carved into the stone walls held torch lamps burning oil in bowls held up by nymphs and satyrs. Their golden light flickered on paint-flecked marble statues of long-gone Roman gods standing in the corners. A life-sized, partially draped Venus, one arm missing, her face still pink, stood at one end of the pool, her toe ready to step down onto the worn steps leading down to the water. Cracked fish and flamingos swam and flew amongst blue waves on a mosaic sea floor. After the heat and noise of the banquet, Ermengard had gratefully slipped her naked body smoothly into the clear water.

She put her head back and stared at the ceiling, allowing her arms, legs, and full breasts to gently float outwards. Above, a frightening creature glared back at her, its grimacing face surrounded by hair snakes moving in the shadows. As a child the face had given her nightmares; but now she understood the story of the Medusa and felt pity for the woman so severely punished by Athena.

Beatritz, sitting on a blue pillow in the corner, sang softly. She was still trying to reign in Ermengard's desire for the Earl.

Let us speak softly my lady,
so no one will hear us.
I do not wish it, yet I am forced to sing.
It is proper and permissible
for a virtuous lady to admit
her love for a good man.

Yet the maiden must be on guard,
for the ending could be good or bad.
One will not stay who suffers wrong
and this can happen many ways.
The fountain may run dry
and a rose has thorns.

Ermengard was barely listening. The forbidden need to touch herself returned. *Mother Mary, help me, for I can't help myself. I want this man. I want to know what his touch feels like. His fingers, his lips, his skin.* Her chest was so tight she could barely breath. *What if he doesn't come to me tonight? What have I done? How could I have been so stupid and childish. I'm so embarrassed to have acted that way at the banquet. A man like him, he could have any woman…*

Muffled footsteps were coming down the stairs.

She looked to the left. There in front of her, wrapped in a dark cloak, stood Rogenvaldr, his blue eyes staring down at her. Frozen with fear, she stared back at him.

Then his cloak dropped to the floor.

Ermengard gasped. *I'm going to die.*

The fine lines around Beatritz's eyes tightened as she stopped mid-verse. *This man is unbelievable.*

The flickering orange lights revealed a lean, muscled body covered, from his neck down to his feet, with astounding drawings of ancient symbols and mythological beasts. Black-edged knot work patterns wound around blue and green trees, all intertwined with dragons and the flowing hair of women warriors carrying round war shields. Strange creatures, half-horse and half-winged eagle, half-fish and half-goat, inhabited his arms and shoulders. His thighs carried a wild ocean with wave-torn sailing ships. Even his member was enveloped by a one-eyed snake!

Most astounding was the large, blood red cross of a Jerusalem bound pilgrim cut into his chest right over his heart.

Tall and silent, he slowly walked down the pool steps to Ermengard. Gradually the sailing ships on his thighs sank into the cool, clear water. His hand reached out to the floating strands of Ermengard's hair and swept it aside to see her shoulders, breasts, and the white angle of her legs moving under water.

I give up. It is not my job to save her. Here is my chance to leave and go to the Bons Hommes meeting tonight. Let them do as they will. Tucking her psaltery under her arm, Beatritz grasped an oil lamp from a niche and turned into a dark tunnel. Quickly she ran up several flights of rickety palace stairs that led to a long forgotten, narrow, dirt-floored corridor with four ancient wooden doors. Grasping an iron latch, she pulled one open on its carefully oiled hinges. An entrance into her private chamber, it was a secret door hidden beneath a tapestry hanging on the wall. Quietly she entered her room. Checking that Alais was asleep, the nurse beside her on the floor-bed, Beatritz hurriedly threw on a black, hooded cloak and rushed out through the same door. Lower down, the stairs intersected with a corridor leading to a small side door of the palace that opened onto the market square. Grabbing a heavy, forged-iron key off a hook on the wall, she let herself out. Struggling to make the lock's metallic clank as silent as possible, Beatritz ran into the dark night towards the bridge and forgot all about Ermengard.

• • •

I feel like a child next to him. He's such a mountain of a man. Caressing her shoulders he slowly pulled her towards him and ran his fingers down her spine. *I can't even get my arms around him. Ah-h-h! Where's he going?* He could feel her stomach trembling. Ermengard put her cheek against the red cross on his chest and looked up. In the orange light his hair flamed around his head. *It's like a lion's mane.* She was afraid to look down. She could feel his hardness pressing against her.

His hands cupped her above the thighs and squeezed her bottom as he lifted her up and onto himself. *Wait! A virgin? Is that possible? She's a widow. I didn't expect that.*

Ermengard flinched with the sharp pain. *It's over! It's over now. Whatever happens shall be a joy to me. I've been starving for too long.*

Firmly he grabbed the back of her neck to kiss her hard on the mouth. Both lovers were hungry for each other. At first there was hard passion in the struggle for release, in the selfish need to obtain satisfaction, no desire for subtlety. After their rapid heartbeats slowed down, there came the luxury of exploration: inhaling the smell of wet hair, tasting salty skin, running fingers over sharp cheekbones, the rubbing of tongues. Another rush of blood, and with it the excitement of knowing it would all happen again.

Afterwards, lightly intertwined, their bodies floated languidly in the cool water. Rogenvaldr, his head leaning back on the edge of the pool, was holding her close with one arm. Fractured statues of strange gods stood in niches lit by oil lamps. In one niche, observing the lovers with a quiet intensity, sat a large white cat. It's bristling fur, lit from behind, was outlined in a halo of light. Burning flames reflecting on the pupils of its wet, yellow eyes gave it the malevolent stare of a demon. Meeting the stranger's eyes, it hissed at him.

Hissing once more, the cat jumped down and slunk towards Rogenvaldr's head, tail twitching nervously. Mesmerized with each other, the two were nearly eye to eye. More hissing—exposing the ridges in its pink mouth, showing sharp teeth, it extended one paw, ready to attack the challenger. Rogenvaldr used one arm to throw water at it, sending it running away, body skulking close to the ground. *If it's not pork loins or troubadours, its cats! It's impossible to get any peace around here.*

The Pilgrim's Cross, shiny, dark red as old blood, entranced her. "Why did you have this done?"

"Instead of sewing a red fabric cross on my tunic as most pilgrims do, I decided to endure a small part of the pain and suffering of Christ. After returning from Jerusalem, most take their cross and re-sew it onto their back to show they have been there and returned. But, in gratitude for my redemption, I will forever carry the pain with me on my heart."

"Did it hurt greatly?"

"Only once. To distract myself while it was being drawn, I composed song-poems imagining myself on Golgotha. If you wish, I'll recite one."

She nodded, watching his wet copper hair gleam in the light outlining the planes of his face, as he sang.

Christ's Cross on my breast-bone
balm of shouldered palm-leaves
placates the poet. SSShh!
Pilgrims crowd the hilltop.

The chamber was quiet and cool. Gently he took her again, touching her between her legs, feeling the water grow slippery. The Earl thought of himself as a generous lover and made sure she had her pleasure. Leisurely moving to depart, he let her float away.

She watched him lithely walk up the steps of the pool, water cascading off his back and muscular buttocks in long sheets. The sailing ships on his thighs arose from the deep. Giving the statue of Venus a pat on the rump, he quickly picked up his cloak and wrapped it around his dripping shoulders. Grabbing a torch off the wall, he padded up the stairs leaving wet footprints on the stones.

Alone, her profile outlined by the dying light, Ermengard lingered in the pool.

The underground spring will soon wash away our passion. Holy mother, have I done wrong to seduce a man on pilgrimage? And as a virgin? I didn't cry out. He'll never know.

By the balls of Saint Peter! How is it possible that a woman twice widowed can have been a virgin? Someone explain that to me. In his heart, under the Red Cross, Rogenvaldr was decent enough to have self-doubt for what he had done. Soon, though, his rights as a noble male erased any qualms. *It's not my fault, she wanted it. And I was good!* Feet slapping he hurried upstairs to get his clothes. Wandering through some strange corridors, he found the main gate and went out into the morning light.

• • •

Tired, and eager to return to the villa, Rogenvaldr turned towards the Porte Episcopal. Annoyed, he was forced to move aside to avoid bumping into a tall, hooded monk just standing there in the shadows. *Why is that monk just standing there? It's the Canon. What could he possibly be up to here in the dark? Who's he waiting for at this hour?*

They nodded formally at each other.

Once outside the city he began walking through the fields to

Coyran. A flicker to his right made him look to see a familiar figure walking determinedly in the direction of the Porte Laurac. The thin, lithe man hopped over vegetable plots, never looking behind. It was Aslak. Silently Rogenvaldr followed him through the gate towards La Capitole.

"By Thor's hammer!" he exclaimed quietly, when he realized where Aslak was heading.

The Roman temple was quiet; dark sleeping figures hid themselves behind broken walls and columns. Aslak turned into the alley of his sister's brothel. Quietly approaching, he expertly knocked the inattentive guard on the head with his sword pommel. Then he disappeared into the building through a door that had been left unlocked to allow customers to leave quietly in the morning

Rogenvaldr saw him go in and ran to intercede. *I should have stopped the idiot in the fields*. The guard, stunned, began to grapple with the Earl.

"Not me, you idiot—inside—!" Pushing the guard away, he ran into the empty courtyard. Aslak was screaming upstairs.

"I'll kill you, you bastard! Get away from my sister."

"Get out of here! Get away from me. I don't want to go with you. Leave me alone! No-o-o!"

A half-naked man tore down the stairs in fear for his life, then rushed out the door without his clothes. Behind him, Aslak stomped down, dragging a naked, kicking and screaming Nila by her arm. The guard pulled out his sword to cut down Aslak, so Rogenvaldr had to parry him off. "Leave it," he snapped. "He's, my man. I'll deal with it."

At this point everyone was awake and watching from the balconies.

"Stop! Everyone stop!" yelled the madam at the top of her lungs.

"She's coming with me." Aslak was attempting to drag off the struggling girl.

"No, she's not," replied Rogenvaldr firmly.

"She belongs to me, you devil!" Lomanha began to hit him on the back of his head with a flowered pitcher.

Nila sat on the ground gasping. She looked up at her brother. "I don't know you. I belong here." She grimaced as he tightened his grip on her hair.

"No. You belong home with your mother!"

"Let her go." The Earl spoke quietly to his crazed young charge. "Or I'll make you let her go. I'm ordering you."

Reluctantly, Aslak let go.

Speaking to the madam, Rogenvaldr bowed graciously. "It won't happen again." He put some coins on a tiled table.

"It better not," she growled. As Nila scrambled to run upstairs, Lomanha slammed the pitcher down so hard that the table broke, scattering the coins in every direction.

Aslak was stomping out ahead of him.

"I should send you back to the boat right now. You're a danger to everyone: to yourself, to Nila, to me, and to every one of us here in this foreign city. You just can't do whatever you want. And you'd better remember that in Jerusalem. You're a soldier under my command."

"Then buy her back—why won't you buy her back?"

"She doesn't *want* to be bought back, nor does the madam wish to sell her. Understand that. Or you go back to the boat."

Exhausted, he led Aslak back to the Villa Limon. Wishing for nothing more than a long sleep, he entered the courtyard to find Sancha sitting on a couch with a lizard-like man dressed in black. His flat, triangular face, topped with oily slick-backed hair, was a mask of anger. Hard narrow eyes glared at him.

"My Lord, this is Dalmu d'Perpinyá. He owns the slave Bathsheba."

"And what does that have to do with me?"

"Your Bishop William has hidden her upstairs," Dalmu claimed. His pointy tongue flicked out of his lizard mouth.

"My who? What are you talking about? William!" he screamed up the stairs. "Get down here! And you," he looked at Aslak, "get upstairs and make yourself scarce. What's going on with everyone here?" *I'm really too tired for this.*

William slowly came down the stairs to the courtyard. He looked very determined.

"Have you got the slave-woman Bathsheba upstairs?" Rogenvaldr demanded.

"Yes."

"Well bring her down. She doesn't belong to you."

"No, I can't do that."

"What do you mean, no, you can't?" Rogenvaldr challenged. "Obviously you mean no, you won't."

"She's mine," the lizard cried, "give her back!"

"No. I want to buy her," said William.

"Have you been knocked on the head? What makes you think you can bring a female slave on our boat?" Rogenvaldr said.

"I want to free her." William was insistent.

"You can't just go buying and freeing slaves—what are you thinking?"

"This one is different. Bathsheba is an Ethiopian priestess who was kidnapped by pirates. She wants to go back to her church."

"She's w-what? Is that what she told you?" Dalmu began to laugh in a high-pitched screech. "And you believe her?" He was bent forward double, slapping his knees. "They all say that! They're just whores!"

"William—" Rogenvaldr was losing patience.

"She proved it to me."

"And how did she do that?"

"By chanting the Liturgy of Saint Yared. She knew the correct Zema form."

The three of them stared at William.

"And how do you come to know this Liturgical chant of Saint Yared?" asked Rogenvaldr.

"An Ethiopian priest in Paris chanted it for us in the Kings Chapel. I remember it well."

"Well, now she's a whore," Dalmud reminded him.

"I'm not leaving Narbonne until she's free and on her way home."

Saint Magnus, help me. "How much?" Rogenvaldr asked Dalmu.

"Twenty silver solidi."

"What? Are you out of your mind?"

"I'm being very generous. That is only slightly more than I paid for her."

"But she was pure then," interjected Sancha, not wanting to lose a possible commission.

"Hold your mouth, woman!" snapped Dalmu.

Rogenvaldr had had enough. "Do you have the money?" he asked William.

"No. I was going to borrow it from you."

"And how long would I have to wait to get it back? The Second Coming?" He turned to Dalmu. "I'll give you five silver solidi."

"Seven."

"Done. Now can I get some sleep?"

As they went upstairs together, William asked, "do you want to meet her?"

"Absolutely not. Go away. Leave me alone." *I can't believe what being in Narbonne is doing to all of them.*

CHAPTER 14

In the ether I saw a great fireball
filled with great shining energy. . .
and around it were many burning stars
into which the white fireball discharged its energy. . .
— *Hildegard of Bingen, 1098-1179*

I hate crossing this bridge. The stinking animal blood being sucked into Beatritz's sandals made her gorge rise and her throat burn. Swallowing the bile, she hurried across through the endless, black tunnel of wooden-shuttered butcher stalls.

Cautiously she side-stepped the slimy lumps of fish entrails on the other side of the river. Empty carts stacked up against cracked walls blocked her way as she moved nervously past a narrow alley. *What the—?*

She jumped as a clowder of cats came rolling out, hissing and scratching each other, all fighting for the same torn-up fish. They got entwined in her skirts and nearly knocked her over. *Get away from me!* Kicking at them finally let her get away. Howling, they disappeared into the dark.

Beatritz skimmed the shadows behind streets teeming with taverns and brothels. *Satan is busy tonight! I pity you revelers— you will all be reborn into another lifetime of Hell here on this earth.* The thought made her stomach shiver.

Passing the flickering oil-lamp lighting the entry to the Hospital of God, she felt her way through the dark until she arrived at the curved wall of the Basilica of Saint Paul-Serge. Her fingers, following its rough, pebbled surface, guided her around to the necropolis behind it. Others never entered the cemetery at night for fear of spirits and demons, but Beatritz had no fear of the dead; they were blessed. A moving spirit herself, she finally arrived at the Toulouse Gate.

"Ps-s-t! Armond— it is Beatritz," she called to the guard, fortunately also a believer.

"Hurry—before the militia notices." Quietly he opened the gate's inner door, stopping just before a known squeak. "It will be a joyous night," he whispered. "I wish I could join you."

Beatritz put her hand on his arm and squeezed it lightly as she stepped over the high threshold. The old ramparts loomed black over her in the dark. Rickety huts and shacks leaned crookedly on the walls. The air was heavy with the ashes of cold cooking fires and dung. Following a dirt path through a field of cabbages, she eventually came to the road that led to rich grasslands around the small village of Saint-Crescentius. Here, away from the safety of the ramparts, merchants hid their fancy homes behind high walls. Everyone was asleep. Ignoring all the barking dogs, Beatritz slipped under the shadows of rustling trees. Rattling noises came from a leper house set far back from the road.

She sniffed the air—bread baking! It was Ermengard's bread oven. The smell from the communal bread oven wafted through the air. *I can't have the bakers recognize me*. Wrapping her hood around her face she wound her way behind the lit-up, bustling bakery.

Finally, breathing a sigh of relief, Beatritz saw the wooden sign of The Golden Lion Inn hanging from the gate post of a two-story stone building set in a grove of chestnut trees. Jaufré Rudel had used a coded troubadour language called "the language of the birds" to sing to her the name and place of tonight's meeting. A dove had been drawn in white chalk on the post; before dawn it would be washed away. A faint light dimly outlined her face as she slid through the narrow slit she made when she opened the heavy wooden door.

Unnoticed, the snake-like figure that had followed her slithered back to Narbonne.

Pierre, the man who let her in, was the husband of a middle-aged couple who managed the inn. They had renounced their marriage and former life, and where now living as Bons Hommes. The spotless dining room was empty, the tables bare of food. A door in the floor was open. Wooden stairs led down to a spacious underground chamber in which a Roman family had once stored its wine and grain. The room was lit with dozens of candles placed in a circle on the edges of a cracked floor mosaic that illuminated a flickering, grinning Dionysius drinking amidst naked, dancing nymphs.

Along an old stone wall were six old brick alcoves with no doors. One to a room, six emaciated people, a candle at their head, were lying on wooden biers. They appeared to be sleeping but were really dying of self-imposed starvation.

Beatritz rinsed her hands in a large basin of cool water set on an altar made of an old grinding stone, drying them with a nearby damp towel.

Sliding silently into a circle of about twenty people, she nodded a quick greeting over praying hands to Mabilia D'Coumic and Adalais D'Ouvelhan.

Pierre's voice whispered excitedly from upstairs. "Henry the Monk is here! And The Shadow is with him!"

Feet shuffled on the stairs and an emaciated man with dirty, bare feet, draped in an unwashed brown robe entered the room. Behind him followed the woman known only as The Shadow. Her tattered black veils, like the feathers of an aging raven, dragged in the dust. The candlelight glowing behind her revealed the body of a small, hunched woman, with the timeless profile of a crone, all sharp chin and hooked nose. The Shadow silently took herself to one side to sit down on a stone bench.

Henry went over to the altar and rinsed his hands. Everyone turned to face their spiritual angel, their guide to God's side. Unshaven, he had the haggard face of a shipwrecked sailor, yet his black eyes were sharp and keen. His back was long and straight. Clasping their hands in prayer, the group knelt to perform the ritual greeting for a 'perfect Bishop'. Touching their foreheads to the floor three times, they chanted three times:

"Bless me, Lord. Pray for me. Lead me to my joyous end."

Holding his hands out, palms down, in a low voice that could turn fearful, Henry the Monk intoned, "May the Lord bless you and console you at your end."

"But," he continued. "Before we begin tonight's consolamentum, I must give you dire news. Satan has arrived in Narbonne in the persona of Canon Hugon of the Abbey of Prémontré. He is an evil and hateful man who would burn everyone he even suspected of heresy. Once, when told he might be burning a true Christian by mistake, his response was: 'It really doesn't matter. God will know his own'.

"His papal mission is to identify those who are Bons Hommes, those whom the church calls Cathars, and give their names to the church to be destroyed. Please, we can't all be martyrs. This movement will not grow if we all die. Hugon believes the real reason for his presence here is a secret, but our troubadours are spreading the word. He dresses in a wool habit and hood, even in the heat, to conceal his hawkish nose and staring eyes. There is a large lump on his throat hidden by a beard. If a tall, emaciated monk tries to engage you in conversation, or even if you even *suspect* you are in his presence, speak carefully. Eat meat if necessary. We must protect ourselves.

"If you go to a meeting, watch behind you. Warn others. There are Bonnes Filles in Toulouse that he has exposed and burnt. It is too late for them, but the fire will bring them to God. Hide amongst the Catholics." He turned to Beatritz. "Be watchful. He lodges with the Archbishop in his palace and will endeavor to engage Ermengard."

He paused to collect his thoughts.

"And now it is time to accompany Sibyl to God."

They gathered around a bier in the center of the room on which lay Sibyl, a meretrix publica, a licensed prostitute well known in Narbonne. At her breast was a newly born infant. Engulphed in a shroud, only their faces, as pale as the cloth, were showing. Under her hips dried black blood swirled together with bright red blood. Sibyl's breathing was shallow, her eyes closed. The still infant occasionally moved an eyelid.

I envy her, thought Beatritz. *I wish I was ready. But I must work for the better good. My time will come.*

When Henry went to kneel beside Sibyl his long, stringy hair fell forward over his face. Beatritz caught a glimpse of the frayed hair shirt on his neck and arms. Vermin crawled around on red sores.

The dying woman opened her thin-lidded eyes. When she saw Henry at her side, her face glowed with happiness. "I waited for you, my teacher," she murmured in a soft, dry voice.

"I'm here now to give you the consolamentum," Henry murmured.

"Please, be swift. My daughter is not long for this world. The townswomen tried to make me overlay her to death, but I wanted her soul to go with me up to God. We can be two sparks together in the night sky." Her eyes became bright.

"How long is it since you have eaten or drunk water?"

"I began the endura two days before I gave birth. For seven days since the birth I have not eaten, nor had water, nor fed my daughter. I want to die—I beg you, release us from Satan's world."

Henry reached into an old wool bag hanging from his shoulder and carefully took out a heavy, large book. Dry, wooden covers, held together by flax twine, contained a high stack of thick, ragged-edged pages covered in brown uncial script. The book was a heretical copy of the Gospels written in the Occitan language. He brought forth a long linen cloth which he laid over the woman's body. Each believer moved forward to touch it.

Leaning closer, Henry solemnly held the book over her head.

"Sibyl, do you renounce the harlot Catholic Church with its sham baptisms, fake crosses, evil persecutions, simony and worship of earthly wealth?"

"I do."

"Sibyl, do you renounce the magical rites of the devil that tempt one to sin, which ensure rebirth in Satan's kingdom here on earth?"

"I do." The words were very faint.

Henry touched the foreheads of the woman and her child with the book. He lit a candle, and holding it over both their faces, he dripped some wax. A fiery look came into his eyes.

"I anoint thee with fire and absolve thee of thy sins. We will now escort you to our heavenly father who will greet your souls with joy."

He gestured to The Shadow, who rose and walked into the center of the circle.

"It is time for you all to kneel and receive your wings."

The Shadow took a glass vial out from under her veils. She opened a stopper connected with a twisted leather cord and placed a glass straw into the bottle. Going to each kneeling person, she dipped the straw, allowing only three drops of the viscous, bitter liquid to fall onto each tongue. The sacred hallucinogenic oil was so old that there was no memory of the first priestess who had used it in the Eleusinian Mysteries, but the effects were just as strong. The formula of poisonous frog extract, black nightshade, opium, ergot, wine musk, and other secret ingredients had been handed down from initiate to initiate, known only to those who practiced the ancient arts of the Mother Goddess, whose statues of a woman with a hundred breasts were hidden in sacred groves in dark forests.

The candles flamed like sparks in their minds; soon each participant fell to the floor as if dead.

Beatritz felt her spirit rise into the air on six beautiful grey feathered wings that swished through the air, pulsing her upwards. Reaching out her arms, hands outspread, she cried out joyously.

Sibyl, let us go together and ride the cosmic wind with our wings! I want to move among the stars with you, above the moon and beyond the sun. I'm climbing the ladders of the prophets, my toes barely touching— Oh, dear God, I see the golden face of Jean smiling in a star. My child, my child, I will join you soon. My wings are golden songs in the blue sky; I hear the voices of angels, those who have gone before me never to return. I hear the music of the stars. My God, take me now, I am the fiery life of your divine essence, I am a flame beyond the beauty of this earth encircled by the hidden wonders of love. Discharge your energy into me, keep my soul with you for eternity.

The light—it's extinguishing! Oh Lord, no, no—it's too soon to return me to the dark earth! Why must I be in exile and walk the path of evil? Farewell, my child, I am in the darkness falling backwards, downwards into Hell— no, no..."

• • •

Heavy-headed and exhausted, Beatritz made her way back through the early morning haze, only stopping at the oven to pick up some bread in case someone asked why she was here. Either way, she hadn't eaten since the banquet. The hot and chewy loaf was full of toasted rye seeds. The bell for matins was ringing, so she put in an appearance at church before rushing home.

Near the side door of the palace she was jostled by a tall, hooded monk heading towards the bridge.

"I beg your pardon," he murmured in a low voice, "but, isn't it a bit early for you to be out alone, my lady?" His foul breath dirtied the cool morning air.

And what business is it of yours? she felt like answering. Rapidly lowering her face, she answered, "Matins, sir, are always early."

She ran for the door. *Why is this taking forever to unlock?* Slamming it shut behind her, she leaned against the wall, her heart beating painfully.

Was that Satan who just spoke to me? His breath stank in the air, and she felt as if it had followed inside, stuck to her.

Shivering, she grabbed a small clay oil lamp, lit it with shaking hands, and ran up the creaking steps to her chamber. A candle flickered behind the tapestry. Alais and the nurse had not stirred all night.

CHAPTER 15

A book of verses underneath the bough,
a jug of wine, a loaf of bread—and thou
beside me singing in the wilderness—
Oh, Wilderness were Paradise enow!
  —Rubaiyat, Omar Khayyam, 1049-1131

The rising sun skimmed the ramparts to outline the sharp edges of Saint Paul-Serge's orange towers across the river. In a cerulean sky, great flocks of pink and white flamingos, gorging on crustaceans, rose and fell over flat lagoons. The confusing languages of people arguing in the market, combined with the warm scent of spices—cinnamon, pepper, and cloves—floated up to Ermengard's bedroom at the top of the palace tower.

Rogenvaldr, sitting idly on a window seat, gazed out over the river and inhaled the smell of burnt sugar from the kitchens. *One could live here. The endless grain, fruits I never dreamed of, the hot blood of the women—this woman.* Vgret in her grave with the twins flashed into his mind. *Forgive me for forgetting for one day, Vgret. But Ermengard must be as fertile as those pomegranates people eat around here all the time. What future does a man without a son have? And she's a very rich Viscountess—it really is tempting. How could she be so young and yet run this whole kingdom alone?*

He'd received a flowery invitation to dine with Ermengard two days ago. William, who was wary of the Viscountess, objected.

"Don't go, you'll just get more entangled with her. She's naïve and desperate for a husband. Anyone can see that. Get the money so we can leave. Is it in the Gold Exchange yet?"

"No," Rogenvaldr had admitted. "She says she has to mortgage her mines and the Jews take their own time about these things. In the meantime, I'll enjoy her company. Why not?"

"You know why not."

"Oh— you just want the money to buy Bathsheba."

William had turned away.

The invitation had led to her bed, and two days later, Ermengard was watching him from that bed with a soft smile on her face. The sharp light outlined his naked body, revealing the ridges of sword scars on his ribs and thighs, mountain chains in a landscape of mythical beasts. Rogenvaldr was not used to sleeping naked; it was too cold in *Orkneyjar* for that. It made him feel so vulnerable that he kept his sword next to the bed where he could reach it all night. He also kept one eye on Luna who, grumpily guarding his mistress against this intruder, slept on a nearby cushion. *Who knows when that thing will try to get its nails into my balls.*

Ermengard shook out her black hair and stretched. He watched the brightly colored blanket slide down to her waist.

"Really, so many tattoos!" Leaning on one elbow, she pointed, laughing. "And what's the story of that one-eyed snake all around your member?"

"Aah! That's Sigurd Snake-in-the-Eye, a Viking warrior two hundred years ago when we were still pagans. When he was born his mother, Valkyrie Aslaug saw in his eye the mark of a snake eating its own tail. She prophesied that his father would be killed in a pit of vipers. She was right, that's how it happened. So, my little lark-eyes, I want you to meet Sigurd-Snake-in-the-Eye." His slid over to her on his hands and knees, his tongue darting in and out of his mouth, until it reached her breasts. Her eyes glowed as she pulled him down into her arms, wanting his weight on her chest, craving him inside her.

Afterwards, her skin wet with the sheen of their efforts, she announced, "Yes, we must travel on a passage through my domains."

• • •

An early summer mauve sky lit up the lagoons; it was always the forerunner of a hot, sultry day. The passage had started out early to make some distance. Ten Norsemen and six soldiers followed at a discreet distance behind the two ladies-in-waiting in a covered carriage. Another large, covered wagon carried the tents, pots and pans, bread, wine, sundries, and a cook who specialized in freshly hunted cuisine.

Ermengard, riding Orian, was happily wearing a new, daring outfit she had just designed for riding. With loose turquoise pants gathered at the ankles, covered by a red silk skirt that fell in sheer layers, she was able to sit comfortably astride on a cushioned yellow saddle. She enjoyed all the women staring when she rode out of town on the Via Domitia.

Rogenvaldr was pleased with his new soft gloves, pants, boots, and linen tunic. *My jeweled sword looks very fine with this outfit,* he thought.

The land around Narbonne had been leveled of trees to grow wheat, chickpeas, and cabbages. Each rough stone village along the road had a small parish church often built on the ruins of a Roman temple and had a strange half-pagan, half-Christian appearance. The smell of citrus floated out of orchards ripe with pomegranates, oranges and lemons. Upriver, the Aude was crowded with colorful rope-towed boats carrying produce to markets. Fisherman stood knee-deep in fresh-water ponds casting their lines for trout.

In the crush of the worst afternoon heat, they reached the cooler, rugged Corbiére mountains northwest of Narbonne. "This is the way to the village of La Grasse," Ermengard explained. "I want you to meet my Uncle Berenger who is Abbot of its Cistercian Abbey. While I'm there, I also will pray at my parents' tombs."

The mountainous pebbled path crossed over stone arches that stretched over narrow gorges a thousand feet deep. Fan-shaped pine trees, over-harvested by the Romans to heat their baths, stood in lonely splendor. The trees had long ago surrendered their habitat to the garrigue, low growing shrubs and scented bushes clinging to the dry hillsides. Rogenvaldr was curious. "Are those really pine trees? I could never have imagined them shaped like that."

Small pieces of gravel slid under their horses' hooves. Above them towered thin pillars of eroded, naked rocks, pushed to edges of cliffs by the winter wind. Hidden rivers roared through underground caverns, the sound of rushing water thundering through the echoing walls of now dry caverns that, in winter, would fill with flash floods from torrential rains. The landscape twisted around itself, disappearing into dark crevices.

Eventually Rogenvaldr became wary and annoyed, thinking, *this sliding path is going to kill us by causing our horses to fall, or heaving falling rocks down on us. And these insects are driving me crazy.* Ineffectually he swatted at them. *They're an enemy seeking my blood.*

Eventually the horses picked their way down a ravine to a level dirt path on which they could ride side by side.

"Now you are now my liege lord, my chevalier!" Ermengard said teasingly, looking at him sideways. "According to paratge, you must submit to me. I am your Domina."

"And what does that mean in these parts?" he exclaimed, astounded at her temerity.

"According to the rules of chivalry, it means that you, as my knight, must honor me beyond the love of any other woman."

"That doesn't sound so difficult. And what are the other rules?"

"Don't you live by these laws? Surely you must, even by another name. Here in the south these rules bind people together. One must live in the proper way, for the common good, always with courtesy. Courtesy is not just for a knight to know how to conduct himself at court; it is for everyone. Life is infused with joie de vivre, the joy of life, if everyone has balance and spiritual equanimity. It is, how shall we say it? Right living."

God help me. What is she talking on about? Rogenvaldr used a blunt edged sword to reply. "Of course we have rules. But they're not made to curb a warrior's instincts for earning the wealth and honor of battle. Frankly, this all sounds like a woman's invention, a story put out by those troubadours to gain patronage from rich ladies. It sounds like a female Christian hope based on the Virgin's tears!"

Startled, she looked at him.

He looked straight back. "Even though God has blessed you here with good soil, fruit that literally falls ripe from the trees and the sea's bounty, your nobles, in their own world of avarice, pride, and need for power still fight each other constantly. How do you explain that?"

"Isn't that what yours do?" she countered.

"Of course. But we claim we're warriors and we act like warriors. Which is why I'm on my way to Jerusalem to repent."

"Only arrogance and pride will prevent you from true repentance. And you've got plenty of both," she snapped. Kicking Orion, she pulled ahead of him into a cantor.

He spurred to follow, watching her hips bump up and down.

They slowed the over-heated animals down under the thick canopy of a grove of chestnut trees. Grateful for the shade, all walked next to each other in a gentle amble, four hearts beating as one. Chestnuts crunched under hooves; rotting stumps gave off a musty smell as they spread old roots over pillows of moss. The unending calls of birds looking for each other, their black nests hanging from branches, mingled with the rustle of animals fearful of capture. Occasionally a beam of sunlight flew through the darkness like an arrow to skim light across shivering spider webs holding ferns together.

Despite the damp heat, Rogenvaldr suddenly shivered. *I can't see the sky; I can't find the sun. It makes me feel as if I'm on an endless ocean of darkness without a sail on my way to the ancients' river Styx.* He came to feel an unsettling unease. *How different from the vast fjords and snow-covered mountains of Norway, the black volcanic beaches of Iceland with its steaming pools, or the flat vistas, cliffs, and fog of Orkneyjar.* He fought a yearning for home, the roar of the ocean and hiss of the waves. *This land is so fertile and crowded! So many people—I can never relax. There's so much complicated history buried here. The Romans, the Caliphate, the Franks—what would Norway have become if we had been over-run so often? Our history is simple, a tale of heroic survival in a bitter winter. Yes, we are still warriors, no matter how much we pretend to ourselves that we're merchants, we're still simple, plain-speaking warriors.*

Ermengard interrupted his thoughts. "Ahead is La Grasse."

Compared to Narbonne, La Grasse was a colorless, grey town strung along one side of the high banks of the Orbieu River gorge. Its narrow cobblestone alleys were lined with attached two-story stone buildings. There was no air between any of them. Thin roots clung to crevices, sprouting a thick green ivy that grew over open windows like curtains hiding secrets. Neither the summer sun nor the winter wind could ever enter. The wooden roof of the market square shaded a well.

"Let's stop here and water the horses before we begin our climb to the abbey. It will be a hard, stony path. Because he is an Abbot, my uncle will not approve of our relationship at first. But after he sees your nobility, he will be quite gracious." She smiled to herself.

Ermengard was wrong. Seated alone with her uncle in his study, Abbot Berenger, tall and lean, crossed his long legs and knotted his bushy black eyebrows together over his narrow nose. "I have absolutely no desire to meet with this Viking," he brusquely told his niece. "I was in Paris when they attacked, and a more brutal sort of animal I have never seen since. I don't care what they claim to be now, Norsemen or Christian. Dismiss him from your presence immediately."

"But—"

His angry aquiline features, so similar to hers, spoke of their common Roman ancestry. "I said to get rid of him. This man from the north will bring destruction on you. I have already heard that you were so foolish as to buy that unicorn horn. It is beyond me why D'Anduze allowed it. Everyone is gossiping about your relationship. It is a sinful affair of the heart.

"I will never condone it," he snapped. "Besides, you're a married woman. I know what you're going to say," he held up his hand for silence. "While it is true that Bernard has long been gone, there is no report of his death in the Holy Land or elsewhere. Be forewarned of the sin of adultery, Ermengard."

Ermengard sat stiff, her fists curled on her lap.

He turned to his servant monk. "Make sure all Rogenvaldr's men are housed separately from the abbey. Use the guest cells across the river."

Enraged, Ermengard got up. Bowing as little as possible, she stormed out of the parlor to the abbey's church.

The dark atmosphere, heavy with the scent of burning wax, calmed her down.

The marble sepulchers of her parents, Aymeri II and Ermengard, stood side by side in a circular chapel. Four twisted stone pillars supported a richly woven purple cloth embroidered with the Aymeri coat of arms. Shadowed stone faces of Saint Peter and the Angel Gabriel watched from the corners of the vault in which flickered four very tall candles on gold floor stands. With their hands in prayer and features softly modeled by the moving candlelight, the two sleeping figures appeared to breathe.

Ermengard placed her hands on her father's cheeks and kissed his marble lips. The familiar face, a hazy childhood memory, was friendly, faint, transparent. She leaned over to kiss her mother's forehead, an unknown person who was only a thought, a desire for love lost to death giving birth to her sister Ermessend. There were times, when half asleep in her chamber at night, Ermengard had vague dreams, like torn veils, of screaming women and flashing white sheets covered in blood. No one had paid any attention to the child huddled in the corner, staring in fear, inhaling memories.

She held the woman's marble face in her hands and spoke to it in a low voice, "my mother, watching over me from the side of Jesus in heaven, please help me. I am in love with a man from a land so far away. I barely know him, yet I've never met anyone like him. He is a nobleman, a true chevalier. So strong, an honorable Christian. He is going on pilgrimage to Jerusalem, and I am determined to marry him before he leaves. Everyone is against me in this. They warn me of destruction, of terrible consequences. How can wanting a man be so dangerous? I've been told you and father loved each other, so you will understand. Speak to me, tell me what to do."

"Ermengard," she heard a tremulous voice in the air. "I know you are lonely and bereft of love. But do not be impetuous. Remember who you are. If you bow to your desires and marry him, you will give him all your powers."

"I am twice a widow. I want a child, an heir. This man's children would be strong and beautiful." Tears were dropping on her mother's lips.

"My child, wait. You must wait to see what unfolds. What if Bernard lives?" Her mother's voice was losing strength.

"He's not, he can't be! It's impossible. He would be ancient. You are in heaven—find him! You must find him and tell me if he is there with you!"

"I cannot help you. But understand, because you are a woman, a time will always come when all the men around you will be faithless. It is our destiny. When you are in the greatest pain, always pray to the Old Madonna."

"No, I want. . ."

"We are all the Madonna's children. She will give you the strength to survive. She is all we have my child. . ."

The voice grew faint and dissolved into the warm air wavering above the candles.

Lost in her desires, Ermengard sat leaning against her mother's tomb for the rest of the afternoon. When her ladies came to fetch her, she was sound asleep.

• • •

The next morning, when Ermengard met Rogenvaldr at the abbey gate, he was in a noble's nasty mood.

"First the Abbot insults me by refusing to meet with me. Then he boards me in a cell fit for a monk. And the food—bread, mushy porridge, and ale. Well, at least there was plenty of ale—we had to drink ourselves asleep on those straw mattresses. Let's get out of here. Where next?"

"We will go north. I want to show you the toll road I'm building. It will by-pass Narbonne and go through my dominions from Spain towards the Kingdom of France. It will increase my income considerably when merchants have to pay for my protection."

"You are building a road?" Rogenvaldr made a mistake in the inflection of that question.

"These are my lands—I build the roads! After my victory at the battle of Tortosa, I can certainly build a road!"

After picking their way through a narrow gully they approached a white gash in the rocks, a small marble quarry worked by Arnaud Gerardi.

The quarry-master was standing on a cliff watching them approach. Under his arm was a Roman statue of a nymph with a leg and arm missing. His fifty-year-old face lit up with the hope of opportunity. Throwing down the statue he loped down from the top of the rocks to rouse his two daughters.

"Quick!" he yelled, "Wash yourselves up! The Viscountess is passing this way—I want you to stop her and beg for a place at the palace. Your mother is dead and there's no money to buy husbands, if any would even have you. If I have to sell you, you'll spend the rest of your lives as slaves hauling pig-shit, so you better impress her. Clean your faces!"

When the two girls suddenly ran onto the road, they startled Orion, Ermengard's steed. She regarded the girls with impatience as she struggled to reign him in. An older man stepped forward onto the road.

"Domina, I am Gerardi, your humble servant," he said anxiously, kneeling down in the middle of the road. Years of breaking rocks had turned his hair brittle and his skin dry. White dust filled the deep crevices of his tired, sunburnt face. "And these are my daughters."

He gestured at them with the cap in his hands. Shyly looking away, the two barefoot girls were thin and unwashed, wearing faded, yellow-flowered frocks.

"What are your names and ages?" Ermengard asked, as kindly as possible, still struggling with Orion, who was hot and tired and saw no reason to stop here with no oats in sight after a long day.

Trying to curtsy the older one answered. "I am Ermessend, and I am twelve, my lady. My mother, may she rest in peace with the Lord, named me after your sister. Gauzia is ten."

The little one was nervously stepping back and forth.

"Stand still, you idiots!" the father snarled, slapping Gauzia on the back of her head. "Now, ASK!"

"M-m-may we serve you in the palace?" stammered Ermessend, twisting the torn fringe of a sleeve too short for her bony arms. Her tangled brown hair had been hastily braided and framed a round face with sad, heavily lashed large brown eyes. Gauzia had the features of a fawn, doe-eyed, with pointed features.

She actually has some beauty to her face, thought Ermengard. *I don't want to say yes, but I can't say no without appearing callous.* She turned to the father, "Send them to the palace kitchens. Perhaps they'll find a place for them."

Tapping Orion with her foot, she moved forward.

Gerardi had to rise quickly to escape the feet of the annoyed horse. "Get out of the way, you miserable girls! Thank you Domina, you won't regret your kindness."

Ermengard was relieved to move on and put them out of her mind. She knew the kitchen would have no place for the dirty little peasants.

The rode passed sun-etched valleys, with sharp shadows under vines heavy with grapes originally planted by Romans. Their rich flavors went well with the spices used in Narbonnaise cooking. These vineyards, formerly owned by the same families for hundreds of years, had been taken under the rule of abbeys like LaGrasse and Fontfroide. The families now worked the land under the authority of the church, receiving bread, absolutions, prayers and the promise of salvation. It seemed a fair enough trade to the peasants.

Wind gusts were blowing hard enough to knock down some of the vines. In the distance, birches were bent into arabesques to create a row of white arches.

"How can one grow grapes with the wind blowing all the time?"

complained Rogenvaldr, spitting his hair out of his mouth. Unlike cool winds of Orkneyjar, it was hot and dusty.

Ermengard, her hair neatly tied under a red, pointed hat, smiled. "It would be much more difficult to grow grapes without the tramontane wind. It comes from the north star above the mountains to blow away the clouds. It keeps the sky blue and sunny. And should there be rain, the breeze dries the leaves so there is no rot. So we appreciate the wind. It is part of our joie de vivre. It gives us wine." *Sometimes I wonder what he does know, sometimes his knowledge seems so limited*, she thought.

• • •

Her road project was a complicated endeavor. Bypassing the congestion of Narbonne, it followed a winding path around stone waves of escarpments that rippled across rolling hills beneath vertical walls of sliding rocks that only sheep and goats could climb. At the top, the animals ate the scrubby grass and plants of the garrigue and eroded maquis bushes that were used to infuse meat with oregano and thyme.

When Ermengard appeared, hundreds of slaves knelt down. At her signal they rose and continued breaking rocks and tamping down gravel. She turned to Rogenvaldr.

"It's definitely not a Roman road. There's no one who knows how to do that. We will have to be content with what it is. It will do the job. I just wish they were better at making water drainage ditches."

"Well, I think it's quite impressive. Roads in Norway crack and melt and most of the time they're mud."

Ermengard didn't like being on this part of the road. It was too near Toulouse. She feared that Count Raymond IV would come thundering down from his fortified city once again to capture her, and claim Narbonne as his own. Her Spanish allies had fought him off once, in the process killing Alphonse Jordan, the husband the Count had forced her to marry. Alphonse Jordan happened to be the Count's nephew and he was still aching for blood revenge.

It was already too late. The thundering hooves of revenge could be heard in the distance. Soon a cloud of dust rose above the next ridge as a dozen riders bore down on them, reigning in their steeds not fifty feet away.

Looking down from atop a huge black mount, Raymond IV glowered at them. The man had the size and red-eyed eyes of a wild boar and was as black-visaged as his horse. Covered in black leather from head to foot, his sleeves were studded with spikes, and his thick, graying hair and curly beard bushed out from beneath a carved iron helmet that curved upwards over his ears. A red-veined bulbous nose spoke of indulgence as much as the paunch hanging over the front the saddle. His legs, too short to go completely around such a big horse, stuck out straight on each side.

The animal, its eyes wild, wouldn't stand still, and jumping on its hind legs from side to side, tried to bite any other horse too close to him. The other steeds, knowing of its proclivities, had arranged themselves out of reach of the chomping teeth. A pack of barking mastiffs ran wildly around and under the horses, expertly dodging kicking hooves.

Focusing his wild eyes on Ermengard, the Count sneered through a large hairy snout of a mouth full of broken teeth, then shouted over the noise of the dogs. "We meet again, my lady. We'll escort you to my tower now."

He laughed, very pleased with these circumstances.

What an enormous horse, Rogenvaldr marveled, *and what an enormous man. I think not!* The Earl moved his horse forward. As if one with him, his men also moved forward.

"And whom do I have the honor of making the acquaintance of?" he asked with casual courtesy, and restraint.

"And you are?" growled the Count.

"I am Rogenvaldr Kali Kolsson, Norwegian Earl of Orkneyjar."

Looking him over carefully, the count announced, "I am Raymond IV, Count of Toulouse and Narbonne."

"That is quite a mount. Where was it bred?"

"I just purchased it from the Count of Percheron. He's been breeding them for the King of France."

"A very noble steed."

Raymond IV, sensing a snide tone, turned to Ermengard who had backed up the nervous Orion. A huge mastiff, sensing the Viscountess was the quarry, broke loose from the pack and aimed its teeth at Ermengard's foot.

"No, stop!" She quickly pulled her leg up over the saddle as the mastiff reared up on its hind legs, opening a broad, fang-toothed jaw to clamp down on her thigh. Orion aimed a kick at him, but missed, which annoyed him no end. Baring his own teeth he raised and lowered his huge head, a bad sign.

"Caesar! Arrête! Bon chien." As the dog retreated it took one last look at the piece of forbidden meat, its jowls dripping with spittle. Orion reared up to stomp on him, but the clever animal, used to this maneuver, easily avoided the two anvils aimed at him.

"Excuse him, my Lady. My dog must be spoken to in Northern French. He's nobility." Suddenly Raymond snapped to two of his men "Are you ready? Go get her—"

Jesus save me! Ermengard twisted Orion's neck around and began to gallop down the road, hooves scattering rocks into the air.

The Count's men started after her.

"Stay here," Rogenvaldr ordered his own men as he went after them. Closing in on the two horsemen, he drew out his sword. The jewels flashed in the sun when he slashed the first man's arm to the bone. It hung, separated from his shoulder as he slumped in the saddle. When the other rider saw his companion spurting blood, he stopped, alarmed.

Rogenvaldr raced to catch up with Ermengard. Grabbing her bridle, he made her stop.

"Why are you stopping me?" she gasped. She was panting as hard as Orion. "That man wants to force me to marry his son. Is that what you want?"

"It's alright, my love. Come back. You are safe with me."

'My love?' Did he just say, 'my love'? Oh, Mother Mary, how wonderful! Her thoughts flew.

Did I just say, 'my love'? Why did I say that? What's happening to me? His thoughts stopped.

When they arrived back, the Count's men were milling around the hurt man. Blood was running down his horse's flanks as they tried without success to attach the arm back onto his shoulder.

"Do you want our men to settle this now?" asked Rogenvaldr.

Raymond IV had heard of these Viking living in Narbonne, and about the rumored affair from his spies. There were fourteen more boats filled with these wild northerners who had burnt out the Saxons, pillaged

Paris and Bordeaux, and were now living in Normandy. *Hm-m-m.* His mind began calculating. *Isn't he supposed to be leaving for Jerusalem? Not if he marries Ermengard, he won't. Yet that is still to be seen, after all where is Bernard? He must be still on pilgrimage. Surely the Earl must first go to Jerusalem, and, by the time he returns, many things can change. And I don't need three-hundred Vikings over-running Toulouse.*

"I have no quarrel with you," Raymond spat out. "I do have one with you!" he snapped at Ermengard. "Prepare yourself. Not today, yet soon. I will own you."

Sharply reining his mount around, he slammed his heels into its flanks. Holding up a leather gloved hand as a signal to his men to follow, Raymond led them away at a gallop, leaving a dirt cloud around the mountain and a red puddle sinking into the road.

"Thank you," Ermengard said quietly, shuddering. "I'm afraid that churl will never give up."

• • •

The royal procession wound its way leisurely south to the lagoons. Fig trees lined the road, glowing in the afternoon light. Reflections of rose-colored clouds floated on the shimmering pools ahead of them. As the horses avoided sand traps full of crustaceans, small birds followed behind greedily eating the clods of shrimp sucked up by hooves.

"Finally, the beach!" Ermengard kicked Orion forward into the water and started galloping through the waves. "Come follow," she yelled, "all horses of the Camargue beaches are water lovers."

A wind-driven, sandy spray blew into Rogenvaldr's eyes, half blinding him. Riding through the ocean was not part of his world. Eventually the horses grew tired, and with his clothes completely drenched, they slowed to a walk. "I don't like all this riding in the water. Up north the water is much too cold and wild, and it will ruthlessly pull a man under. Now," he said testily, "which of your winds is this?"

"It's the blood wind," replied Ermengard. "It's a hot, dry dusty wind that blows for days from Africa, depositing red desert sand as far as Narbonne. You will soon get used to it."

I doubt it, he thought, rubbing blue eyes whose whites were blood-shot from grit.

Blood wind is right. Between the water and the sand, how do they stand it?

"Ah-h! Let's eat!" She raced towards a blue tent set up on a sandbank. On the wet, brown sand, fishermen had built a fire to grill octopus, scallops, shrimp and mullet. Fried sardines, salty and oily, had been heaped on plates with salt-cured lemons and oysters; fresh white flatbreads were smeared with tart goat cheese marinated in oregano oil. Soft silk carpets, their arabesque patterns flowing in waves, had been laid out for their comfort. White cotton napkins dipped in cool water were handed to them to wipe their noble hands and faces. Pitchers of yellow wine stood cooling in mountain snow.

"These are remarkable," Rogenvaldr said, holding his clear glass up to the light. "One can see the bubbles so clearly." In the late sun, one could see the sea through the glass.

"They are blown in Alexandria; its glass is the finest in the world."

Seafood was piled on gold plates around them. "Where do you get all this gold from?" Rogenvaldr picked up a heavy, gleaming bowl of almonds to inspect the engraved birds and leaves.

"Oh, my gold mines east of here. Our Jewish goldsmiths from Constantinople are very skilled."

That's right, her gold mines. How many of them is she selling to buy the horn? Guilt bit him like an insect. *Forget that. She can afford it. She rules a land of milk and honey, the Bible's Garden of Eden. . .*

His thoughts were interrupted by plates of sweet, flaky cakes covered in crushed pistachios, jellied coconut pies swimming in caramelized honey, and bowls of cold mango sorbet with fresh cut fruit.

Rogenvaldr kicked off his boots with a sigh. Too full to move they lay on the carpets and watched the waves climb the shore. The sea's fingers moved closer and closer as the tide slowly rose.

Ermengard rummaged in a small silk purse hanging from her waist. "I have a gift for you." Ever since he had called her 'my love', she had been thinking about it, repeating it to herself every night. As they slept in their tent in the woods, she had sent a servant to fetch it. "Here." In her hand was a man's gold ring. "This belonged to my father." Taking his left hand she put it on the middle finger.

Rogenvaldr studied the heavy, ornate ring closely: an open-beaked falcon with eyes set with brilliant red stones. *I really hope this isn't because I called her 'my love'.* "It's truly magnificent. How can I accept it? I have no gift for you."

"You bought me the unicorn horn. What gift could be greater than that?"

The insect bit him again as he leaned back against the pillows. In front of him the sand drew the tide sideways as the evening tamped down the wind. Gulls flew along tidepools, diving down to pick at little crabs hiding in their translucent shells. Overhead, hawks rode on circular currents of air, watchful for fish or fowl. An osprey flew into a wave to rise up with a snatched silver fish in its beak, its dinner's tail flapping helplessly.

In the near distance, silhouetted against the setting red sun, Rogenvaldr could make out Eindredi's ship, its shining, gilded prow bobbing in the light. There was a haze that made it difficult to see things clearly. He shook his head sharply to focus his eyes.

During these five days spent in a languid summer daze, in her warm world of turquoise sea, lavender skies, and fruit-filled valleys, he began to feel a personal sense of peace that he had lost a long time ago with the death of his family. The un-asked question arose from deep in his mind: *Do I really need to go to Jerusalem?*

CHAPTER 16

Behold now, I have two daughters
which have not known man; let me,
I pray you, bring them out unto you,
and you can do unto them as ye please…
— *Genesis, 19:8, King James Bible*

Gerardi woke up angry the next morning. "Get up, you vermin! It's light already. I'm sick of you hanging around here eating all my bread and sleeping in my house. Clean yourselves up and go down to the palace kitchens. Maybe your ruler will give you some work. Earn some money!" Snarling, he chased them down the road throwing rocks at their thin backs. Holding hands, the barefoot girls half ran, half hopped down the rocky hillside.

"I'm really hot," Gauzia complained.

"Here, I've made you a lovely hat out of vine leaves. Now you look like a nymph!" She smiled as Gauzia danced in a circle.

"My feet are burning!"

"Here, I've found you a stream. Put your feet in to cool them off."

It was near noon when they arrived at the Raymond-Jean Gate.

"Are you two children going alone into the Bourg?" The guard had three of his own.

"Yes," Ermessend answered putting a serious expression on her face. "Ermengard has told our father that there is work for us in the kitchens."

"Oh she did, did she?" He looked skeptical, then decided it was none of his business. "Go on, then." Sad-eyed, he watched them go into the city. "Poor things."

"Look, the Square of Four Fountains! Let's wash our faces!"

The cool water ran through their fingers. Gauzia bent down to put her face into the basin. Seated cross-legged in the shade of nearby walls, old men leered at the girls and guffawed. "C'mon, girl, drink some more!"

"Let's get out of here." Ermessend grabbed Gauzia. With hands and faces dripping, they ran to the bridge, leaving wet footprints and obscene calls behind them.

A guard at the front gate of the palace looked down at them and smirked.

"Down there, at the side of the palace," he said, pointing.

"Is all this food for her?" asked Gauzia, staring at the wagons heaped with lemons, bags of grain, and chicken cages. At the end of the alley was an open gate where a guard counted the carts of figs and firewood being pulled up from Ermengard's river dock by weary donkeys.

Holding hands, they wandered timidly into a courtyard filled with men frenetically unloading carts who, after nearly trampling them, began shouting curses.

Ermessend was used to being yelled and cursed at; stubbornly she pulled Gauzia over to hug the wall.

They crept towards a door occupied by a well-muscled, pig-faced woman in a bloody apron who glanced at them and yelled, "What do you want, filthy vermin! Get out of here before I have you gutted like the pigs!"

"Please, lady. The Viscountess Ermengard herself told us to come here and ask for work."

Putting her hands on her hips, the woman sneered, "Oh she did, did she? And why would she do that?"

"Because my name is Ermessend. My mother, may she rest in the arms of the Virgin Mary, named me after her sister. And we are hungry."

The woman felt her heartbeat more softly. She pitied the two little ones but could offer them no hope. Bending down, she said as gently as possible, "There is no work for you here. But I will give you something to eat to speed you on your way." Reaching into her pocket she brought out two soft milk rolls.

It was her lunch, but Jesus was whispering over her shoulder, "Marcia, give bread to the children."

Straightening up and tightening her bloody apron, she snapped. "Now, go back where you came from."

Back in the street they munched the rolls. "These are so delicious. I've never tasted anything so good," said Gauzia.

"Come. It's a long way home—to nothing but a beating."

Silently, Gauzia began to cry. Her tears salted the bread.

When they passed a man pissing against the wall, his water a foaming stream running down the cobblestones, their bare feet didn't even notice the warm liquid as it ran between their toes.

But the marble floor of the church was so cool. Ermessend had said, "Let's stop and pray for mother. Maybe she can ask the Virgin Mary, who loves all children, to help us."

No one paid any attention to two little peasant girls praying at the feet of the Virgin, until the sacristan saw them and chased them out.

· · ·

The girls' wobbly shadows slid over the dead grasses on the side of the road. As slowly as possible they dragged their sore feet home.

"I want Mama," Gauzia whimpered. "I want to die and be with her."

"Someday you will."

"But I want to die *now*."

"God will tell you when."

"Why did God take her now?"

"Father told you—she hit her head on a rock."

It was late afternoon when a wagon passed them. The driver was a nun in a white habit. Around her waist was a woven rope belt with a large, black onyx crucifix hanging from a loop. Very large iron keys hung from another loop. Stopping the cart, she eyed them from head to toe.

"And where are you two sturdy young girls off too?" She spoke in a pleasant voice through a thin-lipped mouth. Her dark eyes were round, and heavy lidded, with sharply drawn eyebrows. The wimple was so tight that her white skin bulged out around its edges.

They curtsied, as was proper to a sister.

Ermessend answered truthfully. "We're going home to our father who sent us to Narbonne to find work in the palace kitchen. We couldn't find any; so he will be very angry and beat us."

Gauzia began to cry again. Her face was smeared with dirt and tears.

"There, there now. Don't cry. You must trust in the Virgin. And where is your mother?" Her nun's eyes showed concern.

"She is with God," Gauzia said between sobs.

"It is hot, and you are tired, my little one. How far is your farm?"

"It's not a farm. It's a quarry up in the mountain," said Ermessend.

"Why don't you ride part of the way in my wagon? I pass that way. Go on. There are some stacks of wheat you can rest on. Mirelda, help them up." A thin girl with short-cropped hair and cracked lips had been sitting wordlessly in the back of the wagon. She jumped up to obey. "And give them some apples and wine."

The apples were sweet, and the wine was strong; soon the girls were deeply asleep.

They didn't even wake up when they went through the convent gate; or when nuns lifted them out of the cart and took them to a small stone chamber in the back of the nunnery.

It was only when sunlight crept into a small crack between some stones high in the wall that Ermessend woke up. She shook her sister. "Gauzia, wake up. Where are we?"

Gauzia stirred. "I have to make pee-pee."

"Wait I'll call someone." The door was locked. "Hello! Is anyone there? My sister has to make pee-pee. Hello?" Banging and calling produced no answer.

"I really have to go."

"Go in the corner. What am I supposed to do?"

Gauzia squatted down in the corner, wiping herself with the hem of her dress. She crawled back to her sister. "I'm hungry."

"Stop! I can't think when you keep whining."

Gauzia began crying again. Relenting, Ermessend held her, feeling her little bones shake with each sob. In the dim light she could see her face, tucked for comfort into her big sister's chest. Fear made her nauseous. They fell asleep and woke up, stomachs aching with hunger and fear. No one came that day. Or night.

The following day they heard a woman's stern voice outside the door. "Open it." A key rattled in a big lock. Then a thunk. The sister from the cart was framed by the door. A tall, manly-faced nun stood beside her.

"Please, sist—" Ermessend began.

"Quiet! Never speak again unless I give you permission. Sister Anglesa, take these two: wash them, shave their heads, and clip their nails. Then they may eat. Afterwards I will see them again."

"Yes, Mother Superior. I must say, very well done."

"Of course."

Hungry and bewildered, the sisters were scrubbed in warm water from the laundry. Sister Anglesa washed them gently around the dark bruises and the blotchy red switching scars on their backs. Carefully she asked them about their father. What was he like? Did he ever hurt them? What the girls told her was very unsettling.

"I will pray for you," said Sister Anglesa.

The girls were ravenous, and the bone broth and bread were delicious. "Eat slowly or you will bring it back up," warned Sister Anglesa. Then she took them to a spotless white room with some wooden chairs. "Wait here. I must go in first to talk with Mother Superior Thérèse."

In a short while she returned, then ushered them into a bright, round chamber where the Mother Superior was standing by the window waiting for them.

She spoke firmly. "You are in the Covent of the Three Marys. You will live here from now on. You will work for us. There is no escape; no one will find you. You must give in to the will of God; this is his plan for you. With His grace, you may yet become nuns. For now you will do as your told or suffer the consequences. Follow me and I will show you the wages of sin."

The four went outside into the blazing sun and down a rocky incline to a small cave cut into the rock. The entrance was blocked by large stones bleached white by the sun. She ordered the girls, "Clear open the entrance."

Panting with the effort, the children pulled the stones away. Inside, now exposed to the light, were skeletons wrapped with thorns. One leathery corpse, hands tied behind, was bound tightly around the breasts with huge thorns stuck halfway into wrinkled, brown mounds.

"Those thorns are the same worn by Christ around his head at the crucifixion. They will be wound around your head and bound into your body if you ever disobey any sister in the convent. Then you will be taken here and left to die alive in Christ's agony. Have I made myself clear?"

The girls' legs were shaking with fear. A puddle began to form under Gauzia. "Now put the rocks back."

Ermessend felt dizzy and had to sit down. Suddenly she threw up.

"Are you a woman yet?" Sister Thérèse asked sharply.

"Yes," gulped Ermessend, heaving and spitting.

"When were your last courses?"

"I don't remember. Not for a while."

She glanced at Sister Anglesa who sadly nodded *yes*.

"Take them to the back to the laundry. Those monks from La Grasse just dumped another big load of laundry on us to wash. Bunch of pigs. Go now! Hurry."

• • •

Two days had passed, and Gerardi couldn't find his daughters. "Wait till they get back. I'm going to beat them bloody" Furious, he went to town to find them.

The guard at the gate remembered them. "Two little ones, eh? About three days ago? Yes, they came and went out the same day. You shouldn't be letting your girls run around alone like that. Lots of slavers around looking to make some easy coin. Probably long gone by now."

Gerardi felt like punching him in the mouth, but the guard was armed. "Just shut your mouth," he groused, then decided to walk down to the wharves. No one knew anything. Shrugging their shoulders, they became very busy.

One man suggested, "Why don't you try the convents? Maybe they got lost?"

He was tired and hot by the time he rang the bell at the Convent of the Three Marys. A small square window opened, and a nun looked out.

"Have you seen two young girls, ten and twelve? They are my missing daughters. I've been searching everywhere."

"I'm so sorry. We have seen no young girls here. God help you in your search. There is a well just at the corner if you wish to drink."

The voice was sweet and kind, so he believed her. She slammed the window in his face.

CHAPTER 17

When I breathe this air,
the scent of Provence is in my nostrils.
All that comes from there delights me,
when people speak well of it,
I stop and smile with such pleasure
that for each word I ask a hundred more,
for such is the pleasure it gives me to hear it.
—Peir Vidal, troubadour, 12th cent.

*B*y the arrows of Saint Sebastian! How do I get that Viking to leave* *and go on to Jerusalem?* Archbishop D'Anduze was sifting through the bills and payment demands from the mason, artists, carvers, and stone suppliers scattered over the table of his study.

I've got to get rid of him. Why hasn't Ermengard given him his money gift yet? Because she doesn't want hm to leave, that's why. That horn is worth a fortune. If I sold it to King Louis, I could pay all these bills and build twice as fast. An alarming thought came into his mind. *If they marry, I'll lose all control of her! I must separate them. . .But how? Wait. . .*

A plan came to him. *Devious—but, I must admit, clever.* Scrabbling for quill and paper, he wrote two letters. One he sealed and put into a leather messenger pouch together with a dark red bag of one hundred moribatani gold coins. The second was a travel pass for the messenger.

"I need a Templar rider!" he called to a monk standing outside the door.

Later that afternoon, Guilliam Maurs, a young Soldier of God from the nearby Commandery in La Couvertoirade presented himself. Knee bent, one arm across his thigh, he kissed the Archbishop's ring. "Your humble servant."

"You will accompany two of my monks to the Priory of Ganagobie near Fourcauquiè in the Alps of Provence. Give this letter to the Abbot. Make sure you put it into his hands *before* he speaks with my monks. Him only—no one else."

Bishop D'Anduze showed Guilliam the pouch. "After the monks have signed and witnessed the document he must write for me, leave this on the altar as a gift for the Abbey. Return here as rapidly as possible. Change horses, ride all night. Leave the monks behind to make their way back by themselves. I expect your return in three weeks or less."

"For this effort I will pay you five gold moribatani," D'Anduze continued. "For every day sooner than three weeks there will be an extra twenty silver solidi for you. Here is a pass to change horses and to stay in monasteries, plus a travel purse for three people. You must leave immediately. The monks will meet you in the courtyard. Now go."

Brother Ramon and Brother Gilbert were getting on in years. They were startled to find themselves wrenched out of their daily routine to be sent traveling on an arduous mission.

"You are to go to Ganagobie Abbey in the mountains of Provence," D'Anduze began. "There you will bear witness to an exceedingly important missive which must be returned to me in all speed by the Templar accompanying you. The Abbot there will himself create the document and instruct you in your duties."

Then he stared at them so long in silence that they became very uncomfortable. "You will return together by the same road on which you went there. You cannot get lost. I will find you if you tarry."

"If that's what the Archbishop demands of me, I'll go. Though these donkeys will be hard on my bones," Brother Gilbert grumbled. "Why don't you send younger monks?"

"These papers must be witnessed by two monks of the utmost gravity and dignity. No one must doubt the signatures. Stop complaining. I'm losing patience."

"Your Grace," Ramon pleaded. "I've hardly had time to copy the new music I have on loan from the Avignon archives. It has to be returned soon. And there will be no feast day rehearsals if you send me on such a long journey. Can't you send someone else?"

The Archbishop had no patience for recalcitrance. His response made Ramon cringe.

"How dare you question me, you misbegotten Son of Satan! Either you go to the priory, or you can go be a hermit in a borie in the Corbières where you can freeze or starve, I don't care which."

The thought of living in a bee-hive shaped stone hut alone in the mountains terrified Ramon. His big belly was evidence enough of his love of wine, bread, and cheese. The only thing he loved more than food was music. Music was his connection to God. He came from a family of poor wood-gatherers. A monk, hearing him sing in the forest, asked to take him into his monastery. His family, happy not to feed him, for he was already growing in girth, gifted him to God. Fortunately for Ramon, his boyish soprano matured into a lustrous tenor. Now in his fifties, he still had a warm true tone. The monk's knowledge of music was profound, but underappreciated by the Archbishop, who took his work with the liturgy for granted.

"Hah, Plautus is going to suffer!" Gilbert joked, referring to Ramon's donkey. Justus, his own mount, was waiting placidly, ears twitching at the noises of the courtyard.

From atop the church steps, D'Anduze watched them leave. Guilliam, on Alphonse, a sturdy brown gelding, was already chafing at the monk's slow pace. Brother Ramon's brown bulk was hanging over the backside of his annoyed mount.

Sighing, D'Anduze turned to go up to his library.

• • •

Brothers Gilbert and Ramon, urged on impatiently by Guilliam, with monk-like diligence began to follow the Via Domitia to their distant destination of Notre Dame de Ganagobie Abbey.

Most of the towns along the way had been built by the Romans, but in the intervening years had been ransacked by northern hoards come south for treasure, or the Caliphate come north for land. They were now a shrunken version of their former glory, the inhabitants living a meager existence from travelers crossing the crumbling bridges and unkempt roads. Most temples had been reduced to rubble by pillagers in need of stones to build a house. Only the churches were a stronghold, a place of refuge and holy beauty.

The road they traveled was the only route to their destination; they could not get lost. They would ride from one abbey to the next and there would be simple food and shelter. Leaving Narbonne, they found the road congested with farmers, merchants and wandering pilgrims. It was wide, carved with wagon ruts worn into the stones by a thousand years of wheels. At its edges, the paving stones of the old water channels were loose and falling away. Most of the Roman fountains didn't work anymore.

Leaning stone distance markers were covered with dry moss and graffiti. Local merchants had set up modest stalls along the way to sell food, drink, fortunes and sex. Occasionally everyone had to jump to the side as nobles or messengers came storming through on horseback. No one really cared, that was the way of things. With the weather hot and dry, the days were good for travel.

Having made a late start, it was already dark when the trio crossed the bridge over the Orb River into Beziers. Sleeping comfortably at the hostelry of the Saint-Marie-Magdalene Church, they rose for matins at first light, packed water, bread, and cheese, and impatiently urged on by Guilliam, moved quickly east over the damp sands towards Maguelone. Under their broad straw hats, the monks dozed on their mounts. Plautus and Justus found their own way forward by following the tails of other donkeys ahead.

On and on the flat Via Domitia dragged on monotonously across the brown lowlands of marsh and lagoons frying in the sun. On their right, a now sandy wind carried the crashing sound of waves endlessly chopping away at the strand. Thousands of birds were screaming at each other, diving for food, then fighting for space in the air to eat it. Honking and growling flamingos rose in flame-colored flamboyance, taking over the sky until they settled again in a new feeding ground.

Silence would be a true blessing here, thought Brother Ramon.

"Jesus save us!" shouted Brother Gilbert as some large flamingo excrement landed on his knee.

"That is definitely good luck!" Ramon laughed, then ducked as Gilbert tried to throw it at him.

Dense clouds of biting black flies, gnats, and mosquitos loved travelers, as they were an endless source of fresh blood. Ticks jumped from tall grass to boots, to bare neck, to eyes.

"Help us, Saint Christopher," Gilbert prayed, as they rubbed citrus oil on their skin. He looked at over at Ramon who didn't seem to be bothered so much. Unbeknownst to him, Ramon had made sure to take a good supply of garlic in a sack under his cassock. He was chewing on it now and was delighted at its effect.

"This is a punishment from God!" cried a bony, leather-skinned man driving a cart laden with a stinking mound of dried fish.

When the road to Montpelier branched right, Guilliam led them past the city to which many of their companions were headed. "Keep moving. We're going to Maguelone," he informed them.

The trio eventually came to a stone roadway that led to the little island of Maguelone, where the Cathedral of Saint Pierre-of-Maguelone took in pilgrims. Passing under a crumbling carved gate left by the Saracens, they stopped to marvel at the beauty of the scene. The red sun turned the island forest into an emerald in a gold setting.

"By the eyes of Saint Faith it is beautiful here! And trees, shade— what a relief," sighed Ramon, crossing himself. "Let's hurry. The bells are ringing for compline."

The shade cooled their red-splotched skin as they rode towards the orange walls and flat-topped towers of the newly rebuilt cathedral centered in the pines. A vineyard rolling up the hill was watered by a miraculous spring that had first flowed when Saint Pierre kissed the ground here.

The tired donkeys, stumbling on sore legs, were urged forward. "Move Plautus, soon there's a nice stall and straw for both of us." Understanding the tone, Plautus lurched ahead, nearly unseating the monk.

There were twelve Augustine Canons praying at the far end of the enormous stone-vaulted church, small black dots in the vast gloom. Grateful for the cool darkness, the trio knelt down against the back wall.

Guilliam gazed up. It seemed more of a fortress than a church. Narrow window slits to the south seemed merely loopholes for archers; the rest was all thick, high walls barely lit by tiny openings thirty feet up. It all felt ominous, as if any minute an army of demons could attack through the air.

Eventually a wrinkled monk came limping over, silently gestured for them to follow, then led them through an arched entrance to a four-sided courtyard. Gesturing to three small, windowless rooms, he hurriedly left. Exhausted, they sat down on stone benches set against the walls.

A bald young boy, clasping the rope handles of two wooden buckets in his tight fists came scurrying into the yard. Kneeling down by the side of a flat well in the center of the courtyard, he earnestly prayed: "Jesus, we thank thee for this water."

Lifting the wooden cover of the well, he used the buckets to fill a low marble basin in the corner. He stood up and looked at them. "I am to wash your feet. You should not have entered the holy church with soiled feet."

The monks crossed themselves and made abject apologies. Gratefully, they let him wash their feet. Guilliam washed his own feet.

The old monk brought them grilled fish, cabbage soup, fresh barley bread, and a thick red wine. Fatigue overcame them.

At daybreak more bread, cheese, and wine was left on the benches. They chased away two mottled cats helping themselves to their breakfast and ate quickly. Hearing prayers in the air, the monks rushed to the cathedral hoping to participate in matins before leaving. Standing in the open door, they found the cathedral empty. The Canons were using their own private chapel and did not invite them to join in.

Knowing that the monks wouldn't leave without saying matins, Guilliam said, "We will pray on our own."

They began walking determinedly down the center aisle, tripping as they gazed up at the grinning skulls staring at them from the tops of pillars. "Jesus save me," the Templar mumbled.

The distant apse was dimly lit by two high, deep-set arched windows, one glowing with red glass, the other with lapis blue. Red and blue stripes of light fell on the ancient tomb slabs lying askew on the floor, clattering under their feet. The stone forest of enormous columns held up a ceiling lost to darkness. *It would take the outspread arms of ten men to encircle one of them,* thought Guilliam.

The monks felt alone and vulnerable. God's face, painted on the round apse, was an echo of man's deepest soul; a dark, all-knowing presence demanding total obedience, a strike-you-dead-and-blow-you-into-the-sea God. The Almighty's black rimmed eyes looking down on them could see all the evil in their hearts. Against a red sky, guarding the heavenly throne were six angry angels, each with six grey feathered wings that crossed over each other as they flew. To God's right side, the Archangel Michael used a spear to pierce the heart of the dragon of Evil threatening God's feet. On the left, twelve saintly elders of the Apocalypse stood over orange flames with unburnt feet. Below them, horror of horrors, piles of white skulls with grimacing teeth stared out from the flames of Hell.

Even the Templar, who had fought in the Holy Land, was terrified. "Lord Jesus, save us from perdition," he cried, falling to his knees.

Ramon and Gilbert were trembling. As they lifted their eyes to pray, high overhead, hanging from the ceiling, they saw a huge wooden cross bearing an emaciated skeleton of Jesus. The ropes holding it up disappeared into the darkness above. Glowing in the light of a circular window, the Savior floated in the air like a soul rising to God.

They were sinning ants about to be crushed under a mighty foot.

Ramon sang some prayers in a quavering voice and rushed out into the sunlit square. Plautus, Justus, and Alphonse waited calmly for them under the trees.

"Get on your mounts and let's go," nagged Guilliam. "We are on a mission for the Archbishop, not on a retreat."

CHAPTER 18

And the Unicorns shall come down with them,
and the bullocks with the bulls;
and their land shall be soaked with blood. . .
                    —*Isaiah 34:7, King James Bible*

D'Anduze had an impressive library, filled with tagged scrolls in
latticework cubicles built against the walls and books stacked
on shelves, all organized by the author, the way he preferred it. A
comfortable room, it was furnished with a large marble-topped table by
a north-light window and a slanted writing table nearby. He was looking
for ancient reports of unicorn sightings to use in his sermon at Saint
Paul-Serge Sunday. *There must be words that will put awe and fear into
those worshippers. Above all, they must believe!*

At first, he just pulled out scrolls and books and spread them out on
the table. Then, feeling great pleasure, he sat down to read. The soft light
flooded through the arched window making the colors of the illuminated
letters and paintings glow.

One especially magnificent book, its gold-painted wooden covers
adorned with red and blue gemstone set into a filigreed gold cross, was
Saint Basil the Great's *Homilies on the Psalms 13:5*. It clearly explained
the unity of Christ and the horn:

> Now, since it is possible to find the word 'horn' used by Scripture
> in many places instead of 'glory', as in the words 'He will exalt the
> horn of his people' (Ps. 112:9), and since the word 'horn' is frequently
> used instead of 'power', as in 'My protector and the horn of my
> salvation', Christ, as the power of God, has one horn, one common
> power with the Father.

Hm-m-m. A little complicated for the masses, yet a good explanation, he thought.

Enmeshed in ancient writings about the One Word of God and the One Horn of Christ, with aged scrolls, bound psalters, and missives covered with faded brown ink, he jumped, startled when the dark voice of Canon Hugon floated across the room.

"Are you looking for something in particular? Perhaps I can help?"

Hugon had been seen around the palace so infrequently that D'Anduze had almost forgotten the Canon was staying there.

"I'm seeking knowledge about unicorns for a sermon this Sunday. I need to make the townspeople understand that a unicorn horn can be dangerous if not properly worshipped."

"The horn is indeed dangerous. Its power can make people act in ways they would never ordinarily behave. There will be those who lose their way." *Like you.* Hugon lifted his black eyebrows, his round eyes looked down his beaked nose at him. The swollen lump on his neck poked through his beard. "I have a suggestion. Try an ancient Greek text titled Physiologus. St. Epiphanius transcribed it from the writings of King Solomon."

St. Peter's balls, his breath could keep Satan away. D'Anduze held his breath and looked over some scrolls. "Physiologus. Here it is." He had to exhale.

Hugon bent over D'Anduze's shoulder as he was unfortunately forced to inhale.

However, the Canon was correct: the Physiologus was very informative. When he saw the Archbishop beginning to write, Hugon quietly left the library.

More facts about unicorns were in Pliny the Elder's *Naturalis Historiae*, and in a rare copy of Hildegard of Bingen's *Physica* which he had bought from a Rhadanite Jewish merchant passing through Narbonne on his way from Augsburg to India.

As the light faded, he leaned back on his creaking chair, gray eyes reflecting the dusk. *I really want to sell that horn to the King, even if it's a fake.*

• • •

News of a sacred unicorn horn at Saint Paul-Serge brought an onslaught of pilgrims from all around the region, even from as far as Barcelona. The Via Domitia was almost impassable. Merchants sold passion-crazed pilgrims small tin unicorn heads for the price of silver ones; farmers charged a high price just to allow families to sleep on their fields. The alms boxes at the church had to be emptied every hour.

It was Sunday, and once again, in full regalia, the Archbishop stood in front of the huge crowd packed into the old cathedral. Instructed to keep order, dozens of armed Templars, chain-mail hoods hanging like metal hair over broad shoulders, stood in the apse like Soldiers of God on a battlefield.

The unicorn horn rested on the altar surrounded by candles and flowers, its jewels sending out sparks of fire in the light.

Rogenvaldr had not wanted to attend church, but William had pushed him.

"You don't have the money yet. What's taking so long. Is this her way of keeping you here?"

Rogenvaldr had shrugged, but here he was, kneeling in front of the altar next to Ermengard, who had refused cushions, again. *This stone floor is killing my knees.*

Bored, he contemplated the wooden figure of Jesus on the huge black cross hanging from the ceiling above the altar. The flesh was painted a pale ivory, with impressively realistic rivulets of blood running down his arms and chest from actual iron nails hammered into his hands. This Jesus did not, as was usual, look down in sorrow. His gaze was turned upwards to his father in heaven. *Is it for guidance?* Rogenvaldr mused, *or is he also just begging for escape from this overdone papal farce. If I had only known. . .*

"People of Narbonne! Fellow Christians!" The Archbishop spoke in his most thunderous voice. "Be forewarned! The presence of a unicorn horn here is not to be taken lightly. The whole town is now under the eye of God; you must be exceptionally virtuous and generous to the church. For this church is the only thing that stands between you and the fury of the unicorn: a unicorn that has had its horn broken off and sold to the highest bidder—a sacrilege! It is being sold by the sons and daughters of Mammon! I bear witness, the fate of Sodom and Gomorrah may befall us!"

Fear sent a sudden shudder through the crowd. "I'm leaving—let me out," cried one man as he pushed his way to the door. "Before God smites me dead!"

Ermengard became flushed with fury. *How dare he?*

"But first, we must learn to recognize the animal if he appears. The Roman philosopher Pliny actually saw one and described it thus:

> The most fell and furious beast of all other,
> is the Licorne or Monocerous:
> his bodie resembles a horse,
> his head a stag,
> his feet an elephant, his tail a boar;
> he loweth after a hideous manner;
> one horn hath he in the midst of his
> forehead bearing out three feet in length . . .

"This is a dangerous and ruthless animal that will kill those who abandon humility and penitence. Yet, it has one weakness which, if exploited, allows it to be captured and maimed. Saint Epiphanius tells us how it's done:

> All the natural world arises from God's nature—including
> the unicorn, a beast that embodies the Passion of Christ and
> the One Word of God. It is a fleet and strong animal,
> considered impossible to capture.

> Yet it can be caught, but only one way. Just as Jesus,
> the One Son of God was put into Mary's virgin womb
> and born to save us, one must entice the unicorn to put
> its horn onto a virgin's lap. To do this you must tie a
> true virgin to a tree in the forest. There she waits, alone
> in the woods until the unicorn spies her and approaches.
> Gently it puts its horn onto her lap. The virgin grasps the
> horn, and strokes it until the unicorn is fast asleep. Now
> the hunter can trap it! But if the beast hears the hunter and
> wakes up too soon, beware the horn— it is long and hard
> and a fierce weapon!

"And now we are here with a horn obtained by stealth. Think of the magic available to the person who has it in his possession. If poison is put into the drink of a cup made out of the horn, the cup will sweat, and the poison will be rendered neutral. If the horn is dipped into brackish water, the pond will turn sweet. A unicorn's body has miraculous healing powers: egg yolk and powdered unicorn liver brushed on skin will cure pustules, and, with proper prayers to Christ, leprosy! Clothes made from his hide will protect you from plague. Rub a balm made of sheep's fat and powdered horn on a birthing woman's belly and the child will be a sound and well son! It is the miracle of Christ!"

The Archbishop had been shouting at the top of his lungs, now he lowered his voice to a harsh whisper. "Pray for redemption—pray that God will forgive you for killing his son once again. For surely someday soon, the unicorn will appear in our midst and demand the return of the horn."

He stared at the crowd, moving his eyes from one side of the church to the other.

I don't believe this! What's he talking about? Jesus help me. Rogenvaldr was speechless, completely aghast at all this belief of miracles attributed to the horn. This was a Christianity from another world.

Suddenly a gasp went through the crowd. A black cat, totally accustomed to large crowds, was attracted to the strange object lying on the flat stone that was his bed many a night. He jumped up onto the altar and sniffed the horn, smelling the narwhal. Tapping it with one black paw, meowing at the townspeople, it jumped off, slowly going on its way to the sacristy. One could practically hear the soldiers' chain mail shaking as it walked past them.

By all the Saints, God is truly with me! D'Anduze, smiling to himself, decided that now was exactly the time for the benediction. Afterwards, the congregation rushed out of the church in a disorderly mass, faces tight, discarded tin unicorns under their feet.

Rogenvaldr was in no mood for romance. "I'm going back to the villa tonight."

"I understand," Ermengard said sadly, watching his back as he left.

Locking their doors in fear, old townswomen began to murmur. "We didn't kill the unicorn. It was that heathen Viking who did it. He's a Christ killer, no matter what he says about being on crusade. If something evil happens, it'll be his fault. And he's weaseling himself into our Viscountess's affections too, that's for sure. Oh, by Holy Mary's blood, this will end badly."

Hugon had listened undisturbed to the Archbishop's rantings. He was following the flame of his own mission. Having earlier divested himself of his Canon's habit, now dressed like a common worker, he wandered freely, listening to whispered words. *I must find the heretics. Especially those women with their daughters who don't always cross themselves and show no fear of the horn. It is time to act.*

• • •

Arnaud Gerardi left the church in a foul mood. He had pushed through the crowd from one end to the other yet couldn't find his daughters. By now he was convinced they had run away. Kicking aside a large rat, he turned right towards the seedy taverns of the Carreira de les Bracariá. Pushing through a thick studded door with no sign, he loped down worn stone stairs, into a dark tavern so ancient that the kitchen must have fed Domitian's legions.

From the corner came the music of Hopla the Goliard, a tonsured former cleric turned itinerant minstrel, singing some ribald verses. An outcast of the church, he lived the life of a vulgar performing vagrant, living on the coins of charity and sold gossip.

Crossing the slanting flagstone floor, Arnaud sat down at a knife-scared wooden table. His friends were already busy drinking: Feris de Roci, a merchant who rented a cloth-fulling mill just up the river, and Piers Miro, a salt merchant who had grown wealthy transporting the "white gold" from Narbonne up north. Without being asked, a hairy arm plunked an ale down in front of him.

Bleary from too much ale, the conversation soon turned to the usual complaints about taxes. Gerardi was particularly harsh on the Viscountess.

"Satan take her taxes!" Gerardi growled, leaning on arms thick-muscled from hauling stone. At the naming of the Unholy One, the other two crossed themselves and spat over their right shoulders. The quarryman's bulbous hands banged on the table with stubby fingers. "Now she's taxing any old, buried statues I find. Not worth selling anymore; I just break them up for gravel. How am I to earn a living?" He coughed through dust-filled lungs. "Now, because of her, my two daughters have disappeared. Just like that! I send them to the palace to find work, just as she promised, and they never come back. If I ever find them . . .!"

"He's right," Miro interrupted him. "Between the tithes to the church, the road tolls, and the salt thieves, my profits are getting less and less." A whiney, lanky fop, Miro was oblivious to the jewelry he wore that attested to his lie. Thinking about his new mistress, he ran long, painted fingernails through his black hair, oiled and curled up at the ends.

"The mill rent went up, as did the river tax—and now I have to give a share of the earnings to my uncle because he's sick," de Roci groused into his wooden tankard. His squinty eyes, topped by eyebrows that looked like two millipedes crawling over his nose, glared bleakly over it. "And did you know that our Viscountess is giving that Viking one-thousand Almoravid Moribatani pure gold coins?"

"For what? To ransom Narbonne and make them leave without burning us to the ground?" asked Gerardi.

"No, you ignorant fool. To thank him for the unicorn horn he gave her as a 'gift'. Some gift!"

"One-thousand Moribatani? Are you sure?"

"Yes. Of course, I'm sure. I myself saw the entry in the money ledgers of the bank registry. The bankers of Narbonne speak of nothing else."

"I'd sure want to get hold of one of those horns myself," Gerardi growled.

"You're crazy!' the others said, looking at him warily.

"A dangerous mission—but one I'd gladly attempt. Look at these arms—no unicorn could get away from me. I'd just punch it in the nose, break off the horn, and make it run for its life! Gauzia's still a virgin—where in the name of Satan is she? She'd be perfect to trap it."

His friends were in a stupor, but his words began to frighten them out of it. Rising, staggering heavily, they left as quickly as they could manage.

The quarryman just sat there, too miserable to go anywhere.

A bearded man who had been sitting at the next table came over and put a bony hand on Gerardi's shoulder. Startled at being touched, he looked up.

Speaking in a weaselly tone, the hooded stranger said: "Perhaps we might speak, now that your friends have left?"

The man's hawk-like face had black eyes that grabbed Gerardi's attention like talons. Hidden by a beard, one side of the man's mouth was turned up in an attempt at friendliness. Buried in the depths of the hood, it was difficult to make out his features clearly.

"Another drink for my friend here!" Hugon called to the tavern keeper. Uninvited he sat down on the bench beside Gerardi.

"And who might you be?" The quarryman was suspicious.

"I am Ramon D'Amenara, a tradesman recently of Barcelona."

By the balls of Saint Peter, Ramon D'Amenara, your breath smells like the devil himself is sitting here. Roman's next words gave him a shock.

"So, do you really think you could catch a unicorn?"

I don't care if he is the devil, as long he makes me rich. "Of course I could. You have one to catch?"

CHAPTER 19

My Lady hears grass rustling
as the pale Unicorn comes to her.
The twisted horn is laid on her golden lap.
Distracted, he doesn't see the guile in her eyes.
Gently she strokes his horn,
The touch of her fingers is soothing.
Soon she will capture him.

— *Countess Beatritz de Dente, trobaritz*

The heat in the back garden wilted the green leaves of the fig tree into silver, yet Garsend didn't care. Black curls fell out of her yellow headscarf, clinging to damp cheeks as she ran around in a futile effort to catch wary birds. A bright blue one fluttered just out of reach of her fingers over the stone wall. Frowning, she stopped short in over-heated disappointment; it was forbidden to leave the garden alone.

A dove cooed softly from the other side. *Oh, a dove. I so adore doves.* The dove cooed again, more softly. *I must catch it!*

She glanced at her nurse who, bored with the incessant bird-catching, dozed open-mouthed against the base of a marble statue of Orpheus playing his lyre. *Good—just for a few minutes. I'll come right back in again and play with my dove.* She lifted the wooden bar across the door, put it softly down on the dirt and ran out into the olive grove. *Now, where is it?*

Gnarly brown trunks and twisted branches turned around each other, hiding her from view as she jumped over roots and fell forward onto her knees into the red soil.

"Coo-o."

Garsend looked up and ran towards fluttering white wings.

A rough hand grabbed her tightly, snatched her sideways, and put a dank bag over her head. She tried to scream but felt pressure on her throat. Everything went black as she was lifted up and carried away.

Azalais, Garsend's mother, found the nurse asleep. "Where's my daughter? Oh God in Heaven, the gate is open! You old cow, you were supposed to watch her!" Frantic, she ran out into the grove crying out at the top of her lungs:

"Garsend—Garsend, you naughty child! Come here this instant— you're too old for this behavior!"

Azalais ran among the trees, ducking low branches, looking up into possible hiding places. *Mother Mary! Help me find her . . .*

There was no sign of her child. The panting mother ran into the house and came back with her raging father. The nurse was cowering in a corner. The father picked her up and threw her roughly across the garden. She hit the statue so hard that it fell off its base and crack into large chunks. The smiling head rolled off into the thyme, to lie there with its blind eyes staring at the sky.

• • •

Rising from the flat plain north of Narbonne was Le Montaigne Noir. A rugged rock of a mountain, pine and beech roots barely clung to its black cliffs; the garrigue covered sharp edges with its prickly shrubs. Women healers scoured the dark crevices of its vertical slopes for secret plants that could heal or kill.

A shadowy chestnut forest hugged the base of the mountain. No one would dare enter without intoning a protective prayer. In the center of the forest, a clear waterfall ran down a narrow gorge to a pool encircled by tall standing stones. Behind the falls was a crack in the rock, known by the ancients to be an entrance to the underworld; through it the dead emerged and returned.

The ancients had built a stone altar here, its weather-worn edges long ago crumbled away, the barely visible outlines of a bull and a grimacing god-face bulging on its pedestal. The dry white bones of a large, strange bird-shaped animal lay on the altar. It had huge claws on its front feet and horrible hooked claws on the back ones. No one knew where it had come from. Some said it was from deep in the crevice behind the waterfall, others said it was a dead demon. The bones of sacrificed cats, roosters, and rats were scattered around, their tiny skulls grimacing in anger.

A single pomegranate tree thick with ripe fruit stood in the center of the clearing.

Hugon, waiting impatiently at the edge of the forest, looked out from under the leaves of a tree. *I hope I picked right. Yes, I'm sure I did. But he's taking his time.*

Gerardi had argued with him. He didn't want to go into that forest. "It's evil in those woods. There are dark spirits wandering. Why take the girl there?"

"Because that's where you can trap a unicorn! Where else would one live? I spoke to a man who saw one run into those woods two days ago. He tried to chase it, but it was too fast. The fool didn't know you can't chase it—you have to trap it with a virgin. That's why we leave her there. Just kidnap the girl I told you to get, and I'll prepare everything for you. All you have to do is hide in the bushes."

"W-what do I do then?"

"Just watch and stay alert," Hugon snapped. "When the beast puts its head in her lap it will fall asleep. Grab it! With those powerful arms of yours it won't have a chance of escape. Break off the horn and run away. Then we release the girl. I have found an apothecary in Montpelier who will grind up the horn so we can sell the powder. You'll be a rich man! Isn't that what you want?"

"But Ramon, what if it kills her?"

Hugon was losing his patience with the man. "Why would it kill her when all it wants to do put its head in her lap?" He spoke with as much calm as he could in the face of such stubbornness. "Do you want the money or not? I can find someone else if you're too much of a coward."

"No, no. I'll do it. I'll do it."

Finally he saw Gerardi, carrying a bundle across his back, come walking tentatively into the forest. His eyes were darting from side to side, as if a demon was going to jump on him from a tree branch. "Are you sure we should be in here?"

"Don't be such a coward. I've been preparing everything for two days and seen nothing. Follow me."

Hugon had cleared the bones off the altar so that Gerardi wouldn't run when he saw them. They climbed over a low, circular fence made

of knotted branches that he had built around the pomegranate tree.
When they spilled Garsend out of the bag she was unconscious. She
didn't move when they tied her to the tree with a long hemp rope
around her waist.

"Hold her while I tie her wrists."

Hugon noticed him lingering too long. "Enough! She's not for you.
She's for the unicorn. Remember that. Now go and hide under those
gorse bushes to wait. It's nearly dark, it will come soon. I'm leaving."

Crouching under the bushes, staring at the girl, the quarryman's
mind wandered to his daughters again. *Where could they have gone that
I can't find them?* There was a cry from inside the circle.

Garsend's eyes had opened. Shivering, barefoot in her thin chemise,
she stared up at the rattling leaves of the pomegranate tree. *Why do my
wrists hurt?* In confused horror, she saw the raw skin of her wrists
tied by a rope, felt the twisted hemp tied around her waist. *God in
heaven, that rope hurts! Where am I?* Looped around the tree trunk,
the rope got tighter as she struggled. Ripe pomegranates thumped to
the ground.

"Mama, Mama, please come get me! Help me! Someone, please
come!" Clumsily she tried to untie the rope around the tree, tripped on
its roots, ran in tighter and tighter circles, and finally collapsed to the
ground. Crying, she struggled onto her knees, terrified.

Am I going to die now? Whispering hoarsely, bending her head down
to her bloody wrists, she tried to recite the consolamentum: "Do you
renounce the harlot Catholic Church with its sham baptisms, worship
of earthly wealth, with its, with its. . .?" but she was too frightened to
remember the words. *Do I really want to die? No, no I don't. Death isn't
supposed to be like this. It's not joyous at all!*

"Help me! Someone please come untie me! Father, mother, where
are you. . .?"

The shuddering child's black curls brushed against scratched knees
slowly sinking down into the mulch of decayed leaves and poison-
topped mushrooms.

Garsend heard field mice rustling under nearby ferns, squirrels
cracking twigs. *Satan has come for me. I've sinned, and now I am going
to live in Hell forever. Please God, forgive me for my sins of omission,
for speaking badly to mother. Oh, I beg of you, forgive me . . .*

The still, warm air carried the sweet scent of wild strawberries and pale five-petaled swallowwort. As if warned of something coming, frightened rabbits crushed dry leaves as they hopped quickly past her to hide in their warrens. A sudden damp, salty wind blew the scent of oregano into the clearing. It chilled her damp neck, worsening the shivering.

Sitting in the bushes Gerardi's thoughts rattled around in his head. *I wish she'd stop that sobbing and praying. Will she die? No. Ramon said she won't. And anyway, I don't care. It's a lot of money—I'll be rich. I'll buy a young slave.*

Her voice had dropped to a low murmur, and he began to doze off. His head snapped up when he heard the sound of hoof-beats approaching. *The ground is shaking! God in heaven help me—it's a large white beast with a horn!* It flashed by on his right.

A sudden pain in the back of his head made everything black.

Garsend heard the hooves pounding and looked up. She barely saw a white shadow come from behind the tree and jump over the fence. *There's someone*—a hand grabbed her hair and pulled her head back. There was sharp, intense burning in her chest as her wide eyes recognized her attacker.

He left the small, slight body, its shift torn to shreds in an angry fury, lying face down on the tangled, blood-soaked vines.

The ripe pomegranates in the tree above dripped sweet, red juice onto the bloody earth and hoof prints below.

CHAPTER 20

As is the mother, so is the daughter.
—Ezekiel, 16:44, King James Bible

The word went out that Garsend, Raymond D'Ouvelhan's daughter, had disappeared. The frantic parents had assembled friends and neighbors to scour the neighborhood.

Her distraught father was pacing back and forth in Ermengard's solar. "Could it have been slavers? Or pirates? How could this happen to us in our own home!"

"When did you see her last?" Ermengard asked as gently as possible.

"She was in the backyard with her nurse. The incompetent fool fell asleep, only waking when my wife began to scream. The gate was open, and Garsend was gone! She's nowhere to be found—please, send some soldiers to search outside the walls. Oh my poor daughter—." He fell into a chair, wiping tears from his eyes.

"Yes, we will send out the military," Ermengard said, *though if she's beyond the walls, I doubt there is any hope.*

She turned to Beatritz and beckoned her aside. "Beatritz, go now to Raymond's home and comfort Azalais. While you are there, I want you to have a look around. Keep me informed of what you find. You are a keen observer with a logical mind. A woman might understand the subtitles of behavior that a man would overlook. Question the maid. Examine the garden and olive grove. Look for anything that might hint at an answer. As a widow and trobaritz you can ask questions in a way I cannot. The law permits me only the decision of torture and death after I am presented with the facts."

"Surely, with God's help I will be of service," Beatritz answered in her low, calm voice. *The girl is dead and with God. Be joyful.*

"Take Thibaut De Plaigne with you."

194

"But I don't want him to. . ."

"You need protection. Those are my orders."

"Yes, my Lady." *Just what I need. That old love-starved fart with me. Why couldn't she have just sent a soldier along?* Shedding her linen slippers, and donning outdoor shoes made of stout fibers, she strode to the door, looked sternly at her daughter. "You stay here. And go nowhere alone. Take a servant if you have to relieve yourself. Have I made myself clear, Alais?"

• • •

The d'Ouvelhan house was across the river in the southern part of the Bourg. The family lived near their olive mills in a wealthy neighborhood of stone houses near the church of Saint Marie-Lamourguier. Behind the homes were old olive trees growing in rich, red soil. It was the only large grove that remained inside the walls because it was owned by the church. The mills produced the fine "Òli d'Oliva de Narbonne" favored throughout Occitania. Ramon owned three of the mills and would be seen as a rich target for a kidnapping. But no person had, as yet, sent a ransom note.

Beatritz, aware of the secret heresy of the mother, was worried that this could be the beginning of an ongoing blackmail ruse. It would be impossible to speak to Azalais in front of De Plaigne. He was a virulent heretic killer, having himself once lit the flames to burn some Bons Hommes martyrs in the town square of Minerve.

When they arrived, Azalais could be heard sobbing upstairs in the solar. Beatritz decided to speak to her later.

The house was built in the more modern style with the garden in the back instead of confined in the center. They walked through the long central hallway with its flowery silk hangings, Egyptian style chairs, and Greek-patterned mosaic floors. Through an open door she noticed a water clock in a room with actual books among the scrolls. Outside the rear of the house was a kitchen and a modest, elegant garden enclosed by a stone wall. Looking at the still open gate Beatritz mused *there must be something here to help me unravel this.*

An old marble basin, cheerfully bubbling cool water, stood on a flower mosaic against one side. The sun fanned the leafy shadows of two date trees across a pathway of old, interwoven, red Roman bricks. A broken statue of Orpheus had its head lying in some herbs. Vegetables covered with white gauze were growing in plots under an apricot and orange tree. Ivy grew on a kitchen that had its own oven—truly a luxury. As was usual, the enclosing wall was built of stones and marble quarried from the ruins that littered the hillside. The bar that would have locked the gate was lying in the dirt. Either the child opened it to let someone in, or someone could have lain on the wall and pulled it off with a hook. *Could the nurse, promised her share of the ransom, be part of the scheme?*

Accompanied by De Plaigne, she went down to the storerooms to speak to the nurse. Locked up with bags of grain, she was hysterical. If the child wasn't found alive, she would be thrown alive into the Aude River in one of those bags to punish her carelessness. Deep, breathless sobs made it difficult to get any information out of her.

Beatritz squatted down. Her sharp blue eyes frightened the nurse to even greater tears. "Was the gate closed or open when you fell asleep?"

"My Lady, the d-door was closed, I swear by the H-holy Mother!" she sputtered through lips wet with tears and spittle. "P-please, I didn't see anyone open the door. We were alone in the garden. I woke up when I heard the mistress calling! Mother Mary, help me!" Clasping her hands she began to pray, swaying back and forth.

Beatritz didn't believe her and knocked the hands down. "Pray later. Was the statue broken before or after you woke up?"

"Raymond hit me so hard I fell and knocked it over," she wailed.

Here's an opportunity to speak with Azalais alone. "Sir De Plaigne, could you please continue this interrogation while I go upstairs to speak to the mother?"

The nurse's screams followed her all the way up the stairs to the solar. It was the only way—she had to speak to Azalais alone. The mother was lying prone on some cushions, her eyes bloodshot and squinting.

Beatritz leaned down to her, embraced her and whispered, "Does anyone suspect you? Have you been followed? Remember what Henry warned us about. . ."

"Not one person has made me suspicious. I have been *so* careful. I go to church, I cross myself, I stay at home. I went to a wedding and actually ate a little meat because someone was staring at me when I avoided it. No, it's something else. Slavers, or pirates, or a ransom. Oh, Beatritz, I so pray she wasn't tortured and had a good death!"

"Yes, so do I. But you must remain vigilant. This may endanger all of our children."

Back in the garden again, outside the gate, Beatritz began to look around the wall. *Hm-m-m, a high pile of rocks against it. From atop the rocks someone could have easily gained the top of the wall. Then, they could have seen the sleeping nurse and child, have opened the gate from above and grabbed the girl. But surely that would have woken up the nurse. They must have enticed the girl out into the olive grove. But, in heavens name, how? I must check amongst the trees. It must have happened somewhere near the house.*

Dark green olive leaves rustled sharply under her shoes. Flickering shadows disguised gnarled roots. The air smelled of fallen ripe olives piled up everywhere. The hard fruit crunched under her feet. Stooping, she picked up a white piece of cloth. *What's this? I'll keep it.* Beneath the branches of a tree so ancient that its branches hugged the ground, there were crushed olives and footprints of hobnailed boots—and a shred of yellow silk. *So, he enticed her here . . . and grabbed her. And the white cloth?*

The screams of the nurse were silent. De Plaigne was waiting for Beatritz in the house.

"It's no use. Might as well just throw her in the river," he said matter-of-factly.

• • •

"This was carefully planned," Beatritz reported to Ermengard. "And I don't know if the nurse was involved."

"I've ordered soldiers to collect all the townsmen for a search. Every house, every tavern. I've sent Raymond with them. It's no use him sitting around here crying."

As she left, Beatritz turned her blue eyes to Ermengard, "Corruption rules our sinful lives on earth. We are all evil until we shed this earthly body."

Ermengard looked at her, turned away and crossed herself.

• • •

A hunter tracking a boar found the awful scene. Unaware of being followed, the pig had trotted into the forest for a meal of chestnuts. Ignoring his fears, first crossing himself three times, the man followed it as far as the clearing, where he saw the girl's body. Knowing there was a reward, he raced out of the woods to the palace.

As a result, Beatritz, to her distress, had been forced to play the charade of Royal Inquirer.

"Sir De Plaigne," Ermengerd ordered. "Take the Countess to the woods and find out what happened. The child is the daughter of a dear friend, and that this could happen in my city causes me great distress."

The knight had brought Beatritz here against his better judgement. Her tall, willowy blondness, and renewed chastity, was that of a female figure beyond his reach. It didn't matter that she had a child; chastity was a renewable vow made by many older nuns. His code of chivalry required an object of love and desire that was unrequited; she was the perfect woman for him to worship. The knight had no concept that, to her, he was just a reborn, debased soul.

The two of them now stood in the center of the circular fence. The soldiers who had accompanied them, afraid of evil demons, kept their distance. Beatritz's wicker shoes were soggy with blood. The rope was a red snake winding itself around the tree trunk before slithering into the grass.

Garsend lay face down, her half-naked body crushing the blood-soaked ivy. The shredded shift revealed lash-marks on her back, as if a scourging whip had been used.

Beatritz turned to the knight. "These lash marks on her back—were they done before or after death?"

He sputtered at the unexpected question. "I-I beg your pardon?" *What does this woman think she is doing asking me a question like that?*

"The lashes—you've had experience with torture. Were they done before or after death?"

He took a closer look. "There is no blood running from the wounds. She was killed first."

So, even without the consolamentum, she had a good death. She is with God.

Beatritz tried not to let all the blood distract her. "There are hoof prints everywhere. They come and go, jump over the fence, remain a while in the circle, then jump over the fence again and leave. Observe! One rear hoof has its shoe nailed on crookedly. And why are there no human footprints? I'm trying to understand, why did the kidnapper bring her here? The way this is set up— the circle, a virgin tied to a tree, makes me think he was trying to catch a unicorn. So why kill her? He needed her alive."

"Turn her over onto her back," she commanded a soldier. De Plaigne winced to see her bend down to examine the wound under the girl's small, white breasts. It had the appearance of a large black almond. "Ah, this is how she died. This stabbing was made with a long, thick object that came to a point. It could have been any animal horn, not necessarily that of a unicorn." She stood up. "Please cover her up and take her home."

Beatritz was trying to think in a logical manner. *Everyone fears the return of the beast, yet here was someone trying to capture it. Everyone knows about the gold she gave Lord Rogenvaldr for the horn. The kidnapper must have been hiding nearby, watching the girl, then hoping to snap the horn off to sell it. Who would be so craven?* "Search the bushes nearby."

They found the still unconscious Gerardi lying twenty feet away under a bush, a bloody gash on the back of his head.

"Take him to the horreum," Beatritz snapped to the soldiers. "The best place to question him properly is in the old Roman tunnels. He must be interrogated but instruct the jailor not to torture him until I arrive." Startled, they nodded obedience.

Word of the manner of Garsend's death spread quickly. Everyone knew how to catch a unicorn; it was written in the scriptures.

People jeered and yelled as Gerardi was dragged unconscious to prison. He was thrown into a cell in the thousand-year-old underground army grain storage vaults. The Roman warehouse was one of the few remaining ancient buildings still in use. Below ground, its storerooms occupied an entire square block within the city walls. Just like the Romans, Narbonne rented out space to the Arab, Jewish, and Egyptian merchants. Under ground, its tunnels wandered under other buildings as far as the ramparts and under the Via Domitia. Its brick walls, three-feet thick, had only one entrance whose classical portico had collapsed in an earthquake years ago. But the horreum itself had survived intact, for when the residents of Narbonne had dug out the rubble from the stairs, they found the underground chambers still usable, and perfect for a jail.

Beatritz, with the ever present De Plaigne by her side, arrived later. She had never been here before. The steep, curved stone stairs that led down to the underground maze of dark vaults were broken and uneven. The wall she was leaning on to support herself was dank under her hand.

At the bottom, a heavy Roman gate made of flat iron bars was opened by a flat-nosed old soldier. They found themselves at the junction of three tunnels built of rough stone arches, each lit by a few oil lamps placed into the same niches used by the Romans.

The dark tunnels felt endless, smelling of mold and old clay. In her summer shift, Beatritz shivered at the unexpectedly frigid temperature.

De Plaigne was very uncomfortable. "Who knows what unfettered spirits of dead souls are flying around in here?"

Still, if the Countess entered, he would bravely follow. The Romans had built everything to last—even the floor, made of interwoven bricks and cobblestones, was still flat and even. Sounds echoed from the distant left, and the soldier nodded his grizzled head in that direction. Beatritz braced herself and headed forward deep into the dark until, at last, they found Gerardi chained to the wall in one of the iron-barred rooms that lined the tunnel.

Gombal the Jailor, limping around on a leather-wrapped wooden stump, was an ex-soldier who had lost half of his left leg in Ermengard's battle of Tortosa. Just in the process of dousing Gerardi with freezing water, he looked up startled as they walked into the open cell.

The prisoner was shivering uncontrollably. The sight of tongs heating up in some coals to be used for pulling out his toenails made him babble incoherently. His heavily muscled arms and back were rubbed raw.

Beatritz was livid. Fearing for her own daughter, she began to question him. Gombal seemed ready enough to tear the virgin killer apart piece by piece.

"I-I-I-d-didn't kill her, I swear. The u-unicorn did it. I s-saw it—it rushed past me. Its hooves must have hit my head as it galloped by." The gash on his head was leaving a bloody stain on the floor.

"What were you doing there if you didn't kill her?"

"I-I was just watching her, waiting for the unicorn to come so I could get its horn. I k-kidnapped her, but I didn't kill her. I beg of you, on my mother's soul, I'm telling the truth."

"How did you kidnap her?"

"I went to the back of the house and made a pile of stones to look over the wall. The child was running around chasing birds as the nurse slept. I hid behind a tree and called like a dove. Then she opened the gate herself and came running out. I waved a white cloth like the wings of a dove and when she ran to look, I grabbed her." The dry, deep crevices in his face were dripping sweat now. "The unicorn killed her! She must not have been a virgin—she was a whore, a young whore! This is all her fault . . ."

Beatritz lost control. Grabbing the hot tongs, she slapped them onto his mouth. He screamed in agony.

De Plaigne was shocked.

"How did you build that fence around her?" Beatritz demanded.

"I didn't. He did it," muttered Gerardi through burnt lips.

Now were getting somewhere. "Who?"

"The stranger from the tavern. He persuaded me, told me what to do. Said 'bring the virgin', told me what girl to kidnap. We were to split the gold after selling the horn powder." Bloody drool was falling down his chin. "She was supposed to stay safe, go back home."

"And you believed him, you fool? Describe him."

"Tall, thin, grey beard. He was wearing a hood, so I couldn't see his face very well. It was dark. But the evil words he spoke stank from his mouth."

Why does that remind me of something? Beatritz was trying to remember.

"He called himself Ramon de Seville, but he spoke with a Frankish accent." Gerardi's head fell forward.

Beatritz turned to Gombal. "Don't let him die, I'm warning you. And he's not to speak to anyone else. The Viscountess will hear of it if anything happens to him."

De Plaigne followed her out. "Now what?" *It's useless to tell her what to do. The Viscountess told me to guard her, so that's what I'll do. And I will give my life to save her if I must.*

Beatritz didn't answer. She was busy rubbing her freezing arms to warm them up.

• • •

Carved shutters, closed against the heat, threw arabesque shadows on Ermengard's face. "What have you found out? And who was responsible?"

She threw out rapid questions that Beatritz was unable to answer.

Beatritz was thinking aloud. "The real question is: why did it happen? At first, it appears to be the result of greed gone wrong. If the value of a unicorn horn was Gerardi's motive for the kidnapping, then why would he kill her? Or, if as he says, he didn't, then who did? For what purpose? I really can't believe that an angry unicorn stabbed her." Yet, other thoughts kept intruding into her mind. *Surely it has nothing to do with heresy. She was just a child. It's not possible. But it was planned—not a chance murder. And why was the unicorn part of it?*

Ermengard stirred anxiously. "This will give rise to all sorts of fears about the horn. Pilgrims will not come here to worship if there is any hint of wrath associated with it. If they think God will strike them dead, or a unicorn is out for revenge, they will stay away. I've just been informed that the Archbishop has removed it from St. Paul-Serge and put it into his donjon for safety. What does he plan to do with it? Pilgrims are coming to see it. If the purpose of this killing is to make it an object of fear, rather than veneration, who benefits from that?"

"You would be held responsible for any terrible events," Beatritz warned. "As would Rogenvaldr. You have enemies who want to take control of Narbonne, like the Count of Toulouse. People are already calling the killing 'the wrath of the horned beast'; we have to persuade them it's a ruse."

"I don't believe it!" Ermengard heaved a pillow across the room, smashing a luminescent green vase, leaving its purple orchid to float on the wet floor. "I just *know* a real unicorn would never do this, it's not possible.' She hugged her knees. "They are gentle creatures!"

How can she be so naïve? "Wait, I just remembered something." Beatritz pictured the body lying in the mess of hoofprints in the dark soil. "There were horseshoes on the hooves! Why would a unicorn use horseshoes? And one was crooked, as if it became loose and had then been carelessly fixed. It must be a horse, it must. Tomorrow I must go and find out if anyone has recently purchased a white horse, and if a farrier has fixed shoes on it. At least, it's a beginning."

CHAPTER 21

Henry the Monk inflicts evils every day on the church...
He is a ravening wolf in the guise of a sheep...
Churches without people,
people without priests...
Christians without Christ,
the grace of baptism denied...
Oh, unhappy people!
                                    —Bernard of Clairvaux, Letter, 1145

Archbishop D'Anduze, hands clasped behind his back, was admiring the horn now in the treasury of his palace. *Oh, no!* Hugon's dry, musty odor preceded the Canon as he quietly crept into the room to stand beside the Archbishop. *He smells like a crypt with too many cats living in it.*

"How did you manage to attain it?" Hugon murmured.

D'Anduze took a step away. "Fear. Saint Paul-Serge is full of overwhelming fear. I persuaded the sacristan to bring it here until the death of that girl is forgotten. He can't have forty soldiers there all the time to guard it. A vault needs to be built there. In the meantime it's safe here. He can exhibit it when necessary. In any event I have plans for it. All for the glory of God." *Hah! He has no idea of the huge amount I will ask the King of France to pay for it.*

"Good. For I have plans, too, also for the glory of God." Hugon left as quietly as he had entered. Today he felt cleansed and alert. During the days of hysteria after the girl's death, he had sequestered himself in his dark chamber with one candle, praying to his scrawny Christ on the Cross for strength.

Fasting for three days, he had ordered Godfrey to scourge him with thorn-embedded leather straps each morning and evening. When he felt

203

himself purged of evil thoughts and the usual arousing feelings, he had taken some bone broth and bread.

Now, dressed like an itinerant monk, he was again ready to prowl the town to unveil the unmistakable signs of a heretic: refusing meat, linen or straw shoes, a gathering of people that was not raucous, or someone preaching outside the walls at a farm or private home.

What he found was appalling. *The evidence is right in front of my eyes. Holy Saint Peter! Ermengard's city is rife with heresy, yet she appears to have no idea of its presence—even in her palace! And that Norseman she is whoring with—he has to leave the city. I'll let the Archbishop deal with that. I know he wants him gone. And he's planning something, but I don't care what.*

While roaming through the ancient necropolis around Saint Paul-Serge, he had found an unlocked, hidden entrance to the tomb of Saint Paul in the crypt below the church floor. Later that night, cold air chilled his bones when he crept through the door. He could hear the nails of scuttling paws rushing to hide under stones. A flame in the filigreed oil lamp hanging over the marble sarcophagus cast a dim red light on Hugon's bony face, deepening his eye sockets so that he appeared as an apparition of Satan come to gaze on the Saint's remains.

Withdrawing a candle from his pocket, he lit it with the oil lamp and carefully found his way up the ragged steps to the interior of the church. Silently settling down for the night in a corner behind one of the enormous columns, he blew out the candle.

• • •

First light found him praying amongst the many women who had arrived for matins. Nobody paid any attention to the monk in the baggy brown cassock and hood falling over his face. Most women came with their children. He made a mental note of one young mother who, daughter in tow, left the church without kneeling and crossing herself.

Them. I will follow them, he decided.

Ponzia de Coumic, thirty-year-old widow of Jean de Coumic, and her daughter Fabrisse, a nervous twelve-year-old holding her mother's hand, walked briskly along. Ponzia was on her way to break her fast at the home of Adalais d'Ouvelhan. Not only did she want to comfort her Bonnes Filles friend, but she also brought a spoken message from Henry the Monk that set a time and place for a secret meeting with him that afternoon.

Hugon waited patiently in the same olive grove that Garsend had been snapped from to see where she went afterwards. When Ponzia and Adalais left the house without Fabrisse his senses went on the alert, and he followed them as they went to exit the Bourg south through the Porte Lamourguier Gate.

The unguarded gate, hidden behind the old church of that name, was not used much. It led to sea marshes laced with drainage ditches and canals that dried salt for collection. One had to tread carefully on the loose pebbled terraces that connected pathways, aware that a slip could drown you in the quicksand beneath long, tangled grasses. Unkempt dry weeds, sprouting out from under rocks like gray tresses, waved back and forth in the green scum lining the edges of the lagoons.

Insects made an incessant racket, buzzing and sawing their way through grass on sand humps. The occasional snake slithered quickly over the path, leaving ripples in the mud.

The sun got under their hats and pressed down on their shoulders. The only shade was from a little hut behind some rocks that was used by salt-workers. Henry the Monk was in it. Peering out at their footsteps, he quickly beckoned them in, checking to see if they had been followed, and saw no one.

Yet Hugon saw him. Crawling horizontally in the marshes, head down in the ditches, getting slime all over himself, he witnessed the meeting. There was no need to hear what they were saying, so crawling backwards like a crab he left the marshes. Quickly he returned to his chamber to change clothes and instruct Godfrey.

"Get hold of a cart and wait for me by the necropolis gate. I will come for you when I need you. And bring a winding sheet."

After meeting with Henry, Ponzia decided it would be wise to return to church again for Vespers.

'Why must we go again? Today is my twelfth name day—it's not fair!" Fabrisse had complained. "I don't want to go."

But Fabrisse had no say in the matter. Fidgeting, she knelt next to her mother. The cracked floor of Saint Paul-Serge was digging into her knees. *What a way to spend your name day,* thought the restless child.

Knowing that she had to make a showing of prayer and of being a devout Catholic, Ponzia remained praying after the service. As good a Bonne Fille as she was, she didn't want Fabrisse burnt at the stake.

"Stop playing with your hair. Be still." Her daughter had not yet learned patience. Their stomachs rumbled in a hungry chorus.

"I have a cramp in my leg. Let me walk about the church for a few minutes. I want to look at the pictures." Fabrisse got up without waiting for the "NO!"

The child gazed up at the bright paintings telling the story of Jesus. Beginning at the Annunciation, she walked from round chapel to round chapel. Barely lit by flickering red oil lamps their dark corners were vacant shadows. High stone walls, thick and dark with age, felt cool as she ran her fingers along them. She could barely see the gold stars painted on the wooden ceiling dimly lit by window slits twenty feet above her. Thick marble columns hid the girl from sight as she slowly wandered further and further from her mother. The worried eyes of a brown statue of the Virgin Mary, her wooden cloak peeling blue paint, followed the girl in the green dress.

Under the gold-filigreed lamps throwing soft circles of light on the apse of Saint Serge's tomb, she fearfully faced a statue of the saint dying in agony.

This whole church is full of graves down below me. The thought made her shiver. *I must get back to mother.*

She circled around behind a pillar near the stairs leading down to the spirit filled crypt, the netherworld of sepulchers—and didn't re-appear on the other side.

Ponzia heard a muffled cry. *What was that?* and turned to find her daughter. She wasn't to be seen. Twice Ponzia ran around in a circle inside the church—then flew into the sunshine, blinking rapidly. "Fabrisse! Fabrisse!" A crowed formed around the screaming mother as the Sacristan came running.

"My daughter, she's missing! She disappeared in the church. You must help me find her! Oh, Mother Mary, God in Heaven, please help me find her!"

"I'll check the crypt. Perhaps she fell down the stairs. It happens. It's dark in there and children are curious." A few minutes later he returned to find Ponzia running halfway down streets, then running back to the square. "She not in the crypt. I'm sorry."

Ponzia began to cry. "Call for help! Tell Ermengard!"

In the ancient necropolis behind the church, mausoleums and tombstones cast sharp black shadows as the bent form of a tall monk scuttled across the bleached stones to lay a small corpse in a winding sheet onto a cart. His servant drove off with the monk kneeling in the back with the dead, praying and crossing himself, as it quietly rumbled unchallenged out of the city gate.

CHAPTER 22

O that thou hadst hearkened to my
commandments! Then had thy peace
been as a river, and they righteousness
as the waves of the sea . . .
and thy seed had been as the sand . . .
    —*Isiah 48:18, King James Bible*

After dark, the crumbling ruins of the Roman amphitheater just south of Narbonne burst into squalid life. Brick vaulted arches, which a thousand years earlier had led up to the spectators' seats, were now filthy taverns, brothels, cheap inns, and desolate hidden opportunities to buy anything and anyone. In the oval theater, where chariots once raced and Christians were killed for sport, had grown a city that was the stinkweed of the poorest of the poor.

Not far away, in a crescent east of the ruins, was a forest of mastic trees with upswept branches edged in moonlight. Always guarded by Ermengard's military, it was a source of great profit for her. A dense and tangled place, it was dangerous to be caught in its depths, and was avoided at night by the denizens of the coliseum.

Two of Rogenvaldr's men, Gimkel and Blian, tired of being stuck in the Coyran house at night, made a quick decision:

"Let's go to the coliseum. We're dying of boredom while the Earl's bedding the Queen of Narbonne."

After a few nights of serving the two a sour beer, the barman challenged them, "Hey, Vikings, think you can drink a real drink? If it don't kill you, it'll make you strong!"

He taunted them, laughing.

Gimkel was always up to a challenge. "We're strong enough already, but pour it in—!"

The barman, smiling broadly, poured a milky liquid with a resin-like taste to the rim of their cups. It made them ruinously drunk, and almost blind, but they loved it.

At other rickety tables, the fuzzy light of smoking oil lamps on the walls barely lit the faces of sullen, big-knuckled fishermen. Andalusian and African sailors, heavily armed with curved knives, ate dates and cracked walnuts with their fingers. Everyone sat with their eyes down, eating and drinking, elbows on the table.

The open door let in a terrified scream from the night. A woman relieving herself in the field happened to glance up and see the unicorn without his horn. "I saw it!" she exclaimed to the patrons. "Over there, in the mastic grove. Look, Mother Mary of God protect us! It will kill us all—"

A crowd had rushed out to look, but it wasn't there. Suddenly, to everyone's horror, the unicorn appeared again, a bluish white apparition in the moonlight, nodding its head down, so that all could see the bloody stump where once had been a horn. After pawing the ground with one foot, it slowly backed up under the shadow of the trees to dissolve into the night.

There were a few moments of silence, then everyone rushed inside to lock windows and doors. Gimkel and Blian were roughly dumped out onto the cobblestones outside. Holding on to each other, they staggered to an empty patch of ground and fell asleep.

• • •

The day had been a difficult one for Old Porada. Too aged to work on a ship anymore, he had limped from boat to boat seeking small tasks to earn enough for a drink. There was always a fish and someone's fire to cook it on.

Avoiding treacherous cracks in the coliseum's high steps, he settled himself to sleep against the curved stone seats at the top. It was always quiet and cool up here. It was his spot. *Just me and the scorpions,* he mused, sweeping the ground with his hand. He wasn't really afraid of them. Having been bitten many times, he had built up a tolerance for their poison. The bites hurt, which only annoyed him. Soon he fell asleep, just another curved shadow in the night.

A thumping noise nearby woke him up. In the sharp, blue-white moonlight, he could make out two figures climbing to the top of the stairs carrying a large sack. Oblivious of an old man sleeping in the shadows, they dropped it in the corner next to the benches and quickly left.

Strange, wondered Old Porada. *Why would they come here?* Grumbling about his aching bones on the stones, he went back to sleep.

Awakened by the dawn, he got up to relieve himself and nearly fell over the large sack. Curious, he fiddled with the rope tying it shut. "God save us from perdition!"

A young girl was inside it, curled up, her hands crossed over a hole in her chest.

His cries drew a crowd who gathered around to stare.

"I saw two of them bring the sack last night. Woke me up out of a sound sleep. Who could know what they were up to?"

"Two of them?"

"Yes, two."

"The Vikings!" cried the tavern owner's son. "Where are those two drunken murderers? I threw them out last night just after we saw the unicorn. They could have killed any of us."

A shiver ran down every back.

"Let's find them!" cried the crowd, running down the stairs and out into the fields.

Gimkel and Blian were still asleep on the scrubby patch they had stumbled onto in the dark. They awoke to arms hauling them to their feet and an excited crowd arguing.

"What shall we do with these sons of Satan?"

"The unicorn took their souls and made them kill a child!"

"They turned into unicorns!"

"Let's hang them now!"

"No, we'll burn them! Get firewood—"

"Only the Archbishop can burn devils. Let's take them to him," a woman cried. "Drag them with ropes. Don't touch the demons! Your skin will fall off like a leper if you do."

The Norsemen were roped and dragged through the streets to the Archbishop's palace. At the sound of an angry mob in his courtyard, which had grown much larger as it progressed through town, he came out to calm them. The stunned and frightened Norsemen were lying sprawled and bloody on the ground. Blian's shirt, ripped off by rocks, had left his back torn and bloody. Seeing an opportunity, some thugs had stolen the men's' boots, leaving their feet bare and filthy.

"Burn them! Devils, demons, child murderers, a woman saw them mounting the unicorn as it ran into the forest."

Every frightened townsman had a different story, each one more horrible than the last. Finally, D'Anduze put up his hands to appeal for quiet and calm.

"Silence! Silence!" a monk shouted. "Let the Archbishop speak!"

D'Anduze recognized an opportunity when he saw one. *What a gift from heaven—this is a God given opportunity to control Rogenvaldr and get him out of Narbonne!* "Turn them over to me. I'll put them in my dungeons to await torture and justice."

"Burn them now," the crowd yelled.

"We will, we will. Satan will get his own, but first they must confess under torture." He turned to his guards, "Take them away. Hurry. Put them in the Roman dungeon under my palace."

CHAPTER 23

Love was once done right,
yet now that it breaks,
it decides that,
if it can't bite, then
it will lick—
with the rough tongue of a cat.
*   —Marcabru, troubadour, c. 1127—1148*

"Absolutely not." D'Anduze refused to deliver the two prisoners to her; he was a stone wall to her entreaties.

"Please Your Grace," Ermengard begged, "release them. The Earl and his men are furious that they're being held in your dungeon. This is so dangerous, you could cause a Norwegian invasion."

"We are not afraid. God will protect us." *And maybe I can get these Norsemen out of town in exchange for their release. Let's see how she likes that offer. . . they must be gone before I can sell that horn!* "The Norsemen are a danger to the moral soul of this city. Perhaps I will offer to release the prisoners if the Earl agrees to leave Narbonne immediately."

Ermengard was indignant. "No. I will not allow such a negotiation. I will not propose such an insult."

Narbonne was in an uproar. She was besieged from all sides, her relationship with Rogenvaldr questioned everywhere. Townspeople blamed the murders on those who "had killed the unicorn for its horn" and "the one who had purchased it for thirty pieces of silver", meaning her. Throughout the countryside there were suddenly hysterical sightings of angry unicorns murderously attacking children and goring lambs in the field.

D'Anduze warned her again. "Don't you understand? These Vikings are not like us; they are foreigners to our soil. Our holy water is poisoned when they dip their fingers in to cross themselves. I myself have seen it turn from clear to dark. In a fake religious charade they pray to their old gods upon which they have put Christian names."

"That's not true. They have come to us with the holy unicorn horn. I felt its power when he handed it to me." Ermengard couldn't understand why he hated them so much.

"Which you paid well for, might I remind you. And don't think these warriors are going to Jerusalem just to fight the Saracens. Many of these men want to be in the rather excellent pay of the Byzantine Emperor's Varangian Guard. And don't think they are the first fighters from Scandia to be in it."

"I know what you're trying to do—you just want to keep me unmarried and alone, so you can keep dominating me, trying to steal my wealth. All you care about is building your church."

"Which, as all know, is a gift to God. I am left in fear for your mortal soul, Ermengard. You are in danger from this man."

"I'm going to prove they are not guilty. Would it be so against your faith to help me find out who really murdered those children?"

"Perhaps the Lord wanted the children to arrive in heaven in the virginal state in which they were born?" atoned the Archbishop. "Perhaps the innocents have been touched by his hand. May the Lord bless you also, my child, and keep you safe."

• • •

"When the Archbishop sees three-hundred Norsemen about to storm his palace he'll change his holy mind. I'm going to free my men." Rogenvaldr was raging, pacing back and forth in front of her with long strides. *And I'm going to lash Gimkel and Blian to within a hair of their lives*. Ermengard's study was barely large enough to contain him.

De Plaigne, Beatritz and the captain of the military guard were also gathered in Ermengard's study. She was pushing the captain to catch the 'real' killer but could tell that the soldier was not enthusiastic. When it was known that Fabrisse's body had been found in the amphitheater, he had reluctantly sent soldiers to guard it.

"Many of my men are wary of what they believe may be a real unicorn. And anyway, we already have the two killers in prison."

"Go and search. Do as I command." Ermengard curtly dismissed him. Turning to Rogenvaldr she said: "But I'm so confused—if your Gimkel or Blian didn't do it, could it have really been a unicorn?"

"Don't be foolish. There's no unicorn running around killing people." Rogenvaldr was losing his patience with her naivety. "It's not possible."

Startled, she looked at him with hurt eyes, then turned away to hide her feelings.

What have I set in motion? How did these events come to this pass? Perhaps William was right all along—perhaps I should have listened to him. Rogenvaldr walked over to her and took her hand. "I'm sorry, my love. Every choice I make will hurt my men, hurt you, or destroy Narbonne. But I must act."

Ermengard nodded through tears. "I ask that you wait for a few days. Give me the time to find the real killers. Your men will not suffer in the dungeon, I will see to it."

She turned to Beatritz: "Go to the view the corpse, perhaps there will be some revelations to be found. I trust that God will reveal the truth. I will remain here and pray."

• • •

Swathed against the intense sun, Beatritz and De Plaigne were riding south to the ruins. To their right, the Aude River, flat and brown, widened as it entered a delta of lagoons. Along the road drying salt was being moved around by workers, then pushed into mounds.

"This is becoming tedious. I can't keep riding around in circles looking for a child killer. I'm a knight, not a city warden," he complained.

"You're free to turn back at any point."

"Yes. But I'm also a knight charged with protecting you." *And I'm also in love with you, Jesus help me.*

Their mounts, muscles twitching from swarming insects, picked their way carefully across the hard, flat sandbanks. Now exposed by the summer heat, there were cracks everywhere. If the ground collapsed under the pressure of a heavily trod hoof, the horse's leg could plunge into the soft deep of brackish water. Reaching a high mound in the scrub, they halted to regard their destination with mutual distaste.

Arches shimmering in waves of heat, the coliseum's circle of ragged tiers looked like decayed teeth.

"As soldiers are guarding Fabrisse's body, I should like to go first to the mastic grove where the 'unicorn' was sighted," ordered Beatritz. "I'm sure the white horse was used again. Why is it that ever since the Norsemen arrived, the summer has turned dark with evil deeds and fearfulness everywhere. It's frightening. It's as if Satan is devouring Narbonne." *I guess I'm really not surprised.* She turned her horse's head toward the deserted forest.

Usually at this time of the year workers were busily carving small cuts into the bark to allow the resin to form into drops. When dry, it would fall to the ground and be collected in bags. Now the men were too terrified to go near the place and huddled together in the amphitheater.

Ermengard had inherited an enormous income from the priceless mastic trees growing around the lagoon. Guarded by soldiers, no one except her personal workers were allowed near them on pain of death. She controlled the price and sale of the hard, crystal resin drops. Ground up into a powder, the mastic was used in potent skin salves for leprosy, in digestive cures, as a gum chewed to clean teeth and sweeten the breath, and to spice royal dishes.

Beatritz and a nervous De Plaigne explored the grove in silence, completely alone. The stiff stems of leathery branches, with their clumps of red berries giving off the spicy odor of resin scratched at their faces. Soon it would be harvest time, so workers had covered the ground with a white chalky powder from the cliffs of Andalusia. The powder coated the fallen resin, making it easier to gather up the sticky drops.

"The murderer didn't know the ground is white with powder," observed Beatritz. "That suggests he's not from Narbonne. Everyone around here knows about the powder under the trees. Look! We can see their footprints, two people. So he has help. Now, there! Hoofprints!" she exclaimed. "And the back shoe of one is crooked."

The footprints of men and beast wound their way deeper into the forest. They followed. Passing a mound of horse manure, Beatritz asked wryly, "What does a unicorn eat?"

Eventually the tracks met up with those of two other horses and a set of cartwheel ruts, then disappeared in the direction of the Saint Etienne Gate.

"The gate!" Beatritz exclaimed. "Who came through the closed gate last night? Only someone of importance could have gotten in. We must get that information later."

• • •

Fabrisse was lying under a woven straw blanket. Beatritz unwound the top of the sheet wrapped around her body. The buzzing of hundreds of enormous, luminescent blue and green flies rode the still air like the twanging of a mouth harp.

Beatritz sucked in her breath. *Has she been scourged like Garsend?* "Come, turn her over."

The crowd just stood there, staring, afraid to touch a body cursed by a unicorn. De Plaigne, as usual muttering to himself, helped her do it. The child's dress was torn, and her back cut into ribbons.

"Just what I feared." Beatritz stood up. Death never frightened her, but the scourging seemed a vile desecration. *I'm confused. Whom would it satisfy that they needed to do it? Now another child has died without the consolamentum. Wait! There is a pattern here.* Feeling like she had been kicked in the stomach, she saw it. Both girls were daughters of Bonnes Filles. *God, in your mercy, shield us—he's killing those who truly love you. He's killing our children.*

"What? What are you thinking?" asked De Plaigne.

I can't say a word to him. He'd probably praise the killer. "I'm thinking we should speak with the witness."

The reluctant Old Porada was brought to them. He had a gnarled, sinewy body that was bent over to one side. He reminded Beatritz of an ancient olive tree; yet the eyes in the sunburnt face were still sharp.

"What's the information worth to you?" Old Parada asked.

De Plaigne growled. "It's worth your living another minute."

"Patience, De Plaigne." She fished in her pouch and gave him a denarius, which he carefully examined and put into a torn pocket.

"The thumps woke me up. Like someone was dragging something heavy up the steps. I was surprised. In the dark? That late at night? Then I saw two men drop their load near me. They didn't see me—I sleep way in the corner there under the shadow of the bench. I saw them because they were in the moonlight."

"So what did they look like?" De Plaigne was impatient. It was hot
in the sun, and these people were filthy vermin.

"One was tall, thin, bearded, nose like a falcon beak. I couldn't see
the other to well, he kept bent down."

Again the same description. I've heard it before. But where?

"That's all I remember." He turned to go. "Yet, I did think it was
strange that a monk would do that."

"A monk?" Beatritz was startled.

"Yes, a monk—with a tonsure. Aren't they supposed to be at matins
then?"

The news got worse. After ordering the soldiers to return Fabrisse back
to her mother, they re-entered Narbonne through the Saint Etienne Gate.
Dismounting, Beatritz went to the guardhouse and asked if he remembered
admitting into the town a tall monk with a servant during the night.

'I wouldn't know that," he answered. "But Jean was here all night."

"And where would I find him?"

"He's asleep upstairs."

"Well then get him down here," she yelled in frustration. *God help
me, these stupid men!*

"Yes, I let someone of that description in," the groggy guard admitted.
"There's a Canon who comes and goes out all the time at night, during
the day, anytime. He's a friend of the Archbishop—we were told to let
him wander as he pleases."

"A friend of the Archbishop? Then he's not our man," decided De
Plaigne. "I'm leaving, I want my dinner."

And he rode off, happy to get out of his armor. *After all this nonsense
I deserve a nice long sleep.*

Beatritz sat down slowly on a crumbling wall. A memory was
forming in her mind, of a tall, thin man with black eyes and a nose like
a hawk. Henry the Monk had warned her, but she hadn't attended to
his words closely enough. Canon Hugon, of the Norbertine Abbey in
Prémontré. An evil hateful man who would burn everyone. It was said
that, when told he might be burning a true Christian by mistake, he had
replied 'God will know his own'."

And his breath was foul. Now how is that relevant? Confused, she
got on her horse, only wanting to go back to her chamber and hold her
daughter close.

• • •

Tired and hot, Beatritz found it difficult to explain to Ermengard and Rogenvaldr what she had learned. It just seemed so overly complicated.

"A horse that's a fake unicorn? A monk carrying a corpse? Why would anyone go to all this trouble? It doesn't make any sense." Ermengard was sitting on cushions in the corner of her solar trying very hard to understand.

Beatritz was silent, Her stomach roiled with fear. *Oh God in heaven! The foul breath! The Canon! But I'm not going to say a thing, until I'm sure. And even then, only to Henry the Monk.*

Rogenvaldr was adamant. "Now the Archbishop will have to release my men."

As usual, he was pacing back and forth. With his hair tied back in a braid, wearing his leather tunic and boots, he looked the part of a warrior again. His left hand kept playing with the hilt of the long sword on his hip. "My men are gathered downstairs. I'm taking them to get Gimkel and Blian. Now."

It's frightening to see him this way. He speaks as I would have imagined a Viking invader to speak. It's like the fear of Tortosa all over again. "Please, Rogenvaldr, wait. D'Anduze says he's keeping them locked up for their own protection. He believes the town will kill them if he lets them go."

"That's ox dung, and you know it. I can send them back to the ship under cover of night and they'll be perfectly safe." From a tall height, his blue eyes abruptly turned to look down at her. "We Norsemen are capable of taking care of our own."

He took her silence as reticence and was offended. "You're supposed to be the ruler here. Why aren't you ordering the release of the prisoners? Or would you only do that if they were two of your Occitanian nobles, with their fancy manners and Iberian blood?"

"It's not that simple . . . I can't tell the church what to do. Please understand."

"Well I can tell the Archbishop what to do, and my men will help him do it." Turning on his heel, he stormed out.

For once, Beatritz agreed with the Archbishop. *I want him gone too. The longer I know him, the less I like him. He must leave Narbonne and Ermengard, for her own sake. And he can take his horn of Satan with him. Hm-m-m— is Canon Hugon really the killer? For all we know it's Rogenvaldr.*

CHAPTER 24

And I looked,
and behold a pale horse:
and his name that sat on him was Death,
and Hell followed with Him.
                    —*Revelation 6:8, King James Bible*

The black stallion, expecting a sweet apple to eat, thrust his velvety face at Beatritz when she reached to nuzzle his soft nose and lips. Finding no treat in her hand, he blew at her and turned away. Ridden forth and back from the Holy Land, his broad back and thick neck were easily able to withstand the weight of a fighting knight in full armor. De Plaigne, knowing all such steeds were bad-tempered, kept his distance.

A destrier, or Great Horse, he belonged one of Ermengard's liege knights. Ermengard had suggested to ask Sir Pierre Azema about the white horse.

Azema spoke with a thick Iberian accent. "My Lady, you must travel to ask Guichard Maurs, who takes care of the Viscountess's Camarga horses. Guichard knows every dealer and horse sold between here and Arles. You must go to him at his stables near Notre-Dame-de-Ratis, down where the Three Holy Marys arrived by boat from the Holy Land. I warn you, he is a very devout man. I suggest you stop at the church to pray before you speak to him, or he will dismiss you. For certain, he will ask if you did so."

The following day found them sweltering under a yellow awning on a small, blue boat sailing to the low, flat grasslands of the Camarga. *At least the wind is keeping the insects away,* thought Beatritz.

"I feel like I'm in an oven," she gasped.

The sun in their eyes was like the cut of a sharp knife. Both of them were swathed in white and De Plaigne had actually put on a robe and turban. To shade her eyes and shoulders she wore silk veils draped completely over a huge straw hat. The toothless captain was considered dependable enough to get them there, wait for them to return—and not drown them on the journey.

A few hours later, they saw the square tower of Notre-Dame-de-Ratis aloof on its green hilltop, trembling in the hot air winding into the deep blue sky.

The church seems a holy mirage in this Place of the Mary Miracles. Beatritz was surprised to find herself moved when she saw it. *Perhaps it's because they were strong women who survived the dangers of a man's world.*

"Wait for us here," De Plaigne ordered the boatman as they began the walk over the wet sand to the church, which neither of them had ever visited.

The interior was cool and surprisingly simple. The walls were covered with fishing nets heavy with hanging metal replicas of all kinds of fish, as if they had caught them in the sea. A slight breeze clinked them against each other.

In the apse was a large painting of The Three Marys arriving on a sandy spit of beach that quite resembled the one outside. The Magdalene had just stepped out of a boat and was holding to her chest a sacred eight-sided cup from which gold flames emanated. Behind her came Martha carrying a miniature triangular-roofed house, followed by Mary of Clopas holding a filigreed container filled with besamin, fragrant ritual spices.

Over the altar, hanging from the ceiling by ropes, was an ancient wooden boat, its dry, sun-bleached planks a bluish gray.

"*THE* boat?" De Plaigne fell to his knees in awe. "And look, it's not even rotting."

Fighting back her distaste for this worship of Catholic relics, Beatritz went down on her knees. After a few moments she rose, impatient. "We must go to Guichard Maurs. I'll wait outside."

She found a cool spot under a cypress tree and sat down, musing. There were some believers who thought that the Magdalene was the first Bonne Fille. *Anything is possible, I suppose.* She wiped her damp upper lip. *Dear God, give me the strength to solve these murders and stop them. And then what? Would anyone be punished even if I did find out? Who would hang a Norwegian noble or a church Cannon on the strength of a woman's tale? People like De Plaigne would find any excuse not to do so. No doubt some peasant will be executed just to calm everyone down.*

De Plaigne floated out, a beatific look on his face.

• • •

Guichard was in his stable cleaning the hoof of a recalcitrant white Camarga mare. Its huge muscles required two men to hold the hoof in place.

"Wait outside, please," he said as courteously as the circumstances allowed. The horse had twisted its huge head around and was trying to bite him with impressively large teeth.

When Guichard came out, he went straight to the water trough and dunked his head in. Throwing his black hair over his head, he turned to them. Large gray eyes dominated his long, narrow face.

He looks rather like a horse himself, thought Beatritz.

"How may I serve you?" He bowed politely—they were obviously people of quality.

"I am Sir Thibaut De Plaigne, and this is the Countess de Dente. We are both here on behalf of the Viscountess Ermengard. We are looking for a certain white horse recently sold in the Narbonne area."

"Have you prayed in the church? I only speak business with those who have prayed first."

"Yes, we have," replied Beatritz.

"Ah, good. Now what kind of horse are you looking for?"

"One that could be made to resemble a unicorn."

"What? A unicorn? In the name of Jesus, whatever for."

Beatritz decided to confide in him. "Please hold this information between us. Our Viscountess believes that the unicorn rumored to have killed two children is a fake. Someone is using a white horse and dressing it up with a broken horn to distract people and make them panic. We need to know what kind of horse could be used, and whether or not such a horse has been recently sold. Pierre Azema told us that you know everyone who is buying and selling from Perpignan to Arles."

Guichard slowly blew out his breath. "Well let me think on this for a minute. I've been asked many questions about horses, but never one like this. Well, I guess a person could use a palfrey; yet they are very expensive. White ones are usually sold to the nobility before they are born, so it's unlikely that anyone except a great lady could buy one. Of course, there is always the jennet, from Iberia. It's not too small, and very fleet. I could give you a list of various breeders. I haven't sold any recently, but there is always the possibility of a local, private sale."

They left with a list of eight breeders scattered around Narbonne. "This will take days," muttered De Plaigne as they walked to the boat.

"You're a knight. Stop complaining," Beatritz said tartly.

Under a shady clutch of chestnut trees, a yellow-painted wooden tavern was leaning against a stone wall. Out front were four outdoor tables— and a lamb roasting on a spit.

"We must eat and drink or I will not be able to continue." De Plaigne dropped onto a worn bench.

Oh, no, thought Beatritz. As a Bonnes Filles she was sworn to be a vegetarian and dreaded the thought of eating with the knight. "Of course, you're right."

An older woman with a large white hat came to serve them. Her broad, flat face, its skin covered in brown spots, had a pleasant enough smile; however, her eyes were wary and alert under the heavy folds of her eyelids.

"How may I be of service?" Her accent seemed to be from the east, maybe Rus. "We have roast lamb today."

"Do you have any fish?" Beatritz was getting nervous.

"No fish. Too hot. Roast lamb."

"Bring us two platters. And wine." De Plaigne was hungry.

"With water, if you please."

Two platters of meat arrived, hot and juicy, the lamb blood spreading and softening the trenchers.

Beatritz put water into the wine and picked at a dry spot in the bread.

"Aren't you hungry? Eat. Perhaps you don't eat meat?" He looked at her questioningly.

"Yes, I do like it. But it's very—"

"Not one of those miserable Bons Hommes, are you?" He was trying to be humorous, but then, again, he wasn't. Chewing, he screwed up his eyes and stared at her.

"Forgive me, I was being terribly rude. It must be the heat." She took a large cut of lamb and began to chew, closing her eyes so as not to see what she was eating. After choking down half, she pushed the rest over to the knight. "It's too much for a lady; really, this serving is for a man of your strength."

Continuing to eat, he pulled it over.

"Please excuse me, I must find a place to relieve myself."

A narrow path behind the tavern led behind the broad-trunked trees. Her feet crunched on fallen chestnuts as she looked for a hidden spot. She leaned over some roots and stuck her finger in her throat She vomited as silently as possible, took a deep breath as she stood up, then started in fear. The serving woman was standing behind her, watching, a clay pitcher in her hands.

Calmly, she walked over and handed it to Beatritz. In a low voice, she murmured, "It was necessary. May you have a good death."

Rinsing her mouth out, close to tears, Beatritz answered, "May you also have a good death."

Back at the table, she smiled. "Are you ready to continue our search?"

De Plaigne belched. "I am much satisfied. Let us go on."

By the time they arrived back in Narbonne it was too late to go looking for the horse breeders. Exhausted, Beatritz quickly told Ermengard of their progress and went to her chamber. Rogenvaldr was nowhere to be seen.

• • •

The next day was again brilliantly hot, with a vacant, blue sky. The first four breeders had no white jennets or palfreys, nor had they sold any recently. The fifth had sold a white palfrey to a noblewoman in Avignon, and the sixth had sold a white courser to Raymond Trencavel.

"I had no idea there were so many white horses in Narbonne," the knight grumbled.

Will he ever stop complaining? Maybe they sent him back from the Holy Land because they couldn't stand listening to him anymore.

Now they were north of Narbonne, slogging on foot up Mont Laures to a horse farm on its plateau. It was a muddy, rocky path up a strange hump in the flat marshes. Their steeds had been left to graze at the bottom of the mountain. Alongside the way, a fast stream rushed down the mountain, making the air cool, and the mud slippery.

Above the swish of tumbling waves, they could hear the grinding stones of a water mill just ahead. It was solidly built, covered with peeling red paint, with bags of fresh-ground barley stacked on platforms away from the water wheel.

The dusty miller poked his head out just as they passed by. Throwing a bag onto the pile, he quickly returned to his work without a greeting.

Further up the path a barefoot girl, who looked to be about ten, sat on a rock combing her hair. It was blond, very curly, and full of brambles. Her bony arms were attacking it with frustration. Frowning, she looked at Beatritz with envy, noticing the lady's smooth hair carefully braided under her veil.

Beatritz laughed, having seen that expression on Alais's face so often. "Here, let me help."

She stepped over, taking her own ivory comb out of her pouch. Bent over the child, she began to untangle the strands. The girl sat quietly, head tilted back.

De Plaigne was aghast and impatient. "Do you really have to do that?"

"It will only take another minute." She deftly separated the gold strands and braided them. "There. That's better." Beatritz smile at the girl. "Now, can you tell us where the man Helias Theodrik has his horse farm?"

The child nodded and jumped off the rock. Dragging her left foot, she began to limp up the hill, surprisingly nimble. After a hidden sharp right turn they would most likely have missed, they came upon a grove of the twisted, contorted branches of the cu d'ane fruit tree. The bushy green leaves were swathed in starlike white flowers.

"Oh my word!" exclaimed Beatritz, "monkey's ass trees! What are these doing here?"

"Mama planted them many years ago, before she went to Jesus. She would pick them every Noël, put them into sawdust for a few weeks, then bring them down to Ermengard as a treat. She was paid enough coin for us to eat well all winter. But now they rot on the trees for I can't do it alone."

"Well, I will certainly send someone here to help you pick them this year. We noticed at court that the quality of the fruit we are getting hasn't been very good. I wondered why."

"Can we keep going?" De Plaigne was tired of all this conversation about fruit trees and hair combing.

At last they pushed through some chestnut trees into the sunshine — onto a plateau with a magnificent view south all the way to the sea. To the north was the Le Montaigne Noir, at its base the dark wood in which Garsend had been murdered.

The horse farm was large and completely fenced in with an expensive slatted wooden fence. Eight horses were grazing, tails swishing at flies.

A bare-chested man was vigorously rubbing ointment onto the haunch of a black Arabian; the sinewy muscles of his back gleamed with sweat. The girl ran over and tugged his arm. "Papa, we have guests."

When he straightened up and turned around, they could see he was Egyptian, with black eyes rimmed in long lashes, and a straight nose set in an oval face. A long, wrinkled scar over his heart showed white against his tanned skin. He examined them carefully, without fear. "You are welcome, but how come you to the Helios farm?" His voice had a strong eastern accent.

"Guichard Maurs. He said perhaps you could help us find a certain white horse."

"Papa, look how the lady combed my hair! Isn't it pretty?" The girl tugged at his arm until he looked down. A smile lit up his face.

"Did she now," he said quietly. Helios looked up with a much softer expression. "You have made Jacotte happy. Since her mother died, we have daily problems with her hair. It can be quite frustrating. How can I help you?"

"You have no doubt heard about the young girls everyone says was murdered by a unicorn," Beatritz said.

The father nodded and gazed down at Jacotte. Without thinking, he pulled her closer.

"The Viscountess," she continued, "believes that someone purchased, or stole, an ordinary white horse and disguised it with a fake horn to deceive everyone. Guichard Maurs said it could be a palfrey, but that would very costly. Then he suggested a jennet. He sent us to you because you breed them, and that you have been fortunate enough to have had some white ones born recently."

"Ha! Good fortune indeed! Renenutet, the Goddess of Fortune, does not bless one without hard work and careful breeding. I do have a foal. Come, I'll show you. She is a beauty."

Around back of the farmhouse were two paddocks holding three white horses: a male in one, and a female with a foal in the other.

"What beautiful animals!" exclaimed Beatritz. *Stick a horn on one and you have a unicorn.*

"I had recently another mare, but I sold her to a monk. I told him that I thought she was too small for him, upon which he curtly told me to mind my own business."

Beatritz and De Plaigne glanced at each other. "A monk?" she said. "Can you describe him further?"

"Grey eyes, tonsured, thin lips, scruffy looking, like an old and jowly soldier."

Beatritz felt fear gnaw at her stomach again. *He's describing Godfrey. My God, could he be doing the killing? He'd do anything for Hugon. They must be working together.* "Would you happen to know of any poorer farms that would be willing to hide a white horse for a fee?"

Guichard gave them some possibilities.

"Thank you for your help." Before leaving, Beatritz reached impulsively into her purse and pulled out her ivory comb. "This is for you, Jacotte"

The child looked up at her father. He nodded. Excited to go look in her mirror, she made a quick little curtsy, and ran off.

"May Renenutet grant you success in your search."

On the ride back to Narbonne, they didn't notice Godfrey circling around them to get there first.

When told, Hugon was furious. "She's a filthy heretic, poking her nose in where it doesn't belong. Better go to the farm. Make sure he knows enough to keep quiet."

• • •

Hysteria was building in the taverns and churches surrounding Narbonne. Troubadours, always seeking a new tragic tale, sang of lovers dying in the unicorn's shadow.

"Jesus save me—it was going so fast it was a blur!"

"Saint Helena protect me! The creature ate my newborn calf!"

"Yesterday, at twilight, I was sitting on a high rock at Bitter Pond watching my flock. The sheep never drink from it—it's deadly. I saw the

creature come to drink. When he tasted its bitterness, he dipped his horn
in and the water turned sweet! All the sheep came to drink of it. I tasted
it myself—it's now sweet water! I swear on Saint Cuthbert's eyes—it's
the truth!"

• • •

Beatritz and De Plaigne were approaching the third farm suggested
by Helios. They would never have found it on their own. A wretched
shelter in the shade of pine trees, its yellow stones had long since fallen
down and never been replaced. A pile of brown cabbages wrested from
the muddy garden were moldering in a cart. The splintered door was
half open. Yet, a new fence was peeking out from the rear yard.

"Is anyone here?" called De Plaigne as they dismounted.

"What do you want?" a sinewy, straggle-haired youth came
sneaking around the corner. He was pointing a metal spear at them. His
left hand was missing, so he held the weapon lying tightly across his
ragged left forearm.

"We're in the service of the Viscountess Ermengard. We are
searching for a white jennet."

"Nothing here for you. Leave before I use this."

"You, a pathetic excuse for a man, threaten a knight?" De Plaigne
stepped toward him. The young man, his eyes wide with fear, came closer.

Meanwhile, Beatritz had noticed hoof prints in the mud. "Look," she
said, "one hoof has a crooked shoe." She moved to walk behind the shack.

"Stay away from there!" the youth cried again, rushing forward to
stab her.

De Plaigne, useful for once, pulled out his sword and flipped the
young man's weapon skywards. *He's not even worth fighting with,* he
thought, watching him fall onto his rear end and scuttle away. "What do
you see?"

"Look for yourself. A crooked shoe."

Trembling, the peasant stared out at Beatritz from inside a filthy hut.

She warned him, "If you don't want to hang for horse theft, tell us
where the white horse is hidden."

"Please, spare me. I will tell you the truth. My name is Bermund,
and my wife Olan is pregnant and ill. The midwife wants to treat her

with special medicines. I went to town to buy them from Escoralda, but they were too costly. I was begging Escoralda to give them to me cheaper, when a man standing nearby approached me. He asked if I had a farm, and when I said, a very poor one, he said that if I secretly stabled a horse for him, he would buy the medicines for my wife. I agreed, and told him where I lived, and he paid Escoralda for me. The next day he came with a monk and a sweet little white jennet. They even built the fence for me."

"What did they look like?" Beatritz almost didn't want to know.

"The master was tall, very thin, and bearded, with a face like a vulture. And he wore a hooded cloak, even in this heat! The servant was older, with pale eyes and almost bald, like a monk."

• • •

The marketplace around the old Capitole temple, where Escoralda lived in a red wagon covered in mysterious yellow symbols, teemed with unsavory purveyors of everything from sex to murder. Everyone came to Escoralda to buy medicines and to have their futures foretold. A tiny, ancient lady from Byzantium, she knew every cure and remembered every customer. Inside, dried herbs hung from the ceiling and filled baskets. Little stoppered clay jugs were carefully arranged on shelves under the arched wooden ceiling.

"Good morning, my Lady, my Lord," she greeted them seriously when they came to her open door. Her alert black eyes looked Beatritz up and down. "What can I help you with? A pregnancy potion perhaps? I have some of the finest from Egypt."

Beatritz blushed as De Plaigne coughed. "No, thank you. We are making some inquiries for the Viscountess about the murdered children.

"Ah-h-h, a very bad thing. She shook her curly, white hair vigorously. "Give back the horn! Escoralda tell everyone, give back the horn!"

Yes, she remembered the young man with one hand who couldn't afford the medicine, and the man who bought it for him.

"What did this man look like?"

"Wore a black cloak even in this heat! Face like a vulture. But Escoralda is smart—I see he has a large lump in his neck, sticks right out of his beard, and I offer him a very fine powder to put in his drink.

Will sweeten your mouth and make you live longer, I say. 'Curse you and your cures! Only God will decide when I die!' he shouts at me. I see him wandering around town, hiding in the shadows, watching people, stopping to listen. Ah! There he is now—"

Yet in the short time it took for them to turn around and look where she pointed, he was gone.

Escoralda was looking intensely at Beatritz. "Please, come inside my wagon. I wish to speak with you."

Beatritz was curious. Turning to De Plaigne, she said: "Why don't you go to the palace and tell Ermengard our findings. I will soon follow."

Escoralda closed the door firmly behind them. Inside the wagon was warmer than outside and smelled of familiar herbs and strange, oriental powders. A lump of charcoal was burning orange. Its sweet smoke curled up to the ceiling and hung there like a veil.

The old woman offered Beatritz a seat opposite her own. In the small space they had to sit knee to knee. "Please, give me your left hand, I must read your future. It is so necessary . . ."

Escoralda grasped the warm hand in her thin, cool fingers, using her thumbs to rub circles over the palm. She stared at the thin, wavy lines. Her bony finger followed the line of life circling around the mound of her thumb to stop at a star-shaped meeting of lines under her middle finger. Beatritz's eyes were watching her with interest. Then she felt the woman stiffen.

"What I see is very frightening. You are in grave danger and not careful enough, even though you have been warned." Escoralda looked up at her face. "There are flames in your eyes, yes, burning fires in your future."

Beatritz pulled her hands away, then tore her glance away from the strange dark force in the fortune-teller's eyes. "Please, I must go." *Why am I pleading?*

"Go. Have caution, there are evil forces around you. Be more careful!"

Beatritz pushed hard against the door, swinging it open with a bang. The sun was glaring off of the black stones of the Via Domitia so brightly that she was forced to put her hands over her eyes to block the light.

My eyes burn so much. Why is everything so bright? It feels like I really do have flames in them! She walked a short distance and felt the urge to turn around to look. Escoralda was standing in the door of her wagon watching her leave. The sun outlined her form against the dark shadow inside. Is that her? *No—was it possible? Escoralda was The Shadow.*

CHAPTER 25

Rage and longing, fetters and wrath,
tears and torment are thine;
where thou sittest down my doom is on thee
of heavy heart
and double dole.
  —Skirnir's Journey, Old Norse Poem, Anon., c. 1150

The horn is a fake? Frotard nearly fell off his stool. He had been the jailer in D'Anduze's dungeon for many years, yet he never had such a thing to tell his master. As usual, he was listening to prisoners through the clever Roman system of narrow cracks and holes between the floor and ceiling. Thinking they were alone, men confessed things to each other that the Archbishop was always interested in. It was always worth a few coins to report something new to him.

"What are we doing here?" Gimkel groaned, massaging his swollen hip. "I hate Narbonne. I just want to leave, but how do we get out of here? Where's Rogenvaldr? Why isn't he helping us?"

A torch burning high upon the wall showed the crooked outline of Blian's body on the brick floor. "It's Rogenvaldr's fault to begin with." He stopped to work out a broken loose tooth. "We should have gone straight to Jerusalem. That horn will send us to Hell."

"We're already in Hell. Sigurd II sentenced us there when he gave the Earl that fake horn to sell. We'll all die in this insect-filled swamp."

Crossing himself, Frotard stumbled upstairs to the Archbishop's study.

"The horn is a fake?" D'Anduze pretended to be horrified. "Not possible. Don't dare tell that to anyone." He commanded the jailer. "If you do, I will excommunicate you and your family and burn you as a heretic. And you still want your reward?"

Trying not to look pleased, he gave the trembling Frotard his coins.

Once alone, D'Anduze began to pace back and forth. Yes, he was horrified, but not for the reason Frotard assumed.

This is terrible. What if the townspeople find out it's a fake? They'll blame both Ermengard and me for making fools of them and spending their tax money on it. And my secret plans to sell it to the King of France? If he finds out it's a fake, he'll laugh in my face forever. The whole French court will mock me, not to mention the Pope! No one can find out. I can't just kill a noble like Rogenvaldr, but I can put him into prison, so he is unable to speak to anyone. Then I have to make him secretly leave Narbonne. Where in Christ's blood is the Templar with my letter from Ganagobie? I must imprison the Earl, even if Ermengard tries to protect him.

• • •

The Merchant's Exchange, the financial center serving Narbonne's port, was located in the Bourg. It was a thick walled, two-story brick building with no windows at street level. Ship's captains, traveling merchants, Arabs, Jews, Persians, all had to exchange their foreign money here. Upstairs was the Narbonne Financial Council meeting rooms and a large, window-lit auction hall. Downstairs, around a torch-lit central court, protected by bars and thick wooden doors, were the private banking chambers holding wealthy clients' gold.

When Ermengard's gift of gold coins to Rogenvaldr was finally ready, an arrangement was made to meet Eindredi in Ermengard's counting room. It had been previously agreed that one-fifth of the money was to remain in Rogenvaldr's possession. A group of armed Norsemen waited in a skiff moored below the Riverbank Gate to transfer Eindredi's share to his boat, and, as neither trusted the other, each had five armed men to stand as witnesses to the counting.

The sweating Norsemen all crowded into the small, torchlit space, standing crushed against the large, yellow building stones. Rogenvaldr and Eindredi looked at each other warily when the metal bands of Ermengard's wooden chest were opened with three different keys by three different men. Gold coins flickered in the light. The banker counted one-thousand coins into twenty-five stacks.

Eindredi slipped twenty of them into soft leather pouches, leaving five for Rogenvaldr. Embracing the Earl, he whispered, "God be with you cousin. Remember Jerusalem."

• • •

Rogenvaldr had given William the money to buy Bathsheba's freedom. Immediately, William gave the sum to Sancha to pay Dolmus. "Would you please buy her a white linen dress?" William asked. "She cannot travel in whore's clothing. And give her this pocket money."

What a clever woman, thought Sancha. *Well, good for her. Maybe she can start a better life in Alexandria; she's certainly not going back to Ethiopia.*

William and Bathsheba had spent their last night together in his room. They sat apart, not touching, on William's bed. The full moon was a lantern outside the window, making blue half-moons of their faces. Her outstretched legs were shadows. William put out a glowing hand to reach for her arm. Gently she pushed it away.

"No. It can never be. We can never be."

"How do even know your family will accept you when you return?"

"I will never tell them the whole of what happened to me. If I'm rejected, I'll go to a convent outside Lalibela. Maybe I'll just go to it anyway."

"What is it that you haven't told me? At least grant me that before you go."

She put her face down in her hands and began to cry. When she lifted it, moonlit tears trailed down her cheeks. "There were two babies. The first, a boy, was taken away from me at birth, then quickly sold to a slaver. I will never know what happened to him. I did not name him. He does not exist.

"The second was a daughter. I begged to keep her for a while and called her Maienca. One morning I secretly went to the docks to find a captain who would take her to some of my relatives in Alexandria. I found one who appeared to be an honest man and gave him a jewel I had hidden away to pay for the voyage. He took my sleeping child and the jewel, then sailed off. Standing on the dock I could see him in the distance working ropes. Bending over he picked up Maienca and, looking back at me, he laughed heartily, then threw her off the boat into the sea. I screamed and jumped in the water, trying to catch up with the crying bundle thrown up and down by the waves. It was too far, the current pulled me away. I could her my daughter's voice gurgle as the sea pulled her down."

She stopped crying and took his moonlit face in her hands. "We can never be together because I am not in this world any longer. I am with my daughter in heaven at the feet of the Virgin Mary."

At dawn they walked to the wharves near the Water Gate. Sitting together on a pilot barge, they silently floated down to the sea channel. A blue and red boat belonging to a young Ethiopian fisherman was waiting for her, sails tacked and ready. William had negotiated a high price to take her directly to Begwena, from which she could proceed to Lalibela.

"I'll pay you half the money now, and the other half when you return with the secret word that Bathsheba will give you when she's safely there."

Bathsheba stood up, turned to him, and put out both her hands. William grabbed them and put her fingers on his forehead. He held them there for a moment, and looked up, his eyes full of tears. She looked at him deeply and blinked; she wasn't seeing him anymore. When, in her white robe she stepped regally into the boat, the fisherman fell to his knees and bowed until she gently touched the top of his head. Putting a wide straw hat on her head and a white cloak over her shoulders, she sat down facing Africa. The sun carved her form as they sailed off; she never looked back.

· · ·

Rogenvaldr appeared annoyed as he and William, snacking on grilled octopus, walked through town.

"People avoid me when I wander around; merchants are too busy to sell me things, suddenly women are not meeting my eyes. I'm starting to feel torn between leaving and staying with Ermengard."

"Well I'm not torn. I just want to go." William tried to be persuasive. "The horn is sold, we have the gold—and children are being killed. And they're blaming two of our men! How do we get them back? This place feels more dangerous every day."

"Ermengard is—"

"She has no control over the religious fervor that D'Anduze is stirring up. For whatever devious reason he has, Rogenvaldr, he wants you gone. For the love of Christ, man! You're on pilgrimage with three-hundred men; would you let one woman destroy all their chances of salvation?"

"That's easy for you to say. Bathsheba is gone so you have no more reason to stay. But you're right. And I've lost patience. I'm going to force D'Anduze to release my men right now."

"Well, I'm going to Saint Paul-Serge to pray for you."

"Hah! Some help you are." Rogenvaldr threw the remainder of his octopus over his shoulder as he motioned to his men to follow him.

• • •

The angry crowd milling around outside the Archbishop's palace included some of the gang who had dragged Gimkel and Blian into town from the coliseum. When they saw Rogenvaldr approach with his men they were already primed for a fight.

"Child murders! Unicorn killers!" Soon it seemed the whole town jumped on the Norsemen as a brutal confrontation began. One of the first to go down was Thorkell Crook-eye who lay there as if dead, his head blooded by a blow from behind. Unfortunately for them, working townsmen were no match for furious Norsemen—soon peasants and merchants were lying in tangles on the stones.

Panting, D'Anduze arrived with soldiers who managed to break up the two factions.

Rogenvaldr was livid. "Why is this happening?" he shouted, as he bent down to help the now-conscious Thorkell stand up. "I demand you hand over my men."

"As I keep telling Ermengard, it is not possible. Your men stand accused of killing the child Fabrisse de Coumic. They must remain in my dungeons for now. And no, you can't talk to them."

What's going on? Rogenvaldr's mind raced. *Why is this happening?*

And I know your secret now, D'Anduze thought. "Come, let us speak together in the church."

Rogenvaldr walked determinedly after the Archbishop's retreating back and came to a sudden stop inside the half-constructed cathedral. *God in his heaven, this is magnificent.*

D'Anduze turned around, bracing for an argument, but instead found Rogenvaldr entranced at the soaring spires, the towering windows shimmering with all the hues of the rainbow, and the carved columns rising to a partially vaulted ceiling.

As the Earl came nearer, D'Anduze examined him with interest. The Earl was almost two heads taller than himself, all sinew and bone, with long muscular legs and a broad chest. *And that gilded hair, with eyes like a stormy sea.*

"I've made myself clear—I cannot release the men now. It's too dangerous for them."

Rogenvaldr was in awe. "It will be magnificent. How many years have you been building it?"

D'Anduze was taken aback. "Thank you. Too many years. It never ends. I hope to see it completed before I die."

"I too am building a cathedral. In Kirkwall, in Orkneyjar. It is to honor my uncle, Saint Magnus. But it is not as glorious as this is."

"Forgive me—I have never heard of Saint Magnus. And he is your uncle? How did he come to be beatified?"

Rogenvaldr looked down at the delicate features of the Archbishop. He was about to speak when, on impulse, he lay down on his back on the stone floor under the main vault to gaze up at the towers growing to the sky. D'Anduze loved to look up at the towers. He lay down next to him.

"I will tell you. He was a Christian martyr who died praying on his knees rather than fight his enemies. Numerous miracles of healing continue to occur at his gravesite. His bones will rest in the cathedral— if I ever finish it. This is amazing. How do you do it? It seems impossible to get the masons to work for more than a few months. Without a word they disappear, then come back later and demand more money than originally agreed. It takes forever to obtain the red and yellow sandstone blocks quarried on our islands. It's a different kind of stone—much softer than yours. And sculptors are not to be found at any price."

"Abbot Suger hoards the best artists. The ones from Italy are the finest but cost the most. So many cathedrals are being built that no one wants to work in Narbonne."

"Or Kirkwall in Orkneyjar, believe me." He was looking up at the tall windows glowing like jewels in the sunlight. Two men were calling to each as they bent the lead that would hold one together in its arch. A sculptor was tapping away on a column at the base of the vault, putting the finishing touches on a grinning skeleton's teeth. A jagged piece of blue sky was outlined by the lattice of ladders used by the workers. "The four-sided arches are a wonder."

"When complete, my vault will be the highest in Christendom. I will be buried here, and my epitaph will be, 'He built this for the glory of God'." D'Anduze sighed as he stared upwards, his hands on his heart.

The conversation continued on technical notes. Eventually they stood up, brushing off the masonry dust.

"You must free my men."

"When the time is right, I will do so. They are being well cared for."

"The right time is now," Rogenvaldr snapped, turning to leave.

D'Anduze watched his muscled thighs as he strode away. *Sometimes life is difficult; it just doesn't allow one to make friends. Unfortunately, I must force him to leave. I need to sell the horn. How else am I to finish this church he so admires? Those two prisoners may be my only option—unless something else happens.*

• • •

Aslak, left behind in Coyran, was still brimming with uncontrolled rage. *Our family's honor has been soiled by Sigrid's rape. And being enslaved in a brothel! Either I drag her home, or I'll kill her. No! She's not going to spend her life as a whore entertaining filthy, strange pigs. I'm going to end this*—fuming, he slipped out of the villa.

Ignoring hostile looks as he ran into town, he easily found the brothel's narrow alley, still deep in early morning shadow. His banging and yelling on the door rang through the empty courtyard inside and down the nearby streets. Men stopped unloading their carts to stare at him. The rumor that Norsemen had murdered a child had been growing steadily around town.

"I'll kill you, Sigrid! Come back home with me, or I'll kill you!"

Hearing his shouts, the women ran into the alley, pointing at him: "He's going to kill another girl! Stop him! Grab him!"

Sigrid woke up and heard him yelling for her. Running to Lomanha, she begged, "Please hide me—I don't want to leave!"

"Come with me." Hiding Sigrid in her wardrobe, she ran to the front door and opened the little window to yell, "Go away!" She barely ducked the knife that came at her face. "Help! Help! He's trying to kill me!"

Her shrieking voice carried all the way to the Capitole square. "He's the child killer!"

Burly tavern keepers, used to dealing with angry drunks, ran to rescue their neighbor. Aslak's anger riled them with its ravings; it was the lust of a madman. And it proved he was the murderer.

"You are all rapists—you kidnap young girls and ruin them! May God curse you for your sins!" The Norseman was red in the face and spitting at them as he rigidly held out the knife in his fury.

"You are the ones kidnapping virgin girls to sacrifice to the unicorn beast—you Vikings are godless heathens, and you invaded our town with an army of Satan's spawn!" one of the tallest yelled, pointing two fingers in a sign of protection from the evil one.

"Kill the devil's spawn," another yelled from behind Aslak, who spun around to defend himself from the hammer of a well-muscled mason. The hammer hit him on the side of the head, knocking him to the cobbles, where, despite kicking and flailing with his knife, they throttled him to death. The crowd dragged his bloodied corpse out of the town gate and threw it on the closest midden heap.

Hearing silence in the street, Sigrid, looking at the sky, raised her hands palm upwards. "Thank you, Mother Gaea," she sighed, and went back to bed.

• • •

"William, how do I deal this this?" asked Rogenvaldr, holding his stomach with grief. "What will I tell his mother? Both children lost—I promised to watch over him."

He was bent over Aslak, whose battered corpse had been laid down in the courtyard by Gudorm and Thorgeir. Shocked, they had found it thrown on a midden and carried it back to Coyran.

"I hope he has found peace with God now. I will pray for him; there's nothing more we can do." William had been bought to his knees with sorrow. "Aslak brought this on himself: Sigrid didn't want to go home, and he refused to accept that. In his youthful mind, he was doing the correct thing to keep his family's honor intact. I understand it. We couldn't even buy her back. I tried."

Calmly he looked into Rogenvaldr's eyes and said clearly: "I'm telling you, we must leave. Get away to Jerusalem while we can. Girls being killed, our men attacked and imprisoned, another man killed? Forces are working against us. All it will take is one more terrible murder and we could all be executed by a mob; or someone will see a terrible omen and accuse us of heresy. We are very vulnerable here. Remember, the horn is a fake! And this is not our land."

"It is if I marry Ermengard," said Rogenvaldr very quietly.

William inhaled swiftly and crossed himself three times. "You can't do that—you are on pilgrimage. This dalliance has already gone too far. You are being tempted by Eve—you must resist."

"Like you did? No, this place is paradise on earth."

"No. It's the Garden of Eden. Beware of the serpent!" William made the sign of the cross over his friend's head.

"I can't bring myself to bury him in a grave in this land that killed him. We will honor him by sending him off with the old ways."

A pyre was built in a small ship at a bend in the Aude behind Coyran. During that time of blue light between day and night, Aslak was sent to heaven down the river in a burning boat. It was a strange mixture of pagan love and Christian love. The Norsemen, led by Bishop William, knelt in prayer on the riverbank as the floating pyre began its journey downstream.

In the dark, Ermengard sat in the window of her palace, watching with sadness as the glowing embers of Aslak's remains drifted by on its way to the sea. *Is this the end?*

CHAPTER 26

One who is unable to utter a sound
cannot sing
cannot find the words
cannot know how to rhyme,
cannot hear the true reason for a song.
              —Jaufré Rudel, troubadour 1125-1146?

The morning air was still cool when Guilliam the Templar, Brother Ramon, and Brother Gilbert left the Cathedral at Maguelone to continue their journey to Ganagobie. Squinting in the sun they kicked their mounts past a small cove where tonsured fisherman busily gathered nets into their blue and red skiffs before pushing off into the glossy sea.

Leaving the coast behind, they joined up with pilgrims on the Via Domitia to reach the ancient Roman hostel in Ambrussum, a stopping post in use for a thousand years. Mentioned in the Pilgrim's Guide to the Holy Land, travelers paid handsomely for the privilege of eating its bad food and sleeping in its filthy rooms. Yet at least it was here, somewhere in the middle of nowhere, surrounded by sandbanks and lagoons, and high, sharp escarpments running parallel to the road.

The small stone chamber, sized to hold two Roman soldiers, had no windows and an old, ragged curtain for privacy. The monks slept huddled together in the center of the floor to avoid the dark corners which looked and smelled as if they hadn't been cleaned since Domitian's legions had passed through.

Guilliam couldn't sleep. Other travelers were shuffling around in the dark looking for trouble; low rumbling voices, a laugh, a curse; the smell of roast pork creeping in under the curtain. *If anything happens to his cursed monks, the Archbishop will flay me alive. Why is he putting so much pressure on me to bring him this precious missive that he is willing to buy with so much gold?* The bag of gold coins he was to give to the Abbot of Ganagobie was hot and heavy in his crotch. *At the pace they ride it's going to take at least another week to get there. I want the extra payment that the Archbishop promised me for a quick delivery of the document. Merde!* He slapped dead a black insect the size of his thumb crawling down his arm, pulled himself up, and put his forehead on his knees to doze.

Dawn found them hurriedly washing down bread and cheese with local white wine. The long push to Béucaire began. The town of Nimes was on the way, but the Templar had been warned of its dangers to travelers.

"Hurry up," Guilliam said incessantly. "I want to get through Nimes before nightfall." *God save me from these donkeys and the asses on them. I'll be as old as they are by the time we get to Ganagobie Abbey.* "Saint Médard protect us! The Siròc is beginning to blow! Go!"

All the travelers rushed forward, legs fruitlessly kicking up and down on unwilling donkeys to make them trot. The sound of whips and cries blew by them. It was useless to try and outrun the wind. With scarves wrapped around their faces, bodies curled into a ball, they pushed into a stinging wall of sand that blotted out the world. Only the road, with its half-buried stones was left to guide them. Summer-dried bushes tumbled around their heads in the diffuse glow of an unseen sun.

The Siròc died down at dusk, but it had delayed them. The light was blue when they entered Nimes, the jagged black shadow of its Roman coliseum looming ahead. Unsavory eyes regarded the riders with curiosity, squinting with recognition of the Templar's red cross glowing on his white tunic.

Ramon and Gilbert, frozen in fear, had stopped in their tracks.

"Are you crazed? Keep going forward! Those men—pirates, thieves, mercenary soldiers, diseased beggars—they'd slit your throat for your sandals! They all live in the coliseum—it's their fortress, the walls are now their protective ramparts. Whew—what a stink. Oh no! My God in heaven, move quickly! These younger ones are merciless!"

A screaming gang of children arrived, throwing rocks and chasing after them. Under their dirt-caked bare feet, feral cats and dogs swarmed along in the hopes of a meal.

With shaking voices, the two terrified brothers were praying:

Deliver me from my enemies, Oh my God,
deliver me from those who work evil,
save me from bloodthirsty men
snarling with their lips —

Guilliam was frantic. "Stop praying and move! They can get a good price for a donkey, or just eat it." *Or maybe a monk too.* Sounding like an angry shepherd, he herded them around the curved walls while using his sword to mercilessly hack away at the children. "There — go to the right — the road out begins again."

Occasionally he would turn backwards in the saddle, swinging his weapon behind the horse to make the mob keep its distance.

As the cries faded behind them in the dark, exhaustion set in. Plautus refused to budge. Ramon got off the tired beast and held some bread in front of his nose. Pulling his lead they began to walk, Ramon's sandals scuffing in the dirt as he dragged his feet. As always, Justus followed Plautus. A full moon and a sky full of stars illuminated the paving stones and carriage ruts; Roman distance markers gave them hope in the night. Occasionally there was a jingle of another traveler's harness, or the thunk of a wagon wheel rocking a loose paving stone.

At dawn they entered Béucaire, where the comforting vibration of distant bells ringing for matins floated over the lavender plains. To their right was the vast spread of the Rhone River, its silvery waters widening into its enormous delta as it spread across the land, fertilizing soil all the way down to the Mediterranean.

Guilliam asked a thin, hunched-over farmer throwing grayish-green cabbages for directions to the Abbey of Saint-Romanus the Melodist, their next overnight stop. Startling everyone, Ramon climbed back on Plautus, whipping him to get to the Abbey as fast as possible.

Ramon's heart was pounding, his mind spinning. *The revered Saint Romanus!* A Byzantine poet living in Constantinople, he had composed hundreds of odes in the sixth century to become the patron saint of hymns and church singers. Music was Ramon's life. *Saint Romanus! My namesake! You, to whom my life as choirmaster at Saint Just has been devoted, I can actually glorify you in song to God in your own church!*

Built close to God, the Abbey was high up at the end of a rocky winding road that climbed through a cloud to a plateau with a spectacular view of the river valley below.

The Benedictine Abbey of Saint Romanus turned out to be a vast cave monastery in which monks lived in the limestone rock. The young blond monk who came out to greet them answered their questioning looks in a soft, mellifluous voice.

"We are trōglodyta, cave dwellers, and our monastery is a church cave in which we worship God by singing the works of Saint Ramon." Behind him, waves of music surged out of an arched entrance carved into the mountain.

Entering the shaded chamber, they could see at the top of some roughly cut steps, a circular apse cut into the cave wall. The saint's tomb was a grave chiseled out of the rock, upon which had been placed a marble slab. Candles, attached by their own melting wax, glowed around a gold statue of Saint Ramon. Standing on a gold hymnal, arms outspread, his singing face was lifted up to God. The uneven ceiling was supported by roughly cut rock columns.

Ten black-robed monks stood in a semi-circle at the foot of the steps singing in harmony. The low ceiling bounced ringing notes off the walls; the reverberating echoes entered ones very bones. The musical notes intertwined like vines of luscious, ripe, grapes.

Ramon felt light-headed. *I know that ode. It's 'Death of a Monk.'* Joy suffused his very being. *Saint Augustine was right. At last, I have heard the intervals of perfect consonance, the origins of creation!* Forgetting hunger, forgetting his aching tired bones, he moved up behind the ten monks and began to chant the 'kontakion' with them. Hearing the harmonics of his voice, its sweet tone blending perfectly with theirs, they murmured to each other, "by the words of Boethius, he has perfect tone!" Smiling at him, they moved to make a space for him in their circle.

Guilliam and Gilbert looked at each other.

At the end of a long tunnel were the cells in which they were to spend the night. A curtain, straw bed, and a candle were the only comforts; still it was clean and cool. *You could freeze your balls off in the winter,* thought Guilliam.

"We eat at vespers. You will hear the bell even here. The kitchen and food hall are outside the church. The cooking odors of food must never mix with the holy scent of incense or dry our throats. We eat plainly as spice affects the tone of our voices. There is a spring outside by the path. There is a path around the back where you can go to relieve yourself. You must not piss in the tunnels. You are welcome to sit and listen to our prayers; they may quiet your souls."

Ramon never came to his cell. The whole night one heard singing meander throughout the tunnels, on and on and on in harmonic circles.

The next morning Ramon kept them waiting while he went to sing at matins. When he finally emerged, his soft brown eyes were red rimmed in his pale face. Shaking hands were clutched in front of him.

"I don't feel well. I can't ride today."

Guilliam was furious. "By the balls of Saint Michael, you just want to live with your little choir here. Are you such a churl that you have forgotten your duty to the Archbishop? He is impatiently waiting in Narbonne for the documents we are to witness at Ganagobie! Do you dare to make him wait a minute longer than necessary?"

Abruptly dismounting, he grabbed the monk roughly by the arm and dragged him around the cave to a dirt field. Scattered around were flat rectangular graves covered in green lichen. Sculpted figures of knights and monks lay sleeping on top of them. "If you insist on remaining here, this is where you will remain, never to sing again. Do I make myself clear?"

Ramon shrank back, for Guilliam suddenly looked like the soldier he really was.

"How do you feel now?" the Templar asked in a mock solicitous voice.

"Oh, much better. The fresh air has done me good."

Brother Ramon's tears flowed hidden under his monk's hood as he plodded down the path. *Like Satan, I have been exiled from heaven.*

As the riders descended into the mountain's cloud, tendrils of music followed them until the silver floating mist swallowed the notes.

CHAPTER 27

And I saw another mighty angel
come down from heaven,
clothed with a cloud;
and a rainbow was upon his head,
and his face was as it were the sun,
and his feet as pillars of fire. . .

　　　　　　　　　　　　—Revelation 10:1

The sun sat low on Narbonne's horizon; tomorrow would be another sweltering day. A warm banket of mist hung in the air after a heavy, mid-summer downpour unexpectedly drenched the rust-colored fields of millet, oats, chickpeas, and wheat just laboriously tilled by farmers north of the city. The wealth of the salt pans to the south was now soggy and immovable. To the west, endless terraced vineyards happily drank in the warm water to plump up their grapes, as tired workers started the climb up through wet lavender and thyme to their huts. Eastwards grazed the sheep—thousands of soggy sheep, feeding on scrub in the high, jagged limestone plateaus or summer grass in the valleys. Golden rays crept around long shadows still glistening with raindrops.

In Narbonne, crowds of local peasants and merchants mingled with visiting pilgrims. Hurriedly greeting each other they ran anxiously around town to complete final errands before the sun went down and night set evil demons free to roam the streets.

Along the Via Domitia, people slipped on cobblestones wet with slime and manure. Sweating from the sun's sharp rays, annoyed pedestrians jostled each other while trying to avoid carts rushing onto the Roman bridge. It didn't help that, hurrying to close their shops on the roadway, tired butchers left sheep and horse offal on the pavement, ignoring the blood pooling between the cobblestones.

Canon Hugon was pushing through the crowd to get to Ermengard's palace.

Christ help me—how I wish I was in Prémontré. Now I understand that I was truly living in heaven. The peace, the solitude. Not these crazed southerners and their heresies. How many times do I have to warn this ignorant woman of the devils in her midst?

A few days ago, in fear of the Canon's authority, her guards had given him entrance, and he had cornered the Viscountess in her study.

Ermengard looked up, displeased by his unexpected appearance. *As if I have nothing else to do but listen to this smelly old dog.* "Excuse us, Canon Hugon, but we are busy. What is it you want this time?"

Again he lectured her severely. "It's becoming more difficult than ever to walk around without seeing heretics everywhere. The streets are congested with peddlers, beggars, the poor, the maimed, the sick— never mind the thieves and joglars. Heretics are hiding amongst them! Don't think for a moment that they are not there skulking around, having secret meetings, gaining converts!" Slimy spittle was forming at the edges of his lips.

"Unfortunately, I am loathe to burn at the stake every resident of Narbonne at this time; though I am sure you are of the prevailing sentiment that 'God will know his own'.

He left her presence frustrated with the lack of action. *She's not listening...I must be more forceful with her. Who knows, perhaps she's a heretic herself.*

Ow! Christ in heaven! He winced when an elbow struck his back. For the last three days Godfrey had whipped him to atone for sin. The sin was not the murders: it was the tremendous enjoyment he had felt committing them. He needed the release. Now that he had been cleansed, he felt refreshed, his ardor for the work to be done renewed. He kept pushing through the crowd to the palace.

Again the guards had been ordered to prevent his entry. When threatened with immediate ex-communication of their whole families, they nervously directed him to a flight of stairs leading to Ermengard's rooftop garden overlooking the river. When he arrived at the top landing, he stopped to stare through a curlicued arch. The twilight sky revealed an appalling scene of mortal sin.

This woman is debauched and unholy. She is lost, a tool of Satan.

He viewed with disgust the flowered blue tiles on the floor, the blue-and-gold feathered peacock fountains, the purple and green blooming orchids, the pillowed couches, the frosty silk curtains floating in the breeze, the sweating pitchers of iced wine and red glass goblets on low tables surrounded by dried fruits, yogurt, fresh grapes and oranges. *No wonder her city is rotting from within. And that cursed Viking and trobaritz are here.*

Rogenvaldr was in an excellent mood. Blian and Gimkel were now on board his ship. "Yesterday, I went to D'Anduze with a final warning: 'Give up my men or tomorrow three- hundred Norsemen will come to free them.' The churchman finally grasped what I was saying and so, last night, we secretly got them back."

He was sitting close to Ermengard on some floor cushions and wanted to get rid of these other people.

"I want to be alone with you," he murmured into her ear. "Why don't you just let your people take care of it?"

"Because they are the children of my friends."

Hugon stomped forward. "Viscountess, hear me!" he intoned in his most dreadful voice. "Narbonne is swimming in sin! I accuse you of harboring heresy!"

Ermengard was furious. *Oh, no, him again? Jesus aid me. . . I don't need him harassing me in front of everyone. I will skin alive the guard who let him in.*

Trembling at his presence, Beatritz kept her face calm as her heart pounded rapidly. *Don't look at him—he will see your fear, your suspicions.*

But Hugon ignored her to confront Ermengard. "You just sit here while Satan destroys the soul of Narbonne. I see his minions in every dark corner."

"I assure you, Canon Hugon, we are most attentive to our duties and use all our powers to stop the spread of heretical views. My people are faithful Catholics who pray daily for salvation."

Ermengard did not offer him a seat, and the fact that he had to remain standing irritated him to no end. "Obviously, you are just a weak woman. A descendant of Eve is not fit to rule this kingdom. I will insist to the Pope that he replace you. Your negligence allows heretical eggs to hatch!"

Eggs? What is he babbling about? Ermengard thought impatiently. *Is he mad?* "We are on excellent terms with the Holy Father, just as we are with the King of France."

Beatritz had a revelation. *Hatching eggs? Is that what these children are? Little chicks? God in heaven, help us survive him, or we will need to recite the consolamentum each day we live.*

Hugon continued his rant. "You foul yourself with pagans like him," he snapped, pointing at Rogenvaldr, who immediately exploded.

"How dare you! I'll have you know my uncle is Saint Magnus!"

"Pah! Never heard of him," said Hugon.

The next moment everyone's face turned red. The arguing stopped as they all turned to look up at the sky. When the enormous glowing rainbow first appeared to curve across the darkening sky from horizon to horizon, people turned their backs to the sun, looking up in awe. Grateful to see such a fortunate act of God, they all smiled, and crossed themselves with the knowledge that it would bring luck to all their endeavors.

Slowly the rainbow drained itself of all of its colors—except red. As the arc grew stronger, redder, and brighter in the heavens, its light bathed the rolling fields and farms in a bath of blood. The red sun became a glowing, Satanic eye.

"It's the devil's eye!" people cried, kissing the crosses hanging from their necks.

Beatritz raised both hands to cover her eyes and hide the vision. *God protect me from Satan's face!*

Bathed in blood light, Ermengard had cried out, "Mother Mary! Save me!" and clambered forward onto her knees.

Hugon was calculating his options. *Aha! God has sent me a weapon of destruction to use in my mission. I must master Satan and figure out which way to best bend the devil to my will.*

• • •

Towns and villages bled under the red light of Satan's eye. Peoples' faces and upraised hands were edged in red, their white eye globes distorted in fear. Grazing white sheep turned scarlet wooled; the liquid eyes of beasts glinted blood; waves churned up by watermills foamed red. In the crimson mirror of the lagoons, salt fields glistened under bloody blankets. The red shadow crossed the land and, like God's Angel of Death in the Old Testament, stealthily entered open doors and seeped into windows to spread a plague of fear.

Swollen pregnant women turned their backs to the arc, hunched over, covering their wombs with crossed hands to protect their unborn babes.

Salt rakers fell to their knees on mounds of crystals sparkling like rubies.

When the sea turned red, ships stopped sailing, their crimson sails limp in the windless air. Frightened sailors huddled in the bilges with the rats.

Thousands of ravens, flapping black shadows against a sky awash in glowing, fire-edged clouds, screaming raucously, dove down to grab human hair with their sharp, curled claws. People ran, covering their heads, in fear of the demons coming for them.

And the eye of Satan glared from Hell as the red rainbow drowned Narbonne in the blood of Christ.

What are they all upset about? Rogenvaldr had no fear—he knew what the red rainbow was, had seen it in the frozen north sky. Deep inside his heart was pagan knowledge that would forever be a part of his soul. God and Christ's love were everywhere, yet the old gods were still secretly hiding under the rocks and up in the heavens. *I must explain to her*—

"Ermengard, my love. Have no fear. This red light is the Bifrost, the heavenly burning rainbow bridge leading to Asgard, where the Norse road to heaven is guarded by Heimdallr, the one Shining God."

She looked at him with fear—*is he mad? What is he talking about?*

Hugon was elated! *Now I've got you, Rogenvaldr! Thank you, Jesus, for sending this perfect portent for me to use in my mission. Now, where is that Archbishop?*

Smirking, he ran out to find D'Anduze.

"Quick, to Saint Paul-Serge—we must pray for salvation. Hurry, for the love of Christ!" Ermengard wailed as they all rushed out after Hugon.

Luna, unmoving, sat on her haunches, white fur a spiked orange ball, her wet eyes reflecting the flames of Hell.

• • •

Another day of arguing about window construction had come to an end. The light in his study was dimming and soon it would be impossible to calculate the numbers. D'Anduze rose to retrieve another candle and copper mirror from a niche holding the ancient stone statue of Saint Just. *Maybe I should fight Ermengard to increase my share of the salt tax, and maybe build another bread oven. Whatever is that wailing sound? Are those really voices I'm hearing? And it's getting louder, a keening now.*

He went to the window and pushed the shutters back as far as possible. The red arc in the sky frightened him so much that his blood literally ran cold as his knees went out from under him. Leaning out the window, he saw Satan's eye and began trembling, wondering what sin the city had committed to have loosed this awful presence in their midst. Then he remembered one of the ancient writings: "A sanguine arc only appears when a unicorn dies."

Hah! Now I've got you, Rogenvaldr! Perhaps now, if I'm very clever, I can get that horn. Everyone believes its real; those conniving Vikings know it's a fake. A unicorn hasn't really died. Hah! I've got it! I must speak to the Sacristan immediately.

Getting to Saint Paul-Serge wasn't easy. Frightened military guards had to push a way through hysterical crowds until they arrived at the back door of the church and pushed in to where the Sacristan was hiding in fear.

"No one is listening. I can't calm them down," he shouted at D'Anduze when he bolted through the door. "You must be the one to do it."

Just then Hugon, black cloak flying behind him, also ran into the sacristy with the face of a raging angel. Grabbing both of them he revealed what he had just heard Rogenvaldr tell Ermengard about the Bifrost. The three churchmen agreed: Rogenvaldr had to leave Narbonne. Each one hated him for their own reasons.

Canon Hugon despised him for being a pagan, the worst kind of heretic.

The Sacristan despised what he believed was an adulteress affair with the vulnerable Viscountess, who had never been proven a widow.

D'Anduze agreed with the Sacristan, but he really wanted the Earl gone so he could sell the horn.

Together they agreed on a plan of action. "Go get the horn from my donjon," D'Anduze ordered his guards. "And be quick about it. Don't let anyone see you with it."

• • •

The setting sun had taken the blood rainbow with it, but there still seemed to be a brown stain on the land. People from the fields were crawling on their knees over the stone roads leading into the city gates, the surface rubbing their skin raw with a comforting pain. Pain was good, it absolved sin as it joined one's soul with the suffering of Christ on the Cross. Bodies crawled up the steps into Saint Paul-Serge.

As the crush of worshipers surged forward, the air became stifling hot, unbreathable, stinking of fear. Crunched against the huge pillars, no one could avoid the unforgiving stare, the unblinking white eyes and black pupils of saints looking down on the sinners below.

In accordance with Hugon's plan, the rood screen was placed near the altar and closed to everyone except nobility. Ermengard had arrived, crying. Rogenvaldr, perspiring profusely in the heat, knelt on the stone floor beside her.

Beatritz and Alais held hands, pale and frightened by what was happening. Hugon had deliberately placed himself behind Beatritz, examining her neck intensely, enjoying the thought of slicing it in half.

My God, I can smell his breath behind me. Is he going to denounce me now, here in church? She had a vision of herself burning at the stake. At the thought of Alais burning, she nearly fainted. Reaching over, she pulled her daughter closer.

Kneeling next to Rogenvaldr, William whispered nervously. "I warned you in no uncertain terms to stop lingering in Narbonne. These people are more superstitious than they are religious. That frightful rainbow threatens them with God's wrath; and now we are in serious danger because they will probably blame us for it. I pray it doesn't go that way, but I am very fearful it might."

Guarding the Earl, Erling Skakki's tense eyes were watching hands in the crowd for a knife.

Archbishop D'Anduze swept out from behind the altar holding up the horn in widespread arms. Under the gold miter, his face was a mask of fury; rivulets of sweat dripped onto his white robes. Holding it up high, so all could see the bejeweled casement glittering in the candlelight, he turned and slowly placed it on the altar. A moan swept through the crowd as the Archbishop raised his clasped hands in heavenly supplication.

"Save us," he cried, "save us from Satan, save us from God's wrath!"

D'Anduze whipped around to face them, thundering: "Remember the darkness and moldiness of spring before the Vikings arrived? I told you then it was a forewarning from God to stop sinning. But you did not listen! Now, because of your weakness we have been warned again."

Stepping to the side, he turned and pointed to the altar where the unicorn horn rested in its gold sheath.

"Here is the cause of our sins! There you see the horn of a dead unicorn—the original Word of God who sacrificed his only son. We have killed Christ again! I will repeat to you again the words of the holy Father Ambrose of Milan:

> *A red rainbow only appears when a unicorn dies.*
> *And who is this unicorn but God's only son?*
> *The only word of God who has been close to God*
> *from the Beginning! The Word, whose horn shall*
> *cast down and raise up nations! The unicorn is*
> *Christ—God's only son and God's Word.*

The unicorn has been slaughtered and you have paid your thirty pieces of silver to purchase his horn! We are now cursed to Hell by God!"

Tears were flowing down frightened faces. "Save us!" the crowd cried over wringing hands.

"But we ourselves did not do the killing," he shouted angrily. Eyes glaring, he turned, and rigidly pointed his staff at Rogenvaldr. "That man did the killing! From cold pagan northlands he came here with a gold-sheathed horn of Christ in his hands. He came to corrupt us, to corrupt our pure, noble Viscountess Ermengard, to kill our innocent children. He has brought this curse on us!

"And I have proof—the holy Canon Hugon of Prémontré, who has graced us with his presence in Narbonne, he himself has heard with his own ears, the pagan Earl Rogenvaldr tell Viscountess Ermengard that she should not be afraid—that the blood-red rainbow in the sky is the burning bridge leading to Asgard, where the Norse road to heaven is guarded by Heimdallr, the one Shining God." He glared at Ermengard: "Is this the truth? Did he say those words?"

Terrified, she stared at the Archbishop, then turned her head to look at Rogenvaldr, then back at the Archbishop. "Yes, but. . . "

Thibault De Plaigne stood up, pointing a finger at Rogenvaldr. "I myself heard him say those pagan words."

"Earl Rogenvaldr must be burnt for his heresy." Signaling to the Templar guards, D'Anduze ordered them, "arrest the sinner so we can lift the curse!"

Before Rogenvaldr's men could stop them, the guards had grabbed him, dragging him kicking and screaming through the arched doorway behind the altar.

"No, stop this arrest! I command you to stop what you're doing!" None of Ermengard's protests stopped them. When it came to the care of the souls of Narbonne, Archbishop D'Anduze outranked her.

Bound with thick ropes, four men carried the struggling Earl down torchlit stairs, winding around shadowy corridors to finally throw him into the same cell that had held Gimkel and Blian. Quickly they shackled his foot, jumping back when the ropes were taken off. His furious attack was checked only when the chain on his ankle snapped taut, jerking him to the floor.

Once again, the jail clanked shut on a Norseman. When they left, the pounding of their boots and raucous laughter died through the bars. At first, furious, Rogenvaldr fought the captivity, cursing and yelling. Then he fell quietly into thought. The thick chain clanked as he painfully went on his knees to pray. There was a deep chill in the air that held the odor of human waste and dead animals.

Alone, blind in the dark, he gradually gained insight into his deception—and its consequences. *I knew it wasn't a unicorn horn, yet still I sold it to Ermengard as if it was real. Is God punishing me for this? If so, I must be guilty of a great sin. Maybe, like Judas, I have sold Christ for my thirty pieces of silver. William was right; he kept trying to warn me— 'this is no way to start a crusade'. I couldn't hear him. I trusted the king. I should never have given in to the temptation. Lord Christ, forgive me. What disaster has my greed set in motion?*

• • •

Eindredi Ungi was a longtime sailor who knew a bad portent when he saw one. As the blood rainbow grew from one horizon to the other, he ordered the lur blown in a danger signal, warning all sailors to immediately return to their ships. In the red light, scuttling like black vermin, they came running and rowing. Between the time the news of Rogenvaldr's arrest arrived and church bells began ringing for compline, fourteen Norse longboats carrying one-thousand-nine hundred moribatani gold coins were racing eastwards towards Byzantium. Looking back from the prow of his boat, Eindredi could see the silhouette of Rogenvaldr's lone ship, black against the waning light of a setting sun reflecting on the waves.

CHAPTER 28

I, for love of thee, am bound
in this dungeon underground,
all for loving thee must lie
here, where loud on thee I cry,
here for loving thee must die
for thee, my love.
—Aucassin and Nicolette, 12th cent., anonymous

Aching from prayer in a dank corner of the dungeon, he ignored the clay bowl of tepid fish soup that a hungry cat was lapping up. *You eat it. You deserve it more than I do.*

Sandals scraped uncertainly on the stairs as a flame came down the curved stone walls. "Rogenvaldr . . . Rogenvaldr, where are you?"

"I'm here, keep going down."

Framed by shaggy hair parted in the middle, William's face loomed out of the darkness. From below, the lamp defined his lean cheekbones and threw pinpoints of light into his concerned eyes. "Finally, I found you. The jailor wouldn't guide me. Had to give him a gold coin just to get into this rat warren. Fine mess you're in. I bought you some food and wine." He slid it under the bars. "Praying to get out? Well, it just might take God to get you out of here. The Archbishop and Canon Hugo both want you to disappear—permanently."

"Take my confession; I might die at any moment." Rogenvaldr spoke softly.

"Well, you might be right," William replied gruffly, taking an old ivory cross from its pouch. It's gold corners glinted in the lamplit. "Speak, my son, that you be shriven."

"Forgive me Father, for I have sinned greatly. My selling of the horn was against God. To finance a pilgrimage based on the theft of not only coin, but faith and hope, was a sin. I knew that the horn was but the tooth of a sea monster and I sold it as a holy relic, thus deceiving a devout Christian woman. Lust then caused me to forget my dear wife Vgret as I took the virginity of the woman I deceived. And I also broke my promise to Aslak's mother. Now, if I die, I might never see heaven. I accept that. My greed and arrogance deserve death. I wait calmly for its approach and will accept your judgement."

"You're right about yourself. It's about time you understood what you have done," William said. "In nominee Patris, et Filii, et Spiritus Sancti, Amen. We absolve you."

Rogenvaldr fell back onto his heels.

"Wait," sputtered William. "What do you mean you 'took the virginity of the woman you deceived'? Ermengard is twice a widow."

"I swear, I didn't know. Until I realized what I was doing—then it was too late."

"Too late? Too late? What in God's name is the matter with you?"

"I would marry her," Rogenvaldr said. "If she'd have me."

"And stay here with the whole town wanting you burned as Satan's henchman? Your men want to leave Narbonne as soon as possible. Your destiny is Jerusalem! Ermengard is furious at your imprisonment, yet she can't get you out of here because the Archbishop won't release you into her keeping. Probably the only reason you're still alive is the possibility of a war with Norway if he executes you. By the way, Eindredi is gone, with his fourteen ships and four-fifths of the gold. Your cousin left for Jerusalem as soon as the red arc appeared, and word got out you were imprisoned."

"Eindredi's gone?" Rogenvaldr almost laughed at the irony. "So much for family."

"Obviously, he's smarter than you are. And since when did being family keep a Norseman from stealing from his cousin, or for that matter scheming to get his kingdom. May Jesus give you back your senses, you fool. You're really too old for this. Perhaps we can buy your release."

"No. If God wants me out, he'll get me out. Now you must go."

The jailor's grizzled face had quietly appeared in a circle of torchlight.

William put the little oil lamp on the floor and pushed it in front of his friend.

Left alone once more, Rogenvaldr got back on his knees. *Forgive me Vgret and Ermengard. I deceived you both and wronged you both . . . and debased any love we shared.* He sighed deeply with regret.

Silently meditating, he focused on the tiny spot of flickering light left by William. The feeble flame grew larger, then suddenly broke up into long glowing lines of fire that took the form of a church steeple with a fiery cross on top of its point. The spire's light grew larger and brighter until it filled the whole black cell with warmth as a circle of rays streaked out from its center. A golden halo took form in which the face of his uncle, Saint Magnus, was gradually revealed. The Saint was speaking to him, although the words were faint. But as the long face with its triangular beard and round, watery blue eyes became more distinct, he could hear them clearly.

"Rogenvaldr, what hast thou done? Thou hast brought the old pagan ways of deception with thee on pilgrimage. Wouldst thou bring them to the Holy Land? And thou hast been lustful on thy sacred journey."

"Sainted uncle, help me find the way out of the darkness of my soul."

"The light shineth in the darkness; and the darkness comprehends it not. Even in this dungeon is one able to bear witness to the true Light of God. Art thou a simple man who must be nourished by fruit and singing of birds? The fruit is bitter, and the song is false. Haven't I taught thee thus? Thy pride is the beginning of all thy sins. Look into the mirror of your true mind and you will find the Supreme God."

"I truly love her . . ."

"The only true love is the love of God, who gave his Son for our salvation. That love will save you in the trial to come. Remember, only God's love will save you."

"Saint Magnus, stay with me."

"I am always with you . . ." The face blurred as the voice faded away. The empty halo glowed for a short time, then the rays contracted back into the little flame of the oil lamp. Saint Magnus had taken the warmth with him. Rogenvaldr felt the dank cold of the dungeon settle into his shoulders as he continued to meditate on his uncle's words.

As soon as William left, the jailor sprinted up to the Archbishop to report the conversation.

"Bishop William wants the Earl to leave. He's afraid now because the other Norsemen have left for Jerusalem."

"Good." *Now where is that misbegotten Templar Guilliam with my testament of proof from Ganagobie Abbey? Why are those monks taking so long?* He grumbled to himself. *That letter will get rid of all these cursed Norsemen once and for all, including Rogenvaldr. And then I can sell the horn. All this waiting is frustrating and irritating.*

The jailor, head down, was still standing there hopefully.

"Here." The Archbishop handed him a silver solidus. "Continue to let me know of any other information you hear."

"Yes, your holiness. By the way, it seems that Ermengard was a virgin when she met him. He took her maidenhead."

"He what?"

"Yes, he told this in confession to Bishop William, who seemed very put out and called him a fool."

"Well, well. Go now. And keep all this to yourself." *Who would have thought. God in heaven, I hope she isn't with child. He'll never leave.*

CHAPTER 29

Be sober,
be vigilant,
because your adversary the devil
walketh about,
seeking whom he may devour.

—1 Peter 5:8

"Captain Breuil, go now and slip the remaining seven men out of Coyran after dark. Make sure they get safely back to their ship. The last thing I need is for a bunch of ruffians to attack and massacre them. I don't understand why the other Norsemen left in such a hurry, but it's just as well. We could have all been massacred in our beds if they had decided to attack us to get Rogenvaldr out of jail. It's all beyond my understanding."

Ermengard rubbed her bloodshot eyes as she sat down on a sofa. "Now, Beatritz, what have you found out? We must still solve the mystery of who killed the children. If the town thinks it's Rogenvaldr, he'll never get out of the Archbishop's dungeon. He'll rot there, just as my first husband did."

Beatritz was very matter of fact. "I've been searching for the horse that was being paraded out as a unicorn, and I've found it. Now I need to find out who purchased it. But I'm not getting much help. Your military guard claims no one has seen anything, but the truth is, they are men, and don't much care about the killing of two maidens. The general feeling is that the dead girls concern only the parents; they should have been more closely watched, should have been kept at home, should have been married off."

"Well, I care," said Ermengard. "They were the children of friends. It's my city, and I'm still commanding everyone to keep searching for the killer. D'Anduze will never release Rogenvaldr unless the real murderer is found and executed. He so generously claims that it's for the Earl's own safety. But he didn't have to arrest him in the first place. This is all against me, I know it. For the love of Christ, how do I get him out of there?"

"I shall keep searching, my lady." *Another day gone. It seems hopeless. Why am I doing this?* Frustration and fatigue colored Beatritz's tone. "I just wish I knew why the killer chose *them*. Was it random? On purpose? They died virgins—doesn't that mean something?" She looked up; someone was coming. *Oh God in heaven, let it not be the Canon again.*

"Bernautz de Ventadorn!" Ermengard's face lit up.

The singer, who was known as the perfect troubadour glided into her solar outfitted in a blue robe cut up the side to reveal a red floral design and green hose, all set off by tight yellow sleeves. Bowing, he extended a pointy green shoe and doffed a huge floppy hat topped with lustrous peacock feathers that swept the floor.

"Yes, Viscountess. I come from Toulouse, where tales of the red arc have caused a great stir." Bernautz crinkled his blue eyes and shook a head full of blond curls. "As has the news of two murdered maidens. Some say it is the unicorn who killed them, some say the Norsemen"

"I have such a pain in my head from it all. I am so glad you are here. Please, play some music so I become calmer."

"I'm here to serve you." The troubadour pulled his portable organ out of the case swung over his shoulder and put its strap around his neck. Stopping a minute to take a long drink of chilled wine flavored with orange zest, he casually remarked, "I recently learned this in Toulouse."

Beatritz looked up at him. He had a message for her.

After a short bow, Bernautz started pumping the bellows with his left hand as his right fluidly played the horizontal keys. The air soon rang with his lyrical tenor voice:

> *I will not hide my love for you*
> *For, at least, I'll make it clear that*
> *though you behave unpleasantly,*
> *God does not blame you for your folly.*

I will not hide my love for you.
Though I die for that love tomorrow
flames of passion would be a solace,
or they come from a heart unanswered.

I will not hide my love for you.
Though tortured by your downcast eyes
I will wait tonight in our meadow
beneath the tower of love's perfection.

Beatritz took a deep breath. Bernautz had just told her that a Bonne Fille was going to be burned at the stake tomorrow in Toulouse. She was instructed to come to a meeting tonight in the ruins of the old Roman water tower east of Narbonne. Catching his eye, she gave a thin smile, as if in appreciation of his song.

After a few more verses he claimed fatigue. "By your leave, my lady, I will retire. I must go to Carcassonne tomorrow."

"Yes, go, go." Ermengard waved her hand in dismissal, distracted by her yearning for Rogenvaldr.

"I also need some rest if I am to continue my search for answers tomorrow. With your permission." Beatritz bowed herself out. She felt bad for leaving her mistress alone, but she had to go to that meeting. Upon her arrival, everyone was still awake in her chamber.

Alais was too troubled to sleep; her nurse was sitting on the trundle bed at her side. A chamber maid was carefully putting freshly cleaned clothes into a chest.

"You may leave us," she ordered, a bit too abruptly.

The girl curtsied and left the chamber, but carefully made sure that the door was left slightly open. Watching Beatritz through the crack she saw her grab her hooded black cloak and pull back the tapestry covering the door. "Ah, I know those stairs!" the maid thought.

"Mama, don't go out tonight. I'm afraid to be alone." Alais reached out to her.

"It's alright, my child. I won't be long; stay calm. You'll have Alana with you."

"I can't sleep. Those two girls—"

Beatritz returned and sat down on the bed. "I'll stay with you until you sleep. Now lie down and close your eyes. I'm here. Alana, lie down near her."

The chamber maid hurriedly ran down the regular palace stairs.

Later, when both Alais and Alana finally slept, Beatritz wrapped the cloak around herself and pushed through the tapestry. Avoiding well known creaks she slipped down the ancient wooden stairs.

• • •

Hugon was just preparing to be scourged when there was the sound of loud banging on the hidden entrance of the Archbishop's palace near his chamber.

"Hurry up and see who it is before the guards notice the noise."

Godfrey put down the whip and ran into the hall to open the door. When he saw Beatritz's chamber maid, he dragged her abruptly into the corridor. "Stay there. Don't move.."

Hugon immediately came to speak with her. The terrified girl had been turned into a spy when the Canon threatened her whole family with ex-communication if she didn't give him the information he needed, and some coin if she did.

"H-h-holy f-f-ather," she stammered in fear, barely visible in the unlit corridor, her white hat quivering. "The Countess de Dente is leaving the palace by the old Roman back stairs."

"Where are they? How do I find them?"

"The stairs go down to the small door on the side of the palace opposite here." By now the maid was quaking.

"Thank you, my child. You are doing God's work." A solidus slipped into her hand ensured more of God's work. After checking the alley to make sure it was deserted, he turned his iron gaze on her: "Now return, and not a word if you love your family and Jesus."

Without a backwards glance, she skittered back to the palace and the safety of her own chamber. *That man is a friend of the Devil, I just know it.*

Hugon ran to his chamber to grab a vial of poppy juice and a blanket. *No time to change out of my habit. Must hurry.*

"Godfrey, wait for me outside that side door of Ermengard's palace she described."

Racing across the square he calmly appeared at the front gate, where the guards, in fear of him, allowed him entry. Once inside the hall he turned right into a long corridor that he suspected would lead to the side door by which the Countess left at night. The way was usually pitch black, but a full moon was shining its beams through the narrow archers' windows that regularly pierced the thick walls. Stripes of moonlight illuminated his face at regular intervals as he silently moved forward. *Yes, here it is.* There was a curtained off alcove for boots and cloaks just before the staircase. Moving quickly, he grabbed the large iron key hanging by the door, made sure the door was unlocked, and stuffed it into his pouch. Praying that he wasn't too late, he hid in the alcove and waited for the Countess to leave.

It wasn't long before he heard footsteps. He glanced out. Light from a small flame flickered down the stairs. The dim, hooded figure of a woman emerged to glide silently to the door. She reached for the key; it wasn't there. As her fingers scratched along the wall to find it, her hood fell back. *Yes! It's her!*

• • •

"Where is the key? Who has taken it? But I still must go to the meeting. I won't stay long. Alais will be safe for this one time. She's in the palace. What is that strange smell in the air?" Beatritz put the oil lamp on a small shelf and opened the door to make sure no one was in the marketplace. Quietly closing it behind her, she scurried over the bridge into darkness, wrapping her cloak tightly around herself.

The wind had picked up a chalky dust that blew into her eyes. In the gauzy moonlight, the ruins of the old Roman tower looked like a pile of white rocks. It appeared deserted. *This is a night of ill winds,* she thought, a shivering in her bones. *I feel as if something terrible is going to happen.*

The thick smell of old clothes and sweat led her to an underground chamber where the Bons Hommes had gathered.

"You have to inform everyone else." Speaking in a low, hoarse voice, Henry the Monk was warning everyone as she arrived. He was holding the only candle in the room. In the moving flame she could see that his mouth kept twitching back in a grimace as he spoke. Glancing quickly at her, he turned back to the men leaning against lichen covered walls. Peter Maurand and Raymond d'Ouvelhan were among them.

"The Pope has unleashed the Fallen Angel of Death to cut us down with his scythe. He has orders to 'sow the wind, reap the whirlwind, and harvest the heretics.' We know this is Satan's realm," he rasped, grimacing again, "and now the Beast wishes to destroy any future we have on earth. If we cease to exist, we can no longer spread the word of our truth; the world will belong only to him, and to him alone.

"To this end, we have determined that daughters of Bonnes Filles have been killed in Narbonne, Beziers, Montpelier, and Carcassonne. The Beast is murdering our unborn children by eliminating those who could be future mothers—no mothers, no future believers born. Virgin maidens are being sacrificed in a death scythe that has come from the north."

Beatritz gasped. *From the north—of course. The vulture of death. Is it him? Is Hugon really the one? I must find proof.* She turned to leave.

"Beatritz, wait. I must speak with you alone," Henry said, pulling her to one side. His long hair covered his cheekbones, and the flame of the candle was reflected in his dark eyes. "You must tell all mothers that sacrificed daughters will be held in God's arms; it will help them survive this time of travail. And I beg you, be more careful. You are too close to this business. Your investigations are being closely watched. Be less diligent, and don't wander around so much with that De Plaigne knight. He may be old, but he is dangerous. If he finds out the truth about you, he will kill you."

"But I have been ordered to do so by Ermengard. How can I avoid obeying her orders?"

"Dissemble. Just do less. I fear for you."

The same warning that Escoralda gave me. What fearful knowledge of the future do they see? Nodding her head in acknowledgement, she hurried back home.

I must tell Ermengard what I now know: Hugon is probably the murderer. Yet how do I tell her that it is we, the heretics, the Bonnes Filles, that are being murdered? If she knew, would she even care anymore? Henry is right, I must be very careful of what I say and do.

• • •

Hugon waited silently, barely breathing, for he knew his breath would give him away. *Ah, finally, she's gone.* Taking the oil lamp he examined the stairway. It was narrow, a blackened part of the old Roman house that the palace was built over. *It will creak— I'll have to walk on the ends of the stairs. Never mind. There are no guards.* He slid up the three flights until he came to the corridor. *Now which door? Ah, footsteps in the dirt. Here it is.*

Slowly moving aside a thick tapestry, he was deeply joyful to see that God had granted him his prayers. Oil lamps lit up the daughter, soundly asleep in a small bed against the wall, the nurse asleep nearby. Putting down the oil lamp, he glanced around the room, surprised to find it spare, unadorned. *No jewelry cases, no fancy furnishing, no lust-inspiring fabrics—this is unexpected. Ah, of course, books! I should have known Satan would own her. Now, to work!*

He was a silent nightmare entering the nurse's dreams. Sitting on her chest, covering her mouth with one hand, he slit her throat with the other. When he smelled the warm blood, he once again felt that familiar sensual pleasure.

Going to Alais, he threw back the coverlet and climbed on top of her body, holding down her arms with his knees. The girl's eyes opened and grew wide with terror. When she opened her mouth to scream, he held her nose and poured the poppy juice between her gasping lips. A moment later he wrapped her limp body in his blanket. Heaving Alais over his shoulder he went down the stairs, bent double, banging against the walls until he stumbled into the street.

Godfrey detached himself from a shadow.

"Here," whispered Hugon, dumping the blanketed body into Godfrey's arms. "We'll hide her in the horreum. Wait outside of it with her. I'll meet you. I'm going back to leave by the front door."

He hung the key back on the wall and raced to the horreum. There was only one soldier guarding the gate to the tunnels at the bottom of the stairs. A torch above him lit up his metal helmet and bearded face. He was sitting on top of a section of an old Roman column, his elbows leaning on a pair of oversized, muscular knees that poked out from under the studded leather uniform.

Waiting, Godfrey had one foot on the bundle at his feet.

Hugon ran down a nearby alley and grabbed some rubbish. Using his flintstone, he started a fire.

"Help!" he yelled. "Fire, help me!"

The soldier ran up the steps towards the flames down the block. He didn't notice the dark figure running past him the other way.

"Hurry," hissed Hugon to Godfrey. "Let's get her down there."

The gate was unlocked and there was no one in sight in all three tunnels. "Let's go to the right. Jesus, it's cold as a crypt in here."

Moving carefully, they went down the dimly lit passage, hurrying past faint lamps burning in cracks. The ancient brick floor was still fairly even. At the end of the tunnel was a corner room with a sound wooden door. Hugon held it open as Godfrey lay the unconscious girl down inside, then tied her hands and feet. "Gag her, just to be safe in case she wakes up. Now let's go."

He shut the door, leaving the girl in the dark.

Continuing further, he went around another way to leave the tunnels, and stopped short. In front of him, brightly lit by torches, was a cell with an open gate. A shackled man was lying on the floor. Nearby, sitting on a stone bench with his wooden leg stuck out stiffly in front of him, was the jailor Gombal holding a tankard of ale.

In a fury, Hugon turned to Godfrey. "That's Gerardi! You fool—I told you to finish him off in the woods. The unicorn was supposed to have killed him at the same time as the girl. Why is he here?"

Godfrey went pale. "Forgive me, master. I thought I did."

"He knows my face! He knows who hired him!"

Gerardi must have heard his name. Before Hugon could pull back out of sight, he looked up and saw him. "You! I know you!"

Gombal also looked up. "Who are you? And what are you doing here?" he growled. "No one is allowed to be here."

Hugon pulled himself together. "I am Father Aubusson here to confess the prisoner. He is scheduled to be hung tomorrow."

"Tomorrow? No one told me that. Does the Countess know of this? She's not done questioning him."

"She is aware and has sent me. Please leave me alone with the prisoner."

Gerardi was moving as far as possible from the open gate of the cell.

"No, no. I don't want to confess!" he whimpered, a frightened look in his eyes.

"Shut up," Gombal said, going over to him. Bending over him, he started dragging the prisoner over to the gate.

Gerardi, his stinking breath feverishly hot, whispered quickly into Gombal's ear. "He hired me. He is the child killer. He's not Father Aubusson. I swear on Jesus it's the truth. Hurry, get the Countess here before he kills me."

The terrified look on Gerardi's face was very convincing. The guard turned slowly to Hugon. "You may enter the cell. I'll wait out here."

"No. I need to be alone for a proper confession. Go wait at the entrance to the tunnels." Hugon was sneering and Gombal's unease turned to fear. The Countess had warned him that he would be severely whipped if anything happened to the prisoner. *This priest is not what he seems. I must bring the Countess immediately.*

Hugon could hear the man's rapid leg tapping become more distant. He had no idea Gombal was running to the palace.

• • •

Beatritz arrived home to find the door entry as dark as her thoughts. *Where is my oil lamp?* Absently she felt for the key and was startled to find it. *How did it get back here?*

Her stomach was turning itself into a tighter and tighter knot as she felt her way up the stairs in the dark, sliding her sandals forwards on each rough step. A metallic smell in the air made her nose twitch; it came from behind the tapestry. Throwing it aside she ran in and stopped as if she had hit a brick wall. Alais was gone.

"Mother Mary help me!" she cried aloud. Rushing to the sleeping nurse, she began to punch her, screaming, "Wake up! Why are you asleep you incompetent fool? I'll have you whipped!"

Beatritz felt the sticky blood on her hands. Holding them before her face, she fell to her knees, and saw that the nurse was dead.

Chest heaving, she tried to think. *Tell Ermengard, don't tell Ermengard—what should I do? She's not here. Kidnapped. I must find her. I'll go outside, look for someone in the market. Somebody must have seen something.* Banging down the stairs she threw herself out the side door and bumped into Gombal hobbling towards the palace, his wooden leg sounding like a hammer on the stones.

"Lady, thank heavens I've found you!" He was bent over gasping from the pains in his lungs. "No, wait!"

"I have no time now. I must find Abbott Hugon."

"Lady, please," he looked up at her fearfully. "Is it true that Gerardi is to be hung tomorrow?"

Startled, Beatritz snapped at him. "Why are you bothering me with this right now?"

"Come quickly! A strange priest has come to confess Gerardi, but Gerardi whispered to me that the man is not a priest, but the murderer who hired him to kidnap the child who was murdered in the woods. Gerardi knows too much. The priest is going to kill him. Come quick!"

"Alais, he must have Alais! Run immediately and inform the guards to awake Thibaut De Plaigne and send him to the horreum, armed. I'm going there now."

"No, don't go alone!" the jailor cried. It was too late; black cloak flying, Beatritz was running past the looming palace of the Archbishop and down the Via Domitia.

The torch burning above the entrance gate blinded her. She was standing at the top of the stone steps leading down to the tunnels. *If he is the killer, then I must confront him alone. He has my daughter.* She held onto the cold wall as she went down.

"My Lady, isn't a bit late to be coming here alone?" The astonished guard looked at her.

"I have my reasons. Please stand aside. Sir De Plaigne will arrive soon, send him in."

"Yes, my Lady."

Slowly, frightened at what she might see, she crept along the dark tunnels. Step by step, cringing at every crunch of gravel, she inched her way to a light up ahead.

A tall, brown robed figure stood in the entry of Gerardi's cell, looking at the floor. The quarryman's body was lying there face down in a pool of blood. His throat was cut. One arm was flung half-way out of the cell, as if he had been trying to escape. Keeping to the shadows, she crossed the tunnel to see who the man was, then had to put a hand in front of her mouth to keep from crying out. *Hugon! He murdered Gerardi so he couldn't identify him.*

"Will I have to kill you too?" Hugon turned around, a vulture seeking a victim.

So, the she-devil is here.

"You! *You* are the killer!" The reflection of torchlight in his pupils led the path to Hell. Stepping back in a panic, she began to shiver. *Can his eyes really be on fire?* "Where is my daughter?"

Leaping forward, Hugon grabbed her arm. "A murdering unicorn! What utter nonsense. Yet, it suited my mission, and my mission will continue to be served by whatever means possible."

"And what is your mission?" Beatritz could barely speak. Her trembling was uncontrollable. *We're facing death without the consolamentum. Another rebirth. I beg of you God, save Alais and me, I beg you.*

"No more Bons Hommes children! And you can't stop me. I should kill you and your heretic daughter now."

"Alais! Where is she?" Beatritz was struggling so hard to get out of his painful grip that she didn't even defend herself against his accusation.

"Come—" Smirking, Hugon grabbed a torch and began to pull her down another dark tunnel.

Beatritz was tripping and grabbing the edges of stones in the walls to keep from falling. The struggle stopped in front of an arched wooden door.

"Godfrey, open it."

Godfrey complied. The torchlight revealed a small figure with bare, pink, feet sticking out from beneath a crumpled white nightgown.

"Alais!" screamed Beatritz.

"Get her out of there."

Grabbing her by the hair, Godfrey dragged the limp child onto the tunnel floor and flung her at her mother's feet.

"No, no! How could you." Beatritz fell to the floor and wrapped her warm arms around her cold, limp daughter.

"What's happening here?" cried a familiar voice. Thibault De Plaigne ran up, his armor clanking, his hand on his hilt. Seeing the Canon he stopped himself from drawing his sword. "Why are you here with the Countess de Dente?"

"Help me, De Plaigne!" She was trying to remove the gag from Alais's mouth. There was a faint pulse when Beatritz put her cheek to her daughter's throat.

"Do you really want to come to the aid of Satan's wife and their spawn?" snapped Hugon.

"What do you mean?" De Plaigne asked, his eyes widening?

"This woman is a heretic, a Bonne Fille, a believer who kisses the filthy cat's ass of the Devil. I'm warning you—this child is his progeny on earth. Stay away, I say—they should both be burned."

De Plaigne sucked in his breath. If the Canon declared her a heretic, he believed him. Falling on one knee, he bent his head. "I beg forgiveness. I was seduced by the feminine wiles of this Lilith."

Rising up, he drew his sword, holding it in the air with both hands, ready to cut off Beatritz's head. The lines of his face had deepened and were drawn into a steel mask of hate. Guilt for the love he felt for her turned into fury. *I have been duped by a stinking heretic!* "Should I execute her now?"

"No. Leave her to me. I need her alive," Hugon growled.

"Then I will leave. She disgusts me. Her presence sickens my soul." Putting his sword away with a clang, he turned his back. Running as fast as possible, he left the underground tunnels, muttering *I must go to church—I must pray and fast—I must cleanse myself.*

In despair, Beatritz watched him desert her. Now she knew it was true, both dead girls were the daughters of Bonnes Filles. "Why are you killing our children?"

"A cracked egg hatches no chicks! God has spoken to me, and I am his willing executioner."

Heaven preserve us! He is a madman. "God will help us for the evil you bring here." Alais was waking up. Holding her daughter against her chest Beatritz began to cry bitterly. "God will punish you!"

"God? The Pope himself will soon be rewarding me."

"The church is behind what you do? Then you will never be punished." *Except by God.*

"Pah! You *should* die—it is frustrating, yet in her ignorance Ermengard loves you and your daughter. That will save you." Spittle formed at the edges of his mouth, his face was glowing red.

Is that a tail waving behind him? Beatritz was in a panic.

"If you ever speak of what has occurred here, I *will* have you both burnt at the stake—like this!" He waved the blazing torch back and forth, so close in front of her face she had to close her eyes at its brightness. There was the sharp tang of burnt hair and her scalp felt on fire. As her hands tried to protect Alais from the flames, the heat blistered her skin. Terrified, she raised her eyes to him and looked into his soul. *God protect me, I have now met Satan.*

Hugon stared at her and hissed, "Yes, I see future fires burning in your eyes. Your turn will come."

With that warning, like a serpent in the night, he slid around the corner and was gone.

Sobbing, bent over Alais, her mind reeling with fear, Beatritz remained on the floor long into the night.

My child, what is your fate? Nothing will ever be the same. We are now hunted heretics, like beasts in the forest. The future is more dangerous than ever. What will happen to all of us? I pray we shall all find our wings and die a good death. Yet it could not come soon enough.

CHAPTER 30

When I see a lark flying against the sun,
joyfully beating its wings,
swooping up, letting itself fall,
with such sweetness filling its soul,
Oh! I envy those who feel such a marvelous love.
    —*Bernautz de Ventadorn, troubadour, 1135-1194*

"Tf you're in such a hurry all the time the Archbishop should have sent younger monks to get this *very* important missive," Ramon snapped at Guilliam. They were now traversing the high peaks of the alps in Provence.

Pale limestone crags poked up from the dark green scrub as the road rose and fell with the temperature. Drenched by a cold downburst, they were forced to spend the night near the Roman ruins of Glanum, where an enterprising old soldier, who swore he was a descendant of one of Caesar's bastards, ran an inn for travelers not prepared for the damp, cold weather in this intense, sharp mountain range. The trio collapsed on thin straw pallets after hot bean soup in the inn's barely lit, but relatively clean, tavern.

For the next three days they doggedly trudged along the slippery road, fording streams swollen even in summer, walking through an unexpected forest of kermes oaks, to arrive in the town of Apt on the Calavon River.

By now, Brother Gilbert had developed a racking, deep cough and in fear of losing one of his witnesses, Guilliam allowed them to stay for two nights in a warm, dry corner of the Cathedral of Saint Anne.

A beardless young monk took pity on Gilbert and gave him a pallet near the altar. It was an old church, small, with crumbling walls and peeling paintings of Saint Anne and her daughter, the Virgin Mary. The

Holy Mother's bones and sacred veil had been saved from destruction by barbarian invaders when Saint Auspicius hid them in a grotto beneath this same altar. After being martyred by Trajan, Auspicius was then also buried here.

From his bed Gilbert could see the veil and wooden box that held Saint Anne's bones. *Saint Anne,* he prayed between racking coughs, *heal me with your love.* He was too weak even to kneel. *In your mercy, let me live to do God's work on earth.*

"How are you feeling?" asked Father Urbac, the church's infirmarian.

"The pain is getting worse," rasped Gilbert.

Father Urbac returned to feed him a thick brown syrup. "It's a mixture of crushed licorice roots, willow bark, maidenhair, honey, and purslane seeds, all of which have been boiled down and strained."

"Will he live?" asked Guilliam.

The Father shrugged his shoulders and drew a cross in the air over Gilbert.

Gilbert coughed, slept, and prayed all night and through the next day. Ramon sat by him chanting psalms. The Templar was sick of sitting around all day. *Maybe I should just leave him here to die.*

That night, sweat running down his face, Gilbert prayed, *please, beloved Saint Anne, either cure me of my pain or take me to Jesus.* Then he fell into a deep sleep.

Ramon cried, "God help us! He has died!"

Father Urbac ran over and touched his neck, "No, there is a faint pulse. Let him be."

The next morning, when the monks were chanting at prime, Gilbert woke up and began shouting. "A miracle, a miracle! My cough is gone—Saint Anne has made me whole with her love and the strength of her bones!" Upon which all the monks ran over to him, calling excitedly to each other:

"Come look—listen to his breath! He is healed! Let us pray and give thanks for another miracle!"

Father Urbac put his ear to Gilbert's chest while thumping on his back. "Yes, he is whole," he said calmly, using a matter-of-fact tone. "As always, with her blessings, Saint Anne has cured him."

Shaken by this miracle, Guilliam was unusually sober that morning. He even put off leaving a while longer to hear the monks sing hymns of praise, with Ramon's voice the loudest.

After a meal of porridge and honey, which Gilbert gulped down, they continued their journey. The monks, in a state of euphoria and gratitude, endlessly sang hymns in praise of God.

The air was clear and fresh when they came to the edge of a sharp cliff overlooking a dark valley. Across its depths was a mountain upon whose height was visible the sunlit church tower of Notre Dame de Gangobie. According to a monk at Saint Anne, they would have to go around the valley, through Fourcauquier, after which one could cross the old Roman bridge south of town to get to the east side of the Durance River, thence to proceed to Les Mées.

"Let's go, we've got to get through Fourcauquier before night. It's too dangerous to stay there, the spirits of the many who died there live in the kilns."

The monks decided to lead the donkeys on foot, carefully picking their way through the grey rubble of Roman conical lime kilns scattered across the ground. A broken slab at the side of the road labeled the town Furnus Calcarius. Centuries before, worked by an endless supply of slaves, the furiously hot kilns had burned day and night, extracting lime from these craggy hills to feed the insatiable Roman need for concrete. The trees, as far as one could see in any direction, were just distorted dead stumps, the sad remains of those used for the fires.

Gilbert was saddened by the destruction. "It looks like the path to the inferno below, all gray, no color, no life. No wonder they say the slaves live here still. Their spirits will never escape this hellish landscape."

The road went downhill to the bridge, crossed east over the Durance again, where they plodded north along the muddy path through the spray of the river's white rapids. It was slippery, and the river so fast moving, it would swallow a man in seconds. The tired monks moved very slowly, placing their feet carefully.

Will we ever get there? Guilliam was worn out from the slow pace. *Despite the fact there is less distance covered, it's more tiring than racing along.* Then he stopped short and stared.

Before him was an astounding sight. As a Templar, he had been to the Holy Land and back, yet he had never seen anything remotely resembling the tall, human-shaped rocks that rose three-hundred feet above the small valley. Gray, silent sentinels, the stone men stood in

long rows, one next to the other along a green ridge, giants guarding the
way to the Ganagobie monastery they had once inhabited.

The monk describing the way to Ganagobie had warned him.
"Beware Les Mées, 'The Penitents', don't stare. Saint Donat petrified
the monks because they had dared to gaze with lust on some female
Saracen slaves brought back from the Holy Land."

In the sharp light of the late afternoon sun, the rocks had the silhouettes
of monks in procession, complete with pointy cowls and hoods, and
hands in prayer. With their faces in shadow, they were terrifying.

"Lord Jesus, preserve us from harm," cried Brother Ramon as
Gilbert repeatedly crossed himself.

"Don't stare at them, or they will curse you. Let's just get away." In
spite of himself, Guilliam was unnerved.

A narrow wooden bridge led west over the river to Peyruis, a field of
wildflowers that was the site of the dilapidated church of Saint Donat.
From here, Donat could forever keep a stern eye on the monks he had
turned to stone. Built over his original borie, the bee-hive shaped stone
hut in which he had lived most of his pious fifth-century life, the site
was still visited by pilgrims who came to this lonely spot to seek the
intervention of the Holy Hermit from Orléans.

"Oh, God in heaven, not again," fumed Guilliam, shifting on his
horse as the monks stopped for a quick prayer. He was bursting with
impatience as the goal of this endless journey was now just ahead. "We
must ride! We're not on a pilgrimage—we are here for the Archbishop!"

Olive trees spread out in every direction from the bottom of the
road and across the fields. Gilbert longed to get off his mount and
wander among the gnarly branches, to watch their leaves flicker from
silver to green, to pick a ripe fruit so he could bite into the hard flesh
and taste its bitter tang between his teeth. He missed his olives trees,
they were his real family, giving back their perfect oil for loving care.
As they climbed higher, thick clouds began to stack up, blurring the
path. Ghostly whiskers stroked the trees, frightening the larks into an
unearthly silence. Ramon began to sing again, his disembodied voice
floating above the mist.

Abruptly, the wall of clouds ended as the road opened up onto a
sunlit, pine-wooded plateau.

• • •

Ganagobie Abbey sat upon a hill of snow-white rocks. A carved wooden gate large enough for a carriage was part of a stone arch cut into the neatly built wall. Guilliam pulled the bell rope of a small door in the gate.

The monk who came to answer was old, and bent sideways, so much so that the hem of one side of his habit dragged on the ground. His right eye was totally white, but the left orb examined them, an alert black bead. "What do you want?"

Guilliam took the initiative. "We are here on a mission from Archbishop Pierre D'Anduze of Narbonne. We have an important document for Abbot Armond. But Brothers Ramon and Gilbert are exhausted. Could you please show them to their quarters so they can rest?"

"No, no. We're fine, we want to meet the Abbot too."

"No! Go eat and rest." As usual, the Templar bullied them into submission. "I'll arrange a meeting with the Abbot." His orders were to speak with the Abbot first, to explain what D'Anduze was asking of him. Nervously he ushered his charges into the care of the old monk.

Ducking behind a pillar in a courtyard, he got the pouch holding the gold out from his crotch and stowed it under his Templar overcoat. Thus prepared, he went to find Abbot Armond.

He found the Abbot's square, stone house set in a clearing within the priory walls. The peaked roof was lined with slate tiles that overhung a tiled walkway leading to a rear vegetable garden, its rows of cabbages, gourds, onions and peas carefully weeded and pruned. A patch of purslane was growing in a corner against the wooden fence. Bees hummed just outside of the abbey wall.

An annoyed looking monk ran out. "Who are you? And what do you think you're doing in the Abbot's garden?" He grabbed the offered letter of introduction out of Guilliam's hand, then escorted him back through the front door into a spotless, neat parlor. "Wait here," he snapped, going through a nearby door.

The Templar examined the room carefully with an eye to valuation. Fresh flowers in a silver vase sat on a polished table; wine was in a polished quartz carafe with matching cups. The sun illuminated stained glass windows set into deep arches. *This place has wealth,* mused the soldier, impressed, as the Templars always were, with evidence of money.

"Please, come in." The smooth voice startled him. A tall, well-built man, his silvery hair hanging to his shoulders, stood in the doorway. Blue eyes looked down a prominent nose. The jaw was pointy and firm. A simple white cassock of the softest Egyptian wool was girdled with a braided hemp rope adorned with a large wooden crucifix that hung almost to the floor.

Guilliam went down on one knee in homage, noticing the finely tooled leather sandals the man wore. Strangely, the toes and skin had red sores and peeling skin. Small, painful looking ulcers encircled the bottom of his feet.

"So," Armond began, when they were seated. "Why has the Templar Guilliam Maurs of the Commandery in La Couvertoirade, traveled here with two monks?"

Guilliam handed over the papers from the Archbishop. Armond's eyebrows went up to his silver hairline. The Abbot took the time to read them over, twice.

"So it seems that my old friend Pierre needs a favor. A big one." He looked up at Guilliam. "I am to 'produce' his brother Bernard and have the monks witness a certification that he is alive. It is a dangerous business. Are you aware of this?"

"I'm only aware of this." The Templar dropped the pouch on the polished tabletop. The Abbot looked dismayed and wrinkled his nose, then nodded sideways when Guilliam tipped several of the gold moribatani out to clank on the wood. "This should help. There are thirty of them here."

Picking up a gold piece with his manicured nails, the Abbot looked at it closely. "Moribatani? Thirty of them?" Inhaling deeply, he looked up. "Give me two days to arrange the meeting and draw up the documents. Then the monks can be witnesses. Do they return with you?"

"No. I don't care if they stay or go. I have to return immediately. I don't have time to deal with them any longer. This is a matter of the greatest urgency. Can't you do it in one day?" Rudely, he took back the bag of coins, suggestively leaving one glinting on the table. "I will leave the rest of them on the altar when I depart with the document."

I will not be bullied by this Templar. "These things are not so simple to arrange. It must be done absolutely properly. Besides the monks, we have fifteen lay brothers living here, and eight older oblates whom we care for till the end of their earthly lives. On the morn after tomorrow, your monks will see their man.

• • •

Gilbert and Ramon were kneeling in front of Abbot Armond. "As I have told Guilliam, the morning after the morrow you will sign papers attesting to the fact that you have witnessed the living person of Bernard D'Anduze, the brother of your Archbishop. I myself will witness your signatures. In the meantime, pray with your brother monks and help them with their work."

"May I have permission to visit the oil mills we passed on the way up?" asked Gilbert.

"You are acquainted with the process of producing olive oil?"

"Surely, yes. My family once owned a very large olive grove near Toulouse. Our oil was known for its clarity and purity everywhere in the region. I was thirteen and already my father had taught me his secrets. I was in charge of crushing the olives—it is a very delicate process, or the oil will be bitter—then lightning started a calamitous fire, and all our trees and mills were burnt to cinders. My father couldn't feed his family, so he gave me to the church. The Archbishop knew of my family, and he put me in charge of his mills in Perpignan where I now oversee quality."

"H-m-m," said the Abbot. "Stay. I would speak with you further." He dismissed Ramon, who was happy to go to the church and listen to the choir rehearse. "Continue, tell me more about your knowledge of olive oil. We have some problems here."

Gilbert needed little encouragement to talk. "I have been trying various ways to crush the olives so as to make the oil even more pure: using three stages of milling helps. Lately, my reputation rests mostly on my knowledge of the medical and practical uses of amurca, that evil-smelling, bitter tasting water that is the natural result of the milling process. I have sold a written thesis '*On the Benefits and Properties of Amurca*' to numerous monasteries. Even Hildegard of Bingen has purchased a copy," he said, sitting up proudly. "The Archbishop makes quite a good income from the sale of them. But he makes most of his profit from my amurca ointment, which is my secret recipe."

"And what are its uses?"

"Well, after you add some additional herbs, you have to boil it until it becomes a paste; a smelly and laborious job that requires constant stirring. The resulting paste can be used to tightly seal honey jars and wine amphorae, soften leather, and imagine this: if put into plaster it will harden it in such a way that it actually seals out bugs and insects! Not to mention its uses on bodily illnesses such as leprosy, burns, and chilblains—of course, only with many prayers," he added quickly.

"Did you say chilblains? Like these?" He put one of his painfully sore feet on the table.

"Oh, absolutely!"

"Hm-m-m," said the Abbot, looking thoughtful. "Go now, and speak with my olive millers."

In the meantime, Ramon had wandered into the courtyard in front of the stone church. He stood there admiring the carved figure of Our Lady of Ganagobie in the tympanum over the door. Set into an oval of praying prophets, the sculptor had also carved a marvelous curtain of flower petals falling all around her.

A friendly monk came up and opened the door, gesturing for him to enter. He was very blond and very thin, with kind blue eyes that blinked often and very rapidly.

"Please enter. I am Brother Michelle. You are?"

"Brother Ramon of Narbonne."

"Welcome, Brother Ramon. Allow me to show you Our Lady's home."

The church interior was spare, with undecorated columns holding up a barrel vault. *Prayer here would be comforting,* he thought. The apse was decorated with a colorful painting of the Virgin Mary, dressed in a lapis blue robe and little red slippers. She was gazing fondly at the Christ Child in her lap. White-robed smiling angels with gold wings held her veil in delicate fingers. From the ceiling above the altar, in contrast with Mary's joy, hung a sad, emaciated figure of Christ on the Cross. *What does the Virgin feel every day to endure the vision of her son's crucifixion?* The pity of it made him feel like crying.

"Would you like to see our cloister? Let me take you there."

"That's what the Archbishop was building. I'd like to see it."

Strolling in the shade on a mosaic floor made of animals and plants, with the fountain gurgling in the center, Ramon understood. *It's the perfect place to meditate and pray—how delightful.*

Outside the walls more herb and vegetable gardens were carefully laid out on the terraced southern plateau to get the most sun. A hazy mix of lavender and pinewood floated in the air.

The bell rang for compline, followed by a silent meal.

The following day passed in quiet work: Gilbert helped with the oil crushing, and Ramon taught the choir a new hymn.

• • •

On the morning of the third day, Guilliam and the monks stood in front of the Abbot's desk as he regarded them with his serious blue gaze. Finally, he rose.

"Follow me."

As they walked behind him, Gilbert noticed the man's silver hair shining in the sunlight. A narrow dirt path led them to the covered courtyard of a low, rectangular stone building. One of the doors stood open.

"Here live the oblates of our monastery, those who wish to end their days peacefully in prayer. Sometimes a family will bring someone they cannot care for and pay us to do it. Everyone here is here voluntarily; but they must give us all they possess to remain.

"One day, about seven years ago, a man came to us carried on a pallet by fellow crusaders on their way home. They maintained that he had been injured fighting the heathens. His wounds had healed, but his mind had not. Subject to terrible, painful headaches and crying fits, he had exhausted their ability to care for him. He has remained here since then. His memory of those awful events is gone, as is his memory of who he is. Please come meet Bernard D'Anduze, brother of your Archbishop Pierre D'Anduze, husband of Viscountess Ermengard of Narbonne."

They all crowded into the small, dark chamber. A pale, ravaged man in a clean cotton shift lay on a simple rope cot covered by a light blanket. The curled fingers of his bony hand were lying palm up on his forehead; pale, red-veined eyes were open, staring at some unknown vision in his mind. Neither man had ever seen Bernard, yet even if they had—how was one to ferret out the original man from this disaster of a human being? Was he sixty or ninety? His eyes moved towards them as the shadows of his visitors blocked the light.

"Bernard, you have visitors. Will you speak?"

The ghostly apparition began to silently cry. Tears rolled down to puddle in his hollow cheekbones. His toothless mouth opened in a sad grimace.

Moved and saddened, Brother Gilbert said, "I shall now go pray for you in the church." He turned to leave.

"First you must sign the documents attesting to your witness of his being here alive," Guilliam interjected. "Then you can pray till Doomsday. I must depart. The Archbishop awaits news of his brother."

Abbot Armond had all the papers ready in his study.

"Firstly, here is a missive from Ganagobie Abbey relating the story of when and how Bernard came to be here, and the gradual deterioration of his health to this sad condition. It also explicitly states that he wished for no one to know that he was here except his brother. His wife was to be kept in ignorance; he did not want her pity, nor that of his acquaintances. He wanted to be remembered how he looked in his prime when he went to the Holy Land. We have adhered to his wishes until now. We don't know how long this will go on. He does eat a little soup each day.

"Secondly, here is a document attesting to the fact that you, Brother Gilbert, and you, Brother Ramon, have seen him alive, albeit in frail condition. Please sign here."

The two monks did so. The Abbot signed his name and affixed it with his seal. He handed the papers to Guilliam, who raced for the door.

In a panic, the two monks followed him.

"Wait! How can we go alone? Aren't you going to accompany us home?" cried Ramon.

"No. Find your own way."

Stopping by the church as promised, the Templar left the pouch full of gold coins on the altar. Kneeling, he quickly crossed himself, praying, "Protect me Saint Christopher." *Riding hard I will make Narbonne in four days.*

Throwing himself onto his horse, he galloped across the courtyard yelling, "Open the gate!" The two monks stood there, staring after him, watching the dust settle.

"What do we do now?" asked Ramon.

"Do? Hah! I know what I'm doing. I'm staying here for the rest of my life," said Gilbert, a broad grin on his face. "The Abbot has given me permission. From now on I am named Brother Olivius. Excuse me, Brother Ramon, I have work to do. God be with you."

The last Ramon saw of him was his back.

"God be with you, too," he murmured, startled to have lost two of his companions at once. Not knowing what else to do, he went to the church. During vespers he began to cry. Kneeling in the rear, listening to the monks chant the liturgy, he made up his mind. During the evening meal, he didn't eat. After everyone had gone to sleep, he took his portion of bread and cheese and put it in his pouch. After matins, he silently wrapped himself in his traveling cloak and went to the church to pray one last time to the Virgin Mary of Ganagobie. As the altar candle illuminated her face, she spoke to him.

"Go with my blessings, Ramon. I understand. Sing for the glory of God eternal."

Comforted, he now had strength for the journey ahead.

He found Plautus fast asleep under a tree. *Where's his blanket? Never mind—no time for that. I'll ride without it.* As usual, the recalcitrant beast had to be led by the nose by the cheese and bread. Silently opening the gate, he mounted the animal and began down the mountain. The hazy light of a gibbous moon barely lit the way. The helpful Virgin kept the fog at bay, or he surely would have gotten lost.

Plautus clopped over the wooden bridge to Les Mées. The brothers loomed above him, stony faces now lit by a sun just rimming the mountains. He heard them say, *We envy you leaving. Go with God.*

The stones of the Via Domitia were solid and smooth here. The early morning light reflected off their black shiny surfaces. During the night, a heavy rain had washed them clean of the animal waste that filled the crevices and stank in the heat. The air was damp and invigorating. The chanting of the larks made him sing. Breathing in deeply, singing a hymn to the Virgin, Ramon turned Plautus west and headed back towards Apt.

Gradually other travelers joined him, happy to have a monk amongst themselves. An older merchant, with a very young blond wife and infant, offered to let him sleep in their wagon that night. In thanks, he blessed their marriage, made the sign of the cross over the child and sang it to sleep with a hymn. For a prayer and a blessing others gave him food. All were grateful for the presence of this gentle monk. Occasionally they stopped and picked berries together in the sun, then drank the fresh rainwater that ran down the rocks in slender waterfalls.

"God is watching over us!" Ramon laughed, then sang a song of thanks to God as they all joined in with glad voices.

When the road broke north to Béucaire, Ramon set Plautus's nose in that direction.

"No Father, stay with us! Your faith has protected us on our journey."

"Bless you all, but I must go my separate way. God's love be with you!"

Once again, he took the road to the Abbey of Saint-Romanus the Melodist. Voices floating down the mountain led him to the cave. Entering the cool chamber with its glowing altar, he once more walked up behind the monks and began to sing with them. They recognized the pure voice ringing off the ceiling with joy as, without a glance, a space was opened for him in the circle. He stepped forward into God's love.

Thus, Brother Ramon, Brother Gilbert, Justus, and Plautus simply vanished from this earthly world.

CHAPTER 31

The cold time is here,
with its ice, snow, and mud.
Birds sing no more,
branches are dead.
Neither green leaves nor
flowers grow.
The nightingale, whose song
woke me in the springtime,
is now silent.
—Azalais de Porcairagues, trobaritz, 12th cent.

T*hat odor, why does he always have to come up right behind me?
And why just now?*

"I must speak with you."

"What is it that you wish, Hugon. I am pressed for time with church business." Guilliam the Templar had returned yesterday and D'Anduze was busy double-checking the documents, extremely satisfied with the wording and witnessing. *Yes, the Abbot did an excellent job.* When Hugon approached closer, he quickly turned the papers face-down. *How do I get rid of him?* Fully dressed in his vestments, D'Anduze was expecting to meet Ermengard and Rogenvaldr in the church this very morning and had no patience to deal with the Canon.

What insidious plot is this old goat setting in motion? Hugon wondered. *Why is he arrayed in his vestments? And a gold miter?* "You should know that I am departing Narbonne today. I have to report back to the Pope about the rapid growth of heresy in the south. And he won't be pleased. I will return through Albi. Hopefully, it won't be as diseased as this city is."

It's about time he left. "Breaking more eggs?" D'Anduze said it in jest, tired of the Canon's constant muttering about the cursed eggs.

"Why, yes, now that you ask. I still have many more fertile *Bonnes Filles'* daughters to be rid of."

God in heaven—it was him—he killed them! "So, killing the virgin daughters of mothers judged to be heretical by you is your holy mission?" D'Anduze was shaken. *The man is mad. No wonder they sent him wandering.*

"Yes—and the Pope will reward me for it."

"I have no doubt," he replied wryly, turning back to his papers. "Well then, may God protect you on your journey." *And keep you far away from here in the future. I only wish I could warn the people of Albi that a killer is coming to their city—but I can't; what he is doing is the will of the church.*

"Thank you for your blessing," Hugon said to D'Anduze's back. "You may soon have need of God's blessing too. I'm warning you. I'll have much to say about the state of heresy in Narbonne in my report."

No one paid any attention to the darkly clothed monk on his donkey, followed by a servant leading a white jennet, riding out the Raymond-Jean Gate north to Albi. At the same time, not by coincidence, a red wagon with strange yellow symbols was being driven through the cobbles of the Perpignan Gate, south to Iberia.

• • •

The Archbishop had sent a monk to the palace with an urgent message: Ermengard was to attend D'Anduze in his church the next morning, without fail.

"Well, Beatritz, what scheme has he got planned against me now? I've just *got* to persuade him to let Rogenvaldr go. What is he up to? He can't think to leave a Norwegian Earl in prison to starve to death just so I don't marry him. I don't trust him."

That same morning Rogenvaldr was hurriedly dragged out of his cell by soldiers and brought to the church. Surprised by the sudden turn of events, he suddenly found himself kneeling on a church floor in a filthy, dirty state in front of the Archbishop. His eyes, blinded by the light, could barely make out the glittering form looking at him from under a gold miter. *Why am I here?* The rising sun, shining through the window glass, threw a red rainbow onto the altar where the horn sat, glowing in a bloody light. *That cursed horn! I can't look at it. I can't even speak of it. This deception has been the source of nothing but death for me.*

"Welcome, Rogenvaldr Kali Kolsson," the Archbishop said. "I'm warning you in advance. In spite of what happens now, you will remain silent about the horn. If you speak of it, you will return to my dungeons, and probably a hangman's noose. If you hold your tongue, I will allow you to leave Narbonne today, never to return. Do you understand? Am I being perfectly clear?"

Rogenvaldr mutely nodded agreement. His stringy hair stuck to his shoulders as he rubbed his swollen ankles, wincing at the weeping rat bites. *I just want to get out of that dungeon.* Dressed in gray veils from head to foot, Ermengard entered the church. *Here I am,* she thought, *obedient as usual. But why is the Archbishop all fitted out in his vestments? And who is that figure on the floor? Oh, God in heaven!*

"Rogenvaldr!" she called, running towards him, veils flying.

Hearing her voice, he turned his head to see her, and quickly looked away, too ashamed of his deceit to meet her eyes.

"Quiet, Ermengard! You are in my church; you will kneel and be still."

His arms look so thin and his eyes so. . . She was about to bend down and embrace her lover, but something in the Archbishop's loud voice frightened her. Wary, she pulled her arms back and knelt down a short distance away.

"I have brought you both here together because we must speak of the unspeakable: a great sin. My children, your uncontrollable lust has thrown you both into an unholy state.

"You, Rogenvaldr began a crusade to the Holy Land with three hundred men in your care. You traveled far, often through great danger, and were in close sight of that goal. Then you lost your way. You became mired in sin with a woman who has deceived you."

What is he talking about? I'm the one who deceived Ermengard with that horn. And why can't I speak of it?

"Yes, of course you are confused Rogenvaldr. Many years ago, Ermengard was wed to Alphonse Jordan, who, shortly after, left her a widow. For her own safety, as she was only thirteen years of age, she was then married to Bernard D'Anduze, a brave warrior who soon left for the Holy Land. A Christian wife would wait for his return even though it would be until her death. Yes, many years have passed, but patience is rewarded by God, faithlessness is not.

"Ermengard is a lost sheep. God says to the sinner: 'Your sin will find you out'. I have proof here of it here." Composing a morose expression on his face, he produced some papers from behind his back and handed Ermengard the testaments from the Abbot of Ganagobie. With difficulty he kept the feeling of triumph from his eyes.

Ermengard held them up to the light in order to read them. *What is this? It cannot be true.* The officially sealed and witnessed documents burned her fingers. They were tinder in her hands, any minute they would burst into flames.

"No! No! It's not possible," she cried as she read further. "It's been nine years—he's been gone nine years! Not a word, not one letter, not a rumor; he was your brother, why didn't you tell me?"

"As you can read, after his terrible injuries in the Holy Land, he was carried to Ganagobie Abbey, where he has been discretely taken care of for all these many years. His pride explicitly demanded that no one was to know. Not even you. He was afraid you would visit and see him in such a disfigured condition. And, you must admit, you were never shown a corpse, nor received a word from his military commander of his death."

The parchment dropped to the floor as she covered her face with her hands.

"Her husband—he lives?" rasped Rogenvaldr.

The terrible truth was written on her face when she spoke. "I didn't know—I thought he was dead." Slowly she sagged to the floor.

The tawny smooth mountains and black rocks of Iceland floated up to the surface of Rogenvaldr's memory. As a very young child, he was standing beside a hot, steaming fumarole that was rising into the crisp air from a boiling spring. There was a large chunk of ice on the stony ground, sparkling like a white jewel when he held it up to the sun. Then, on impulse, he threw it into the hot waters. He could still vividly recall his sadness and disappointment watching the beautiful crystal dissolve. The love he had shared with Ermengard melted away, just like that icy jewel.

Raising his hands in prayer, Rogenvaldr looked up at the figure on the cross above him. "Jesus, only you can help me now. Is the River Jordan wide and deep enough to cover me?"

A heavy wooden clunk behind his back startled Rogenvaldr. Looking over his shoulder he saw Bishop William looming above him, gravely holding the huge wooden cross. "Rise, my son," he intoned.

Rogenvaldr rose unsteadily on his weak legs and grabbed the offered cross, embracing it, hanging on, as a man whose ship has sunk would grab a piece of flotsam to save his life.

Ermengard jumped up and threw herself onto him, yelling, "I did not know! I swear on the blessed Jesus, I did not know!"

Rogenvaldr staggered, nearly letting the cross fall. He forced himself to straighten under its weight and walked on. There was nothing left to say. Whether she knew or not didn't matter. They had committed an unforgivable sin. And they both would suffer for it.

"Please believe me—!" Ermengard wailed, as she collapsed in a heap. She covered her face with her hands, *Blessed Madonna, don't let him leave!*

All the way out of the church Rogenvaldr dragged the heavy cross on the dusty stones, leaving a snaking trail in the dust.

His longboat Hjálp was manned and ready. The crew hung over its rails, anxious to see their captain arrive. A little blue skiff was winding its way toward them over the lagoon. In it, standing bent over with its weight, stood Rogenvaldr carrying William's cross.

"Holy Father," Blian said to Oddi. "I never thought I'd see the day . . ."

The Earl staggered aboard, carefully lowering his burden into the prow. The crew ran around manning the sails, grabbing their oars.

"Quick, let's get out of here before he changes his mind," urged William.

White sails snapped their red cross as the Hjálp skipped over curling waves, the blue dragon again leading the way. When the sun rose, they were already racing east past Marseilles.

Rogenvaldr, determined to live out his destiny, stood upright in the prow facing the sunrise, his eyes focused on the horizon.

Suddenly, as a flash of lightning reveals an iceberg dangerously close to one's ship, a profound revelation came to him.

I innocently entered the Garden of Eden and Satan tested me with a poisoned apple. When I was almost lost, God gave me the chance to repent.

"God has saved me! Onward, to Jerusalem!" he cried to the fiery light rising ahead of him. The salty wind wet his radiant face, the pounding oars echoed the rapid beating of his heart.

To the rhythm of waves hitting the keel, Armòd sang a new ballad:

> *Long in the Prince's memory*
> *Ermengard's soft words shall linger;*
> *it is his desire to*
> *ride the waters out to Jordan . . .*
> *While she lives beneath the sun-ray,*
> *may her lot be ever happy . . .*
> *Unless hard changes his fate,*
> *he shall fair Ermengard*
> *ne'er meet again.*

• • •

The Archbishop waited until he could see the church door close behind the Norsemen before he stepped over to Ermengard sobbing on the floor. His gold slippers and embroidered hem glittered in front of her eyes in a blurry haze. "I told you your husband lived, but you wouldn't listen. You have consciously committed adultery. God will punish you as you deserve. Pray long and hard for forgiveness."

Ermengard kept her eyes down, refusing to look up.

D'Anduze walked to the altar, looked around, saw no one, quickly grabbed the horn and rushed to the sacristy. Out in the courtyard six Templar soldiers were waiting for him with the horn's box.

"Here. Be careful putting it in. Now, get it to the King of France with as much speed as possible." The messenger strapped the precious object to his back. "Die to protect it. Go directly to Notre Dame. You will be met there by the Sacristan. He's waiting. Now go!"

He watched the crowd jump out of their way as they thundered through the Royal Gate to Paris. *I'll just tell everyone the Viking stole it back and took it with him when he suddenly escaped and left for Jerusalem. And you can go to the devil, Bernard of Clairvaux, I will build my church in spite of you!*

• • •

Alone on the floor, her chest pounding, Ermengard wrapped her arms around her body to keep it from falling to pieces. *I love him as I will never love another man.* In the chaos of her mind her mother's words came to her. "A time will come when you have been abused and deserted by all the men around you. It is then that you must then pray to the Holy Madonna for strength."

Slowly, on all fours, she crawled over to the statue in the darkest shadows of the round chapel. Trembling, she lit a candle and stared with swollen eyes at the weathered brown wooden face of the ancient Mary, with its white Moorish eyes outlined in gold and robe of peeling red paint. Pockmarked with age, the wood appeared to have absorbed centuries of women's pain-filled prayers.

"Madonna, help me! They have torn me apart. . ."

Uttering a cry, Ermengard threw out her arms in the shape of a cross and fell face down onto the floor. The mortar was rough on her cheeks, her tears wet the cold stones. As the rays of the setting sun turned floating dust motes into little sparks of fire, she lay there, unmoving. At night, the darkness of the church became her blanket. The morning sun rose to stream through the stained-glass windows, covering her body in a melting glow of colors.

The old women veiled in black arrived at the chapels of Saint Just to light candles for morning mass, only to discover their Viscountess lying on the floor in a halo of light, dry rivulets around her face. Understanding the pain of loss, they knelt in a circle around her, praying to the Madonna to save Ermengard's lonely soul.

When the bells tolled sext, Ermengard opened her eyes. Going back on her knees she clasped her hands in prayer and nodded to the statue. Looking around she saw the women in prayer.

"Thank you," she murmured.

Beatritz, a tall narrow figure standing in the shadows like a stone sculpture, approached her.

Arm in arm, the two slowly walked down the columned aisle to the church door. Ermengard stepped into the sunlight and raised her face to the sky. The heat dried the last drops of moisture in the black tendrils of her hair. Turning to Beatritz, her honey-colored eyes shaped like a raptor's wings, she commanded in a strong voice, "Come, stay by my side. I have a kingdom to rule."

AUTHOR'S HISTORICAL NOTES

In 950-1250, during what is now called the Medieval Climate Anomaly, the weather throughout Europe was exceptionally warm. The melted sea ice made it much easier to sail from the lands of Scandia south to Jerusalem. There was actually a Norwegian Crusade led by King Sigurd that lasted from 1107-1111.

This novel is based on a thirteenth-century manuscript called the Icelandic *Orkneyinga* Saga. There are four facts in that history that appear to be true: Rogenvaldr Kali Kolsson was Earl of Orkney, Norway and Viscountess Ermengard was a young noblewoman who ruled Narbonne. They met in Narbonne in 1152 when the Earl went on a pilgrimage to Jerusalem. The saga clearly states there was a romance between them, and that marriage was in the air. Then, he abruptly left Narbonne, never to see Ermengard again.

Why did Rogenvaldr suddenly leave Narbonne? Later, when leaving Jerusalem to return home to Norway, he took a northern land route, giving Narbonne a wide birth.

Ermengard's story is a scant one. Born around 1127, she was orphaned at age five by the death of her father and inherited the kingdom of Narbonne. In 1152, she was the rich and powerful ruler of Occitania, a land known today as France's Languedoc. Ermengard never married a king and had no heirs. Even though she was friend and equal of Aelinore of Aquitaine, and devoted to King Louis VII, the monks who wrote the history of those times did not bother to include the story of her long life.

Could Ermengard and the Earl have had a future together? Six years after their romance, he was killed in 1158 in Norway by another chieftain. Later declared a Christian saint, he is now enshrined in a tomb in the Saint Magnus Cathedral in Kirkwall, Orkney.

Ermengard never married again. She ruled her kingdom for another forty years until she was deposed by her nephew Pedro de Lara in

1193. He expelled her from Narbonne. Alone and destitute, she died in obscurity in 1196, buried in an unmarked grave.

The summer of 1152, when they met, was a turbulent time in the Languedoc region. The *Bons Hommes* were a rapidly expanding southern sect whose views about Christ were deemed heretical. The church was resolved to stamp out the threat of a religion that had no need of the Pope or mass. They came to be known as *Cathars*; a derogatory term coined by the church. Their hierarchy, which included priestesses as well as priests, were named *Parfaits*, or Perfects. The *Parfaits* had no possessions, were vegetarians, wore no animal-based clothing, and were chaste. They believed that Satan controlled human beings on earth; they all desired to die and be with God.

Troubadours, patronized by royalty, were accomplished musicians who wandered through the land, ostensibly to entertain, but also to pass along secret messages, gossip, and deliver the latest news. Undoubtedly, some were *Bons Hommes*. The lyrics of still extant troubadour songs originally written in the Occitan language have been loosely translated. My historical model for Beatritz was the 12th century female troubadour La Comtessa Beatritz de Día of Provence.

My characters could never have foreseen the venal, callous rage, akin to the Four Horsemen of the Apocalypse, which descended on Ermengard's lands within seventy-five years of her romance with Rogenvaldr. Thus we see how, little by little, the future consequences of her heresy dawns on Beatritz. Before this, it was other people being burned at the stake. It could be her turn next, or her daughter's.

Unicorn horns were objects of veneration, held in a much the same awe as a saints' relics or vials of Christ's blood. The confusion as to the origin of such a horn is explained in the text. The monetary value of such a powerful object was enormous.

The money in circulation at the time varied and often was minted in various cities. I chose to use the moribatani, a gold coin first minted in North Africa and named after the Almoravids. It was considered to be made of the finest and purest gold.

The least valuable coin was the silver denarius, twenty of which made up a solidus.

The cities, towns, holy sites, and geographical formations I cite in the countryside around the Languedoc and Provence regions are still in existence, some in ruins, some as restorations. Many of them are actively in use and have informative websites. The Via Domitia, broken up into marked sections, can still be traversed today by an intrepid walker.

The ingestion of hallucinogenic substances in religious rites and mysteries goes far back in time. Did the Cathars use them? I didn't find any references one way or the other, but as archeologists are fond of saying: "Absence of evidence is not evidence of absence."

The quotes introducing each chapter date from the year 1152 CE or earlier.

I have quoted Earl Kali Kolsson's actual poetry as translated by Ian Crockatt in his book *Crimsoning the Eagle's Claw*.

Excerpts from religious texts are from early church writings and the Saint James Bible.

The quotes I used from the *Orkneyinga Saga*, written by an anonymous author in the late thirteenth century, were translated from the Icelandic by Jon A. Hjaltalin and Gilbert Goudie, Edinburgh, Edmond and Douglas, 1873.

Koli Kolsson's description of Icelandic volcanoes is from *The King's Mirror*, an anonymous thirteenth century Norwegian manuscript.

I would like to thank Frederic L. Cheyette for his rich exploration of Ermengard's life: *Ermengard of Narbonne and the World of the Troubadours* and also Jacqueline Caille for her highly researched book *Medieval Narbonne, A City at the Heart of the Troubadour World*.

AUTHOR'S WEBSITE

My website lists some of the books that I used through four years of research. There are also links one can click on to visit the many ancient, still-extant sites in France through which my characters lived and moved. Being a photographer, I have posted images of the places mentioned in the book to help readers better imagine the twelfth-century world of Narbonne. My Medieval Blog has interesting articles about life in 1152.

I invite you to visit me online:

Website: www.peggyannbarnett.com
Facebook: www.facebook.com/peggyann.barnett
Instagram: @Peggy_Ann_Barnett

ADDENDUM

THE ORKNEYINGA SAGA
(excerpt from *THE ICELANDIC SAGAS*)
Written by a 13th century Anonymous Historian

Early in the spring Earl Rögenvaldr called a Thing meeting in Hrossey, to which came all the chiefs residing in his dominions. He then made it known that he intended to leave the Orkneys and go to Jórsalaheim saying that he would leave the government in the hands of his kinsman Harald, and praying all his friends to obey him, and help him faithfully in whatever he required while he was obliged to be away himself. Earl Harald was then nearly twenty, tall and strong, but ugly; yet he was a wise man, and the people thought he would be a good chief.

In the summer Earl Rögnvaldr prepared to leave the Orkneys; but the summer was far advanced before he was ready, because he had to wait a long time for Eindredi until his ship came from Norway. When they were ready, they left the Orkneys in fifteen large ships. The following were commanders of ships: Earl Rögenvaldr; Erling Skakki; Bishop William; Aslák, Erlend's son; Guttorm; Magnus, Hávard's son; Swein, Hróald's son; Eindredi Ungi; and the others who were with him are not named.

From the Orkneys they sailed to Scotland, and then to England, and when they sailed to Nordymbraland (Northumberland), off the mouth of Hvera (the Wear), Armód sang:

> High the crests were of the billows
> As we passed the mouth of the Hvera;
> Masts were bending, and the low land
> Met the waves in long sandy reaches;
> Blind our eyes were with the salt spray
> While the youths at home remaining,
> From the Thing-field fare on horseback.

Then they sailed till they were south of England, and so on to Valland**.

There is no account of their voyage until they came to a seaport called Verbon***. There they learned that the Earl who had governed the city, and whose name was Geirbiörn, had lately died; but left a young and beautiful daughter, by name Ermingerd.

She had charge of her patrimony, under the charge of her noblest kinsmen. They advised the Queen to invite Earl Rögnvaldr to a splendid banquet, saying that her fame would spread far if she gave a fitting reception to noblemen arrived from such a distance. The Queen left it to them; and when this had been resolved upon, men were sent to the Earl to tell him that the Queen invited him to a banquet, with as many men as he himself wished to accompany him.

The Earl received her invitation gratefully, selecting the best of his men to go with him. And when they came to the banquet there was good cheer, and nothing was spared by which the Earl might consider himself specially honoured.

One day, while the Earl sat at the feast, the Queen entered the hall, attended my many ladies. She had in her hand a golden cup and was arrayed in the finest robes. She wore her hair loose, according to the custom of maidens, and a golden diadem round her forehead. She poured out for the Earl, and the maidens played for them. The Earl took her hand along with the cup and placed her beside him. They conversed during the day.

The Earl sang:

> *Lady Fair! thy form surpasses*
> *All the loveliness of maidens,*
> *Though arrayed in costly garments,*
> *And adorned with precious jewels:*
> *Silken curls in radiant splendour*
> *Fall upon the beauteous shoulders*
> *Of the goddess of the gold-rings.*
> *The greedy eagle's claws I redden'd.*

The Earl stayed there a long time and was well entertained. The inhabitants of the city solicited him to take up his residence there, saying that they were in favour of giving the Queen to him in marriage. The Earl said that he wished to complete his intended journey, but that he would come there on his return, and then they might do what they thought fit.

Then the Earl left with his retinue and sailed around Thrasness.****

They had a fair wind, and sat and drank, and made themselves merry. The Earl sang this song:

> *Long in the Prince's memory*
> *Ermingerd's soft words shall linger;*
> *It is her desire that we shall*
> *Ride the waters out to Jordan;*
> *But the riders of the sea-horses,*
> *From the southern climes returning,*
> *Soon shall plough their way to Verbon*
> *O'er the whale pond in the autumn.*

Then Armód sang:

> *Ne'er shall I see Ermingerda*
> *More, from this time, if it be not*
> *That my fate shall be propitious;*
> *Many now are grieving for her.*
> *Happy were I if I could but*
> *Be beside her just for one day;*
> *That, indeed, would be good fortune,*
> *Once again to see her fair face.*

*Jerusalem

**Norse name for Gaul-land, the west coast of France

***Narbonne

****Thrace

ABOUT THE AUTHOR

Peggy Ann Barnett grew up in 1950's Queens, New York. In 1965, after earning a BFA from The Cooper Union, she embarked on a successful career in photography. In her Manhattan studio she photographed the first covers for New York Magazine, did corporate work for the Fortune 500 in the 1970- 80's, and produced many assignments from great designers like Milton Glazer.

When she moved to the Pacific Northwest in 2006, she became a poet. Her creative background as a photographer makes her writing extremely visual and full of vivid imagery. In 2010 she published *On Your Left!*, poetic memoirs about growing up as the child of holocaust refugees, her marriage to Ron Barnett, and the move of a city girl to the country. For five years she studied meditation with the Thai Monks of the Forest and helped them develop a curriculum for English speaking students.

Peggy has always been drawn to the Middle Ages. She spent many happy hours sketching medieval art in the Cloisters. In the Cluny Museum she sat for hours contemplating its Unicorn Tapestries. She loves researching and wandering old castles and medieval streets.

Her passions now are travel, hiking, and reading her poetry at open mics.